WILLIAM SCOTT holds three university degrees and is a Fellow ᴏ. the Institute of Mathematics and its Applications. He served on a national committee and has published many articles and papers on science, teaching mathematics and philosophy, education, history, religion and current moral problems in society – a particular concern. He has taught in Scotland, England and Brunei.

Born and bred on the Isle of Bute, he returned there after many years of working and travelling to devote himself to writing. He was twice runner-up in the Scottish Association of Writers' Constable Trophy before winning the prize in 1997.

For most of his life an atheist, he now enjoys few things so much as the services at St Giles' Cathedral, Edinburgh, where the intellect is not offended but stimulated.

His favourite sport is hashing: cross-country running, especially in the jungle of Borneo where there is some danger of getting lost in the dark in a swamp and even being swallowed by a crocodile or python – a perfect antidote to a dependence on civilised comforts.

First Edition 1997
Reprinted 2003

Details of titles currently available from
Luath are set out on the final pages of this book.

This book is made from low chlorine pulps produced in
a low energy, low emission manner from renewable
forests and from recycled materials, the latter
comprising at least 50% of the pulps used.

The publisher acknowledges subsidy from

THE SCOTTISH ARTS COUNCIL

towards the publication of this volume.

Printed and bound by Gwasg Dinefwr Press Ltd., Llandybie

The Bannockburn Years

WILLIAM SCOTT

Luath Press Limited
EDINBURGH
www.luath.co.uk

Dedicated to my good friend,
Col. Bruce Niven, MBE, MA, PPA
of the SAS and Gurkhas,
who will recall a conversation in his Singapore bungalow,
surrounded by his beloved, magnificent, wee men.

ACKNOWLEDGEMENTS

I am very grateful for help given by Allan Grant, Duncan McIntyre, the late Ronald McNair Scott, Councillor Robert McIntyre, Robert Reid, Sheriff David B. Smith, Eddie Monaghan, Jess Sandeman and, most of all, June Stewart and Bruce Niven.

William Scott
November 1997

Contents

CHAPTER I

Edinburgh, 1996

THE QUESTION WAS THIS: should my country become independent again—after three hundred years yoked to the rest of the United Kingdom? On it depended my future, for on the desk lay a letter inviting me to stand as a candidate in the general election. It was from the independence party, assuring me that acceptance would mean automatic selection, and, given the seat and my credentials, guaranteeing success.

I wondered whether this was true, or merely an expression of confidence to encourage me to accept? As I looked out across the broad expanse of Princes Street Gardens to the castle, on its towering edifice of rock, I realised that if my country called in this way, I had a duty to respond, but, and it was a vital but, only if I believed in the cause. Years of legal training and the almost daily examination of my integrity demanded I should first explore the case comprehensively.

Far beyond the window, my eye rested again on the very route where William Francis had led Randolph's force up the rock, when the castle was retaken from the English in 1313, during the War of Independence. And something happened which I never experienced before: my flesh goose-pimpled and my hair stood on end, as if the spirits of that long-departed medieval world suddenly flew out of the great rock opposite and called to me.

Puzzled and unsure, I set the issue aside and tried to think of my work; took the file on Tom Stewart, put it in my briefcase, collected hat, coat and scarf and began to make my way downstairs. 'I'll be back tomorrow,' I assured Margaret, my secretary, and soon the taxi was speeding along to Waverley Station, where, like many another professional, I boarded a train for some distant extremity of the realm.

As hedges and fields flew past, and the great gaunt medieval Palace of Linlithgow, I contemplated the question of independence again, but soon gave up and returned to the file, never imagining that the answer would lie within, or take me back to that very bygone age.

Tom Stewart had just died. As his solicitor—a job I had somehow acquired unknowing, from a long dead senior partner—my task was to settle his affairs. The will, written in a flowing hand in ink, was simple. As he had no relatives, everything of value was left to Edinburgh University, his alma mater; everything else to the Salvation Army; on the face of it a simple task, except for this: anything of national importance was to be made available to the state, and he made it clear that the state was the Nation State of Scotland. And that is where I sensed difficulties. For who represented the Nation of State of Scotland? Was there one? And was there anything in this unknown man's property which might be of national interest?

It was to answer this last question that I embarked that day on a trip to Rothesay, on the island of Bute, where for many years Tom Stewart had lived, before entering a nursing home. Of course, I rationalised, this was just one of those wills that all lawyers come across, full of whimsy and, despite protestations to the contrary, even outright craziness. And yet, the man was a university graduate. Second class honours in English, class of 1939. I looked out the window again and wondered what it meant. Of course it did not mean he had a second-rate mind. English is notoriously subjective and the award of a first a guarantee only of conformity in critical opinion. No, this man had ability, or at least, must be given the credit for the possibility.

What had been his vocation? No clear answer: joined the RAF, Sept 1939—that would be soon after graduating. Served in number 603 Squadron, based at Turnhouse. Crashed 1940. Invalided out of the service, 1941. Medical problems unstated. Medals none. Mentioned in despatches, none. Enemy planes shot down, none. What did this mean? An undistinguished war? Perhaps, but only perhaps. Maybe he was one of the unknown heroes. I could not tell, then, but something about this odd request that his executor should decide if any of his belongings were of national interest, made me pause and wonder again.

Had he anything of national interest? I would soon find out. I had the key to the house he had left in 1945. So what had occurred between 1941 and 1945? Injuries in the crash had brought about a paralysing stroke, requiring his admission to hospital and then the nursing home, where he had spent the last fifty years. Ruefully, I saw that I would have to go to this place and enquire about him.

From the rail terminus at Queen Street, I crossed to Central Station and boarded another train to Wemyss Bay, where a ferry conveyed me to the island nestling in a fold of the land, three miles into the Firth of Clyde.

The air was balmy, suggestive of a storm, or some event of mystical significance. And yet we passed Toward Lighthouse to starboard, tall and straight and white and rational; and small houses, and a castle on the shores of the Argyll mainland. Maybe it was the island itself. All hills and hollows, it lay, unmoving, like a sleeping tiger, waiting for any small prey that passed.

From the pier, I journeyed a mile inland by taxi to the top of a hill. The house was a cottage, once white, now a dirty grey, with ferns growing out of the slates in places, and windows opaque with grime. Inside, dust lay thick everywhere. There was no pile of uncollected mail, which was odd. Why had this place not been sold—to ease the man's declining years, or pay his costs?

The filth made me pause. Should I not go to the town and hire some help? Have it cleaned before I did my work? No, I decided. Anything of value might be stolen. Of course, it was ridiculous that there might be something of value. I almost laughed at the idea, until my eye penetrated the gloom to the books which lined the place. A man with so many books might know what he was about.

I took the scarf and rubbed the grime off the window and the light grew stronger. Then I rubbed the inside of the door and hung my outer clothes on the hook there. Finally, I advanced upon the desk which sat proud of the bookcases in a corner, cleaned the chair with a handkerchief and sat down. Around me, close to hand, would be the most important books. There was Barbour's *Bruce*—the poem written in 1375 by John Barbour, Archdeacon of Aberdeen, about Robert Bruce and the War of Independence. *The Scalacronica* by Sir Thomas Grey, translated from the French by Maxwell, a lovely volume with coloured plates showing the more important armorial bearings of the time. I had never seen this book before and was excited. I soon read that it had been written by the son of an English knight who had been captured on the first day at Bannockburn. These and many others I found, Froissart, Bower and Lanercost among them, each with its view of the War of Independence and, apart from these primary sources, a large number of secondaries: academic papers and histories by everyone who mattered, and some I'd never heard of. And notebooks— stubby, red-covered books filled with the accumulated thoughts of Tom Stewart, as he plundered these rich treasures. But something of national value? No. This was a good library but it was not unique. The shelves further off contained a large part of the best literature of the world. So he liked novels? Well, any graduate in English would do no less.

Was there a journal? In the desk drawers I found them: thick, unlined notebooks, filled with the same neat handwriting. There were six, in black leather bindings, and they covered the period 1930 to 1944. Should I read them? It would take hours. I would carry them away with me after my search.

The rest of the desk, this room and the others, revealed nothing except more books, old furniture of no particular interest and, finally, I found myself again in the hall, clad once more in my outer clothing, somewhat dusty, and ready to leave. The journals were in my case.

What more need be done? And yet I lingered, and knew not why. It was as if some departed spirit was urging me to remain, held me in its thrall, and would not let me go until I had done its bidding.

By now, I could hardly see for the gloom which had descended upon the house on that late winter afternoon. There is nothing here, I said to myself, aloud, and immediately doubted it. If I did not hurry, I would miss the last boat. And so, with a strange reluctance, I closed the door and began to lug my case downhill towards the pier.

As luck would have it, I arrived to see the last ferry setting off; and was immediately annoyed at myself for becoming marooned on this island, when I should be at home in my Colinton mansion attending to my political future.

The best hotel on the sea-front was third-rate, which increased my irritation. The room—the finest in the place, I was assured—was plain and cold and without charm. With no enthusiasm, I took the latest of the journals and set off for the bar where I found a roaring fire, a tumbler of malt and began to read.

> 20.9.41 Unable sleep. Greenock being pounded again. Christ! Wish I was up there among the bastards! Legs still giving me jip and bloody headaches a nuisance. Can hardly think straight. That's the worst of it, being no bloody good for anything; have no will; and nothing to do. Home guard won't have me. All I do is totter about the place among all these Polish troops. A woman gave me the glad-eye today and I could do nothing about it. There's just nothing there any more. My life is bloody awful.

There was more of the same, much more. Twice, German aircraft, pursued by Spitfires, jettisoned their bombs on the island, but not much was interesting. The talk was of troops in training causing the kind of havoc all troops do, especially when heading for a violent and probably terminal future; and the townsfolk, women mostly, the men being at the war; and his own efforts to recover health and happiness.

Gradually there is less about headaches and something like a return to an intellectual life. Books start to be read or re-read. But there is a sense of lost purpose, a life unfulfilled, because the author is denied his rightful place at the heart of the battle.

I soon gave it up and went in to dinner, a solitary affair, except for a newly married couple from the south with nothing but each other on their minds. And so it was that, afterwards, I retired again to the bar and took up my former comfortable position in the leather chair beside the fire, with a glass for company and the journal, which had begun to pall.

Thirty pages in, on the point of giving up, I saw my first exclamation mark, wondered at it and paused, for here was something new. This was not a man to express excitement and yet there it was, writ large. Not one exclamation mark but a page full of them. What was this? I read:

> *27.11.41 Wakened at six by gunfire! Came down and made tea. Looking out of window at church, saw chapel wall dissolve in cloud of dust! Direct hit from artillery on Toward Point which is firing across the island to a target on Inchmarnock. Stupid buggers! Imagine using this place as a range! As if some shell would not be underpowered and fall short!*

I remembered the chapel. It must be the small stone building adjoining the Church across the road. But it had seemed intact except for the roof. There were no signs of shell-fire now. Inchmarnock is a small island to the west of Bute. They must have been firing right across the island of Bute.

> *28.11.41 Nobody came to see the chapel! Imagine it, nobody cares that a shell fell short and blew up an ancient building! Christ! They are obsessed with their war. Nothing else matters to them! Maybe they are right. Maybe nothing else does matter!*

> *29.11.41 Decided to restore chapel. Maybe I can do that much good. All I should need to do is rebuild the stones. From the window, it looks like the shell hit the north wall and blew it inwards. It would be something for me to do. It might be satisfying. At least it would be something! Christ! I wish I had a God! Somebody! Anybody to talk to about*

The entry ends abruptly in mid sentence. But no action is taken for some time. Maybe it is the illness, I mused. Perhaps he has not the will necessary for such an undertaking. He reads books, fitfully, spends his afternoons foraging for food at the shops and the harbour from fishermen. He thinks about gardening, and wonders where seed potatoes might be obtained. But it is still winter. Maybe the weather is against his rebuilding project.

> *4.12.41 Went to chapel at last to estimate difficulty!! Wall is very thick. very!! With air space between. Found heavy leather bag full of papers!!! Treasure! Oh treasure!*

There is no entry for the next day! For the very first time since he began the journal, eleven years before, there is no entry!

6.12.41 To hell with rebuilding the wall! What I have here is another man's journal written in the fourteenth century!! I count 427 pages of script! I will make it my task to edit and translate this so that scholars may read it and understand it more easily!!!

I was astounded. And when the barman came to me with polite requests for a refill, I could not reply for the sheer wonder of the discovery. For this is what he intended me to find. An ancient document written by a medieval person which would provide a window into his world, that extraordinary world; a document that would take its place alongside Barbour's *Bruce* and *The Scalacronica*, Bower, Froissart, Lanercost et al. This was a major discovery!

Tom Stewart had spent an entire day deciphering the ancient manuscript, forgetting the habits of a lifetime, his daily entry in the journal. Similarly captivated, I ordered an entire bottle of Drambuie and when it arrived, poured a treble. Then, for good measure, invited the barman across to take a stiff dram with me.

'You've had good news, Sir?' he said, standing sipping the drink.

I said nothing, for I was speechless again. Good news indeed! With tears in my eyes, I nodded, but could not say anything. I had been given a great secret and secret it must remain until I had sifted it comprehensively and decided what action to take.

That night, I read my way through the journal, pages full of the great task of translation and amplification, written in a gradually less legible hand as exhaustion took its toll. Yet there was an air of great excitement in it, as of a high purpose nobly engaged. The problems were discussed, as he ruminated to himself what their solution might be. How to set the scene, what the characters would have looked like, what their way of life must have been, down to food, clothing, conversation and attitudes, those above all. The credo of the times, the belief systems of an ancient race of men and women. I began to see that more than translation was involved. What he was trying to do was create a work of literature, and for a university graduate in English, unhappily incapable of other employment, that must have seemed a high purpose indeed.

At dawn, I had read all of it and failed to find what I sought: no mention of the whereabouts of the manuscript or his 'translation' if that is what it was.

I slept late and rose at eleven. After a full English breakfast—I can laugh at the adjective now, given all that transpired—I phoned Margaret to tell her of my delay, and then went shopping for cleaning tools; hired a high-powered vacuum and a small generator to drive it, amongst other things.

An hour later, I was throwing open windows in the cottage and hoovering madly. When several loads of dust had been deposited out-side at the back, I started on the windows with soap and water, won-dering as I did so, where the hiding place must be. Finally, having done enough, as I judged, to make the place habitable, I began to look under carpets at floor-boards, and tapped the walls for hollows, going from room to room, but finding nothing. Yet somewhere there had to be a secret place.

It would be in a box of some kind, with a metal casing, to protect the manuscript from fire. It would also have to be inside the house or it could so easily be dug up by someone accidentally. Yes, it would definitely be in the house. It must be handy, for it would be used constantly and would have survived only because it had been carefully preserved. What if another shell had fallen on the house?

But after three hours of searching, I could find no trace of it. Would he have told anyone? I thought not. Else why had it come out in this strange manner in the will? Would there be a clue to its whereabouts? Perhaps not. Had he refused to sell the house because of the document hidden here? Maybe he was taken unawares, the stroke which paralysed him being so unexpected that he had made no preparations to tell anybody—except for the will.

I fetched the will from my brief-case, looked at it again with care and saw that the statement about the national treasure was in a slightly different hand. Was this his hand, or someone else's? Maybe he had been unable to communicate by then and someone had helped him by making this small but important addition—before he became utterly incapable of communicating his wishes.

It was disappointing. I knew I had to leave, but was reluctant to do so. At four o'clock, I tore myself away and began to walk down the hill towards the pier for the last boat, leaving the equipment outside at the back to be picked up before the shop closed at five. I even boarded and sat down in the saloon; but before the ship departed I rose again and stepped back onto the pier. Leave I could not. I would try again the next day.

Dinner was a fraught affair. I would far rather have been at the cottage hunting, but there was no light, the generator would have gone, and therefore no point, until morning. Reading the journals again, I was startled to realise that if this were a sample of Tom Stewart's writing, his effort at modernising the text was probably wasted. But it was the text that was the prize. It would be a national treasure and I must have the honour of finding it and making it available to the world —if it existed.

I fell asleep that night dreaming of an honorary doctorate, awarded for my discovery of this new primary historical source.

At nine the next morning, I stood again in the hall facing the stairs, inspecting the woodwork carefully. There had to be some secret cupboard and it had to be close by. The box must be big enough to hold the manuscript and his own transcription. It would have to be lead or steel; and yet metals like these would be difficult to acquire in war-time, everything being commandeered by the military.

Finally, I saw what had been staring me in the face. A small knob of wood protruded from the side of the stairs, and when moved, released a catch on the upright between the first and second steps. Inside, I found two ammunition boxes and inside these, the manuscript and its translation.

Of course he would use ammunition boxes! The island would be littered with them, hundreds of shots being fired by every man in training.

The ancient manuscript was on sheets of parchment or paper, which I fingered delicately. Each was about 7 inches by 9, the lettering upright, in black, faded ink, each line effortlessly written below the one above, every line straight as a die. I saw immediately that this was the work of a scholar, one used to writing such documents. And then the Latin! Even my rusty acquaintance could see that this was first rate, reminiscent of Julius Caesar: a spare, clear, pure prose. And as soon as I began fitfully to translate, I knew that here was another de Bello Gallico, except that it was not about Gaul but my own land and its powerful neighbour.

I began to translate.

CHAPTER 2

The Island of Bute, 1375

'IOANNIS BANNATINUS TO WHOMSOEVER shall discover this, greetings. I tell the tale of my life, for that is the only truth I know. I do so in Latin and not Scots or English or some other bastard language because these have nothing to communicate to peoples from other lands. What use then to write in Scots as Archdeacon Barbour does? Who can understand it? Even the spelling is his own. And what use to tell a tale made up from so many men's lies? Barbour was not born until after Bannockburn, so what does he know of these things? Besides, the fool wrote in verse as if that conferred some distinction, when all it does is make it more obscure. And his inconsistencies are legion, a merry joke to any head of sense. Did no one teach him figuring? I listened to it all at the castle last night, and, as the king nodded his white head gravely at the end and awarded him a pension for it, shook my own in sorrowful amazement that our new Robert cannot discern a fuddled cleric when he sees one. But it were useless to complain. I might lose the very head on my old shoulders or, what is worse, the spartan fare which keeps me in freedom to think. For this I still do well, though I am eighty-eight years old, and my body no longer answers my demands, so that I have given up making them.'

By now, as you will have guessed, I had moved over to Tom Stewart's version, the effort of translation being beyond me. The king would be Robert II, for this must have been penned in 1375, the year Barbour's poem was read at court. Where was the castle? Rothesay, most likely. Robert II was crowned in 1371, I remembered, and the kings often stayed at Rothesay. His son, Robert III had died there in 1406.

I read:

'I do not know why I write this for it will not be read; yet write I must to correct that travesty by John Barbour. So I suppose it is from fury that I take up my quill. I will convey the facts truly, in the hope that some person in days to come will find this and behold the truth. I was, you see, present at Bannockburn and even played a royal role— which Barbour knows quite well but will not say for jealousy and also because he wishes to make a god of Robert Bruce, when the truth is

9

that he is a god without need of lies to amplify his achievement. And then, the King would have it so, wishes to believe that his grandfather was the greatest all round man who ever walked the earth, and what the King wants is done.

To begin to set the record straight. I was born—so at least I judge— a few years before 1290, when all our ills first befell us. For it was about then that the fools in charge of our government invited Edward, King of England, to decide between competitors to the throne of Scotland.

Living at Ardmaleish, on the island of Bute, with my family, I was not then much disturbed by it. At first, my days were filled with life on the croft, tending the animals and the fishing which we increasingly took part in as we grew up. Besides Eck, my barrel-shaped elder brother, four years older than myself, there were my mother, Alis, still slim of figure and hale of face and my younger sister Isa, a red-haired wildcat, if ever there was one, and my father, Fergus Bannatyne.

Of middle height, my father had piercing blue eyes and dark hair; great energy and enterprise; full of ideas for the improvement of the farm and the making of trade in fish and cattle and anything else he came across—subverted at every turn though he was by the guilds and his feudal superior, the Steward. And he was demanding of us. My mother must take to the loom and make our clothes and, when she had done so, for other folks too, because of the merks they brought, as if there were not tailors enough in Rothesay, the town of the island, with its castle and market, or folk to do their own.

Myself? I was marked out from the beginning. It was something I knew early at the breast, for my consciousness was almost immediate and all-embracing. I sensed, even as a boy, wilfully seeking diversion about the croft, that this life was not for me, that out there somewhere, across the seas, was a wide world, and that I would explore it and maybe turn it to my will. And father knew. It was in his eyes from the first. Soon after I began to speak, he was deferential at my enquiries and depth of insight, and I was expected to play the man in his absence and take the blame for my older brother's scrapes.

Schooling, I had a little, in Rothesay, to which I walked the three miles every day, in grey kirtle and knee-length trews, barefoot, in all weathers, as boys are meant to do—or at least my father's—for he had ideas about making us tough. The dominie, a forbidding man, with a long body, short legs and dark hair, known as Weasel Willie, was soon charmed with my ready response, and not too overborne by the many questions I fired like arrows, at every opportunity.

The schoolroom, where I first beheld the universe of knowledge, was like most other dwellings hereabouts: whin-stones piled randomly, the holes filled with mortar and the roof thatched with reeds from the loch nearby. The floor was beaten earth, which would turn to mud in rainy weather, the level being below ground, a little. We sat on benches, a dozen or two of us, at a rickety table, much scarred by earlier scholars, one of them Weasel Willie himself, no doubt.

The first word I ever saw written was like an act of magic to me. Willie wrote it on a slate and said it was the name of our country. Other words followed and each was like a new friend to be known fully and enjoyed. Now, so many years later, it seems as if I never had a friend like them; well, maybe one or two. She that I loved, Signore Dante Alighieri, whom I met near the end of his life, and my mother, perhaps. Was Robert Bruce a friend? Yes, of a kind; but his ambition and noble blood placed limits upon what he would do for any man.

That very first day, when other scholars left in boisterous glee at the end of lessons, I remained to practise scribing on my slate, only giving up when the charcoal had shrunk to an unmanageable fragment. Before long, my tentative trials became writing fully formed. Within a few weeks I was reading—anything: parchments of Willie's and whole books; understanding only in part, but so fascinated that, like a dry clout, I absorbed anything I came across.

It was this, of course, which came between me and my brother, who cared nothing for such matters, and at first berated me for conforming to the rules of the schule. He resented my progress, the praise heaped upon me, and was offended by my facility. I took a few beatings until even he saw that my lack of size and bulk were no match for his. So I was ignored thereafter and we went our separate ways.

I can still remember Weasel Willie yet, his excitement at the intensity of my own, standing there, hands black with charcoal, in moth-eaten black gown and breeches that had been dyed red once, but now were faded and holed like cheese, along with the brogues he wore. Yet to me then, in my patched kirtle and bare feet, such raiment was finery.

It seemed that my head was made for words and in a few years I had read every book in Willie's possession and then cried out for more, and at worst, threw tantrums of fury that there were not more words to read. Given the opportunity by him—and even denied it—I would spout words, glorious resonating torrents of them. But better than words were ideas. These early sprung into my head as if by magic and were a constant source of delight to me; and many of them were questions, quaestiones, as I still call them when they are of the intellectual variety; which lead to others and so on and on, *ad infinitum*.

Thus, I wondered how a bird could fly, and why the grass was green and not some other colour like red or blue, and where was heaven, where God lived? Among the stars? And why were fish fooled into giving up their lives with hooks trailing chicken feathers? I was surrounded by a universe of whys—mysteries without end—which it was a pleasure to explore and speculate and wonder at, when quaestiones produced no answers from the adults in my world; and ecstasy, later, when I went beyond that simple world of Bute and discovered many answers in higher spheres, and even for myself.

I still remember the day I saw the map, a rough drawing on animal skin of the countries of the world, and my excitement was utter, total, as I took in its import in an instant. Here lay the island on which we lived, and the very croft, my finger showed, must be at the north point of the next bay north from the town, Rothesay. There, round about, were the other islands, Cumbrae and Inchmarnock and Arran—and the further Hebrides, which I had never seen, and the mainland, with the capital: Edinburgh. And then England, of glorious name, and Wales, an English province now, and France and Holland and Spain. And beyond, Italy, where lived the Pope, descended from the great Peter, apostle of Christ—so at least I believed. And not for a moment did it ever occur to me that I would not visit these lands.

Farther off, were Greece, the Holy Land, Persia and India, but what lay beyond, according to the mapmaker, were dragons. I wondered at these too, imagining them standing at the edge of the world, breathing fire on all who dared approach. Was hell underneath? I wondered. How foolish I was in those early days.

Yet even I could see the defects of the map, for had I not stood on the highest points of Bute and taken in the shape of the island at a glance? It was not shaped like a boot but a sleeping cat. It must have been the first time I noticed a mistake in a scholar's work; there were to be many others. Instinctively, I knew that this map was about as accurate as my brother Eck's drawing of a horse: four stick legs, one wider stick body and two eyes in the backside with the tail sticking out between. Still, in the unbridled pursuit of knowledge, I easily forgave the mapmaker his imperfections. He had given me an idea and it did not need to be accurate to be of value.

It began one summer morning when I attended the market in Rothesay, with my father. We were selling our produce from a cart, among a motley throng of townsfolk and crofters similarly engaged, when I espied the dominie in conversation with a youngish man in clerical black with a head prematurely grey. Weasel Willie called to me and I went.

'This is the laddie I telt ye of,' said he to the man. 'John Bannatyne, aged about ten years. And this', to me, he said, 'is Master Baldred Bisset.'

All I could think of to say was: 'Why are you called Master?' which provoked laughs all round.

'Because I am *Artium Magister*,' said he. When my puzzled look told all, Baldred said, 'So you have not started on the Latin, then?' and my tutor, shamefaced, admitted it, slapping a large carbuncle which stuck out from the crown of his scalp, with a reproving forefinger, as if in penance. Whereupon I dumbfounded him.

'*Amo, amas, amat, amamus, amatis, amant*,' I chanted, which embarrassed him further.

'Where did you learn that?' said Master Baldred.

'From a small book of parchments,' I said. 'I found it in the chapel.'

'And have you read all of it?'

'Yes—well almost. I read it whenever I'm in church and things become boring. I hide it behind a loose stone.'

Master Baldred smiled then, and after other questions to see what more I knew of Latin, said that I must go to Glasgow and he would undertake my instruction.

My father was against it at first, declaring that my aptitude in counting and instant appreciation of what to do in every situation were qualities the family could not well do without. But Master Baldred smiled patiently and explained that a mind like mine should be trained for some higher task than farming or fishing. My country had need of me, he said, finally; and that, so far as my father was concerned, was enough, for we were all patriots in those days.

They were dark days indeed. A great battle had recently been fought at Falkirk, against the English, and we had lost. The few survivors among the participating Butemen, had brought news. The cavalry, led by the Red Comyn, had fled the field without a blow struck, the shiltrons shattered under Bishop Bek's repeated cavalry charges and our good Scots pikemen were trampled under the hooves of armoured horses ridden by armoured knights, squires and men-at-arms.

Now the country was leaderless, Wallace having fled to the continent, some said, and our castles yielded up without a whimper of resistance. News of these developments was slow in arriving, but came in dribs and drabs from fishermen, mostly. Reality hit us when a shipfull of English arrived to take full control of our castle and our conditions of life changed immediately.

The new governor, Sir Hubert Cressingham, was a tall flaxen-haired person with blue eyes and fine silver armour which he liked to wear as he rode on his high white percheron around the island, at the head of a troop of men-at-arms. And he was right to protect himself, for not a few Brandanes, as we are sometimes called, would have put a shaft through him without it, from the security of our many woods.

Under his government, taxes were trebled, regulations quadrupled, and freedom curtailed. Orders were read out at the Mercat Cross to desist from making weapons, or training in their use—except if we enlisted in his troop. All our goods and provisions were at his beck and call; even our women. This took time to become apparent and I missed most of it, for I was soon transported across the Clyde by a galley, made my way on foot to Glasgow at my father's side, and enrolled as a scholar in the small school run by Master Baldred at the Cathedral.

Before he left me, my father looked into my eyes and said gravely, in the gaelic, 'Master Bisset says you are a genius. All I can see is a skelf of a laddie. But maybe he is right. We will see, by and by. Just don't let us down, boy. Remember you are a Brandane. You must work and work and work and do what you are told.'

As soon as he said this, I knew there would be times when I would not; and events have proved me right; for what person of spirit always does what he is told? And so, what some men never learn in a lifetime, I knew instinctively. However, work has ever been my God, for a long time, the only one.

Many years were to pass before I saw my father again and some of them were deliberate and there was good reason on both sides for the breech.

As payment for my learning I spent my days, part of them, cleaning the Cathedral and the offices around and serving the altar at matins, compline and the like. Then it turned out that I had a voice, a very high soprano, which some liked the sound of, and sing I did too. In between, I studied: read every book set before me with a hunger worse than many days starvation, made notes in fine writing on every spare parchment I chanced upon, scribing as small as possible to save space, and committed to memory, as easy as blinking, everything of interest. Once seen, never forgotten, became my watchword. My mind was like a bottomless urn, which held everything that fell into it, and I had only to incline my head slightly to one side and I could recall everything in the past, as visual images tumbled out into my consciousness, and things said—no matter how long ago—were heard again in my ears.

Then there were the disputations, mostly with Master Bisset, but often with my fellows, when words would fly from me like flights of arrows, cutting into my woolly-headed opponents till their faces blanched or reddened. After only a year, a year in which I had surged far ahead of every other, I was suddenly introduced to the scriptorium and given instruction in copying manuscripts. I began writing letters for the Bishop—copies for his records—but soon I was copying whole books.

Four hours a day I spent on this task, bent over a sloping desk, rounded knife blade in left hand to hold down the parchment, which tends to curl, and for cutting my quill—a task I was forced to do half a dozen times an hour, as the tip wore down—writing with the right hand, in an upright style, the quill between middle and forefinger, as I'd been taught.

At first, I concentrated on accuracy and speed, this being what I imagined was wanted, but before long I was reading with fascination. I began with Aristotle's *Organon* and loved the power of the reasoning, and when I had finished and made some enthusiastic remark to my tutor, was set to copying Euclid, which I liked even better. Of course I did not understand everything, was too busy copying to grasp all of it, but much of it went into me and took root there as if I were designed for no better purpose than to grow a whole universe of knowledge within myself.

I remember one of the later syllogisms in the *Organon* which puzzled me. I did not understand it, but had such respect for Aristotle, that I took it at face value. Not many years later, in very different circumstances, I was to recall this moment with frustration and excitement.

Geometry, Arithmetic and Algebra I copied, and after each section, Master Baldred would question me, and even set me problems to solve which I attacked with gusto, though I soon found that some defied my best efforts at first. Then, during the night, when all around me slept, the answer would come magically to mind, usually when I was on the point of dropping off to sleep, so that by morning, all was clear again.

And so I found myself picked out from all others at the school and compelled to copy book after book in every hour of leisure, so that I had no time for the temptations other boys engaged in. Parchment being hard to come by, paper would be made and this I would use instead, so that the books I made were a hotch-potch of both, bound between boards of wood and held there by leather thongs.

Illustrations there were none, only the bare essentials of figures in the texts. Evidently, these copies were not for some important personage.

Thus my life continued, winter and summer, for the next few years, because I did not go home when the others did, but was kept hard at it; and minded not at all, for I loved the scriptorium and the wonders that I copied, and I left my fellows further and further behind me.

It was not all plain sailing of course. There were vicious battles of words between myself and others, Baldred worst of all, who taxed my patience continually by his criticisms of my arguments and style of speaking; but the effect of it was to compel me to organise what I said at speed and utter the points in the best order and most concise manner conceivable.

At times, we fell out; and I would be enraged by his failure to see what was self-evident to me. There were even occasions when he imposed his authority, berating me for unconnected things because, I expect, he had no better escape. At the time, I often thought ill of him, but his goodness would re-assert itself and the breech would mend. And so the years passed, until, one day, when I was fifteen, Master Bisset sent for me to see him in Bishop Wishart's house.

Robert Wishart was writing at a desk in a corner facing the centre of the room. My tutor stood to one side, leaving me in the intense rays of the sun which streamed through a small window, high up. The walls were bare except for the cross and some shelves of books.

Presently, the bald head with the white wisps lifted and the blue eyes surveyed me as he laid down the quill. 'Master Baldred says you have become impossible,' he said stiffly, accusingly; and my heart sank to my bare feet. I was going to be expelled.

'Me? No! How? I pr...pr...protest!' I stammered, out of a red face, horrified at this judgement.

'There you go again,' said Wishart, sternly. 'You have just proved it. You *are* impossible! You challenge every thing we say.'

All I could think of to reply was: 'But you have never stopped me asking quaestiones.'

'But there is a limit,' said Baldred. 'When we don't have the answers.'

They laughed then, both of them, and after he had asked me many questions of his own, Wishart said, 'Well, laddie what are we to do with the likes of you? What would you like to do?'

'Continue learning, my lord.'

'He has little left to learn from me,' said Master Bisset. 'He writes and speaks English, Latin, Italian, Greek and French as if he were a native. He knows more mathematics than I do myself and as for philosophy, natural and metaphysical'—laughing with delight—'he kills anyone foolish enough to dispute with him. In short, my lord, there is nothing else to be done except find him some higher place.'

'Then he must go to Cambridge,' said the Bishop.

'But that is in England,' I protested.

'Aye, it is,' said the Bishop, 'and that is where we want you. Scotland has become a vassal province of England, now that John Balliol has fled. What we are to do now is in God's hands. Your part can be to study the English, understand them, befriend them, if you can. Rise in their service if possible. And while you do it, sharpen your intelligence in one of their universities.'

I was given much advice. Especially about making efforts to lose my accent. As Master Bisset put it, I must try to distinguish myself, of course, for along that road lay advancement, but my Scottishness should be submerged as much as possible.

'Were you not at Oxford?' I quizzed the Bishop. 'And is not that the best place to study?'

'There you go again!' said Baldred, 'Who are you to question the Bishop?'

'Never mind, Baldred,' said Wishart, wearily, dismissing him with a wave of a wrinkled hand. 'Oxford is no better than Cambridge, which has the advantage of being smaller and newer.'

'What is the good of that?' I insisted.

'Because there are fewer temptations,' said Master Bisset, who had been at Bologna himself. But I was not satisfied by this and showed it.

'Well, you will just have to bide your time,' said the Bishop, testily. 'You will find out in due course.' And this mystery they would not explain.

'What will I do for money?' I objected. 'Won't I need books and things?'

Bisset laughed. 'You already have a set of books. What do you think you have been copying all this time? Anything else you can borrow and make copies when you get there.'

What I did not have, as they pointed out, were clothes and shoes. These I was supplied with, out of the cathedral funds.

CHAPTER 3

London, 1303

AND SO, WITH SAFE CONDUCTS from Sir John Seagrave, the English governor of our part of the realm, we took the road south on horseback, the Bishop, my tutor and I, with a few soldiers for protection, first for York, where we met up with Bishop Lamberton of St Andrews, and his escort, and then towards Nottingham and London.

When I protested that we were passing Cambridge, the Bishop said, 'You will come to the English court with us. Who knows what you will learn there. You will be installed as a scholar on the way back.'

London announced itself to us by the approaching stench of so many people crushed together, every narrow street a running sewer carrying everything human beings did not want; and the smoke of the cooking-fires rose in clouds blotting out the sun; even, as we watched, actually setting fire to the very dwellings themselves. Near the Thames, a deep, stinking flood of effluent, plied by craft of diverse sorts, we came to the Palace of Westminster, gave our names and were told to attend the next day, promptly, at noon.

Lodging, we found in a tavern hard by, crammed into a tiny chamber, and, with Master Bisset as my protector from the legions of rogues with which the place abounded, I wandered the markets and trading places of the many guildsmen.

I had never seen so many fine buildings. Westminster Abbey was magnificent—towering above all with delicate carving in stone—astonishing to behold—and then the high battlements of the Tower and bridges with shops upon them and great halls erected by the guilds. Such riches! Silks and satins of every colour; glovers and shoemakers, cabinetmakers and candlemakers, apothecaries and pastrycooks—every trade imaginable and some I had never heard of; and foods and drinks of a diversity I never dreamed existed. And the incessant noise! Armourers were making everything from swords to mail and the new breastplates; fletchers and bowmakers worked side by side turning out enough weapons for an army and everywhere around rang the sound of hammer on anvil; for, indeed, an army was assembling.

'It is always thus, here,' said my tutor. 'If it is not war against the Welsh, or Irish then it is against the French or ourselves.'

The next day we were admitted to the palace and, after a short wait, to the throne room itself, where I beheld for the very first time the great and puissant king, Edward Plantagenet.

He was six feet two, still spare of figure, in spite of his great age, which showed in his white hair and beard and rather mottled face, as if it had been pickled inexpertly; except for a small pot belly under the great chest encased in a red velvet doublet and white hose, with an outer full-length silk robe of silver and gold, edged in ermine.

I stood beside and a little behind the others of our small embassy and copied all their movements. How we had to bow and kneel and scrape before we were deemed fit to advance and converse with this great personage.

Around us were guards by the score, some with cross-bows at the ready, should a move be made against their lord; others in full armour with sword or lance or halberd in hand; and nobility and officials of many kinds, often in uniforms, emblazoned by the brilliant reds and yellows of the royal house; and ladies, the first I ever saw, in ermine-edged silk robes of red, yellow, green, blue, apricot and peach, wearing tall conical hats of matching colours, some with veils, mostly white, like wisps of cloud. What beauty! What splendour!

At last, enough obeisance had been undergone to satisfy his liege-men and the talk began.

'And is all rebellion at an end?' said the King, sitting tall on his throne above us, lisping slightly, left eye drooping, like his father before him.

'While Wallace is at large, Sire,' said Lamberton, bowing again, in black gown, holding his flat black velvet cap humbly in hand, like the other churchmen, 'men will flock to him.'

Displeased, the King bellowed, 'When every Scottish castle is in my hands, and every noble is my sworn vassal?'

No one could think of anything to say.

'If every noble is my sworn vassal what has England to fear?'

'Some of them may feel that they have been coerced, Sire,' said Wishart, small, old and wizened, with a white tonsure like a halo.

'Coerced is it! Did they not agree to be my vassals before this sorry affair ever began?'

'Well yes, Sire, but—' said Wishart.

'But me no buts, sir priest! Wallace is my vassal because his feudal superior is. Swore an oath by God! And Bruce, and every other worth a fig in that northern wilderness. They are my vassals, as you are, all of you! So if there is any talk of rebellion it will be met with vigour!'

As there was nothing worth saying to such an implacable message, no one did. The King said, 'I am soon off to Flanders and would know what trouble I leave behind me. Do I have your assurance of peace in Scotland?'

When no one would answer, the King exploded. 'Will you answer? What did I bring you here for, but to receive your assurances of good conduct?'

'Sire,' said Wishart, 'I can give no assurances. But the country is peaceful now.'

'Is it so? Maybe that is because I have just taken Wallace. My agents have taken him in Flanders and hold him for me.'

As the world now knows, this was not so, for, even before this, Wallace had escaped to Paris; but we did not know it then, and were much affected. I saw Wishart stiffen and grow sad, all in a moment; and something like a tear deposit itself on Lamberton's cheek. Master Bisset said, 'Sire, I urge clemency.'

'Clemency is it? The rogue is my vassal yet he killed my men and led a rebellion, causing much trouble and expense to put down. I will make an example of him. Bits of him will hang from every town-wall of significance as a lesson to others. This I promise you!' After another silence, the King said, 'You boy, lurking back there, step forward. Let us see what you have to say, since these cravens are silent.'

Nervously, I did as ordered, flushing under the stares of the multitude around me.

'Well, boy, what have you to tell me about the Scots? They are your people. Will they cause me trouble?'

'Yes, Sire,' I replied, levelly.

There was a surprised silence and then the King laughed and others soon joined in. He said, 'You are bold. Why do you think so?'

'Because they want their freedom, Sire. They did not ask to be your vassals and most do not consider themselves vassals.'

The King exploded again. 'But their superiors have sworn! Do I have to make every menial swear? Is it not enough that the nobility and burgesses have sworn? Does it not follow that those who must follow them are my vassals and must do my bidding?'

'No, Sire. No Scotsman would ever blindly give up his freedom just because his superior was compelled to do so.'

There was a sudden dead silence, and every eye in the great court was turned upon me to see what terrible event would ensue. Behind me, I felt Lamberton's tall figure grow rigid, as if he might be wounded himself by the very blows soon to fall on my slight shoulders. Wishart laid a hand upon one of these, comfortingly.

The King surveyed me imperiously. 'Well, have you nothing further to say? Don't you know you could be killed for less?'

'I spoke the truth, Sire. It was what you wanted, I think.'

He seemed taken aback at this and it halted him for a moment while he considered me, out of that drooping eye which mesmerised me, as if I were a terrified rabbit in the presence of a golden eagle.

'And you have shown me how matters stand,' said he. 'If they are all like you I will yet have trouble.' He rose and swept off the dais, petulantly, as I judged, and then, at the door, turned again and waved me away with an imperious hand. 'You may live, boy. But begone from here today, before I change my mind and throw you into the Tower. I do not make war on boys, today.'

Our party left the city quickly, but late that night, as we lay safe in the Benedictine monastery of St Albans, full forty miles north, so fast had we travelled, there was general rejoicing, over tankards of ale. 'God be praised!' said Wishart. 'That was a brave thing!'

'We should keep him clear of England,' said Master Bisset.

'No, it must be Cambridge as we agreed,' said Wishart. 'Now more than ever. This steel needs tempering.'

'But what if they hear of this?'

'Why should they? He'll soon be lost in Cambridge among the other scholars.'

CHAPTER 4

Cambridge

AND SO IT CAME ABOUT that I was enrolled as a subsizar in Granville's Hall, a four-storied building of wood, wattle and daub, the largest private building of its kind I had seen, outside London. In the morning, the others said farewell and I soon found myself performing the same duties as before: emptying chamber pots, and latrines, serving at dinner, and clearing up after the young, and often wealthy, scholars who abounded in the place.

Lessons there were many, some of them in our hall, many more elsewhere in other halls being erected almost every year. A man would undertake to speak and scholars would come and hear him, and if he were any good, they would return. After the talk, there would be many questions. Sometimes the talk was nothing but questions and answers, in the style Abelard adopted in Paris, two centuries ago. Thus, for most of the time, my mind was on fire with the heat of new ideas that struck into me every day; and which I argued over within myself and marvelled at, and disputed the truth of, with anyone with the patience to listen.

For a long time, no one would listen. What could a youthful subsizar without money or connexions have to say that would be of value? But my enthusiasm was boundless and would not be denied. Sooner or later, it had to emerge.

Eventually, one day, one particularly fateful day, it did.

The bell for dinner had struck and the gentlemen were well into the meal, the ale and wine beginning to take effect, when, outside, there were hoofbeats and the sudden clatter of steel horseshoes on the cobbles of our courtyard. A minute later, the door crashed open, and a tall ginger-headed figure in black cape, helmet and coat of mail strode into the room, divesting himself of gauntlets as he came. This was Giles de Montherlant, a man full grown, too old to be a student, some said, and one who had set himself above the college rules without demur from anyone. This, because he had been well-trained in arms, had killed his men in battle and, even now, was on the verge of knighthood. If that were not enough, his family had lands in both England and

Gascony, and power of that sort was a disincentive to interference with his wishes.

Rowels ringing on the flagstones, he clattered to a place at my table, sat down, shouted for food and raised the half-full, quart jug of ale, which he quaffed in one long thirsty slurp. Finally, he laid it down and looked about. 'I have seen Wallace. His entrails are twenty feet long.'

All talk ceased.

'They are green and slimy like a giant eel.' Again he was met with silence, as everyone present tried to comprehend. 'They cut his cock and balls off and fed them to him. Then they slit him from neck to crotch and pulled everything out. The stink of it on the fire was most foul.' Silence again. And Giles, smiling at the effect he had produced, said, 'He was still alive, you know. Even then. He did not cry out. Then they stretched him a bit and you could hear the joints cracking. And his eyes still shone with life. Then they cut the head off and a great gout of blood spouted clear across the yard and still the body trembled with life, though the head, with these burning brown eyes, was some distance away. Even when the limbs were chopped off, the torso struggled and writhed with life.'

The silence was palpable, so worrying, that no one would break it. Until Giles himself said in a quiet voice, full of wonder. 'I never saw anyone killed like that before. It means something. Maybe someone will tell me.'

Gilbert de Clare shouted. 'A rebel got his deserts. That's what it means.' But from another table a man said with conviction, 'A brave man was foully murdered. He was no rebel. He fought for the independence of his country.' The voice was fine and contained more than a hint of the north. But a fair-haired youth declared: 'Scotland? It no longer exists except as a province. Your baronage and clergy all submitted to the King. They gave up their independence and now they do not have it. Every Scottish castle is in English hands.'

'No, Cressingham,' said the dark youth, 'it has no validity, because they swore fealty under duress. It was either that or die. No one can be expected not to swear in these circumstances. Homage is a voluntary procedure and if it isn't, it has no compulsion.'

That was when I first realised that the fair-haired speaker was the son of the governor of my own castle in my own home town.

'Damn you, Bruce! No!' said Cressingham. 'Your grandfather and Balliol—and the others—all became the King's vassals before he decided who should be King of Scots. They did this voluntarily, knowing that the man who was made king had agreed to be King Edward's vassal. It follows that every other Scot became King Edward's vassal as soon as Balliol did, for he was their superior.'

Now I understood why I had been sent to Cambridge. To consort with the Bruces. This dark-haired youth must be Alexander de Bruce, brother of Robert, Earl of Carrick, and Edward de Bruce and two others I knew nothing of. I also knew that Alexander was considered the ablest student in the town, a genius some said; and the argument rooted me to the spot, for he had surely lost this one.

While Alexander sat silent, on the bench among the other students, pensively trying to find a riposte, I could control myself no longer. For I knew the only way out. Had I not been along that same path with King Edward himself? I said, 'No Scotsman considers himself any man's vassal unless he has voluntarily sworn to it.'

At first there was amazement that a sally should be made from such an unexpected quarter, but then laughter followed, and I soon saw that my accent was still far from their strangulated vowels. In the midst of it, Cressingham shouted, 'No Scots peasant is expected to have the wit to put the words in the right order. So why would he be asked to swear?' This was accounted a master stroke by most of the company, some of whom laughingly began to vacate the tables and the hall for the taverns outside. Then Montherlant seemed to awaken from a sleep and shouted at me: 'You boy! Fetch my dinner and stop this useless chatter.'

Cheeks burning with the rebuke, I fled to the kitchens and returned with a platter of stew. When I had angrily plunked it down, I was rebuked further and given a buffet on the ear for good measure. 'Mind your own business in future, boy,' he told me, but I stood my ground.

'You want to know what the death of Wallace means?' I said. 'I'll tell you.'

All movement stopped and in the silence, I said, 'It means that Wallace was an exceptional man, one who loved life and would not easily give it up. Above all, that he would never give up his freedom voluntarily. It means that you can take his life but never his soul; and that his soul will live for ever. And every Scotsman will be inspired by his deeds today, and in the past, in dying as he did. It also means that your King is cruel, covetous and unchivalrous. Wallace was never his vassal and yet he was treated as the worst criminal.' And then, inspired myself, I added. 'It means that Wallace is like Christ and those who killed him today will pay for it in all time to come.'

They hated me for this. Called me blasphemer and vagrant and offspring of a cow and wolf and many things far worse. Instead of leaving, they used me as sport that night. I was punched and kicked and then roasted over the fire like an animal, kindling added to keep up the heat. Once, Master Granville himself came in, but soon went out quietly without saying or doing anything. By the time they tired of it, I was unconscious. That night I lay, burning all over, and the next day I was left to my own devices to heal and mend or not, as the case may be.

My sleeping place was a broom cupboard with scarce space to lie down on the floor. I had filled a sack of reeds for my mattress. There I awoke, and for days I lay upon my belly naked, burning and shivering by turns, in utmost agony. A few people looked in on me and someone brought a pitcher of water and kept it filled. Finally, having become less heated, I knew I had to get up and move around or I would die there. And so I got up and left the hall and walked by the river, where the cooling breeze was like healing balm on my skin which had attained the consistency of crumbling parchment. Later, I returned and ate in the kitchens. That night I really did sleep, and the next day I knew I had survived.

In the morning, Master Granville sent for me and told me I should leave.

I refused. 'If I am thrown out of here I will go because I must, but I will not go voluntarily, for there are things I crave to know. I have done no wrong here but have been maltreated. I will not go.'

'You must go to another college, then.'

'No, I will remain here, sir.'

'Then they may kill you. You have seen what they are like.'

'And you have heard what we Scots are like. We do not give up.' I burst into tears and swore I would still remain if they cut off my limbs, so long as my mind was left intact. Master Granville sighed then, and said I could take my chance.

I served, as usual, at table that evening, and my flushed face and burnt hair caused much amusement, Cressingham suggesting that some roast pork had just been served, inviting anyone to cut a slice, but when I ignored it, the talk turned to other things.

As the days passed, I sensed a grudging respect in some that I had survived and had not fled in fear; but a few others, of course, were encouraged by my continued presence to try to achieve the very flight I had stubbornly refused. There were many taunts and buffets and once a dagger point entered the soft flesh of my backside as I stooped over my work. I berated my tormentor loudly, comparing his treatment with that of the unthinking cruelty of the Romans at Calvary.

At first, I thought I would be killed, for the youth stood up and drew his sword, but others calmed him. Thereafter, somehow, I ignored it all, listened to the debates and attended the lectures as before, eagerly, like a love-struck calf.

And then it was that fall in love I did.

Visitors came and went continually, scholars mainly, but members of the families of the students also. One evening, I found myself serving flaxen-haired Sir Hubert Cressingham himself, resplendent in a white silk surcoat adorned with small blue chevrons, who had come to see his son. They were dining together at High Table among the fellows;

and, beside them, I beheld a girl with auburn hair and blue eyes in a gown of pale green silk, bound with a gold belt, from which hung a mauve escarelle.

Because of my burnt skin, I suppose, she stared at me and I returned her look; and in that moment I was lost forever. I went off to the kitchen in a daze, struck dumb by the image of her and when next I came near, I heard them talking about me. Plainly, no one knew that my home was in Bute.

She glanced at me often, with a level gaze that was unnerving, but I could not look away, for I was entranced by her; and I knew that she saw the captivation; and I instantly judged that it was not an unusual experience for her to steal a young man's heart, and feared for myself.

They stayed a few days and every day my capture became more complete. Her name was Eleanor de Rognard, daughter of a landed Norman knight, now dead, along with her mother. Sir Hubert Cressingham was her guardian.

Eleanor was tall and auburn-haired, with blue eyes and a slightly freckled face, smooth, shapely and honey-gold; an elfin nose which turned upward slightly, and bright, even, white teeth which lit up her face whenever she smiled. But it was the eyes which held me. Once, as I served her, I looked into them directly and saw that they were composed of hazel-blue segments, which reflected light like coruscating sunbeams on a bubbling river.

At table she shone like a star, flashing witticisms in every direction, not all kindly. Yet, to be put down by her was accounted an honour of a kind among the young aristocrats who soon deemed it part of their education.

This revealed an unexpected side, one day, when the subject of fleetness of foot was discussed. As usual, everyone thought it was properly an occasion for men; and as usual, Eleanor was determined to prove everyone wrong. A race was suggested, around the very building itself. And so, soon after, a party made of young Cressingham, Clare, Bohun, Montherlant and others made ready to begin, Eleanor having been rudely laughed to the rear of the line.

How her eyes flashed then! I saw her take off like a hare around the outside and race as if made for the purpose: chest thrown out, head laid back, arms and legs going like metronomes, but in a blinding rush of speed which had her hair streaming behind like a blood-red war pennon and the skirts of the green dress rising in the breeze she herself created.

Clare was quick but Eleanor quicker. As they neared the finish line, her eyes seemed to blaze determination and she slowly drew ahead, to win by a clear margin.

Every day, every hour and second of my life was filled with thoughts of her, so that all work stopped abruptly. And yet I never spoke to her, for to me she was a goddess beside whom I felt a worm, and a badly singed one. Of course, my interest was soon known to all and I had to suffer the additional humiliation of taunts about my love-struck condition. The lady herself did not share in these, but smiled upon me kindly. Once, when I appeared at table to serve wine and blushed as I poured some for her, Clare said, 'Here's that love-sick calf, again. Must we put up with it still?'

And Gracie chimed in, 'True. We should have roasted him for longer, the Scots pig.'

But Eleanor defended me. 'You will make fine candidates for knighthood. Putting down the servants is of course a useful training for dealing with rebels.'

Missing the irony, or choosing to ignore it, Montherlant replied, 'There is something I don't like about the Scots peasant. He does not know his place.'

'Yet he serves you and I well enough from it,' said Eleanor.

'He is an upstart and should have stayed where he was.'

'Why did you come here, Scotchman?' said the elder Cressingham. 'It is such a long way.'

'There are no universities in Scotland, Sir,' I said.

'But what use is learning to you, boy? What prospects have you?'

Another would have told him then: about my home Bute, about being one of his own feudal vassals. But I did not. Instinctively, I kept my distance and my own counsel. If I had declared myself then, everything would have turned out very differently.

I said, 'I crave knowledge for its self, Sir, and do not care what difference it will make to my prospects, whatever they are.'

Sir Hubert was surprised. 'You mean you like books? How can this be? Any boy of your age likes hunting and adventure. Surely, you have some spirit?'

'That is not for me to judge, Sir. For now, my only concern is knowledge.'

'Not so!' said Clare. 'You crave Eleanor more than any book. You cannot deny it.'

When I said nothing, stood uncertainly, blushing as I never had before, he said, 'See, he does not deny it.'

'Since you told him he could not, why would he bother?' said Eleanor.

Young Cressingham said, 'Why must you take his side?' And then Eleanor seemed taken aback, as at some interior revelation. 'I do not know, quite. Perhaps because he has no one else on his.'

I should have been pleased at her support, but was not; for I saw instantly that she simply sided with the underdog, who ever he was. I could not know it then, but this very trait in Eleanor was to be an important factor in her life and mine.

Everyone knew that there was no hope for me, and yet I would not quite believe it myself. And I was soon trapped into a sword fight with Giles de Montherlant, for challengers were invited and when none came forth, someone suggested that the Scotch peasant would provide rare sport. There were cries of approval, for all enjoyed the prospect of entertainment; and who cared if a supporter of Scots rebels were gutted?

The issue was the difference made by years of training in arms. Montherlant undertook to force submission on anyone not trained, with four blows.

Thus was it that Giles and I were stripped half naked and stood facing each other in our breeches across the hall, in the space before High Table on its dais, at which dined Master Granville, the Cressinghams, Eleanor and half a dozen fellows. There were gasps when my back was bared, for the skin was like parchment, that part of it not peeled or flaked off. And there were suppurating sores still.

When Sir Hubert called 'begin', Giles lunged at me with the sword and I was driven back against the table with the point at my throat. There were roars of approval and a few catcalls at my ineptness. I cared nothing for these, as the pain of my burnt skin had almost unmanned me.

I laid the sword down and prepared to return to my work, but young Cressingham would have none of it. 'Another trial, Giles. Damage him a little and we'll see if he has any mettle.'

'A shilling, Scotchman, if you can show some fight,' said another, Annesley, by name, but I shook my head.

'What would you need to fight bravely?' said Clare.

'Instruction and practice,' I replied, which provoked some laughter.

'A kiss from the fair Eleanor, if he does well?'—this from young Cressingham—which brought far more, some oohs and ahs, and a hint of a blush on the lady's cheek.

And so it seemed to be agreed that if I acquitted myself well, this would be the reward. Mindless of it, anxious only to do well before her, I held the sword grimly and waited. And yet I did not crave a kiss, for what was that beside knowledge of the person herself? A kiss was a triviality. Yet I felt the pressure of humiliation and that moved me to focus on my predicament.

What could I do? Of course I had seen men fight with swords, watched them training beside the castle in Bute and even in Cambridge, on the grass by the river. I gripped the hilt firmly, more strongly than before, resolved to move aside as soon as I was attacked and then attack in my turn, once my opponent was off-balance, as he lunged.

'Don't kill him, too quickly, Giles,' cried Bohun, and there was more laughter. In the midst of it, Montherlant lunged forward and sent down a swinging blow with the sword, towards my left shoulder. I immediately stepped to my right and lunged for his belly, driving in with all my strength.

Surprised that he had missed, Giles made an effort to recover and stepped back to his right, but I pursued him with the point, mindless of his blade and he, for once, was driven backwards across the flagstones. As I came on, a flashing arc caught my hilt and in a sudden jerking movement, the sword was plucked from my grasp and fell among the scholars. Giles smiled and, responding to the applause, dropped his guard.

Anger erupted in me like sickness. I launched myself into the air, feet first, directed at him, and luckily caught him in the throat. In a heap we fell, arms and legs together, and I began to pummel him with my fists. His head cracked against the floor and he went limp under me.

There were cries of 'shame on you!' from some round about and 'pure luck', from others, but a few whoops of glee also. I stood up and said, 'Where is the shame in dealing with my torturer the only way I can?' I waited for a reply and when there was none, I left them. No one followed to make further sport of me.

That night I lay awake as usual, dreaming of Eleanor, rigid with desire and incapable of thinking of anything else. At dawn, still restless, I got up and paced the corridors of the place, mournfully mooning in the general direction of the guest quarters.

For an hour, I walked up and down silently, as if compelled to remain there by her presence somewhere close by. Finally, I gave up and made off again; but I had gone no distance when behind me a door opened and a figure wrapped in a grey night-shift emerged. It was Eleanor.

I stood unmoving at first, and she; and then, like a moth to a flame, I was silently drawn towards her.

In the half light of early morning, which streamed through the windowed cloisters, she looked naked, for the shift was of flimsy material and the sunbeams poured through it, illuminating all her majesty. I had never seen anything like it before and was dumbstruck.

'You must say nothing of this,' she whispered; and when I made no reply, she made to move off; but then turned. 'Why did you not stay to claim your kiss? You won it fairly.'

I said nothing, could say nothing for the paralysing embarrassment at seeing her thus, rendered naked by the morning light.

Two quick steps brought her to my side and, before I knew what she was about, she planted a gentle kiss upon my cheek; and stood back

with an expression of such warmth and generosity of spirit that, all these many years later, I weep to think of it. It was a blessing; she was a blessing; and I suddenly felt privileged to be alive to see it.
• When I continued to say nothing, she gave me a kindly smile and left me to my lonely vigil.

What lay behind that other door was no water closet but another bedroom; and the mystery of her movements was to lie at the back of my mind for a considerable time, before it was resolved.

The Cressingham party left the next morning and I stood in the yard, watching. Then, filled with anxiety that I might never see her again, I took a horse from the rail and galloped after them. At the north gate, I tethered the animal and climbed up onto the town wall, for, having no money for the tolls, I could not follow.

For a while, I watched from the heights as the party wound its way northwards. Once, Eleanor half turned in the saddle and made some sign. I imagined that it was a wave and that it was to me, and my heart sang. When they were out of sight, I stood at a loss, as if my very soul had just departed. Then, I shook my stupid head and gazed into the distance, remembering her, the shape of her lips when she smiled, the elfin nose with its slight upward tilt, the blue eyes shot with hazel, the sheen in her red-brown hair which rippled like a magic river down her back; and the broad, high forehead. What power of thought lay behind that honey-hued cliff? Most of my contemporaries seemed to think women devoid of brains, but I knew better. I knew that my own mother was resourceful and capable, with all the qualities of man, and more: warmth and kindliness. Eleanor was like that too. My heart told me it was so and I believed it, for the knowledge was in her smile.

I was in a turmoil for days and could think of nothing but her; lay burning with desire at night, composing verses which I wrote down the next day at dawn, for I often had no candle. And the worst of it was that I could not send them to her. Of course I gave them to travellers to the north with what few coins I could scrape together, going without food because of it, but they would not reach her, that was certain. Who would go out of his way to Bute for me? And yet, though I knew the futility, it helped somehow, and made me feel more at peace. It was a time of craziness, when I felt ill, more ill than ever in my life, vulnerable and powerless, an easy prey to any predator.

A week later, I again attended a lecture and then everything looked up; for the sheer fascination of the limitless universe of knowledge held me in its grip even more effectively. Here at least was something I could do, an activity in which I could take part meaningfully. At first, though, I was an onlooker. That first lecture after my hiatus, as I think of it, was on Aristotle. Master Jean d'Arcy was expounding the *Organon*, one of the books I had copied with such pleasure, for what we had were all the possible true syllogisms. It was a wonder this classification. To think that Aristotle had exposed and resolved the entire matter!

And yet, he had not.

At the end, Master Jean remained for quaestiones and a soft northern voice like my own spoke up. It was Alexander de Bruce. He stated that the last syllogism was wrong and produced a counter example which displayed the issue conclusively. At first there was a hush, as men everywhere around considered the point, and then a growing hubbub, as a few were converted to this radical idea. Some, of course, were so wedded to reverence of Aristotle, whom we all held in awe, that Alexander had to be wrong; for how could he be right in opposing the greatest thinker of all time, as many thought?

Alexander was questioned, aggressively and contemptuously, but answered calmly, clearly and with authority.

Within a few minutes, I saw that he was right and Aristotle mistaken. Arguments raged for an hour or more, but, by then, some at least were convinced. Alexander was borne off in triumph to a hostelry, where extraordinary celebrations occurred.

My own advancement began at another lecture one day, when the speaker called for an answer to an arithmetical computation, needed for some related question. While my peers busied themselves with quill and parchment, I looked on with amazement, for I knew the answer and shouted it. Master Catchpole told me to hush, as if I were mistaken, but when first one and then others announced the same result, he began to consider me with greater interest; enquired my name and how I knew, and I had to explain that multiplying two double digit numbers in my head, without benefit of scribing, was very easy; one I had always been able to accomplish without effort. Of course, I had to demonstrate this small gift and did so for every pair of numbers called out to me. When these were checked and found to be correct, I was accounted a genius of a kind myself, though I have always thought the gift of no particular value. It depends on estimating the size of the number and multiplying the two ends; this, with a little knowledge of the properties of numbers, makes the answer obvious, without the labour of calculation.

From then on, I was talked about and questioned and my tutors took an increasing interest in my progress. For myself, the lesson Alexander had taught me was one of the most important I ever learned: never to assume that authorities, however revered, are right. The shock of it affected many of us, I suppose; some of them were masters. In a way, I believe that Cambridge took a different line from Oxford because of it and other like occurrences. For a while, I naively imagined that this was why our masters had left Oxford in the first place: because there, quaestiones, especially of great authorities, were not encouraged.

How could we progress unless we questioned everything? So at least it seemed to me. There was, however, a limit to this thesis which I soon discovered for myself: some things were beyond question; and to do so, was to court disaster and even death. So some quaestiones had better remain unstated.

It happened in the philosophy schools, to which I was invited a year or two early—a rare distinction occasioned after I came first in Logic and Latin in the examinations. We had been doing Aquinas, considering the various arguments to show that God exists. At the end of the disputation, just as the lecturer was leaving, a scholar, Norbert Wendover, suddenly objected: 'How can God be omnipotent and yet do nothing about the pestilence? How can he be all-loving and yet allow people to die in agony by the thousand? Do not the observable facts of the suffering of humanity contradict the very definition of God?'

The shock in the hall was immediate. Every eye turned upon the speaker. Here was a man who challenged God! It was unthinkable! And yet the idea instantly seized hold of me and I was captured by it.

For once in my life I said nothing and it saved me I think, for they took Wendover and gave him the most terrifying inquisition imaginable, firing questions at him, demanding that he recant from his heresies, cursing him for his failure to acknowledge his creator, and, finally, ducking him near to death in the river, holding him by the ankles from a bridge, with his head under the surface; and all the while abusing him in other ways too terrible to report. The cruelty was inhuman; and yet it was all too human. I wanted to protest that this was not what Jesus died for; that compassion was supposed to be our watchword, and yet I knew that if I had done so, I myself would have suffered a worse fate. At least Wendover was an Englishman.

A month later, Alexander de Bruce was pronounced *Artium Magister, summa cum laude*, and a dinner was held that night by his eldest brother at which I attended high table.

It was the first time I met Robert de Bruce, Earl of Carrick, of whom I had heard and was to hear so much more and even to come to know.

He was six feet tall, clean shaven, with dark-brown hair. His skin was unmarked by the pox and his cheeks ruddy with vigour and health. I suppose he would have been about thirty years old then. He was clad in a scarlet corset sangle, the height of fashion then. It was adorned with highlights of cloth of gold, and he wore dark-green tight breeches and poulaine shoes, with a fine black felt hat on his head from which a long peacock's feather curved upwards proudly. Except the king, I had never seen such rich raiment or such an aristocratic air. Here was a person of consequence; everything about him proclaimed it.

Talk crossed and recrossed the table, one and then another holding forth, as men accustomed to lecture are apt to do at every opportunity. For a while, the earl was content to listen and savour the best minds of the time, like sage rooks, white-faced in their black gowns. Much was made of Alexander, also done up like a prince, though in blue and grey. He was half drunk pretty quickly, but firing off flashes of light in every direction as usual. Then the talk turned to the realm, or rather the new realm which had been created by the addition of Ireland, Wales and now Scotland. England had become a far larger country and all present were delighted by this extension to her power. The Bruces had lands in Norfolk and Yorkshire as well as in Carrick and Annandale, and were as Norman in origin as any of the others. So no one expected that any would dissent, but the earl did.

When a toast was proposed: 'to the King, confusion to his enemies,' the earl did not stand up and drink like everyone else, including Alexander. When the others sat down again, there was a silence, until Master Granville enquired of the earl his objections.

'I accept fully that Scotland is now a part of England,' said he, 'but I am not happy about it and I do not approve.' The man's high complexion was flushed redder than ever with embarrassment, as if he had been caught out in some strange way or forced into a false position after many days concealment. Pressed by the Master, he explained, 'I am of Norman stock, as some of you. But I was born and grew up in Scotland. My mother is wholly Scottish—so I am at least half Scottish.'

'Half Norman, too?' suggested Master de Coverly, one of the fellows.

'Perhaps', said the earl, 'and yet I am the seventh of my name to live there. Even my great grandfather considered himself Scots. It is at least clear that I am not one whit English.'

'But you are on good terms with the king, are you not?' said Master Granville.

'I would not keep my lands or my head, otherwise.'

'Yet he is your friend, so they say?'

'He is. And a nobler knight and more able king I do not know. I am proud to count myself a friend of his, if indeed I am; and I do think I am.'

'Well, how can you view the extension to his kingdom as anything but desirable?' said Granville.

The earl quaffed a chalice of wine and pondered for a moment. 'Because it is at the expense of my own country.'

'Surely, you do not mean that you imagine you should be King of Scots?' said de Coverly, a nervous, delicate don with brown hair and black robes, pointing a long-nailed finger at Bruce.

'That was not what I meant; but John Balliol having been deposed and banished, who else is there?'

'But this is treason!' said Master Hemmings, a large, rough Dominican with a Cornish accent, 'for our king is now King of Scotland. Edward, King of England.'

Bruce seemed to agree. 'The king as superior overlord has the right to banish the King of Scots and has done so. And if he wishes, under that law, he can make himself King of Scotland.'

'Well then?' said de Coverley. 'What have you against it?'

'It was badly done and never should have been done, this overlordship. My grandfather and the others were duped into agreeing the overlordship, thinking that they themselves would become king. They should not have done it.'

'Since they did,' said Granville, 'that is an end to it.'

'No,' said Bruce. 'No one else agreed then. And if they did later, it was under duress. How could it be otherwise? How could a country be given up in this fashion? It is impossible except through stupidity and fear. Fear of Edward did it. Fear of his power. That was what lay behind the Ragman Roll at Berwick, when every noble, cleric and burgess was forced to swear allegiance to an alien king.'

'But they did so swear!' said de Coverley. 'Yourself among them!'

'Only to save our skins! Is that so bad? Would not anyone else do the same?' The English were irritated. Granville said, 'Well it's over now anyway. Nothing can undo it.' And many there nodded sagely. But the earl did not.

With a smile like a razor, Master de Coverley said, 'There is talk that the king will make you governor of Scotland. Is it true?'

'I do not think so. Sir John Seagrave is governor now. Why would the king change?'

'Perhaps, so that you might go down better with the Scots than a foreigner.'

'It is a post I do not covet,' said Bruce.

'But why?' said Granville innocently. 'It would bring you great honour and wealth.'

'And the same difficulties as Balliol.'

De Coverley said: 'Balliol was a fool. He disobeyed the king.'

'He merely governed according to the customs of Scotland,' said Bruce.

'But Scotland is part of England now!' said de Coverley.

'Not to the Scots,' said Bruce.

'Then it is treason,' said de Coverley, 'for you say you are a Scot!'

Wearily, Bruce replied, 'I am the king's sworn vassal. I speak only of those who are not.'

'But you excused it on ground of duress!'

'Only for the others,' said Bruce, flushing slightly; but I wondered if he meant it.

He sat on with his wine after the others had left, pensively, his face crossed by shadows which flickered from the fire nearby. Standing behind and a little to one side, I said, 'And how is it in Scotland?'

Alexander, who alone remained with him, said, 'This is the one who defended Wallace.'

Bruce turned in his chair and eyed me. 'Not well. The land is laid waste, the people are starving and miserable.'

'It is said you played your part in this,' I told him. 'That you fought for England at Falkirk. That it was you who chased off our cavalry.' Bruce looked bleak, downtrodden, and his head drooped. When he made no reply, I added, 'How could you act against Scotland?'

'The Balliols are my enemies. So long as they were in charge I would not fight with them. If fight I must, I fight against them.'

'Against your own country and against Wallace?' I was shouting, and noticed just in time to quieten myself, before others in the hall further off came to listen.

'They fought under Balliol's banner. Their chief noble is John Comyn, leader, now that Balliol is in exile. I could not fight with them under his command.'

'So it was pride, then?'

Bruce's hand went to his scabbard and he looked at me as if I were a small animal he would smite to shreds; but as I stared him out, his eyes softened and he said, 'You have smeddum, then. You were right, Alexander, this one is the kind of Scot we need.' But when I smiled with relief, he added, 'Watch your tongue, however, or someone will cut it out.'

'Is there nothing you can do to stop this misery in my country?'

'It is my country too,' said Bruce. And after some reflection, 'No, there is nothing I can do.'

'Surely something can be done to redress this . . . this travesty of justice! They have taken our country. It has been given away, for nothing!'

'You are right, but might is on their side. Our army is scattered; tiny by comparison and ill-equipped. Edward has only to snap his fingers and twenty thousand well-armed men will carry him over our border and lay waste the land again, burning everything and killing men, women and children. With that army and his fleet of supply ships he can go anywhere which we, lacking arms and food, cannot, even in our own land. Edward has already been to the far north of Scotland where few Scots have ever been. He has the power and the skill and he is ruthless. We have nothing. Are just beetles by comparison, to be crushed underfoot.'

'So you will do nothing?' I said.

'There is nothing to do!' said Bruce with force.

'But how can you sit there and say that? How could you fight against Scotland? You have played your own part in this loss of freedom, in all this misery.'

'I could not prevent it.'

'But did you have to join in?'

'Yes! Otherwise I would have been stripped of my lands and my men, and would have been no better than the worst peasant.'

'At least you would have had your honour,' I said finally, and made to leave.

'Stay,' said Alexander. 'Sit down with us.'

But I was angry and did not want to sit with a traitor. Alexander smiled at me winningly, 'I have been saying the same thing to him myself but less effectively.' And he laughed. 'You don't know what a terror he is, I can tell you. But sit now, please. Join us. Take some wine. Here,' and he poured wine into a tankard someone had left and motioned me to sit. When I still refused, standing doggedly, as if in the midst of enemies, Alexander, added, 'It is clear that you have an uncommon mind. We need the use of it. So will you kindly sit down and lend us your aid?'

There was no answer to this. As usual, Alexander had the clinching reply. I sat down on the earl's left and faced Alexander across the board.

'What are we going to do, Robert?' said Alexander. 'There must be something we can do.' But the earl was disconsolate. I had given him every reason to be. He shook his head sadly. 'We must wait for some good luck. Maybe something will happen.'

'That's no good,' said Alexander. 'The problem is that they are stronger and better armed and more numerous and better trained. How do we deal with that? There must be a way.'

'Why must there be?' said Robert, irritably.

I said, 'I was shut up in Cathedral school with my head in books and missed it. What happens when the English come? I mean how do they exert their power over us?'

Alexander grinned at the earl. 'See? I told you. He asks good quaestiones.'

Robert said, 'They gather an army at Berwick; then they cross the border. They take everything they find: cattle, goods, food, fodder, weapons—everything, including women and anyone else they want for servants. They burn the houses, destroy everything they do not need. They take the castles with siege equipment. We have nothing like their mangonels. I saw one at Stirling, the War Wolf. It knocked a huge hole in the wall, but long before that it had terrified the occupants into submission. When they have taken a castle, they reinforce it. In Wales, they built the finest castles you ever saw. They can be defended by thirty men. Thirty! These castles dominate the entire countryside. You would have to see them to understand what I mean. The Welsh are reminded every hour of every day that they are under the yoke.'

'But the army cannot stay forever,' said Alexander. 'It must be paid and fed. The King will send it home eventually. What then?'

'The land is ruled by the castles, as now.'

'Can't we take the castles back again?' I said.

'No, we do not have the equipment.'

Alexander said, 'Then some other means must be found.'

'But they will just send another army to take them back again,' said Bruce, wearily.

I said, 'If we did this over and over, perhaps they would grow tired of it and leave us alone.' There was a silence then as they considered this. I added, 'What is the use of them claiming our land? I mean, if we have no money and the lands are laid waste all the time, what profit is there?'

There was another silence then, and I knew I had said something worthwhile.

Robert said, 'You mean that we should flee before any army, burn our houses and destroy all our crops, leaving them nothing? Would the people put up with that?'

'Yes,' I said. 'Anything rather than lose their freedom.'

'That's it,' said Alexander. 'The strategy! If there is nothing to be got out of Scotland but starvation and death for an invader, they will lose the taste for it. The country is wide, with many hiding places. We must hide from their army when it comes. And if they send out scouting parties to find us, these we must kill. Prick it at the edges and when it finds no food to sustain it, they will go away.'

'What about supply ships?' I said.

'Ships are difficult to handle,' said Robert, thoughtfully. 'A good gale would sink them. Maybe we can do something even there.'

'Feeding an army, even from supply ships, is impossible,' I said. 'The army must go to the ships or send men to collect the supplies. These men can be attacked and the supplies captured and made available to us.'

The earl laughed and we began to laugh too. 'What a pair of firebrands I have here,' he said approvingly. 'Maybe all is not lost after all.'

'The question is whether our people will wear it,' said Alexander, pensively. 'Maybe they'll get tired of it before the English. Then subjection is inevitable.'

I have wondered if Robert Bruce was aware of all this beforehand; if the conversation did help to clarify matters. As I found out later, you could never be sure what he had foreseen for himself. Certainly he had a gift for discussions of this kind when anyone was free to speak and new ideas, or more often new ways of looking at old problems, were spontaneously generated.

When they stood up to leave, I did too. Robert took a purse and handed it to me but I refused it. He seemed offended. 'For your studies,' he said, 'to help you on your way.' When I told him I did not need money, he laughed and replied, 'A man who does not need money is one worth knowing.'

'Why won't you take it?' said Alexander, also amused.

'I do not know, quite. I have never taken money before for doing nothing. Perhaps that's it. And there is something about the idea that worries me. I would dislike it to become a habit. Perhaps it never will if I never make a beginning.'

Alexander laughed. 'It is pride, then. The same as you, brother.'

'Maybe this pride will free a country,' said Robert.

'The lack of it caused our country to be sold for favours,' I said, levelly; and knowing I referred to their grandfather, they left me without another word.

My scruples were soon to be tested in an unusual way and found wanting but not morally. The failure was intellectual, a failure of insight. I see that now, all these years later. How important it is to be able to see, to understand fully. It is this fault which lies behind so many men's failures, great and small. If only we could always see how things really are!

One of the fellows, Master Hammond, soon convinced me that he was the best mathematician in the town, and I began to seek him out and sit at his feet whenever I could. He was a rarity, for he easily gave up the use of a text to reveal discoveries of his own—the only fellow to do this. Some condemned him for it, as there was not opportunity to examine his findings with sufficient care. Yet I minded these objections not at all. The frequency with which he produced new ideas and beautiful arguments to justify them was a miracle and I felt blessed to know him. New theorems fell from him every other day, new inventions of notation to manage them and fresh insights into the already known, which astonished those of us with the courage to attend; for of course there was a danger of being condemned for listening to false teaching and misusing our time—it was clear that his work would form no part of the examinable syllabus. And yet one sensed that here was real intelligence at work and the daily acquaintance with it, the flavour of this excess of creative power, inevitably had its effects upon our own.

My education in particular had been awarded an unusual freedom, however, and in it I suspected the hand of the earl who, I knew, had spent some time ensconced with Master Granville on my account, before he departed. For reasons that were unclear, I was encouraged to work far harder than anyone else and permitted to enter any schools I wished, even though I had not taken my Bachelor's degree. But Robert Bruce could not have foreseen that I would fall under the influence of Master Hammond, with whom I spent more time than any other student. He it was bore the responsibility for an alteration in my views that was to have enormous repercussions in my life and to my view of the career of Bruce himself.

Having spent four full hours copying a manuscript for a wealthy burgess—one of the ways I earned my keep, the original was rented for the purpose—I left the shop where I had been employed and met Master Hammond in the street. 'Come, take a tankard with me,' said he. And I felt flattered that my mind should be considered fit company to join him in a nearby tavern. It was there, forgetting my own duties as a servant, that I got involved in a discussion which brought about my conversion.

The subject of my Scottishness came up and Hammond seemed to think that we Scots were far better off under English rule. I pointed out that most Scots were trying to recover from their cattle being stolen, their lands being burnt and the loss of their freedom.

'What is the use of freedom?' said Hammond. 'Why does it signify? Is not what matters most strong, effective and fair government? What is the use of freedom if you have nothing, if you are reduced by poverty to a naked savage? And if you have no law and no redress for wrong-doing? Is not what matters most how men live? In poverty or in comfort? Under a firm, just law or under the barbarity of dog eat dog? And is not Edward Plantagenet the best king this island has seen for centuries? Since you have no king, how could you do better? Now he has gathered together Scotland, Wales and Ireland as well as England and he soon expects to govern France and maybe Spain as well.'

When I queried this, he pointed out that, in marrying Eleanor of Castile, the King therefore acquired title to the throne of Spain—more even, in the person of his son, and was related to the King of France, in which already he owned a large part of the lands in the south.

'You see, what the King is doing is uniting all the countries of Europe under one strong, able, fair and effective ruler. What could be better? For if there is but one country, there will be no opportunity for the constituent small ones to go to war with each other. And the peoples of all these small countries will have the advantage of English law, English fair treatment and English wealth. This is surely to the benefit of every member of those countries. Of course, there will be a time of adjustment, as now, when a land like Scotland must recover, after foolishly resisting the inevitable march of progress. How could a small country like Scotland defeat such a mighty neighbour as England? It is impossible. Inevitable, then, that Scotland has been subsumed under

England's rule. Anyway, the competitors for the Scottish crown wisely saw that vassalage to England was the right and sensible course, which is why they gave homage.'

I was staggered, my senses reeling. Here was an argument for the abandonment of Scottish nationhood in favour of a wider community of several nations, Scotland among them.

'Yes, Master Hammond, but—' I began, only to be told:

'What is this *yes, but*? Let us have no more of *yes, but*. Either it is yes or it is no. Has Aristotle taught you nothing? And who was the scholar who told me only yesterday that one must follow the logic where it leads, as Aristotle recommends?'

I found myself stammering with the shock of it. 'S.s.s.s.o y.y.y.you think this is desirable on the grounds that the larger nation will be stronger and more uniformly fair and helpful to all the peoples?' And then, not giving him time to reply, insights of my own flashed into my mind: 'It will even be better able to defend itself against foreign invasion—such as the Mongols.'

'Right! Divided we fall, united we stand. The Mongols can be beaten if we all stand together. You see, then?'

The shock of these novel possibilities was thunderous. 'Yes,' I replied, 'and the Saracens too. Just think, if all the countries of Europe were under one head, like Edward, we would be able to put a hundred thousand knights in the field! A crusade of that size would win back all the holy sepulchres lost in Palestine!'

As I went back to hall, my senses were in ferment not just with ale, but with this new idea, these new politics. Round and round my mind they went that night as I lay half drunk with the surprise of it.

In the middle of the night I sat up with a start, for I realised that no one in my family would understand this! And yet it was surely right, this idea! It was better for Scotland to be a part of England. Because it was better for every Scot to have the benefit of the good law, fair treatment and the better living conditions of the English. One had only to look around to see how much better off everyone was. By comparison, many Scots went ragged and barefoot—so that they were frozen stiff in the northern winter—or starving because, either there was not enough food anyway, or the English would have stolen or destroyed it.

How could any of that be desirable for the people of Scotland? If only they could be persuaded to give up thinking about freedom, that most iniquitous concept that was so far from their real interest! Why should one care about freedom when one could live and thrive so much better without it? God knows how many Scots men, women and children had died in the past ten years, simply because they wanted freedom! Logically, the very idea of freedom in these circumstances was idiotic!

If all it meant was certain death! Against which, without it, was a very satisfactory life.

And so I was converted. But I was young and steeped in Aristotelian logic and used my mind, as I had been taught, as if it were a sharp knife, without regard to any other consideration. Then there was the influence of Hammond, of course. Him I thought a god, a god of the mind, with the gift of creating new worlds of ideas all on his own. If I could not stomach his conclusions, perhaps I would be denied them and his company and favour in future. There may have been a little of this too. But as anyone can see, he was brilliant, a formidable advocate and he impressed me as no one else at that time.

Hammond was soon at my side next day and, in the course of a few hours walk by the river, reinforced his conclusions in my head. A few weeks later, coming from a class, arguing some obscure point, some-one said, 'You know Bann, you begin to sound like an Englishman.' And, I am ashamed now to admit, I was pleased.

Master Granville called me to see him one day and informed me that I had been awarded a scholarship of some obscure kind and so must now give up my position of subsizar to some other impoverished worthy. I would now sit with the gentlemen at table and 'I had better mind my manners'—except, since I already knew they had none, that presented no difficulty. And there was an allowance too, for clothing and books and entertainments, to be spent as I desired. All this because I had been an exceptional scholar who promised to bring credit to the college and the university.

Of course I was delighted and celebrated by investing in a new kirtle of white lindsey-woolsey, tight breeches of red kersey and a pair of yellow shoes with real laces and red baubles on the upturned toes. I had my hair cut in the new fashion, short in front and long at the back, and wore a tall purple hat with two peacock's feathers. A great foolishness, certainly, and one that makes me blush even now; but I was young and made the mistakes of youth, all the more flagrantly for having had so little opportunity before.

I was accounted a sensation; and others copied my attire or went one better. But everything came to nought within a week, for I was returning from the schools one afternoon, when I was set upon by some ruffians from the town and was soon rolling in the gutter among the filth, fighting as best I could with one of them, amongst a scream-ing crowd of onlookers.

I received a bloody nose and my new raiment was quite ruined, the smell of shit on it intolerable. When this was reported at hall, there was some sympathy. My new friends wanted to seek out the ruffians, but I did not encourage them. 'You must take training in arms,' said one, 'or your life will be a misery; ever at the mercy of any determined thief and ruffian who covets your goods.' Of course it was the gaudy clothes that had been my undoing. They had created a distance between me and the poor of the town, and they so resented it that I was instantly set upon. All this I realised that night as I lay abed, conscious of my bruises. I resolved to dress more circumspectly in future and learn to defend myself.

And so, every day, in the late afternoon, for two hours, I took the training that was available in the fields by the river. The tutor was a man-at-arms who had fought in the Welsh and Scottish wars. His name was Jeb and he came from Lincoln. He must have been about forty years of age. He began by enquiring about my life and how I had been brought up. When I mentioned slaving over books for years, he seemed unhappy and shook his head. 'Books woun't keep you alive, young maister,' says he. 'You'm learn to use a staff first.' But when I mentioned walking to school barefoot, he seemed better pleased, as if I had passed some of the elementary initiative tests of life.

Work with the quarter staff went on for some weeks, and many a blow on the shoulders and head I took in that time, but I did learn the art well enough and even saw why this was a useful beginning. I learned to move my feet quickly, to dodge blows, and timing—that above all. I also gained in strength and stamina and eventually had Jeb on the back foot. After this came the sword—about three feet long. I had to learn the different cuts, how to get under the guard of my opponent, but above all how to defend. Again, stamina was a vital ingredient. As Jeb put it, 'If you'm cain't hould your steel up, you'll get his steel frew yer.' But also speed, for that was the best quality: attacking first, and attacking fast, before your opponent was prepared. Finally, there was deception: making the enemy think you were going to do something else or nothing at all. This, Jeb accounted of greatest importance, having saved his life often. Then I progressed to dagger and sword, both, using the one to catch and hold the sword of my opponent; and all the tricks of limb and torso one could apply, to gain leverage and advantage.

Lastly, there was archery and, as soon as I saw what a bow could do, I knew this was the weapon for me. It was six foot of yew, required real strength and a knack to string it. Once strung, the power was vast. Many times, until I learned, I cut and scraped the inside of my arm while practising in the early days, but persistence had its reward, and as time passed, I became a skilled archer, able to put a shaft through a board at two hundred paces, using a protective bracer on the arm by then. I was shown distance firing, angling the bow skyward for maximum elevation and firing off five or six arrows in quick succession, to increase the chance of a hit. This was how the Welsh fired in battle, Jeb told me. Volley fire, with the leader calling out the range and fall of shot, so that small adjustments could be made to deal with advancing cavalry.

Of course, I was not supposed to fire arrows at all, this having been the true origin of the university. A student at Oxford had shot a townswoman with an arrow, whereupon, failing to identify the culprit, the townsfolk hanged three students from the town-walls. Masters and students then fearing further reprisals, the university dispersed. It happened that several masters had homes around Cambridge and, knowing the folk there, were able to rent rooms to continue their classes. Thus, about two centuries ago, began the second university in England.

So long as I did not speak of it and kept myself out of sight of the masters, no one much cared that I broke one of the regulations, for most were absent-minded about anything unconnected to ideas. Of course, had I, too, been unfortunate and shot one of the townsfolk by mistake, there would have been a cataclysm, and maybe the university would have had to move off elsewhere. In that case, I would have been dangling from the walls of Cambridge. I was lucky, I suppose. Knowing the danger, Jeb was careful to supervise me closely.

Suddenly, one day, I saw, as if in a flash of dazzling light, how effective this would be in a battle. A thousand archers each with fifty arrows could fire ten arrows a minute and, if well-commanded, could drop the range by ten yards every time they fired! It meant that advancing cavalry could be under continuous fire from arrows, and since these were steel pointed and could penetrate armour, it entailed certain destruction for most. It took my breath away, just to think of it, and for many years I kept it in mind, for here, surely, was the problem which must be solved in any battle: how to deal with archers, not cavalry, for these could be shot down at will. Everything depended upon discipline; but if that were sure, a sufficiency of trained archers, well-supplied with quarrels, would be invincible.

Long before the expected time, I was capped *Artium Baccalaureus*, but by then I was half way through the Master's course. My standing having been confirmed, I was often asked to help others less well-endowed. And so it came about that I was found useful by my fellows. Geoffrey de Bohun, I helped often with mathematics, for which he had no aptitude. At the end of a term, when for the first time he passed an exam in the subject, he handed me a purse and when I refused to accept, he was astonished.

I explained that it was a pleasure to me to help and I never took money from anyone for it; that being a habit I viewed as unseemly. It was the wisest move I ever made and it was uncalculated, for Geoffrey, thereafter, saw in me not an employee to be patronised, but an equal, with a vision and integrity of my own, worth having on his side. We became fast friends then, and to my surprise, at the Christmas break, I was invited to spend the holiday with him.

I had never been on holiday before, copying manuscripts both for myself and others, being my usual form of life at such times. Groats earned for fair labour I had no qualms about accepting; it was money given for nothing, or for advice or knowledge I happened to possess, that I could not accept. Why would I accept money for activities which gave me so much pleasure? Thinking was so much fun! And teaching others to think almost as enjoyable. The satisfaction arose from the delight one took in their progress. I felt I would taint my natural enjoyment if I were to be paid for it. In truth, I do believe I would have tutored a cat or a dog for the very pleasure it gave me to organise and declaim the ideas I had with such delight acquired.

And so, with a few others, I rode to Hereford with Geoffrey and shared rooms in the great gaunt castle. His uncle the earl, was a forbidding figure, tall and stout and black bearded and rough and ready, like most of the peerage. Dinner was in the great hall, ablaze with firelight and candle-light, amid music and entertainments of diverse sorts: juggling, tumbling, singing and so forth. The tables groaned with food by the pile, some hunted that day: venison and hare and wild boar. Then there was salt fish, always plentiful, and even salmon and trout from the river nearby, which teemed with them all year round. And duck and hens, partridge and pasties—huge pies filled with meat or fruit—and ale and wine and even brandy, which the earl received regularly from the port of Bordeaux, in the king's hands at that time. And honey and cheeses, of many kinds, and pickles and nuts of several sorts. I had never seen such wealth of provender. If I had any qualms about my new allegiance to the English, they vanished when I saw how they lived. Surely it were best that my own countrymen should live like this too? And surely that was only possible if we were, as indeed we were, subsumed into the English state? In time, we too would be able to live like this.

The idea of my own family enjoying such wealth was wondrous to contemplate, for Christmas back on the island of Bute would, I knew from bitter experience, be nothing like this, nowhere near as grand—or as healthy! That was the true measure of this new life. It was healthier because there was no shortage of anything. At Ardmaleish they would have one goose between the four of them—if one could be captured or shot—a bowl of thin soup made from the same, a loaf of bread and, maybe, a little kail or turnip—if there were any left—and not much else. There was not much else available in winter, except fish perhaps.

Of course I realised that the English peasantry did not live like the gentry, but even they, I knew, lived far better than my family or any others in Bute.

England, I concluded was the place to be, the nation to belong to, if I could.

In pursuit of this aim, I fear, I became more English than the English themselves, so that I almost, but not quite, made a fool of myself on several occasions. But they were tolerant of me, seeing my admiration. My knowledge was valued and called upon whenever a dispute arose, for here scholarship was thought important and made much of, in spite of the earl's heartiness and hunting spirit. Geoffrey was not slow to boast of his new found capability in mathematics nor to give credit for it to his tutor. And then, among the young at table, I was expected to shine, to fire off brilliancies and argue impossible propositions with aplomb, which none could refute except by buffets or swordplay, but there was little of that.

Only at training in weapons, in which I now took the same intense interest as everyone else, was sword-play allowed. By common consent, the college rules still applied; and if they had not, some of us would surely have died of it. We were hot-tempered and we did fall out, but fisticuffs were the methods of settlement and black eyes and bruised limbs were not terminal conditions.

Richard Cressingham was always distant towards me, which was a puzzle, and I knew it had nothing to do with my humble home in his father's bailliwick, which I had been careful to conceal, for these young men were all well-born and regarded birth as the most important aspect of any man. From it came titles and honours; without it, one was a bastard or a common mongrel without pedigree. Inevitably, they knew me for what I was, but time and acquaintance had wrought changes in their view of me and there was the possibility of advancement, even then, for exceptional men of humble birth—like William Marshal who had been the foremost knight of the realm in the last reign, as everyone conceded, ending as earl of Pembroke. And men like him sometimes were promoted knight banneret for brilliant action in the field. Then, in in my own case, distinction was already in the air, on account of my rapid ascent through the schools of the university to the point where I was expected to graduate Magister in half the allotted time.

And so I thrived and grew to think well of myself, became tall and broad and strutted my stuff with the best, sword and dagger at hand if the need arose, which it did when travelling, though I always did so in company, as we all did in those days, for fear of what the English called trailbaston: being set upon by bands of rogues, often deserters from the army without employment.

Yet my mental life continued apace, in spite of my occasional riot of drinking and wassail, for it was a day wasted when I made no intellectual advance, a habit that has stayed with me all my life. And some of it had to remain secret. I wonder that I should reveal it even now, and yet, I am old, too old to persecute for heresy.

It happened in the philosophy class and caused especial problems in the theology school, for, still determined to follow the logic wherever it led and think the unthinkable, as Hammond also recommended—the only way to make progress, according to his viewpoint—I soon had doubts about God, the same ones uttered by the unfortunate Wendover. Aquinas might have astonished the world by giving five different ways of proving his existence, but they quickly dissolved under the intensive scrutiny I now applied to everything, as if it were second nature.

How, I asked myself, could God be both all-powerful and all-loving? This was an unspeakable contradiction, for one only had to look at the world, the world of Cambridge itself, where, every day, people died in the most appalling circumstances and suffering, to see that a loving God had no option but to intervene, if only to moderate the suffering. The definition of God given by Aquinas was patently a self-contradiction. For the same reason, God could not be Good, or he would not hang back when, with his power, he could so easily change the course of events.

None of this could I safely reveal to a soul, though once or twice I guessed that Hammond shared my thoughts, for that route led to ruin and disgrace. It was, and still is, unthinkable in our society to doubt the existence of God. Hell and damnation is nothing to the hell stupid men will make for free thinkers here on earth.

And so in the theology schools I laboured under a disadvantage: since I did not believe in God, I found it difficult to argue from the premises everyone else thought as natural as breathing. Worse, I had to conceal the premises that I supported or the fact that I doubted the ones so readily assumed. And so I did less well in theology than in other things and, for a while, I wondered whether I would receive the distinction I coveted.

My cause was helped one evening in hall when someone mentioned Aristotle's discovery that a horse always has contact with the ground, for otherwise how could it move without falling over? It was here that my acquaintance with Alexander de Bruce had its reward, for it made me wonder seriously whether this were so. In a short while, I found myself defending the opposite proposition: that contact with the ground all the time need not be a prerequisite of motion. The argument raged among us as such things were inclined to, especially when anyone was daring enough to quarrel with Aristotle, who was like a God to everyone. Gradually, I saw that I could easily lose every inch of the small stature I had so patiently acquired by a defeat in front of such an audience, for it would be talked about afterwards; and I would be toppled from my pedestal.

I will never forget the pressure upon me. It brought me out in a sweat and for a while I could do nothing to relieve it. Then, when those around were on the point of concluding that I had lost, I resolved to make one last attempt.

Suddenly it came to me what I must say. 'Why do we dispute such a thing? Why do we not go and look?' And some scoffed at me, as if such a thing were beneath their dignity; others that I was merely seeking an undignified escape. But I insisted, and in the warm evening we repaired to the street outside, where a horse was ridden up and down before us at speed, so that the event could be observed.

At first, it seemed as if, even now, matters went against me; but no! When the horse was at top speed, the hooves were not in contact with the ground all the time; the thing was clear to me. Unfortunately, it was not plain to my companions, who could not see what was before their eyes. The frustration was tremendous. They could not or would not see what was obvious. In desperation, I went to the college pantry and made off with a bag of meal and, with them looking on in amazement, I began to spread it evenly on the flagstones of the hall, to make a track. When there was not enough, I went back for more and even got help with more sacks of the stuff from a store-room, mindless of the cost or the trouble that would fall upon me.

When it was all spread, I crouched my body into the shape of a horse, using arms as forelegs and began to move as fast as possible across the track. At first my efforts were in vain but I became faster and faster. And so surrounded by whoops of merriment, I tried again and again to race along the meal track, and after each journey, walked back pointing to the places where my hands or feet had marked the meal-strewn floor. Finally, I convinced myself I had demonstrated the very fact I needed. The distance between hand marks and foot marks on the ground was greater than they could be if continual contact was maintained. This meant that hands and feet had to be in the air at the same time.

But few others were in agreement.

I resolved to try again the next morning and, after rescuing the meal with difficulty, under the stern gaze of Master Granville, who thought me mad, and called me a peasant with unseemly practices, who had learned nothing from English gentlemen, I purchased many sacks of sand and had a horse ride outside on a track of sand, carefully spread to show the hoof-marks. Would this persuade them?

Not so! Few were convinced.

In desperation, I then called for bed-sheets and had several sewn together and supported in the vertical by posts at regular intervals. Then I asked a blacksmith to fashion horseshoes of a special type: each had a grooved metal spur which projected outwards at right angles. The frustration while this was done was immense! I had to wait for the metal to cool and all the time my fellows were agog at the apparent stupidity of so much needless expense.

'Why not give up and save yourself the money?' said one.

'Because it is an intellectual matter and to an intellectual there is nothing so important!' I shouted, red-faced with passion. What could be more important than proving a thing like this—if it can be proved? For then a real advance in human thought occurs; and that this would be so was self evident from the great number of them who refused to believe it. Few understood.

Finally, when my specially designed horseshoes were in place, in each groove, I set a paint brush and tied it on tight. I even used inks of different colours on the four brushes. The horse was then ridden between two lines of bed sheets so that the brushes marked the sheets showing the positions of the hooves. Thus, on the left side were the marks of two hooves, showing their positions at all times. The right side was now laid against the left and the marks on it pricked through onto the left bed sheets, which meant that now on the left sheets were the marks of all four hooves. It was now plain that at some point in every stride, all the hooves were off the ground.

It was not what Aristotle believed and so, like Alexander de Bruce, I had made some kind of minor original advance. Of course, many did not believe me even now; but enough did, for me to be accounted a sensation of a kind, author of a new method, where the school-room is forsaken for the street, sand laid down or bed sheets joined, and many trials carried out until the reality of nature becomes apparent. Master Granville might call me a peasant, but some laughed at me for a good fellow and a few applauded my ingenuity. Henceforth, I was Bannatyne of the bedsheets.

These events, I think, even though some masters did not approve, arguing that such quaestiones should be resolved by logic alone and not by unseemly experiments, convinced enough that maybe I had something of interest in my head, for I made the demonstration the subject of a lecture to the fellows, which was well-received, even though it had to be done with rhetoric and dialectic alone. This, along with my success in mathematics, philosophy and natural science, together with my competence in music, was such that minor blemishes in the subject where actual belief and religious conviction counted, were overcome. I graduated *Artium Magister, summa cum laude*, and then wondered what to do.

The Church, I knew, was out; and this would annoy my patron, Bishop Wishart. Of course I could try to pretend', and thus could easily become, like Alexander de Bruce, who was now Dean of Glasgow, a cleric of some kind; but my integrity baulked at the idea. That left only a career at court or an administrative post of some kind in a great household, or the army or teaching. Of course teaching urchins of the kind I had so recently been myself, seemed the gravest outcome to one of my new found gravitas, and teaching at the university was not to be considered so soon after graduation.

I was still thinking over what to do, when the king paid a visit to Cambridge and, for a few days, there was enormous hustle and bustle in the town, as scholars and burgesses were turned out of home and college to accommodate the king's retinue: a hundred clerks, numerous nameless functionaries, soldiers by the thousand; servants galore, and women too, camp-followers and the like. All these had to be accommodated and I found myself relegated from the dormitory of gentlemen to the floor of the great hall itself.

Master Granville announced one day that he would present me to the king if the opportunity arose, and I said nothing about my earlier meeting, since that seemed unlikely. But then I learned there was to be a dinner and, with Master Granville and others, I was to attend.

The feast provided by the university was sumptuous, there being roast swans and suckling pig, beef, mutton and pheasant, with the finest wines to drink. With a few hundred others, I over-indulged myself mightily, and then was taken by surprise, for Master Granville rose and signalled me to join him. I had no option but to follow, and to High Table we went, he and I, to stand beneath the tall seated figure of the king. I saw at once, that he had aged. The large figure slumped in his seat and the beard seemed a yellow-stained, white-matted cousin of what it once had been.

When I had been presented and my distinction as the finest scholar in the place made known, the king's eye settled upon me and suddenly lit up. 'You seem familiar, boy. Where have I seen you before?' And he began to rack his brains to remember.

Uneasily, I told him. He laughed, a deep rumble within that broad frame of massive bone. 'So you have become first among the English!' he joked. 'I'm not sure I should approve, for what Scot could be as good as an Englishman, eh?' Around him, others laughed at the notion. 'And what sort of Scot has he become?' said the king at last.

'One admiring of all things English, Sire,' said Granville. 'He is a credit to us, to our education and fairness to all those from the farthest corners of your domain.' But the king was not so sure. 'What is the sign of this? Maybe he is a spy, sent by those rebellious Scots, Wishart and Lamberton.'

'No, Sire,' said Granville, appealingly, 'I would vouch for him myself. Anyone will tell you how English he has become here by contiguity with those who are.'

'Contiguity? It takes more than that I'll be bound! You have to be born to it. Englishmen are not made in a day. How long is it since I saw you at Westminster, boy?'

'About four years, Sire.'

'And in that time you have become an Englishman? How can I count upon you? How do I know this is so? Are you not the boy who spoke of freedom and how the Scots would never give it up?'

'Yes, Sire,' I said, blushing for very shame, for I did not think the concept worth a fig by then, beside the natural desire to see my countrymen live in peace and plenty.

'Well, you were right, by God!' said the king.

The sound fell upon me like a thunderclap and I was mystified. Seeing this, the king laughed. 'Do you mean you do not know?'

Flushing to the depths of my being, I said, 'Know what, Sire? What is there to know?'

Many around me broke out laughing, that the man presented as above all others in learning, should not be in possession of the news.

'Bruce has crowned himself King of Scots, you fool! Even now we are on our way to deal with him. What do you think the army is for? Where do you think we are headed?'

I was completely flummoxed. 'King of Scots? But how can that be? John Balliol is the king—or was until he abdicated and was banished. Who says Bruce is King of Scots?'

'He does!' said a young man who looked much like the king, and this I guessed must be the Prince of Wales. There was much laughter then.

'Well boy, what do you think of that, eh?'

'It is folly, utmost folly! It will cost many lives and achieve nothing.'

The king smiled at me. 'And what would you do about it?'

'What you are doing, Sire. Put down the rebellion.'

'Will you join us, then? Have you training in arms?'

'Yes, Sire, gladly—to both questions.'

CHAPTER 5

Campaigning with King Edward

I HAD HEARD NOTHING FROM Scotland for months and the reason was now clear: Bruce had led a rebellion and there was no crossing the border because it was no longer safe to do so. Some at Cambridge would have known as much, but, as usual, I had been buried so deep in books that I had never surfaced long enough to hear it.

The next day, I packed my library into a cart and bought a horse to draw it. Then I joined the army of King Edward and set off to the north for the first time since my arrival so long ago.

Day followed day, but it was not too boring. I found I could read as I went and in the evenings there were diversions around the camp, for some of my friends were present: Gilbert de Clare, Richard de Cressingham, Ralph Walmsley and others. Even my old adversary, de Montherlant, was of our company, though he had become very grand, having been knighted, not long before, at a ceremony in Westminster, with three hundred young men, the Prince of Wales and his friend Piers Gaveston, first among them. Tied to my cart, I could not disport myself as the others. I was advised to hire a servant but declined, saying that my books were too precious to leave to untutored hands.

Outside Berwick, the entire army was inspected by the king, a king sadly aged and hardly able to keep his saddle. Yet he crossed over to the Lanercost Priory, where for some months he remained, before moving onto Burgh by Sands on the Solway.

The army was chasing Bruce about the Galloway Hills and the pursuit had become so exciting that I soon left my cart with the rest of the baggage train. Aymer de Valence, the new governor of Scotland, was in charge and I was registered as a supernumerary cavalryman riding with my friends, who were as thirsty for glory as it behoves young men to be.

De Valence was eager to close with the rebels, for Bruce had already been defeated at Methven, near Perth, by an unexpected charge from the city at night, which scattered Bruce's forces. They had disappeared for a time, after that, and only recently returned by sea to the south west, where they had murdered the garrisons of a few castles before taking to the heather. Try as we did, they could not be brought to battle.

Gradually, the story of Robert Bruce's defection became clear. He had signed a bond with Alexander Comyn, head of the Balliol clan, agreeing to cooperate for the good of the realm of Scotland. Some even believed Comyn had agreed Bruce should be crowned king in return for the Bruce lands. However it may be, it seems Comyn betrayed Bruce by sending his copy of the bond to the king, in Westminster, who then commanded Bruce's attendance at court.

Before the matter was made public, however, the Earl of Gloucester, an uncle of Gilbert de Clare, sent a shilling and a pair of spurs to Bruce's lodging. Bruce rightly interpreted the spurs as an injunction to flee or face execution; the shilling being the fee to the courier. On the way to Scotland, Bruce had come upon a messenger at the border, who, being apprehended, gave up a letter from Comyn to the king which revealed Comyn's betrayal. At the kirk in Dumfries, Bruce then met Comyn, who did not suspect that he had been exposed. Bruce challenged Comyn with his betrayal, and in the resulting dispute, daggers were drawn and blood shed. Afterwards, Bruce reported the fight and Kirkpatrick, one of his men, returned to the kirk 'to mak siccar'.

Lacking any choice, Bruce declared himself king and persuaded the clergy to support him. At Scone, a coronation of sorts was quickly arranged, even though the coronation stone was unavailable, having been removed to Westminster by King Edward.

Soon after, Bruce marched on Perth but was surprised by a night attack at Methven, where the Scots were routed and fled westwards. After another skirmish at Dalrigh near Loch Dochart, Bruce had sent his womenfolk north to sanctuary and took to the heather with his remaining few hundred men.

After playing hide and seek for six months, he was now back in the Carrick Hills at the head of a small guerilla band, intent upon taking the whole of Scotland.

All this, I gleaned from the talk at firesides, where my English companions often laughed over it. At that time, none of us had the least idea of the momentous changes Bruce would soon wreak among us all.

Our commander sent for me one evening, and ordered me to Carlisle with a request for supplies. Riding through the night under a full moon, I arrived at the castle early the next morning; and after gaining entry and handing over my letters, and feeding on left-overs, I was able to get some sleep on the floor of the great hall of the single squat Norman tower, on the first floor, among other dormant forms, kept warm by the bodies of wolfhounds which shared my hard bed and the remains of a fire.

It was full light when I wakened. In the castle-yard a raised platform had been set up and when I enquired, learned that two Scots had been captured and were to be beheaded on the orders of the king himself, that very day at noon. Imagine my horror when I learned that these were Alexander and Thomas de Bruce!

Permission was easily obtained to speak to them and we conversed in the chill dungeon for an hour or more. It was the worst moment I had ever spent, for I admired Alexander as I admired no other save Master Hammond. Alexander was a genius, that was clear, and it seemed to me the height of lunacy to put to death a mind like that.

They had been beaten after capture by the McDowalls on the beach at Loch Ryan, after landing with a small force of Irish from their own lands in Ulster. Alexander seemed drawn, with eyes shadowed by nights of fear and concern, but he smiled when I revealed my feelings of dismay and my offer to ride to the king and ask him to intercede. 'You are a good soul, Bannatyne,' he told me, 'but you know quite well that it would be wasted. This king does not change his mind. He is merciless with those who cross him, as if he were an avenging God. Remember Wallace?'

How could I forget? When I asked if there was anything I could do, he said, 'Tell my brothers that it was only bad luck. The cause is just and they will prevail.'

My own position was, of course, acutely problematic now. Here I was on the side of the English and two fine Scotsmen by my side were about to be killed! I was nearly sick on the spot at the thought of it and it heralded the beginning of doubts about my situation.

'You don't believe in freedom then?' said Alexander, presently.

'How did you know?' I said.

'News has a way of travelling when it wants to. The Bishop told me, if you must know. You are become more English than the English, men say.'

'It is for the best, I think. What use to fight against the undefeatable? Is it not better to live in peace and prosperity, rather than waste men's lives in a futile struggle?'

'I see what you mean, friend. It is a strong argument as I expected. I heard about the summa. The first since my own.' Then he laughed. 'I also heard you had trouble with the Almighty.'

Truly, this was astounding! How could anyone know about my unbelief? 'Why am I of so much interest?'

'Because you have so much in your head, more than any of those at Glasgow hoped. And then you crossed over. There had to be a reason for that and it had to be a good one. That made Baldred shiver, in case it meant that we were all of us in the wrong!' He laughed then. 'Odd isn't it? How concerned we are when we reach conclusions different from those whose minds we judge to be equal or better than our own. Those who value the mind above everything else, that is.'

'You will have followed your brother, I expect,' I said. 'When he was crowned, you had no choice. But is there a case to answer?'

Alexander was silent for a while, lost in thought, as he often was. Then he said, 'It depends on the people finally, and you haven't seen the extent of their misery or the dreadful treatment they receive from the English. You've been away and that's why you do not know.'

'I can't believe all the Scots want to fight,' I said. 'There are many Scots in the English army and in the castles, under English command. And many people, surely, would prefer English rule, however harsh temporarily, while things are still unsettled, to suffering and death.'

'You are partly right and partly wrong. It's your premises that are at fault as usual. It's always the same in a false position, and I do honestly believe yours false. The harshness is not temporary. The English intend to continue to exploit us, to levy taxes for their wars elsewhere, to enrich themselves at our expense. Many Scots find it deeply offensive to be ruled by aliens. Can you imagine what it is like to have your wife or daughter taken by an Englishman, for no better reason than that he is English, and a conqueror? And if you do anything about it, you are imprisoned or killed out of hand. That is the kind of hold over us that they have here. It is not the decency and fair government you fondly imagine, because that is how they treat each other—some of the time. It is slavery.'

Of course it was a persuasive, powerful argument, but I did not believe it. How could I? I was in love with the English. And I had seen none of the things he spoke of. But I remembered it! Oh, how I have often thought of that last argument from that most able youth!

I had to leave them while they were prepared, first by the priest and then their gaolers. At noon, precisely, they were led out to the yard and up onto the scaffold. The charges were read out: rebellion, murder and so on; it hardly signified, for there was no trial, summary execution only, at the behest of an arrogant, unimaginative and callous king, who could not understand his people; could not see that his was not the only will of consequence in the world.

Around me, were a few guards and serving folk and some from the town, warned of the spectacle and there for the entertainment. It was revolting from beginning to end; all the more so to me who alone knew the extent of the crime about to be committed. The brothers embraced for the last time. Then, as the eldest, Thomas was beheaded first. Alexander shivered when the head flew off at the second stroke. He stood tall and thoughtful, staring heavenwards and then looked down at me and said, 'Bannatyne, do not mourn for me, mourn for our country. We do not die in vain, we are all instruments and must die sometime in any event. It does not matter that we die thus. What difference if it is after a full life in a warm bed of ague or apoplexy, or this way, on a scaffold in a grey castle under a drizzling sky? I am not responsible for this. I am not in control of it, nor ever was. Who is to say what the effect will be? My duty is merely to try my best to respond well to what fortune brings. It is not winning that counts, but trying to win.'

He would have continued with the discourse which was as natural to him as life, once launched, and I hung on his words; but the serjeant would have no more of it. After all, it meant nothing to him, why should it? So Alexander de Bruce, of magnificent vaulting mind, was held down by the shoulders and in a single blow, the head that might have won a kingdom, or written books to rival Aristotle and Aquinas, was rolling on the ground, dripping blood, a plaything for stupid men's feet.

Scandalised by the inhumanity of man, I knelt down in the mud and screamed. Later, I was sick, retching up the remains of last night's dinner.

I think I felt the loss of that life more than anything before that time, and all my life after, I regretted that I had not known him better. You see—especially will it be necessary to say so to those who are not like he and I—insight is the greatest burden of all, for no one, or almost no one else possesses it, and it is such a struggle every time to persuade the ignorant, who are as numerous as fish in the sea, of what they cannot understand; most of whom, will never understand. And often one fails to get through, to convince, and foul things are done out of stupidity, or catastrophes occur that we foresaw and should have prevented.

Alexander and I were brothers and knew it instinctively, on meeting. We belonged to the brotherhood of the mind. And because of the lack, I never had anyone to talk to, to share my mental events, for no one else I have ever met could do so—except perhaps Signore Dante. And the consequence is that I often had to suffer the anguish of silence, when my soul cried out to reveal the full extent of what I knew.

Alexander knew my doubts without asking. He shared them—as his last speech showed so clearly—and knowing my measure, knew I would have them too. After dictating two million words of his *Summa Theologiae*, Aquinas suddenly stopped; and nothing would persuade him to continue. He wrote nothing more of any kind. And Alexander, I guess, had seen what this meant logically, as I did. The difference was that we did not need to plod for a lifetime to reach these conclusions; they were immediately available to us.

The garrison did not understand my sorrow, suspected I was a supporter in disguise, and I could not convince them. How can you explain to swine about the majesty of the mind? As depressed as I had ever been, I set off again for the camp in Glentrool forest.

A few days later, I arrived to discover the aftermath of a battle. Though outnumbered five to one and pitifully supplied with weapons, Bruce and his followers—one could not call it an army, it was too small and untrained—had routed the English cavalry in a series of running manoeuvres. De Valence was beside himself with frustration. Everyone else branded Bruce a coward who would not fight properly as if the laws of chivalry—if there were any—had to be obeyed even when one side was so markedly inferior to the other. But what had occurred, I immediately realised, was something novel and effective, and I sensed it would have repercussions. It amounted to the implementation of the strategy he had discussed with Alexander and I, not so very long ago, in hall, at Cambridge.

Of course I could not speak about the deaths of the young Bruces, even among those who knew them, for were they not rebels? Had we not journeyed so far just to deal with them? But one night, by a flickering fire, the issue of the best way to treat the rebels was tossed about the circle of onlookers. Cressingham could see no difficulty. The rebels had killed some of us and were murderers. Of course they should be put to death. Something, some dark demon within, made me cry out against it. 'You make martyrs of them all,' I said.

After a silence, de Valence himself said, 'It is the king's order and must be carried out.'

'But is it right?' I persisted.

'If they will not desist, what else is there to do?' said he. And I had no answer for him. Recognised that I had done myself an injury by even suggesting clemency and cursed my openness, for it was so much against what I wanted: to be accepted by the English as a full member and find my place and make my way in peace and prosperity.

Events soon changed everything, but before then I was to know my share of shame, and I blush to think of how I was in those days. I cannot plead youth, and given my aptitude, there is not the least excuse for what I did.

For a month, we hunted high and low for the rebels until, finally, Cressingham decided he had had enough for now. De Valence, who was at his wits end after so much wasted effort, agreed that a few of us might travel to Bute for a change of scene. We could report back on news from the other islands and there would be some value in our absence.

Thus was it, that Cressingham led us—Gilbert de Clare, Geoffrey de Bohun, who had lately joined us for the glory he supposed he had been missing, forsaking the chance of a degree, Charles Beauchamp, Augustine de Gracie and myself—to Largs, where we left our horses at an inn and took ship for Bute.

The place was timeless. The beach below the castle just as I remembered, and the circle of white, thatched houses surrounding the moat. The elder Cressingham was away on a scouting trip to Arran, a nearby island, leaving the castle under the captaincy of a formidable man-at-arms named Simon of Nottingham. A veteran of many fights, he was skilled in every weapon, and a forceful commander of his thirty men. Yet he was deferential, quartered us in an upstairs room and laid on a fine feast of venison, veal, the inevitable salt-herring, and a large pike, taken from the moat that day. They were well-supplied with wine and a barrel of it was soon attacked with gusto.

The next day was market day and we strolled around like the young gods we were, examining the goods with none too much respect, and it was then that I suddenly came upon my mother, selling turnips from a hand-cart. I blushed to the roots of my hair and said nothing. At my elbow, Cressingham called out, 'Look at Bann! He has given up the fair Eleanor and now fancies an older wench.'

Indeed, my mother was as comely as I remembered, though her long dark hair had acquired a snow-girt appearance. There was no sign of my father, my brother or sister and I was puzzled, but I dare not enquire, for then my fine friends would know that I was a peasant, without breeding and influence, and therefore not worth the trouble of their company. I stood rooted to the spot, red-faced and silent.

Cressingham said, 'Take her, if you want. She's yours! Father won't mind. He'd expect it. That's what they're for, don't ye know? They're all ours, to be enjoyed.'

If it were possible, my shame was worse than ever, but I stood in silence looking at her and Geoffrey said, 'Well if he won't have her, I will.' And he laid hands on my mother and took her by the hand and ran off with her uphill towards some trees, followed by the laughter of my friends. And all I could do was watch. I felt as if I had just castrated myself.

'See that you don't get more than you expect, Geoffrey,' Cressingham called after him. 'Some of the locals have been ill-used already by the soldiery.' And then to me he grew sympathetic, laying a friendly arm around my shoulder. 'Come, Bann, what does it matter? Feelings like these are natural. Even if you have a secret love like Eleanor.'

I said nothing. He had misunderstood so completely that I was speechless. I walked to the beach alone, in a cloud of self-disgust, and when, at dinner that night Geoffrey appeared once more, after a day of it, and was asked how it had gone, he said, merely, 'What can you expect? It is just like fucking an animal. These people have no wit, no knowledge. She did not understand anything I said.'

'But did you understand her, Geoffrey?' said Gilbert. 'Did she like it?'

'I expect so. Don't they all? Don't women like it as much as men?'

'I have heard they do,' I said out of a red face. 'If they are well-treated.'

There followed the worst bout of drunkenness I ever experienced. I drank and drank and would not stop until I was sick and then drank again, to the astonishment and pleasure of my friends, who were quick to join me. Somewhere around midnight, we staggered out of the water gate, having bribed the watchman with a tankard, swam the moat; and set off around the houses with torches looking for any women who might live there.

I woke up in a small thatched cottage many hours later, beside a married woman that I remembered as soon as I cast eyes upon her. 'I won't tell,' she said in the Gaelic; to which Cressingham, who was lying on the other side, said, 'What's she say?'

'She thinks I should get up and have breakfast.'

'But you've not had her yet.'

'Haven't I?' I replied, but it was dangerous to say what came to mind, for I had never had anyone before, and I realised that if they knew, it would be an issue they would help me with, to my profound embarrassment.

Sir Hubert Cressingham arrived the next morning by ship, with Eleanor and a score of men. She had grown and was almost as tall as me, and filled out, so that her breasts swelled under the green gown and when she saw us, her eyes lit up with pleasure, for with us she could converse on equal terms, sure of our good behaviour.

I was as madly in love as before, entranced by the smell of her as she passed in the hall, and for days I feasted upon her shiny auburn hair and hazel-blue eyes and skin like soft honey; and said little. In truth, I was in a sorry state, the kind that afflicts youth between child-hood and manhood, when they do not know who they are or what they should be doing; when the whole of life seems an unresolvable puzzle.

I despised myself for my conduct with my mother and so I was no fit company for anyone. I drank and listened and then drank again and if anyone tried to involve me, I bit their head off with a boorish epigram or a look of dismay, as if they were not quite good enough to converse with, when it was I myself who was not good enough for anything.

Eleanor observed all this with displeasure and said to me one day, 'I had heard that you were blessed with great intelligence and yet all I see is a sulky child in need of training.' I said nothing; gave her one of my looks, and for my pains, the very next day, was taken in hand by Simon, on the orders of Sir Hubert, to be put to the weapons training.

And so for several days, I and the others were encouraged to practise with arms and, somehow, in the course of all that hard work, my ill-mood left me.

For hours we fought with sword and shield, until we near fell down with fatigue and then it was lances on horseback, which I had never tried before, and did badly, compared to the others, but when it came to archery, I outclassed them all, putting bolt after bolt through the target wherever it was set up.

By then scholar's muscles had been hardened by hard riding and, if I had seen no action yet, I had at least become strong enough to string and the pull the bow as if it were a part of me, and aimed and fired quickly, efficiently and with deadly effect. I won every competition so easily that, soon, no one dared shoot against me. Perhaps it was all the scribing with the quill, or careful study of so many deep books—so critically, looking always for lacunae in the argument—but my eye in those days was a wonder, a miracle almost as much as my mind itself. For a bet, I once shot blindfold and still won! Admittedly, I was against Bohun, who had poor eyesight. I could sense where the target had been set from the talk and noise of movement, and could still hit it, unless they cheated and moved it late in the shot, which they did for devilment.

Then there was to be a picnic. We would ride to the north of the island where, Sir Hubert assured everyone, the view was very fine, with fairy islands in a silver sea and tall trees round about—a place of rare magic, he said. And so, one day, we set off, my friends and I, at speed, followed closely by Eleanor, who was good in the field, with our host and his retainers following at a more leisurely gait.

Three miles out, at the entry to the Kyles, we came to Ardmaleish, which had not changed much except that the thatch needed fixing, the number of cattle had shrunk and the fields were unsown. My heart near burst when I saw the signs of decay. As we galloped past, there was no sign of my sister, brother or father. The grey shape of someone behind a window suggested my mother, but she kept well out of our way.

It was on the return journey that I took a chance. I dallied and then dismounted, electing to walk my horse, which I said was a trifle lame. Thus, after the party from the castle had gone ahead, I stopped at the croft and entered the old kitchen. My mother was standing by the fire and I rushed to her and buried my head in her breast, sobbing.

I was ashamed and showed it; did not expect forgiveness and was forgiven just the same. For an hour, I sat at the old chipped table weeping salt tears which I was powerless to prevent, and trying, futilely, to explain myself, my betrayal; and my mother listened and was understanding and this made it worse. Far better had she belted me about the ears, as in the old days. Then, at least, I would have understood.

'When I first saw you I was so proud,' she said. 'There was my son, dressed like a young squire, and with friends from Cambridge.' She sighed, longingly, and it occurred to me that she might have wanted to study there herself. 'When you did not speak, it was hurtful, of course; but I knew why, could see what it meant.'

'B.b.but I am an abomination! How could I do such a thing? And then . . . and then to allow that oaf Bohun to take you into the woods and d.d.do—whatever it is they do—Mother, forgive me! It is most shameful! I will never forgive myself! I do not deserve to live!'

'Hush, hush yourself! It was not as bad as you think,' she said at last, after considering for some time how she should treat me. 'The young man was very nice. Gentle, as a man should be,'—which sent me into further paroxysms of remorse that I had allowed it.

She took my hand and hushed me, as if I were a child again and said, 'It was not bad at all. I liked it and there is nothing wrong with that. You see, your father has been gone two years and I needed him. Well, your young friend provided what I needed and you could never give.'

I have wondered at this speech, whether it was true or a lie made up to mollify my self disgust. I confess after two normal lifetimes, I still do not know the answer. If it was the truth, it was a bold thing to say to me at that time; and, if not, it was very kindly meant. Ever since, my mother has always seemed like a saint to me, even if she did like it, as she said.

My father and brother were at the war with Bruce. My sister was dead. Shagged by some soldier and killed in childbirth. She was not eighteen then.

I spoke of my life, of Cambridge and the books and my degrees, which she had heard about. Evidently, news had come from Glasgow about me: that I was a great man, with a great future, that I had conversed with the king and could expect a position at court. And she was proud of me, even though I had joined the enemy, her enemy, the enemy of every native of Bute—well, almost all: some of the Brandanes had joined them for the favours received.

Somehow, the question never got asked: why? And I did not want to answer. Debating with one's mother is not a profitable exercise, I decided. But I do not think she expected it; she expected what she had: my defection to a nobler, richer, more comfortable and far more interesting world, all this she could see in my talk: my admiration for all things English. She mentioned Eleanor and saw me blush. 'Everyone expects young Cressingham to marry her, if the elder does not,' she said, finally, and that was a surprise.

I left her then, to walk around the croft, among the by-ways of my lost childhood and I cannot remember a more unhappy time. I was caught between two worlds, the superior English one of plenty, good society and fine talk of chivalry and the new ideas of Cambridge; and the old, inferior Scottish world of deprivation, hand-to-mouth existence, ever fighting the elements for the necessities of life. Yet, to me, the intellectual starvation of a life lived in Bute, had I remained there, was the greatest evil imaginable. Until, that is, I thought again of my mother; how she—not just Scotland—but my own mother!—had been invaded against her will—and by one of my own friends! Had I joined the English aristocracy only to become a party to the rape of the very woman who begat me?

For a few fleeting moments I thought of riding hard to Rothesay, finding Bohun and killing him out of hand with sword or dagger— though the bow seemed best, for then I could shoot him to death slowly, choosing each point of penetration with care and savour his screams. But it was fantasy, mere anger translated into nonsense acts I would never carry out.

Along the beach I paced like a man demented, my sorry head as hot as if it were in the fever-heat of mental attack. Apparently, there was nothing I could do—except conceal my hurts from my friends; and be as kind as I could to my mother. But that conclusion was for the mind alone. As I have come to see, there are other factors in a man than the mind, other demands and motives which over-ride everything else.

I stripped off my clothes and began to wade in the water, thankful for the chill—eager for the penance, by God!—and walked out a way until the wavelets lapped my waist and then I swam out from the white sand among rocks and sea weed and gradually my feverishness was replaced by an icy calm. After a while I swam back to the shore, shivering, and dried myself and dressed in damp clothing and felt much better. Immersion in cold water has ever been my favoured remedy for illness. The cold seems to invigorate the mind and even the flesh, which heals quickly because of the salt, if wounded.

My mother met my reappearance with a kindly face and a bowl of thick soup which I ate beside the fire, savouring the scent of the peats. We spoke little, she and I, for there was not much to be said; the air between us thick with meaning and remembered moments from the past. Then she went out and returned with a stone jar of whisky she said she had got from a neighbour and set out two goblets and poured liberal measures; and so, for a time, we sat in the flickering peat-fire-light, sipping the colourless peaty fluid.

I laughed aloud at the idea that the whisky and the fire both smelled strongly of peat and mother explained. 'The barley is dried above a peat fire for days and days. So why would it not smell of peat? Have you something against peat?'

The enquiry was earnest and without rancour, I saw, with amazement.

Evidently, my mother's concern was solely for my comfort, worried by how I might perceive her small world; and I felt humbled by her, saw that her innate goodness was worth more than any university, and maybe even any country. Tears sprang into my eyes and I stretched out my hand to hold hers in mine; and we sat on by the fire in a communion of spirits such as I had never known.

But after a time, I am ashamed to say, I was bored with it, wanted my lively friends again and I soon set off for the castle, anxious, suddenly, to get back before the watch took over and the drawbridge was raised for the night—in case, left outside, I would somehow fail to regain my former place.

I found them at dinner, round the great oak table laden with venison by the haunch, a whole salmon caught that day in the Kyles, and several roast duck. The wine had been flowing and the talk was becoming riotous.

'Where have you been, Bann?' said Eleanor, and Richard replied with a laugh:

'With the wench, numbskull! The one Bohun had yesterday. That's where she lives, don't ye know?'

I flushed scarlet and made no reply; then took my seat and diverted myself by carving a slice of venison.

'See, Eleanor,' said Richard, 'You have lost him. Did I not tell you how inconstant he would be?'

She surveyed me wonderingly, and replied, seriously, as I thought then, 'I have not known many men or even many boys, but I would have thought sowing wild oats was a thing all men and boys do, from time to time.'

There was a sudden hush; all eating stopped; for every man and boy there present had been somehow emasculated by the revelation that here was someone superior to us all, who understood and maybe forgave us.

'So you forgive him, then, Eleanor?' said Bohun.

'Why would I need to?'

'Maybe he would like you to,' said Clare.

When I said nothing, but chewed on and swallowed wine, she said, 'I don't think he has been guilty of anything of the kind.'

'But he is guilty, guilty as sin!' said Richard, triumphantly. 'Look at him!'

Eleanor surveyed me again carefully, out of that sunlit face with its coruscating eyes and concluded: 'Maybe he is guilty; then maybe he is not; even so, maybe he is not guilty of what you think.' And that did make me awake from my red-faced slumber. Here was a person of insight, one like myself, a little, at least. My heart seemed to fly across the table to her.

'Come Bann, tell us,' said Bohun, 'have you been with a wench or no?'

It was on the tip of my tongue to say: 'I have been with my mother,' but I could not. Unquestionably, she was a wench—at least in the terms of the discussion—but I could not. Nor could I say I had been conversing with a lady, for they would not have believed it or considered her a lady, there being no other within fifty miles, so far as they were concerned.

I said with some force, a force I had never used before in this company: 'I have been with no wench; I have not done what men do with wenches.'

'Then where have you been?' said Richard, disbelieving.

'I will not say.'

And there was at first a general irritation that I should refuse to share with them my conduct; but presently, they ignored me, and left me to my dinner in the absence of any other sport.

It was managed by Eleanor, I see that now, after all these years, for I have thought about her often. Perceiving my plight, though not understanding its source, she diverted them from making sport of me. Stories she told them; and then, when that was over, she took up the harp and began to play like an angel, so that they were all of them captivated, just like me. I was grateful to her then, but thought it accidental; now I know differently: she saw another fellow suffering and tried as best she could to alleviate the grief, whatever its source.

For days, we roamed the island with falcons for sport and bows at the ready, shooting anything that moved, the more especially if it moved quickly. As usual, Richard was the leader, determined to outdo everyone and often succeeding, for he was a fine horseman and skilled in the hunt; but Eleanor too was a surprise. Compelled to watch much of the time, frustration overcame her finally and she unslung a short bow and began to compete with us and shot rabbits and small game with ease.

By the week's end, I wonder that any of us were not in love with her; but then she was like one of us, an active, vigorous force of nature that none of us would tame, that much was clear; and maybe the others were too in awe of her for worship, if it is not a contradiction. She feared nothing, would dare any dyke or fence and once even set her horse at the low wall of a thatched cottage and, because of the slope, soared over it, missing the smoking chimney by an inch. How we did roar then! And none of us would follow her. That was a measure of her stature, she could put us to shame.

Richard tried for his revenge at one of the lochs of the place. 'Come friends,' he said, 'let us bathe awhile in this cool water. A shilling for the first to swim the loch.' And off came clothing in heaps around him and in he went, like a skinned sow, striking out for the far shore, mindless of the pike which swam there.

'Mind they don't eat your ballocks!' shouted Eleanor.

Soon, Bohun, Gracie and Beauchamp were stripped and diving in after him, leaving Clare and me, looking at each other with red faces at the prospect of undressing before our lady.

'Go on then!' she said. 'How can you hang back like two children? Have I not seen ballocks before? What will two more be but more of the same?'

Young Clare hung his head—he was ever a pious youth—and reddened worse than before and made no move. Myself? I stripped and ran away into the water like a man stung on his backside by a wasp, and heard her call behind me: 'I see, Bann, you are the same, except you have nothing between.'

I swear I never swam so fast in my life. It seemed to depend upon submersion, trying to keep my head down low in the water to hide my red face. And at the end of it, I had quite overtaken the others and landed, covering myself, and wondered like a ninny what to do now, for my clothing was where I least wished it to be—in her very hands by God!

Richard, when he arrived, laughed himself into a stupor and then strode off around the loch, naked as before, as if it was of no account, and took his clothing and dressed, followed by Beauchamp, a brainless lout whose body was carpeted with dark hair like an animal. Only Bohun and Gracie and I remained, covering ourselves, ingloriously, until they left us in disgust, Richard seemingly intent on taking away our clothing but dissuaded by Eleanor, a kindness that was appreciated.

Why did we not challenge her to join us? I know not. It would have been the clinching riposte; but we were young and foolish, I suppose; or maybe chivalry prevented it.

The talk among us was the usual: of knighthood and crusades and glory and titles, these too; and for the others there was real hope; some, even, for myself. The example of William Marshal was in every mind; but my scholarship was an obstacle, for I could not bear too many hours away from books and would retire to refresh myself every day when the possibility arose. It as if my mind needed the daily exercise and then there was the talk of ideas, which I enjoyed almost as much; and would lecture to the four walls of any room I happened to be in, arguing, speculating, theorising, above all questioning. Often I had an audience of sorts for a time but, deprived of that, I would take parchment and write down my own thoughts and begin to make plans for writing books of my own.

CHAPTER 6

The Battle at Loudon

WHEN WE RETURNED TO THE mainland and sought and found the Earl of Pembroke with his forces in the Castle of Ayr, it was to learn that a pitched battle was to be fought at Loudon Hill not far from Strathaven Castle. De Valence had challenged Robert Bruce to meet him at any place he chose on this day; and to everyone's surprise the appointment had been accepted. Very confident then we were, riding across country for the fight; and all the young squires, knights and hangers-on were eager to distinguish themselves.

Myself? I was more circumspect. If the Bruces were satisfied with Loudon maybe there was a reason. Robert might not be an Alexander, but he was the elder brother and had earned the younger's admiration and even awe. Plainly, Robert Bruce must have qualities I had not seen. Consciously, I was as pro-English as ever; hoped the battle would see an end to this senseless warfare, when everyone could get back to the main things of life: books, and in my case, more books, and maybe Eleanor, if I could manage it. Unconsciously, I was wary, unsure in my depths about the virtue of my position. It showed in small things: irritability and brooding moodiness.

The rebels were drawn up between two hills, one of them dizzily high on the left. The ground in front fell down towards their lines of spearmen and then, after the last line of this pitifully small force—a third of ours—it swept upward again. Surprisingly, there were no cavalry; every man was on foot at the base of the pitcher, for that was what the hills around had made: a pitcher with a spout and we were lining up at the spout ready to descend and run them down and trample over them.

The position looked so inviting that I sensed a trap. And yet there was not much to be seen but grass. At the edges, at the base of the hills, were swamps, made by rushing streams in winter, which would provide poor footing for horses; but the small force of standing men seemed insignificant by comparison to the one arranging itself around me. Even their bristling pikes looked innocent enough.

Trumpets sounded and the front rank were soon away, cantering, and then galloping, lances and armour glinting in the hot sun, bright banners crossing the valley like bunting on a festival and young knights hallooing as if on a fox hunt.

Just before the lines of men, however, horses began to fall and riders came down, and men screamed, and animals whinnied in fear, as they broke fetlocks in the pits—hidden under a covering of reeds—which festooned the place. And then the next rank fell on the ones already fallen and everywhere men tried to get to their feet among frightened horses out of control, which hobbled about until they fell again and lay dying. Then more and more charged into the melee, making it worse and more disorganised, until De Valence led a troop along the edge and charged into the flanks of the enemy. Pikes screeched on armour till they found holes in visors but lances found their billets aplenty.

My own did, I am ashamed to say. In borrowed mail, I charged like the rest, knocking one man down and then another; then angled the lance and injured three men in one scything movement as I sped across the rear of the enemy and won through to the far side, losing grip on the lance, and drew the sword to return. But where to go? The rebels had advanced into the space around the pits and were cutting down every knight who fought there, weighed down by armour designed for horses, which were all, or nearly all, on their sides, hoping to die soon for the pain. The sight of the battle was startling, as, everywhere around, men killed or were killed or lay down and crawled out of the way, if any would let them. The noise of screaming and shouting, and horses neighing and blade screeching on blade was deafening, horrific. The rebels in the van were redoubtable, cutting swathes through our fine English host.

In desperation, I charged into the rear again and scythed a couple of unfortunates and then I was down, my horse stabbed in the belly, and I fell, head over heels forward, tipping into a cauldron of struggling, fighting men bent on killing each other.

The rest of it passed in a dream. I was fighting one and then another; cut one in the shoulder and then the other in the neck, so that blood spurted out everywhere upon me, and I slid on the mess it made and saved my life from a fierce axe blow; and then I was hit on the head and I fell for the last time.

When I woke up with a splitting headache, it was dark. Around me bodies lay everywhere and, somewhere to the front, men still fought among a great pile of horses and bodies I could not see across. I fell asleep again and woke up to find myself somewhere else, as if I had just been carried. I was too exhausted to speak and lay on for a while, drowsy with loss of blood. I put my hand to my head and found it bound with cloth. It was a miracle! Someone had taken me out of the fight, carried me across the swamp, and set me down in comparative safety behind a gorse bush at the foot of the steep hill.

Slowly, I began to crawl up the hill; on and on in the dark, I went, hearing people walking about not far away, picking over corpses, who missed me in the darkness, and I began to climb, gaining strength as I did so in the cool breeze that blew skywards.

I seemed to climb all night, for it took hours, this ascent. Below me, I sensed disaster, for there were no trumpets now, shouts of jubilation only, but they were in Gaelic or Scots. Finally, I reached the top and there I slept for a time, fitfully, and then when dawn came up I saw. Hundreds of horses lay dead around the pits which had broken their legs and hundreds of knights lay sprawled in the rictus of death, arms and legs askew, like toy soldiers far below. Of Aymer de Valence, Earl of Pembroke, there was no sign, nor of my friends. All was silent, all was lost. Far off, around a farmhouse, the Scots were still celebrating with captured English ale and wine and the noise of it carried across the valley to me.

In a dark depression of spirit, I descended the hill on the hidden side and soon found a horse cropping gently among the grass. I mounted and made off for Bothwell where the tracks led.

A few days later, I came upon the remains of the army and met Bohun and Cressingham and the others; and was glad of their pleasure at my safe return. But it was a sad company, for much of the baggage-train had been lost, with it, all my precious books, and the survivors were short of food. De Valence had aged overnight, a light tinge of silver having appeared on his beard. He and everyone was appalled by the defeat, for it was so contrary to what all had believed: that rebel pikemen were no match for English cavalry. We had been wrong about that. Bruce had found ground suitable for his force and we had been unable to make headway across it.

Sometime during the second day of travel across a bleak moor, I became aware of the prisoners. There were about twenty of them, on foot, in a single line, tied by the neck to each other and led by a man-at-arms on horseback, with one or two others for escort. It was while passing these that I looked down at an upturned face and saw my brother.

He had grown and was almost six foot, having filled out into a broad hulk of a man, with a dark beard, hair streaked with blood. He said nothing when I halted and stared at him; and my heart seemed to swell in my breast, but I, too, had nothing to say.

'They will be hanged of course,' said de Valence, when I enquired their fate. 'They're rebels and will be an example to others.' The grimness of his look left me in no doubt about this. There would be no talk of trials and charges. A crowd would gather and it would happen. Probably, they would suffer more than hanging. It was the way of the English with rebels; it was the times; cruelty being the norm.

Food and drink in plenty was soon found at a monastery and the men became more cheerful. But for myself, there was a dark pit of doubt in me. Could I leave my brother to die without trying to help?

Maybe that was the day I finally grew up, I know not. All my life so far had been easy until then. Now I had to make a choice and blood dictated it, not reason. And I wept bitter tears, for a little, while I contemplated what I was having to give up. All my fine connexions and excellent prospects—for my conduct in the battle had been noticed and I was well-regarded by all.

In the darkness, I easily found my brother, for I had marked the place where they lay down for the night. I cut him free and then had to wait until he freed the others, and in desperation at the time it took, I joined him, using my sword, while he plied my dagger. We crept off after that, moving south, slowly and quietly at first and then, when out of earshot of the camp, running as fast as possible. The pace could not be kept up and yet we had to get away, far away, by dawn.

By first light, tired out, we were not far from some woods and about half the party with us wanted to rest up, but I was against it, said we should put more distance between us. Stragglers from our group would be found and would suggest our route. Perceived as an Englishman, my advice was ignored by all but Eck, and he and I set off by ourselves, westward now, in a loping run through the forest, hour after hour.

How fit we were in those days! The sweat fell from us like rain, but desperation and the immortal stamina of youth held us upright and by noon we were well clear of our party and any pursuers. Weak with fatigue, we sought shelter among some bushes beside a stream and drank copiously and ate some stale cheese and a cooked fowl I had in a knapsack. Then we slept under the rays of a sun which barely heated the grass.

My brother had grown into a fairly taciturn giant, or was it my finery and man-of-the-world-air? I know not, for sure. I taxed him with carrying me out of the battle and he admitted it but there was a distance between us.

'Why did ye niver come hame?' he said accusingly, and when I told him I had just returned from Bute, he asked me for news. But when I had told him all I knew, his own was more impressive.

'Faither's tae'n up wi' a fishwife. He rides wi' Douglas and she gangs wi' him.'

I said nothing about our mother. All he would say thereafter was that he hoped 'the auld bastart wid git a shaft up his erse while he's tumblin' hur.'

My father's betrayal affected me deeply and all the years of my life the wound was never properly healed.

Later, at night, we set off again and knew that we were free. The next day, we walked into the rebel camp.

They were in a valley in the Carrick Hills, awaiting reinforcements, for news of the victory had been sent in every direction and men would join now, who would have been afraid before. The glorious smell of meat roasting assailed our nostrils and we fell down beside it more dead than alive. When Eck appeared there were smiles from the men sitting, squatting or standing about, a motley army and none too numerous, clad in brown homespun cloaks or lowland doublets and tight breeches, sadly torn and stained; everywhere weapons: swords, daggers and pikes being sharpened or repaired and the bustle of cooking and eating. But when they saw me, there was silence.

'He was fighting for them!' said a voice. And others, agreed. 'Aye,' said one, 'he had nae helmet. Ah seen him fine!' In the midst of the growing anger, while my weapons were roughly removed, there was a hush and a tall figure came towards us from one of the small tents pitched around the fires.

Even in the half light, he was imposing, more than I would have believed. It was Robert de Bruce himself, the air of wavering consequence magically transformed into a rock-like certainty. It was there in the step and the look of cold appraisal.

'Explain yourself,' he said to me.

'I'm here because I've nowhere else to go. I set my brother free and cannot return to the English.'

Voices were raised against me for a traitor who deserved a traitor's death and Bruce said, 'Well, are you a traitor?'

'No,' I replied, 'I am still on the side of the English, except I cannot go there any more. They will not have me back.'

I expected to be killed for this but Bruce laughed and said, 'Well then, since you are not a traitor you can live.'

'But Sire,' one protested, 'ye canny lee an Englishman amang us, withoot he'll escape and mibbe gie away oor plans.'

Bruce smiled. 'You must stay with us, you see. Will you give your word of honour that you will not escape?'

Of course I gave it easily. It was better than death.

I often wondered at Bruce's easy generosity. That was one of his great qualities: no one was ever turned away. Everyone was grist to his mill, to be cultivated for his purpose. It was a very wise strategy and it soon began to work upon me, as it worked upon others like Thomas Randolph, his nephew, also captured from the English.

That night was one of the worst I ever knew, for I was in the Scottish army, if you could call it that, but not of it. When Bruce departed, I was left alone, unsure of what to be about. I followed Eck to a campfire, and was rudely driven away by a one-eyed creature in rags who shouted through rotting teeth, 'Keep aff, ya fucken English bastart!' And so I stayed out in the cold, and Eck said nothing. The hate seemed to swirl in my direction and I sensed that Eck would not have the strength to resist.

I found a rock on a knoll nearby and sat there with the light wind in my ears and a pain in my empty belly and listened to the talk of the camp-fire, one of many scattered around. The man without the eye was known as Right-eye, to distinguish him from Left-eye, who sat at another fire some way off. In time, I realised that these were not alone in having been partially deprived of sight. There was another yet, known as One-eye-Cumbrae, from the island, next to Bute, from whence he came.

They had lost the use of an eye by disease or a wound in battle. Right-eye had a red hole in place of the organ, which was not much annoyance to him, for he was accounted a good swordsmen even then. Left-eye's was a suppurating, painful sore, revolting to behold and stinking to be near, yet his companions were polite and made no complaint, for did he not deserve the warmth and companionship? By contrast, One-eye-Cumbrae had a fine-looking bearded face and you would be hard put to tell which eye was at fault, for the whiskers and eye-brows which concealed it, unless you were close.

Then there was Shorty, tallest man in the group, taller than Robert de Bruce but not as tall as his brother Edward or Boyd, who was a giant. Shorty was as thin as a wand and scratched his arse often, an act that long experience in materia medica now makes far better sense to me than it did then—if I take an interest in the peculiarities of the Scots, there is a reason and it will be told eventually—Shorty had a worm. He was pale-faced as well as short tempered, as if feeding the worm left too little for himself.

Girvin was a hunchback, a squat, broad figure on short legs with hands as broad as lintels, as misshapen a creature as any I ever came across, with lumps and odd hairs sprouting forth from his face. When he stood up to piss in the fire I saw that he was barely five feet tall. 'Christ, wull you no' fucken pish elsewhere, Girvin?' said a voice, 'yull pit the fire oot!' and this I learned was Malky, a large, grey-headed cantankerous fellow who minded his comfort more than anything.

Next to him, seated on the same log was an inseparable pair: Torquil Smith and his brother Sheugle; the former of middle height and thickset, with powerful shoulders, arms, thighs and hands; the latter, a runt of a laddie, a skelf of a boy hardly four feet tall; yet as time would tell, the better of the two, for at least he was loyal and had some sort of intelligence.

They ate and drank and laughed and got drunk and farted and pished and shit where they liked and were unspeakably revolting. I watched it all in cold, hungry isolation and said nothing.

But they were not all freakish. There were well-made men too, mus-
cular and hardened like the others by travails too numerous to relate,
and ordinary, among so many others the same or similar. The three
Frasers—cousins or brothers, I forget which—were strong men all; and
five Andersons, brothers from some Argyll village; and Stirrat, a big,
square-set fellow with a dark beard, who could put a bull on its back;
and two long-legged Lamonts, cousins, from Cowal. There was Jinky,
the only fat man about the place and why he never lost his extra flesh
among so many alarms and partial starvations, I never found out. And
Eli, a fair-haired youth of my own age who had been a dominie till he
joined Bruce. And women too; and they were attached to no particular
man as it turned out; women who knew not when their last hour
would come and would take their pleasure where it suited them, or for
a drink or a favour. Bess Morrison was the liveliest: a buxom, brown-
haired wench with a light in her eye, great energy, and as I was to discover, lust for life—every form of it.

They were rough folk, all smooth edges chipped by adversity, but
comrades who supported each other, and, from the pit of my solitude,
I felt strangely drawn to them. By morning, I craved their approval as
well as their company and most of all their food.

Water I had found in a stream which alas, some had fouled with
piss or maybe a horse. Bruce was slow to impose proper discipline
upon such a motley, with new men arriving every day, who had to
be taught the rules of life in an army, or else be the death of it, from
disease and stupidity.

Seeing my woebegone expression as the men ate their breakfast, Eli
threw me a sliver of rancid meat, which I grabbed and shoved into my
mouth. Jinky and others objected: 'Christ, whit wid ye feed yon English
mon fur?'

'Why would you not feed him?' said a voice we all knew, from the
tent nearby, and Bruce appeared.

Right-eye said, 'Ur we no' supposed tae kill they bastarts? Wull, why
no dae it noo?

'A dead enemy is good, I grant you,' said Bruce, 'but better still is
one who becomes a helpful friend. We need him, don't you see? We
need every hand we can get.' When there was no reply, but a few mutters about my being a traitor, Bruce said, 'Watch him then, but show
your good side. You will not win his allegiance by cruelty.'

Right-eye was still not satisfied. 'The Inglish wid hing us or sword
us, so why dinny we dae the same tae thaim?'

'If people see that we are kind to those who help us, maybe they
will. If they know we will hang them, they will fight harder to prevent
it.'

Yet, the camp roused, an hour later, we were on our way 'to take more of the realm into his peace'—a euphemism for: *join us or die, and your lands, cattle and goods become ours.* This was the only pay available to the rebels: loot, so they made the most of it. Had Bruce been too generous to opponents, our army would have frittered away to more profitable ventures. And so Galloway was laid waste. And it was my fault.

We had been preparing to go north to sort out the Comyns who still supported the exiled king, John Balliol, when round the fire, to which I had been grudgingly admitted, I began to talk wistfully of Alexander. It was soon apparent that Robert, who joined us there, knew nothing of his brothers. When I told the tale of how they died, he was enraged, rose and stamped about like a bull. And nothing would do but that I should reveal every detail and when I had finished, he put an arm around my shoulders and comforted me, and I knew that here indeed was an exceptional human being. For is it not written, that those who bring bad news are often made to suffer? I suppose Bruce could see the affection in which I held his brother, for I told the story as it happened, leaving out nothing, not even the tears which came along with it.

And so to Galloway we went, to take revenge upon the McDowalls, trailing southwards, a huge straggling serpent of men, mostly on foot, but horses and carts and women too; and herds of animals, periodically collected, and occasionally slain for their meat.

Bruce was merciless, a man steeled to cruelty, even though I remonstrated with him. Reminded him of his own advice about myself. And was it not the King of England who was to blame? The McDowalls were only doing their duty according to their allegiance.

For a long while Bruce refused to listen to my protests and I was shouted down by him and others, but then one day, I pointed out that cruelty poisons the soul of the cruel and he suddenly knelt down and prayed for forgiveness. The advance stopped, and men milled around wondering. But when he stood up, the madness had left him and he seemed purged of cruelty for a time.

Many small castles and keeps were attacked, but our lack of siege equipment was an obstacle to success. The defenders, be they ever so few, had only to stand protected behind their battlements and we could do little to injure them. If ladders were laid against the wall, as men climbed up, they were shot down by archers, or the ladder tipped over by men standing out of sight, so that all who had climbed up were cast off into the air, breaking bones as they fell. It was an unequal contest at that time. Later, the problem would be solved, but for now, for the most part, all we could do was burn houses, steal crops and cattle and force ordinary folk into submission.

Having cut a swathe through the area, but achieved little, the Bruces left for the north to settle with the rest of the Balliols, chief among

them the Earl of Buchan. Sir James Douglas was left the task of paci-
fying the south. Before that, we went westward and negotiated truces
first with John McDougall, Lord of Lorne, who commanded Argyll,
and the Earl of Ross, who had captured Bruce's wife, daughter and
sisters and sent them to the English. There was great anger in our
leader when we came to the lands of Ross. It was there in the tense set
of the face and the hardness, which came upon him again. At times
like these, he was like a man possessed, stamping the very earth below
his feet, like a percheron anxious to ride down the foe.

The worst of it was that Marjorie Bruce, the daughter, had been put
in a cage hung on the Tower of London, Mary, the sister, in a cage on
the wall of Roxburgh, and the Countess of Buchan, who had crowned
Bruce at Scone, in lieu of her English husband, in another cage on the
wall of Berwick, each of them doomed to remain there in all weathers,
to pee and shit in public, and suffer taunts and missiles from every
person who passed by. It was done partly out of cruelty, to discourage
others but also to entice Bruce to attack a great strong-point and
retrieve them, for then he would be at their mercy.

Elizabeth, the Scottish Queen, being the Earl of Ulster's daughter,
was spared these indignities. Several times I observed Bruce gradually
enrage, face becoming livid, and then seem to rise as a prelude to
giving orders to mount and attack the folk of Ross and murder them
all. But it never happened. Some deep force would assert itself and
he would sit down again, and call for wine and smile and converse,
having put the matter out of mind.

About this time, news arrived that King Edward had died, never
having moved from the Solway, partly, men said, because of the defeat
at Loudon which had enraged him; and the effort had put an end to
his old age. The Scots were jubilant. His ruthless leadership would not
be missed. I was sorry, for he had been an extraordinary man who had
lived for nearly seventy years, become a famous tournament knight,
fought in a crusade with distinction, invigorated the legal system, and
conquered Wales and Scotland, leaving his mark everywhere. The
world would not see his like again and the question in every mind was
how his son would fare; but those who knew him, like the Bruces,
judged him a shadow of his father, lacking the iron will.

I had been given back my weapons, by now, except the bow and
arrows, until, one evening, some of the young men were firing at a
target and Bruce joined in, but could not hit it any more than the others.
'Bring me that longbow of Bannatyne's,' he said, but he was not more
accurate, finding the power difficult to control. He threw it down in
disgust saying it was heavy, clumsy and not as good as the Scottish
bow. Then he halted and turned and looked at me enquiringly. 'Why
do you use this? It's no good. Show me what you can do.'

The target was a large white birch tree with a two-foot circle cut in it. The bark had been stripped off and the area smeared with dirt, ,making a clear target; the range about thirty yards.

I strung the bow, aimed and fired and hit the dead centre. There was a roar of amazement and catcalls that it was a fluke and worse. But I did it again and then again. I shot five arrows and hit the mark every time. There was a hush when I had finished.

Men looked at me with new respect. 'So you are not just a book-worm,' said Bruce. 'Can you teach others to do this?'

'I can try. Whether they learn depends upon them; and practice, much practice. But that is not its strength.' I walked away, leaving Bruce, until I was about two hundred yards off and then turned and tested the wind with a wet finger. It was blowing from the left. I aimed a little to the left, elevated the bow and loosed off a testing shot. It fell twenty yards short and nearly hit Eli standing in the way. There were more catcalls at this failure. I tried another and it was long. The next hit the tree five feet above the mark. Then I fired ten arrows in quick succession and all ten were within six feet of the mark, four of them hit the tree and two the mark itself.

Smiling as if he'd been handed a magnificent gift, Bruce ran to meet me, followed by others. 'So these long bows are useful after all!' he said, with that winning smile of his.

My situation now changed immediately. I was asked to accompany the king on all occasions. It was then that Gloag, Bruce's general factotum, a man of about fifty who had been a kind of tutor in his youth, spoke up. 'Yull no lee him wi' thet weepon? Yull git an arra in yur beck yin day.' As he came from some wilderness south of Carrick, Gloag's style of speech was at times impenetrable.

I was asked again to give my word of honour that I would injure no one in the rebel army or the king himself. When I agreed, I was allowed to keep the bow and arrows, but there were many who thought the action unwise. To make sure, it was made clear that my promise meant I could not escape unless recaptured by the English.

And so every morning, I began to accompany Bruce on his early walk around the camp and its environs to assess any possible danger, consult with watchers and, above all, conduct his early morning evacuation. A youth of about sixteen, Wullie, by name, also accompanied us; armed only with a short bow and a few arrows in case of surprise attack which had happened once before. For a week or so, wherever I went, there was Wullie with his bow, eyeing me suspiciously.

Bruce minded not at all and often presented his back to me so that I could have shot him down easily a hundred times. It was, a very brave gamble for Bruce to take, but it had its good effect in arousing my admiration for his trust.

74

Soon after dawn, then, we three would stalk the sentries to see who was asleep and shoot any small game we came across. Thus, rabbit, pigeon, pheasant, grouse and anything else edible that moved was available for the king's breakfast. Once, I observed the tall skinny, hen-like figure of Gloag following curiously, suspiciously, as if I were a danger to his master, but I put a shaft a yard from his head and never saw him at that game again.

I have often wondered at the risk Bruce took in leaving me weapons. I did not know it then, but I could so easily have altered the course of history, for without him, every Scotsman's story would have been different. I expect he calculated that no decent man, especially one who had given his parole, would be capable of shooting his captor in the back; and that I was a decent man. As we both knew, not all men were.

With Gloag I had trouble from the very beginning. Some men are like that. He had attended Oxford and had a degree. As a native of southern Scotland he had been taken on as a tutor to the young Bruces and spent most of his adult life ministering to them. Robert he regarded as a kind of half grown chick who had still to be reminded of many trivial things and, to his credit, Bruce viewed the old man with amused tolerance; only occasionally erupting into abuse when Gloag crossed some invisible line.

For an Oxford man, Gloag had lost none of his accent or at least had forgotten the English one, after too many years back in Carrick. 'Wull ye ate yer bliddy greeny stuff, Rab,' he would say—the only person to use such a familiar expression—and the king would reply as often as not: 'You know fine, I eat only meat. Haven't I told you a thousand times kail is for cattle?' And when he got wet in the rain or fording some torrent, which he usually did first, like everything, Gloag would fuss about him with rags, drying him off. 'Yull git yer deeth a calt, ya ninny, ye. Kin ye no' bliddy git wan o' they ithers tae dae thet?' which Robert would ignore mostly, only exploding if he were in a particularly bad temper, at which Gloag would slink away like a shot-rabbit to re-emerge later in the day, when the king would have missed his attendance, the re-appearance timed to a nicety and dependent on the extent of the offence taken.

Once Bruce had mentioned meeting me at Cambridge and pronounced me a leading scholar, I became the target of all Gloag's resentment, for, increasingly, my counsel was asked more than his. And so, when-ever I seemed at rest, Gloag would arrive to harry me with this or that minor detail, hoping to score some point against my distinction and recover some of the ground he had lost.

'Hoo many teeth hus a deer?' spiered Gloag at me one evening, out of the dark, as we sat around the camp-fire.

Innocently, I said I had no idea. 'Weel, thet's somethin' ye don't ken,' said Gloag, triumphantly, looking to Bruce for approval.

'And how many is it?' said he.

'Thurty twa,' said Gloag, grinning inanely out of that white-girt, bald, egg-shaped head of his, with the single twist of white hair sprouting from the forehead.

'How do you know?' said Bruce.

'Ma tutor telt me,' said Gloag, 'and noo ah'm tellin' you.'

Bruce smiled tolerantly at having become the pupil yet again and said to me: 'So you are not the best in everything, Bann?'

By chance we had just shot a deer and the haunch was even now turning over the fire. I rose and went looking and soon returned with the head, opened it and pretended to count the teeth. 'I see only thirty,' I said, grinning.

Gloag was angry and pounced upon it. 'Lat me see! Lat me see!' and counted, uncertainly, frantically. At length—and I saw he was unsure, had fluffed the count and was bluffing—he announced, 'Thurty twa! Thur's thurty twa, richt enough!'

'What about these missing ones?' I said, laughing, pointing to a couple of small gaps where teeth might have been or might not.

'Thur's nae teeth there, there's nane there!' said Gloag, angrily, at having somehow lost his advantage.

'But there used to be, anyone can see it,' I replied. Then I looked at the old man's mouth and poked up his upper lip, the better to count his own teeth, and said, 'Open up, now. There you are, you've lost at least five. Why wouldn't a deer be the same as us? Wouldn't it lose teeth too?'

'But...but...but there's nae holes whaur you said.'

'Neither has the deer', I replied. 'The holes have filled up, there's just a gap left.' And Gloag flew into a rage and cursed me for a Cambridge clishmaclaver—and then he remembered he had to see someone about something and left us in high dudgeon.

'Well how many teeth does a deer have?' said Bruce, presently.

'How should I know?' I replied.

Bruce and the others laughed joyously. He said, 'I thought you would know everything, like Alexander.'

'Only the things that matter,' I said, 'and then only a few of them,' which made Bruce laugh again.

'I thought you were a scholar,' said Bruce.

'Being a scholar means knowing how little you know,' I said, quietly, 'not trumpeting what you do.'

'But Bann!' said Gibby Hay, 'You are supposed to know the answer to every question.' And when Bruce laughed either at the very idea, or my discomfort at being so diminished, I was irritated and replied, testily: 'Only if the question is clear. This one isn't. Can't you see that?'

Of course they could not; and I had to explain. 'It depends on what kind of deer it is. Red deer, fallow and roe deer may be different. Then, males may have different numbers of teeth from females. And the age of the deer will matter. A faun, like a human child, may have fewer teeth, which even fall out eventually.'

'Well, what if it is an adult red deer?' said Gibby, determined to find fault. 'You don't know do you?'

'I can count the number in that stag's head, if that's what you mean.'

'Do you mean, you haven't?' said Bruce with amazement.

'Of course not,' I said. 'I guessed the number at a glance. You don't think I'd waste my time counting, do you?' Gradually, they all began laughing. Only Gibby was still unhappy. 'But you told Gloag you had counted them,' he complained. 'That wasn't fair.'

'Fair?' I said. 'What has that to do with it? Gloag asked a stupid question to discomfit me and was being a nuisance. What do I care how many teeth a deer has?¹ Some questions are of no interest.'

---

1. The female adult of the deer in question have 32, but the male red deer has 34.

CHAPTER 7

Arguments with Bruce

THE YOUTH WULLIE, SEEING my expertise with the longbow, wanted to learn and I began to teach him in the manner I had been taught myself. And so, whenever the army halted for the night, he and I would practise and Bruce would often watch.

Of course, Wullie could not manage to pull the bow the full distance, for this was no ordinary bow. It was over six feet of yew, russet heartwood on the inside and white on the outside, the one to aid compression and the other extension; a single shaft of the finest grain, smoothed like one of the pebbles on the shore of the Kyles of Bute. It had taken me months to acquire the strength to pull the bow all the way back, and it would take Wullie years, until he grew strong enough.

As we wound our way north into the western wilderness, making truces first with John of Lorne and then with the Earl of Ross, Bruce would come to my fire every night or invite me to his. There, we would talk about Cambridge and the great teachers like Hammond, Granville, D'Arcy and others, some of whom he had met and even sat under as a student. He had read Aquinas and thought the five ways a miracle of argument, so there was no point in disputing these, for Bruce was as ardent a Christian as any man I ever knew, including Baldred. To have doubted the existence of God, the defined Aquinas version, would have been to court disaster. I expect the excommunication, following his murder of Comyn in the kirk at Dumfries, played its part, for, thereafter, Bruce was like a man living on borrowed time, who could only redeem himself by actions of remarkable nobility. Doubting the existence of his maker never entered into his calculations.

I suppose I quickly came to like and admire Bruce. His skill with weapons, especially with steel in his hand, on or off a horse, was exceptional. He would often contest feats of arms with the men and always came off best, by reason of the very qualities old Jeb had tried unsuccessfully to instil in me: decision, speed, deception, stamina, accuracy, agility and force.

Bruce had wide shoulders, a solid waist and rump, containing much power, but not an ounce of fat—few of us had. The life was too arduous for that, and food was irregular and invariably meat of some kind, or porridge. Very quick on his feet he was, and very fast over a short distance, very fast into action once he knew where action was needed, and he decided very quickly where and how to deploy himself. The years in the hills on the run, on the brink of extinction, had wrought him into a fully-tempered warrior, careful and calculating, but fierce and sharp as the blade in his hand, when danger threatened. I once saw him disarm four men in quick succession, with four savage but accurately directed blows, when they least expected it. This became a habit: fighting several folk in mock combat, as a means of keeping his skill tuned to perfection, like a lyre in the hands of Orpheus.

And admire him as I did, it was an easy step to wish to please him. At first this was difficult. 'Who *should* be king of Scots, then?' he said to me, one evening, over a tankard of ale in his tent, with but one candle between five of us. This because of something I said, which indicated that I did not regard him as king, even though he had been crowned. In that light, Bruce's dark eyebrows were raised to points, which with the firm set to the jaws, gave him a dangerous, diabolic look.

'John Balliol is King of Scots,' I said.

There were explosions of disapproval and snorts all round. 'But he has abdicated,' said Randolph, preening his sandy-haired moustaches. 'Exiled to France.'

'Only because he was forced,' I replied.

'So you are a Balliol man, then?' said Bruce, with that look of steel, a look I had seen before only in Galloway, when he was intent on revenge upon Balliol men, like the McDowalls.

'No, I am a king's man. Edward's man.'

There was a gasp at my effrontery.

Sir Robert Boyd shuffled the massive rounded shoulders, shoved the under lip out of the black beard, pugnaciously, and said, 'How kin a Scot born in Bute be fur Edwart, King o' Inglant?'

'Because he was given the kingdom of Scotland by the nobles of the realm and every one of them has since made homage to him.' As I said this, I saw Bruce flinch, because he was one of them, several times he had given homage. 'Edward had the right to depose Balliol and since he is no longer here, that makes Edward himself overlord and effective king and ruler of Scotland until his return. It is an intellectual issue; unarguable.'

'But how can it be best for Scotland to be ruled by the English? You've seen how they mistreat us?' This from Gilbert de la Hay, Bruce's particular friend, a decent man, warm and kindly, and therefore, above all, concerned for the treatment of other folk. Dark he was, like Bruce, but bearded, with soft brown eyes.

I said, 'I am glad you concede that it is *right* that we are ruled by the

English; and now question only whether it is *best.*' There were mutters at this, but Bruce remained silent, making a sign for quiet with a calming hand, as he often did at such times, interested by what lesser men would say. 'It is best for this reason,' I went on, 'On her own, Scotland can only be subjected to endless trouble, distress and savage warfare at the hands of our more powerful neighbour. It is inevitable, as the day night. And for generations, to escape this, Scottish kings from Malcolm Canmore to the present, have given homage to the king of England, for to do otherwise would have meant being killed. He was, you may remember, captured by the English and forced to pay homage as a condition of saving his life. And every Scottish king is in the same position. If the English come in force, they must eventually take the kingdom because they are so much more powerful; and they will eventually capture the King of Scotland—whoever he is—unless he flees overseas, as now. So, in brief, gentlemen, there can be no lasting independence for Scotland. It is impossible. Well then, let us recognise it! Let us give up this senseless resistance and accept the dominance of the English and with it their protection from future wars; and let us grow in health and strength and prosperity, instead of hunting each other around Scotland, putting every enemy to the sword and making women and children, the realm over, miserable, starving them half to death by burning their crops, their homes and stealing their goods. How many good folk of this realm have been killed-off by this rebellion? Thousands! And yet more thousands must fall before it ends, as it surely will. And even if by some miracle this rebellion succeeded, it cannot last long, for as soon as there are new kings in place, the same situation will occur all over again!'

Nostrils emitting steam, Boyd had risen to his feet and drawn his sword by this time; and I sat still, waiting to be cut down for my impudence—but defiant. Bruce told him to sheath the weapon and then eyed me levelly, as if I were a serious enemy. 'You have gall to argue thus, but you were asked your opinion and it was honestly given. For that you must be thanked, not killed. And yet your views are so opposed to everything we believe. You are a danger to us.'

There were murmurs of agreement from those around. I said, 'The only danger any man faces is the refusal to confront the truth. Was it not Julius Caesar who declared wishful thinking the enemy of success?'

'And whit if ye die of yur truth?' said black-bearded Boyd, with his rough manners and big idea of his own importance.

'That you die is less important than how you die. Alexander said the same thing in Carlisle, just before they cut his head off.'

'Is it not better to live?' said Randolph, who, after his capture at the battle of Methven, had sworn homage to King Edward rather than lose his life. And then, only a few months ago, having been recaptured by the rebels and under the spell of their leader, recanted and given homage to Bruce instead. Logically, his situation was a morass, but I had not the heart to tell him. Probably, if I had done, I would have had my own torn out, for he was not as generous as Bruce.

'Yes, of course!' I replied. 'So why don't you accept the inevitable and make peace. Then you *can* live—*at peace!*'

'Christ, I'll pit a blade through the bastart yit!' declared Boyd, through grating teeth.

'No, you won't,' said Bruce, laying an arm upon him. 'That would be defeat for us and our ideas. We would lose everything then.'

Boyd exploded: 'Wha cares if wan bugger gits kilt?'

'We would all wonder if he was right and we would always remember him with regret. No, friends, we must convert him to our cause, if we can. And I'm not sure we can.'

I said, 'Why don't you convert the Balliols then, instead of murdering them out of hand?'

Bruce shouted: 'I'll tell you why. *They* don't have a case to answer! It's kill or be killed by them! You are different. I must ponder this.'

He was greatly upset by my resistance and went off by himself in a great huff of turmoil. The next day, he was ill, shivering with fever, yet complaining of cold, though the weather was fine. We, Wullie and I, were the first to know, for he had not appeared for the dawn patrol around the marches.

As the light came up and we could see better, it became evident that Bruce had unnatural patches of colour on his skin. His face was clear, but the neck, back and legs were not: red, itchy and like fish scales they were. Worst of all, he tried to stand and could not, for the weakness. All day, he lay down and the army came to a halt without his driving leadership.

Gloag was at his cantankerous best, cajolling and bullying him to eat 'some ae this chaw,' fussing about him like a scrawny hen. 'If ye dinny eat yer chaw, hoo kin ye expeck tae be weel?' In the evening, having been prevailed upon against his wishes, Bruce ate some and was sick an hour later, cursed volubly by Gloag, who complained at 'the waste ae aw thet guid chaw.'

Early next morning, Bruce forced himself up as usual and we did our rounds. The breakfast set down soon after our return was a bowl of green soup, which Gloag declared to be 'the baist bliddy thing fur the "coleric", whit a spae wife had gied him fur twa merks, yin merket day.' Bruce took a spoonful and spat it out, pronouncing it revolting.

'What the hell's in this!' said he.

'Weel, fower leaves ae kail, twa cats een—bit there's nae cats, so a dug's een ull huv tae dae—a puckle ragwort, dandelions, docken and sich, and a big dram ae usquebeatha.'

'You must have forgot the dram,' said Bruce, trying to smile through the discomfort.

'Jist you drink it doon the noo, and ye'll dae fine. Sure, ye ken fine thet potions ur nae guid inless they taste foul.'

When half the appalling mixture had been swallowed, Bruce spat it out and the bullying went on again until, finally, some of the stuff went down, but he was still very weak and had to retire to the tent to rest.

Scouting parties were sent out everywhere and Bruce, from his pallet, ordered attacks on keeps, steadings and any small castles around. Thus was it, one day, that the camp was quite depleted, only a hundred men in all being left as rearguard. As one of them, I was standing by Bruce's tent firing shots with the longbow, showing Wullie the angles of elevation for different distances, when a line of horsemen appeared above the skyline, not four hundred yards away. From the banners, they were not our men. Then they were in motion, a long straggling triple line descending the brae towards us. Three hundred, I made it, galloping like mad with drawn swords and bright lances which glittered in the morning light. At the foot of the hill, they bunched, converging upon us.

The idea that I could gain my freedom flashed into mind, but I said and did nothing. Then I thought of Bruce on his bed and the small force around us who could not possibly defend him. He would be killed outright or taken and beheaded, like Wallace and Alexander. I could not stand and watch; knew it would be the end of me, my conscience shattered.

I called the camp to arms and sent off a ranging shot. Then, the riders being closer, I let go five bolts, waited to see the outcome of the first and when it hit the bunch, dropped the elevation a fraction and let go five more in quick succession, then dropped the angle again and loosed ten. Around me, all was pandemonium, as men struggled to reach weapons, mount horses, put on mail and all the shouts, noise and scurry of preparing for battle. I fired ten arrows fast, at fifty yards—point blank range—and then had no more. Cursing the lack, I seized a lance, and stood to defend the tent with only Wullie beside me. Around us, some went forward with pikes, a few hid and not a few fled to the protection of woods behind.

The attackers burst through the standing pikes like great flying stones from a mangonel. A lance grazed my temple and mine snapped on catching in an armoured knee-joint. The horse and rider crashed into the tent and flattened everything in it. I drew the sword and punctured the belly of a second passing horse, jumped out of the way of another and, as it reared, leapt onto the knight and pulled him off, the fall stunning both of us. Then, unhindered by armour, I jumped up, and slashed him with the blade.

Blood spurted from his neck and I knew it was over for him as he fell clutching the gaping wound. Fighting was taking place around, but here was relative peace. A trumpet sounded and the attackers rode off. By then, I was in a dead faint, kneeling beside the man I'd killed; stupified by the dead blue eyes that stared at me even after the last twitchings of legs and arms. The nose was proud and the hair grey. Here was a person of command and authority, and a moment ago he had been alive. I had killed him! The enormity fell upon me like a dead weight, so that I fell down beside him, clutching the torso, and wept and apologised for the enormity of it, getting my share of his blood on my clothing.

Then I remembered Bruce and let out a yell of self disgust and leaped up and tried to pull the tent apart to get at him, but the horses had already kicked it to bits. I lifted the torn canvas. There was nobody there!

I turned and found Bruce smiling at me, sword in hand, dripping blood. Still unwell, but improved in some strange fashion, as if the tide of battle had been an elixir.

'I have . . . have killed a man,' I said, in shock.

Bruce laughed. 'Just the one, is it? Come and see; and bring your quivers.'

Across the plain we found eight dead horses and six men dead or dying who had been on other horses which had now run off. 'That's fourteen you took out all by yourself, and seven men killed in all, not counting any others who still live but with arrows in them.'

I was shocked at the catastrophe I had wrought. I stammered 'B... b...but some of these men still live,' I said.

'Not for long,' said Bruce, through jaws like man-traps.

'But surely—'

'In Buchan, all our enemies must die.' He turned to me and put a hand on my shoulder. 'Any who are left alive will trouble me further, again and again. Don't you see? They must be taken out of contention. I can't afford to have an army in my rear when I'm trying to deal with the English.'

There was a terrible, cold logic to the decision, and I knew I could not have carried it through myself. That was one difference between us: he was like steel. But then, adversity had made him this way. He had survived great and frequent perils, when only quick thinking, exceptional skill and phenomenal self-confidence had sustained him. None of it helped me. I seemed to have acquired a load on my soul for all the men I had killed.

That night, in the tent, the commanders were told of my part in the defence of their leader. Some looked upon me with a kindly eye. Boyd, though, was still unsure of me.

'So what does this mean, then?' said Bruce, smiling in the firelight, 'this defence of the rebels?' Everyone laughed. I even managed a rueful smile myself. At first, I had nothing to say, for I did not understand it at all. Compelled to reply by Randolph, I said, 'I could not just stand' by and watch him being killed. I had to defend him. Anyone would have done the same.'

'No Englishman would,' said Randolph.

'I am not an Englishman.'

'But you support them,' said Randolph. 'Why didn't you do nothing. You might have been freed?'

'I couldn't do nothing! Would you have stood by if King Edward had been attacked and you had been on parole?'

'I would not have fought Scots to save him.'

'Why not? After giving him homage?'

There was no reply to this and Randolph fell silent. Other men would have drawn swords. 'So you are as pro English as ever?' said Bruce. And when I agreed, he added, 'Well what will they do, if they find out about your fighting for us?'

'That is not my problem, but theirs.'

'Be serious,' said Randolph, with irritation. 'It is your problem! It could get you killed by them.'

'I am serious,' I replied. 'Never more so. My position is that I favour acceptance of English rule, for the sake of the peace and prosperity it will bring, and the extension of the English Commonwealth, so as to increase its power to remain at peace by repelling other nations it cannot subsume. But if Scotsmen I know, and admire, are about to be killed by English supporters I know not, I expect I will continue to defend the Scots. Do you imagine I would allow any Englishman to kill my brother, who is a part of this force? Of course not, for he is my brother.'

'There is a contradiction here,' said Bruce, quietly. 'You cannot do both.'

'The contradiction is only practical, and so far as other men are concerned, some of whom may seek to deprive me of my life, because of it. Intellectually, there is no contradiction. I am entitled to my belief about the best policy for Scots, and to my ambition to aid those of them who may be in peril.'

I doubt if any understood me. It was a strictly intellectual affair, and all of them were practical men, accustomed to make whatever compromises were necessary for the sake of expediency.

'Will you train my men in archery?' said Bruce, eventually. 'If I had a hundred like you, I might be able to deal with the English.'

'You would need a thousand,' I said, 'for they have three times that number, and if pressed, could double it.'

Discussions about how to increase the effectiveness of the few rebel archers continued for some time. Fletchers had to be found, and bowmakers, these above all; and the bows must be the six foot bows like the one I favoured. Fletching, I had taught myself, perforce, because I so often needed to repair arrows damaged by contact with targets or intervening objects. But bows were beyond me, at that time. Good hardwood had to be found, craftsmen to work it and good sharp steel arrow-tips, to penetrate mail and armour plate. All this I told Bruce and he listened carefully and intently.

There is little yew in Scotland—a few old trees, near churchyards, often enough, because they are known to counter evil spirits. God knows, the tree is poisonous, the smell and atmosphere generated show that easily enough. And not all the tree is useful, only the heart-wood or rather, where it meets the outer shell, for the two, with the heart on the inside, give best results. But there is also elm and some oak and even ash, and birch could be tried. I had already made the discovery that wood wrapped around tightly with twine was less liable to bend and therefore generated more power. Crossbows were also mentioned, but I knew them to be inferior because of the time taken to reload. In the time a crossbow fires two arrows, in the right hands, a longbow can fire ten. Henceforth, as we journeyed around the country and over the border—then especially—I was to seek out good hard-wood for bow staves.

It was about that time that Bess Morrison gave birth, and because of it the army waited a full day for her to recover, as leaving her in that enemy-occupied land would have ensured her destruction. Afterwards, Bruce asked her who the father was. 'Christ how should Ah ken?' she replied, brazenly. 'It could be awbuddy,' which produced loud laughter round about. 'Weel awbuddy bit Bann here,' she added, with a grin.

'Could it be a prince, dae ye think, Bess?' said Left-Eye, who had the daring of the least imaginative.

'Och, aye,' she said, 'It micht even be yin ae they. Bit ye ken, it widnay be the furst.' Bruce said nothing and went off to his tent.

In no time, Bess was back at her business, a force of nature beyond compare; but she looked after the child, feeding it regularly when it squalled, and if a man would accompany her into the bushes, she would take it with her and perform on the grass beside it. Eventually, it was left with a guid wife somewhere, to be brought up as usual. Only the ones she liked did she keep around her, and they were left to feed off the scraps of the army, often dying young of minor ailments im-properly attended. But she was kindly too, and had a good way of dealing with rotten meat, for she knew which herbs would reduce the foul taste. In these ways, she made herself useful and was liked because of it, but she was no slouch in a fight either. Her ham fists could give a good clout and she was wont to protect herself with a dagger, if any man seemed to insist on more than his due. Every evening, she would set down the small hand-cart that bore her few possessions, erect her shelter, and set up house while her diverse progeny collected firewood. Her cauldron was always good for a stew of hare or horseflesh, whatever was available; and if she liked a man and he had no better place to go, he would sit with her and feed and gossip.

Her progress was accompanied by several cats and dogs which would occasionally be stolen and killed by folk like Gloag, for potions, or even, in time of want, for food; but as they bred as often as their mistress, there was always a sufficiency. Her face, once comely, soon began to show the effects of too much travel but her body, in spite of all its many occupants, showed no signs of distress. Gloag, she detested, of course, and he kept well away from her withering wit.

'Git tae fuck oota here, ya auld skinnymalink, ye!' she would cry, if Gloag approached one of her many animals or children. Once, a child had gone missing and she blamed it on Gloag. Probably, it had slipped into a river and drowned or strayed into some deep ravine and fallen to its death out of sight.

CHAPTER 8

Miracles in Buchan

THE DAY AFTER THE BIRTH we moved quickly, as far as possible from that place which was known to the enemy, who would be massing ahead. Eventually we came to Slioch, a hilly country, within sight of the sea. It was there that Bruce fell ill again and near to death, and there for some weeks he remained, the army guarding him carefully from the kind of surprise attack before.

Somehow, the Comyns, led by Sir David de Brechin, knew of Bruce's weakness and determined to take advantage of it. One morning, we awoke to find a force twice our size camped within three bowshots of our own.

Bruce lay on his pallet of straw, in agony and weakness, so our situation looked disastrous. Two to one against, and with our leader an invalid some of us had to be used to look after. Every head in the camp was down; everyone expected catastrophe. Until Edward de Bruce, who had also arrived in the night, saw it. He helped his brother onto a litter drawn by two horses and, with a horseman on either side to hold up the man prostrate with weakness, he prepared to move camp to some other place.

Tents were folded and every cavalryman mounted. After that, we marched or rode off at even pace, mindless of the surrounding army, twice our size. It was the bravest thing I had ever seen and, as I was to discover, typical of Edward de Bruce, who was always careless of himself to a fault. Seeing him lead that retreat in those circumstances, I felt like cheering, as we all did later. Ahead, the lines of Comyn, Balliol and English men parted before us like the Red Sea, we passed out of the trap they had set for us, and a few hours later were in lowland. That night, we camped south of Inverurie, amazed that we had not been attacked.

I have often wondered why Sir David de Brechin did not attack, when he had us at his mercy. Later, much later, this same man was to pose unusual problems to the king, with the consequence that I never had the opportunity to question him.

Every day for many days after, I wondered at Robert Bruce. His weakness was awful to behold in one normally so strong and forceful; and while he was incommoded, the army was a restless, rootless thing, unsure and unclear. It needed him, and without his dynamic presence was a shadow of what it had been. At times, we thought he would die. Then Gloag would appear, clucking like a hen about to lose a chick, and force some more 'greeny stuff,' down his throat and he would revive a little.

It could not last. The Comyns came eventually in even greater force, accompanied by Sir Philip de Mowbray and his men, and when they did, when men looked to him for guidance, in a voice cracked with fever, Bruce ordered Gloag and me to raise him up and we obeyed. He ordered us to dress him; and we did that too. He ordered us to arm him with coat of mail, dagger and the axe he was fond of; and, with tears in our eyes, we did that also—for the position was lost, and we knew he wanted to die fighting. Finally, he ordered us to set him upon his horse and fix him there as best we could, for battle; and this, too, we did with ropes and cut branches.

After that, he spurred his horse and every man followed in a last gallant charge right at the heart of the enemy, Wullie, just behind him, waving the brave banner with the red lion on its field of gold, and me at his elbow, ready to fire. And a great shout went up from us all; and then from the massed horsemen ahead—seeing Bruce himself, well enough to lead the charge—Bruce, the victor of a hundred engagements, feared by all—a few of them turned and fled, and by the time we reached them, that few had become a flood no one could stop. Many were killed fleeing: speared in the back, cut down with the sword and some even knocked flat by the one axe which was a personal weapon in all that army.

It was a miracle!

After it, after Bruce had ridden to a halt and those still fleeing had disappeared out of sight, closely pursued by those rebels yet intent upon more blood, he slid out of the saddle and ended up kneeling on the ground; and gave thanks and prayed, as men pray when they have received divine assistance. For myself, I watched it through a haze of tears, and wondered if, after all, there was not a living god who had brought about this astonishing event.

Now, years later, after the benefit of much reflection, I see that it was will that won the day, and not God. The will of Bruce to fight to the bitter end, no matter the odds, and despite his own incapacity. To have been successful—as the Comyns should have been, for they had the superior force, which must have triumphed, if it had stood fast— they needed to have an equivalent will; and because they had not; because they were lacking in confidence, they fled. But then, I expect their men did not support them, because they were not devoted to their commanders, as we were to Bruce. That, finally, was the difference. Bruce was the kind of man to whom one was bound to be devoted. It was only a question of time; being in his company. It was his gift. But, in truth, there was a glorious recklessness about that charge, as if we knew, come what may—and most thought to die in the next moment —that it was right and proper conduct. We knew this, because Bruce was doing it just ahead of us and we all looked to him.

The next few days he spent on the litter, as we moved through the land of Buchan, slaying every man of military age, burning every farm, every field of crops we did not need ourselves, and taking every item of the least interest that we came upon. It was callous and yet necessary. Some of our force did not stop there, but also killed male children who might afterwards prove a threat in the unprotected rear of the realm.

Later, after all the burning and savagery, when we came at last to Aberdeen, bowmakers and fletchers were sought and found. My bow was shown and examined and others made, and Bruce appointed me commander of archers. With his approval, I chose young men, not above fourteen, for then they would not be needed as pikemen. But they had to be strong enough to string the bow and pull it, no easy matter. They were collected gradually, as we moved south again, from the ranks of supporters. No Comyns were left alive to volunteer or would have been admitted anyway.

Thus was it, that the one man in the realm who counselled acceptance of the English as rightful overlords, was set to train the Scottish army because he could not stand by and refuse to aid his countrymen.

All the usual difficulties occurred: having an accent cultivated by design in England, I was viewed with suspicion by every new recruit. And as I had no experience of command, *my* will was tested severely at first. When they saw what I could do, however, both for them and their country, they were more respectful.

Many of the young men could not string the bow, still less pull it as far as needed. In that case, the short Scottish bow was used; but it was accounted a great success by each one when he was able, after many trials over weeks, to string the more powerful weapon and yet more, when he could pull it all the way back and send an arrow over two hundred paces. These were marks of progress everyone soon came to recognise. The final one was the ability to fire ten arrows so quickly that all were in the air at the same time, all travelling 200 yards and all close to the target. Three things above all were inculcated: power, for without that there was no point in being an archer, who fights from a distance. Accuracy, for why shoot at all if you cannot hit? And then speed, for then, so many arrows were fired that some would find their billets.

My small force followed close behind the army towards Argyll, practising as we went, on every occasion, as Bruce determined not to blood them until they were proficient. But we were useful too, for the amount of game shot by them increased and was enjoyed both by ourselves and the full-grown men. And as we passed a house, if a youth seemed impressed, he would enquire and might be allowed to enlist; others, disallowed, would arrive days later, having run off for the purpose, against parental wishes.

And so most took no part in the battle at Brander, but gradually, as things turned out, they began to shoot singly, at targets that presented and, after that, shooting in unison became natural, for then, the target would surely fall to one of us.

With only a score of archers, then, I went with Douglas to the top of the hill above the pass at Brander and fired down upon the enemy until every bolt was loosed. Then we charged down and fell upon the mass of men fighting in the pass by the loch. It was soon over and we chased the men of Lorne all the way to Dunstaffnage Castle, which was given up.

It was there, lingering on the field in the aftermath, with a wound to a leg, which prevented my following in hot pursuit like everyone else, that I saw the awful results of battle. Clansmen were everywhere scattered about, screaming with the pain of injuries soon to be fatal, or comatose with shock. One kilted highlander sat with his back against a tree-stump holding his entrails in both hands, looking at them with wonder as if the inevitability of his death was not yet appreciated.

The pikes of our force had advanced upon the McDougalls relentlessly and been resisted for a time, but then the flights of arrows from the mountain had wrought a terrible carnage among them and the pikes had had their way. Once on the retreat, they were lost, for who can properly defend himself when his back is turned to his pursuer?

I found two of the Anderson's lying together, as if brother had defended brother, one with a sword cut in the neck, half severing it, and the other stuck fast to the ground with a lance which swung crazily in the breeze above his recumbent form. Above them, stood another of the brothers, aghast, inconsolable and speechless at his loss. Then a voice cried to me and I beheld Malky, grey head lying in the mire, where a stream fell down the mountain, his left arm bleeding from a harsh sword cut.

I tore a piece of cloth from my kirtle, bound up the arm, helped him to his feet and together we walked off the field of the dead, in the direction of the fighting, which continued around the corner of the mountain. I cleaned the wound when we came to the roaring river which flows out from the loch; and later, reaching the sea, had him wash the arm in salt water, as was my practice, and in time the wound closed and mended, though there was a wide scar thereafter.

Before long, my command increased to forty able archers and a score of youths in training, not yet able in some particular. I became difficult and demanding of them, as necessity, I felt, demanded. They would only improve if a standard had to be met and so I was inflexible about it. Some youths would never reach it, lacking the eye, the strength, or the application, and were assigned elsewhere, as messengers or trainee pikemen; and there came to be a mystique about us, as of men of skill—self evident, as we practised and shot mostly what we aimed at, so much, that some grown men among the pikemen wished to join our company. Within a year, the number of archers had exceeded a hundred, with half that number still trying to reach the standard.

In time, there were no more areas of the country to be pacified, except for the castles which resisted all attempts at that time. Edward de Bruce was ordered south to Galloway to try and penetrate the Balliol Castles at Dalswinton, Buittle and elsewhere; but there was a lull in military activities, which turned Bruce's thoughts to the administration of government. For most, this was a welcome relief from cold-lying in heather and forest, and many were allowed to visit their loved ones. As someone on parole, my position was uncertain; but the king agreed to my leaving and appointed a commander in my absence.

Jermyn Lindsay was a good archer, if not outstanding, and a man of some forcefulness. To Bruce, he would have seemed a fine choice because his loyalty was unquestioned and he came of noble stock, unlike myself. The matter was also desirable because of a limp I had developed in the leg due to the wound which I had taken too little notice of. The place was red and sore and filled with pus, which I was compelled to lance every night, leaving a poultice over it till morning. But it refused to get better. This sort of injury became of intense interest to me in later life, as you will see.

And yet I left the army with regret, for I had enjoyed success there and delighted in my small but increasingly effective troop. I was ordered back within two months and did not expect to command in future. Of course I was advised to stay out of sight of the English, who might be expected to prevail upon me if I were taken. Accordingly, I had to swear an oath to Bruce that I would not take up arms against the Scots and would return in the time specified. His last act was to send me to Glasgow, where I was wanted at the cathedral.

A day later, I arrived to find Bishop Wishart and Baldred Bisset in close converse in their quarters nearby. There were smiles and congratulations about my successes in the schools and the field. When I enquired why I had been sent for, they took me outside to a stable and pointed to a cart, my own cart, still full of my books and the horse too, none the worse. 'It was taken at Loudon,' said Baldred. 'The king sent it here until you could call for it.' And there followed a discussion about the new books I had brought with me, which neither had heard of until then—though Baldred had been reading them one by one and having others copied.

I decided to leave the books where they were until my position became settled. That evening, at supper, they started on me about my politics and I saw that much thought had gone into the question of converting me to the common view most Scotsmen held.

Wishart began. 'Robert Bruce is the king now, properly crowned and fully in command of the realm. Does that not change your mind?'

'Many castles are still in English control. As soon as they return in force, the country will once again revert to them, at a cost of much bloodshed. It is such a waste,' I said. That and more.

'But you played your own part in freeing the realm,' said Baldred. 'How can you stand aside?'

'I haven't stood aside. As you say, I have taken my turn in the fight. But that doesn't mean that I think it is the proper course to take. I did it because I was in a position where I could do no other. I would not stand by while a single Scotsman is in peril of his life.' And so they made no progress with my conversion that night, or the next seven, for I spent these days relaxing, with my books for company, attending the services again, enjoying the plainsong and the holiness of the great cathedral, and the company of educated men.

The effect of good regular food and a merciful release from travel wrought benefits on my health and the foot improved. Then, one day, it was time to go, time to return to Bute, for which I had a longing like hunger.

Two days later, I arrived at Craigmore on Bute from a fishing smack I picked up at Fairlie, on the Clyde, and three hours later, having skirted the burgh of Rothesay, where the English might be expected to be in control, I came to the farm at Ardmaleish, three miles to the north.

It was late evening, the gloom having fallen, but I knew the way as if by second nature, past the dories that lay on the beach of the first bay, with the shacks and cottages of the fisher folk; around the point and up the hill where the croft stood among fields in the promontory above the Kyles. The water glinted below me, no wave breaking the surface. Clouds lay low over the hills of Argyll, opposite, and a grey mist hung menacingly among the great sea lochs there. The air around was still, as if before a storm. In the fields no animals moved or lowed. Indeed, I noticed with alarm that there was something more important missing, but could not tell at first what it was.

Half way up the hill, I stopped, and suddenly realised: peat smoke from the fire. There was always a fire in our home, or always had been until now, and where there should have been a skein of smoke wending its way skywards, was blankness, emptiness. All around was still and silent as the grave.

The door lay half open and I entered and shut it, and then called out. There was no reply. The place was in darkness. I went to where we kept rush-lights and fell over something, yet found one and managed to strike a spark. In the dim light, I saw that furniture was smashed and things lay scattered about the floor. I looked everywhere and found no one, no sign of life but a smear of blood on the wall. There had been a fight of some kind.

I lit the fire and prepared a simple meal of broth with oats and scraps of cured meat and some kail, long since past its best; and then, having nothing better to do till morning, I lay down to sleep.

In the village at Kames the next morning, I learned the truth. My mother had taken up with a soldier from the castle and my brother Eck had come upon them at the farm. There had been a fight and Eck had done some damage before chasing off the interloper. Later, the soldier had returned with others and Eck was badly beaten before being taken to the castle dungeon, until the sheriff should decide what to do about him. My mother was working at the castle as a cook.

The castle stood on a plateau above the beach at Rothesay, surrounded by a moat, nestling under a steep hill on the east. To the west, the ground sloped downwards to a broad valley with a river, and further off, southwards, a loch. Trees studded the landscape and I had always thought it beautiful. Beyond, were the distant snow-topped peaks of Arran.

Unsure of myself, I skirted the edge of the plateau. Should I approach and announce myself? Or had they been told of my work for the rebels? Bruce had expressly refused this from my parole. Yet, these were circumstances when oaths might hardly apply.

In the valley below, I saw a rider in dark clothing: tall and straight in the saddle, with auburn hair rippling out behind, like the river. I knew her instantly. I descended the hill and stood in the track.

As soon as I saw her I was overborne with delight, and forgot everything else. And she, too, seemed pleased to see me. How can I describe the deliciousness of her presence? The cheerfulness of her laugh and the way her mouth looked when she smiled; the white even teeth and hazel-blue eyes that made mine swim whenever I looked into them. I felt stirred to the bottom of my being by her, overmastered, as men are who commit rapes, mindless of all decency and the infinite reprobation of the world. And yet my own feelings were nothing like, for I would have died rather than incur her least displeasure. I firmly believe I would have castrated myself rather than cause her hurt.

Leaving the horse to graze, we strolled by the river, back the way she had come, and my heart was in my mouth all the while at my good fortune. All I wanted to do was touch her, be near—or so I thought at first—but it was different, of course, I see that now. I desired her with every inch of my being, I who had been a deep scholar all my life, preferring the cloistered world of ideas for the sake of the truths of the mind which then became available.

She spoke of her life. How Sir Hubert was in Argyll seeing the MacDougalls of Lorne—who, since our attack, had regrouped—seeking fresh troops, and Richard was in England with the army, which, some said, would soon be used to cross the border and curb Bruce and his rebels once and for all. Each day, she rode and read and embroidered and helped with the cooking, which she liked. And when opportunity presented, she practised with weapons, for 'who knows when a woman may have to defend herself in such warlike times?' And when I laughed at the idea of her fighting, she shot me a look of granite, unslung my bow from its place upon my back, strung it—to my amazement at her strength—fired an arrow high into the air, and we walked near two hundred paces before reaching it.

I told her the tale of my capture and my work for Bruce, and how I had come home and found the farm empty, the farm that once supported five people. I even spoke of my father, for the first time. How he had taken up with a woman of the camp and followed Douglas, so as to keep away from his son Eck, who despised him for it.

She listened patiently and then said quietly, 'Do not blame your father too much. The flesh is weak. There is no standing against it.' And her expression filled with sadness, sympathy and desolation. 'Your brother will be hanged on market day, when the folk have assembled.'

'I must try to rescue him, then,' I said, and then cursed my stupidity. 'I suppose you will tell them.'

'No, I won't. They are nothing to me.'

'But Sir Hubert is your guardian. Richard, your friend.'

'You don't know what they are like.'

'Why do you stay, then?'

'I have nowhere else to go.'

'Surely you have relatives? Have you not lands in England?'

'Lands yes, relatives no. Sir Hubert is my guardian. I must do his bidding. He has decided I am to marry Richard.'

'And what does Richard say?'

'He will do as he is told, I think. Unless some better prospect comes along.'

'But surely—'

'You don't understand! Already he treats me as his wife. The reality has dimmed his interest. If it were not for that, maybe he *would* marry me.' She looked at me without concern as she said this, but I blushed, reddened to the roots of my hair.

'You mean—' and, I am ashamed to say, my eyes fell, so that I beheld the covered place where the evil deed was done. 'But how? Surely, since you are a ward, you are protected?'

She laughed, a sad laugh in one so young. 'Who is to protect me when Sir Hubert is away? Richard has the run of the place. It started years ago. He came to my room and there was nothing I could do to prevent it.'

'But you should run away!' I protested, angrily. 'Have you no care for your freedom? You are treated like a . . . like a . . . like a whore,' I decided, blushing at the very idea.

'Yes, that is what I am.' Again she looked at me sadly, as if she would say more, and I knew instantly what more there was.

'He is not the only one, is he?' I suggested.

'No. Sir Hubert too. There is bad blood between them and I don't know what will be the end of it.'

At last I understood that strange meeting in the guest quarters of Granville's Hall. She had been coming out of Sir Hubert's bedroom! I was appalled, for, besides her difficulties, my own seemed minor. 'It is so unfair!' I shouted. 'They are supposed to protect you and . . . and . . . they take advantage of your helplessness.'

'It is not so bad,' she conceded. 'I have a roof over my head, I can read—as a scholar you will know the value of that—I live in comfort and have many pleasures. Music, writing.'

'But you are a slave to them, to their fleshly desires.'

She laughed. 'And have you none of your own?'

The question was so boldly stated it took me unawares. I blushed again and blustered that as a scholar, confined to the cloisters, such things were not for me. And she laughed again, a rich rumbling warm laugh that made my fragile sense of self shiver at its roots. 'And yet it seemed to me a few moments ago that there were signs of stirrings within you that might have caused a maiden—which alas I am not—to flee, in case she were molested.'

Again I blushed and did not know where to look, or what to be at, and in the midst of this confusion did not God strike my false tongue by inflicting upon me once more the affliction of projecting flesh, which men are sometimes heir to? And yet I would not, could not, leave her, for her company was a joy to me, as sweet as heather honey. Thus we proceeded, she smiling at my discomfiture and I crimson with embarrassment at my state of arousal.

'If only Richard had your sense of guilt,' she said at last. 'There is nothing wrong with it, you know,' smiling at me now. 'It is natural. Everyone has these feelings. Think of it, if men never became like this there would be no children to populate the world.'

'But it is sinful,' I replied. 'Everyone knows this. I will have to confess my sin at the first opportunity.'

'Is it sinful in marriage?'

'Of course not.'

'Does God positively forbid it outside marriage?'

'Yes,' I said, but, when pressed, could not think of a single instance.

'If it is sinful, why do we have to do it?'

'We don't have to.'

'Don't we? Doesn't everyone do it?'

'No, not monks. Not those sworn to celibacy.'

'But that is difficult? Yes? Then few are capable of it.'

'Yes,' I replied, grudgingly.

'Then there is not much wrong with it, if it is something we are all compelled to do.'

'But it is against holy church!' I protested, weakly.

'When did you ever pay attention to holy church? Theology was your worst subject because you don't believe in it! Think for yourself! It's what you are best at.'

I was dumbfounded, beetroot-red. I the scholar—winner of countless celebrated disputations, who should have been able to rout a mere girl, without one iota of my advantages—I had been shown the error of my ways and I did not enjoy the experience.

She said, 'I tell you these things because it will allow me to say other things about myself and perhaps, just perhaps, you will think less badly about me.'

I waited, wondering, breathless with fascination, while she steeled herself to tell me and the effort of it, as she screwed up her courage, told me what it must mean.

'When Richard or my guardian come to me, I like it. If they did not come I would miss them.'

'So it is not servitude, then?' I said, with astonishment.

'Yes! I am a prisoner of my own flesh!'

'You like it?' I said stupidly, and then repeated it. 'But surely you would rather do it with one you loved?'

'Yes, who would not? But I do not love anybody. I do not have anybody to call my own. So I must take my pleasure where it offers.'

'Offers? But they take you whether you will or no!'

'Yes, and sometimes they are careless of me. But usually, I like it well enough.'

'Why do you tell me these things?'

'Because I know I can trust you and I need to tell someone.' When I looked perplexed, she added, 'I know that you love me and that means you will not act against me if you can help it. I received your letters, you see.'

'You did not write back.'

'No, I had nothing worthwhile to say, except thanks, and that

would be little consolation. Anyway, you forgot me as soon as I left.'
When I denied this, she laughed and said, 'Well, there were no more
letters.'

'There would have been if I had received a reply. How was I to know
they had been received?'

'Faint heart never won fair lady.'

'But how can I hope to win you? I am base born. You are a lady,
daughter of a knight.'

'And you are very clever, men say, though I have begun to doubt it.
Why should it matter that you have no titles or lands?'

'It does and you know it!'

'Yes, but I have a mind to suit myself in these things.'

My heart leaped at this and gave me hope. Then, for a while, we
discussed the possibility of saving Eck before market day. The problem
was difficult because there were so many of them and all well-armed.
The key to the dungeon was kept on the serjeant's person on a chain
around his neck.

Finally, I remembered that the next day was market day.

CHAPTER 9

Initiation in the Act of Love

ELEANOR SOON HAD TO GO, as the castle would be locked up for the night. Promising to meet her again during her afternoon ride, I returned to Kames and entered a few cottages to stir up interest in arranging my brother's escape, but it was no use. Years of striving to be an Englishman had made me into one—or sufficiently like one to deter any locals from conspiring with me, in case it were a trick of some sort. That night, after dark had fallen, I lit a fire in the house, made a simple meal, and then, sitting in the smoky room with only shadows for company, I contemplated the problem of my brother.

The castle itself was impregnable—or so we thought at that time. Castles were built with high walls which could be defended by few men, if only because these walls were unscalable. Anyway, what use to gain entry when I had no means of opening the dungeon? Eleanor's aid could not be counted upon, as she was English—Norman, anyway, which was the same thing—and had no particular interest in me, except as a swooning acolyte, which realism compelled me to admit to myself. In that case, the only opportunity of freeing him would arise when he was on his way to the gallows at the mercat cross.

I saw too quickly that the task was impossible. If I went anywhere near the place with a bow slung on my back, I would be marked out—might have been marked and reported already, by one of those I had consulted. And if I strung the bow, I would be shot down by bows already loaded for just that purpose.

I thought of concealing myself far off, at the limit of my range, but that, too, was hopeless, for I might just as easily skewer Eck as any of his close attendants. If only I had a few men—half a score even, would do—but commander I was not and never would be. Not here at least, when my style and accent and clothing proclaimed me for one of the English most people hated. But surely, if I went around the island looking up old schoolmates, I could collect a force? And as soon as I had stated it, I knew I was incapable even of this.

What Bruce would have accomplished in a word with a short ride, I would not have managed in a hundred years. I had spent my schooldays outstripping my fellows and been resented for it, where Bruce would have won their admiration. There was some deep mystery here I could not fathom, and it was all the more irksome because it mattered so much, so very much! It amounted to this: my brother was about to die because I was not good enough, not well enough equipped, to save him!

In the years since, I have often thought of this puzzle and I see now that it is really about love. The leader has to love his men and they will know if he does, even the worst reprobate! And if he is good enough and really does care for them, they will learn to love in return. But at that time, I understood nothing of leadership. Even so, it has never been in me and the reason has as much to do with my intellect as anything, for how can I be expected to love stupid men or, what is worse, men who are morally inept because they are stupid? And yet, Bruce was neither stupid nor immoral and had a high regard for minds like mine. So how is it that he could lead and I could not? That he could love the stupid ordinary men when I could not?

I am not quite sure that he did love them, though many thought he did. What is certain is that he loved power and would conceal what he felt if it helped him to achieve what he desired. For the sake of this, he would take any amount of trouble and care over his men, and they loved him for it. In truth, if he had loved them truly, as they thought, he would never have been able to expose their lives in battle the way he did, time after time, often to their suffering and death. And yet, he did try to be careful of them, to use them sparingly, as far as he was able, this I concede.

And yet I had commanded archers. Of course, they were young men all, boys really, not old enough for battle; and I had succeeded, I knew well, because I had a skill they coveted; and they would even follow my miserable orders if the prize at the end was the acquisition of it. But men fit for battle? No! Ordinary, rough, coarse men would laugh at my youthful pedant's ways and go their own. Besides, Bruce had ordained that I was in command, and that was worth more than the title necessary to make it possible.

What was it about being a war leader that I lacked? Experience certainly. I had never been in battle, had never fought for my very life. And then I thought of Loudon and Slioch and Brander and knew that I had as much of that as other men. Three times I had killed other men —many! By god, these were battles! Well then, what was the deficiency? And in those days I did not understand and was perplexed, for my mind had proved itself to be such a marvellous instrument until then.

Night fell and I lit a fire; and then sat beside its flickering flames, wondering, speculating, worrying about what I might do on the morrow; and got nowhere. And every time my thoughts reached another dead-end, they turned instead to Eleanor, she of the tall lissom figure, elfin nose, auburn hair and eyes that sparkled, who held my heart so much in its thrall that the thought of her was relief of a kind, a strange pleasure, in the midst of so much dire anxiety.

My flesh lifted, for nothing could keep me still, and I remembered how she had said that no one could stand against it; and I gave way, and it helped somehow, that she had said this, as if the act were made right by it. Certainly, it relaxed me for a while, until again the impossibility of saving Eck once more confronted me, so that I cried out, and tear-drops fell at my impotence. What use were all these years of study, all these things I knew, all my degrees, and all my crafted arguments to which I clung like a limpet, on a drifting, shiftless sea of uncertainty?

Long into the night I kept my vigil and then went out to view the Kyles from the back door and, as I looked across at the sea lochs of Argyll to the cloud-topped hills, it came to me at last what I must do, with the clarity of blazing light, the kind of experience I had enjoyed so often at Cambridge when, after much searching, I found the argument, especially the refined phrasing of it, necessary to establish my position with dazzling insight.

I slept and woke at cock-crow and bathed in the freezing waters of the Kyles and then left for the town, where, in a field on my route, I found a passable stallion. I had no saddle, all that kind of thing having been stolen from the farm, but I had brought a length of rope and with it I made a bridle of sorts. Mounted, I rode towards the castle and the mercat cross close by, and circled the place, until I came to a hill above it, where I dismounted and waited among the very bushes in which Bohun had taken my mother, and watched the crowd gathering for the market with their wares in hand-carts and baskets.

Eventually, the draw-bridge was lowered and they set out, twenty men-at-arms on foot, with my brother in their midst, led by an officer on horseback. At the great hanging tree, that stood near the cross, they halted and I saw that some sort of announcement was made, while Eck, hands bound behind him, was set up on the horse. By then I was off, spurring my mount downhill, like an angry bee diving upon an intruder to the hive, cursing my lack of aid, since I needed six hands for this work: two for the bow and arrows, one for the sword and the rest to stay aboard my slippery steed, which every moment threatened to jettison me and my project before it had properly begun.

A hundred yards away, I began to loose off shafts, as quickly as I could manage. The bumping horse made aiming difficult but the very whirr of my arrows among them put a temporary halt to the execution. One or two soon came back with interest as men dived for cover amid the roaring of the crowd who scattered in every direction. Then, with Eck well-mounted on the horse below the tree and the rope tied tight, a man made as if to kick the animal so that Eck could be hung when it moved off.

My heart near stopped with panic. It was so close, so close! Was I too late?

People were shouting at me, people blurred by the blinding rush of speed. My own island folk were calling to me, eyes alight with the gleam of hope.

I fired again fast, lying low down, close to the mane, and hit the soldier with two arrows, so that he fell in my path. My speed now was like lightning! A flashing surge of movement, horse and man unified with effort and concentration of purpose, as we rode down the inter-, lopers and their vile ambition of summary retribution.

The space ahead was filled with flecks of foam from the stallion's mouth which hit me in the face and my body seemed to travel through the air so that I felt as if I were riding the very wind itself, a storm of avenging fury for every arrogant presumption of the English intruders. Then the sword was out and a quick slash severed the rope which bound Eck to the tree branch and I laughed at the craziness of it, the madness of the fleeting triumph of it, as Eck's horse whinnied and dashed away in a raucous clatter of hooves, and then I felt a blow, a hard, searing thump in the ribs, which threw me sideways.

Retain my seat I could not for lack of saddle and stirrups, my head swam with nausea and I fell hard onto the earth amid sounds of tumult and aggressive intent, and shouts and savagery of every kind. More blows heaped upon me. Finally, I must have lost consciousness.

When I awoke, sore in many places, hardly able to breathe for the pain in the ribs, everything was dark, and, for a while, I thought myself in hell, a stinking, dank, and freezing hell, so something different from what men like Signore Dante imagined. I rose out of the filth on the floor, spat out a foul taste, and felt the bump on my head and then winced at the soreness of my side, like needles every time I moved, and near fell down again at the pain of them and my legs, bruised in falling, but I rose again, unsteadily, and began to explore my prison.

Above, in one corner, was starlight and I knew where I was: the very same dungeon in the castle which once contained Eck. I hunted about, blundering around, but came upon no others. The floor was covered in a mud-like substance, which I knew would be layers of the shit of other men, Eck among them, kept viscous by the piss which also fell among it.

Somehow, in spite of the awfulness of my surroundings, I must have fallen asleep then, for when I awoke, it was to feel a hand upon my mouth. I looked up and beheld a figure in the darkness. It was Eleanor. I would know the scent of her anywhere; it filled me with delight, cutting through the stench. She whispered, 'You must climb up out of here, and do so quietly. Can you?'

She had let down a rope and I used it to climb out onto the court-yard above. In a moment she was beside me, lying in the darkness, shaded by the high walls on every side. She whispered in my ear again, 'The water-gate is unguarded. We will leave that way.'

I almost raised my voice to protest, but she laid a finger upon my mouth. The scent of her breath was sweet, even among the stinks of us both, and I wept a tear of pleasure, and almost choked with emotion, so touched was I by this aid, an event unusual for me who was always so alone. Although the place was silent as the grave, I knew there would be watchers all around us. Half a dozen men would stand in the round towers or battlements.

The gate opened easily without a sound, and we left and crawled down the bank to the moat. 'Are you well enough to swim?' she whispered, and when I murmured 'Yes', she led me by the hand into the dark water which was near as stinking as the dungeon and together we began to swim silently across to the far side. Safely out of it, we walked off quickly towards the beach and then southwards, away from the farm, the first place they would look.

'Why did you come?' I said at last, after we had immersed ourselves in sea-water to cleanse our clothing.

'Because it was no use to remain. Do you think they would not guess who let you out?'

'But why?'

'I saw the whole thing from the battlements. It was bravely done. You had to do it and there was nothing else you could do. So it was not quite stupid. It almost worked, you know. With a good horse and saddle you might have stayed up.'

'What happened to Eck?'

'They hung him just the same. He took four arrows in the back before he fell. You, they kept, because you are a sympathiser, known to be a friend of the Cressinghams.'

'What will they do if they catch you?'

'Not much, I suppose. I have lands they want and I am considered English.'

'I must get away from here, to rejoin Bruce.'

'I know. I think two of those you shot will die. They will not forgive this.'

'What will you do?'

'I have no idea. I do know where there is a cobble. I found it while riding the beach near Kilchattan. The men in it had drowned in a storm, I expect. I hid it, in case I wanted to leave.'

'Then why don't you?'

'And go where? To England? Tell the king about . . . about being used by my guardian and his son? He would never believe it!'

'So you *are* upset by it, then!'

'Of course, what did you think?'

'I thought you liked it! You said you did!'

'Everybody likes it! But I don't have to like them!'

In a couple of hours we were at the beach not two miles from Kilchattan of the red sand, nestling under the hill, by which time I had been trying to adjust to the loss of my brother, acutely conscious of my failure, angry and frustrated, so much that Eleanor chided me for it. 'There was nothing you could do. You did what you could and it was well done, even though it failed. Why must you succeed all the time? Who do you think you are? You are just a man and must expect to fail some of the time.'

Strangely, I was uplifted by this speech, for had she not called me a man? It was the first time I thought of myself as one. Somehow, scholar had never seemed quite the same thing. I also saw that she was right. The man who won all the time had never been born—unless he were Jesus. I said, 'In their failures shall ye know them.'

'Not for the best men,' said Eleanor. 'But I do agree they will have to fail to learn how to succeed.'

In a thicket beside the water's edge was the cobble, a rough wooden boat shaped like half a hazel nut, about two yards long.

'There were no paddles but you may use this piece of wood,' she said, pointing to a branch she had fashioned for the purpose with an axe, during previous visits to the place.

'I don't know what to do,' she said, when I asked the question.

'I want you to come with me,' I said. 'I offer nothing but myself and what I have. I love you to the bottom of my soul and would give my life for you. And now that you have helped me in this way, I am in your debt as I never could be otherwise.' I took her hand in mine and looked into the eyes that made mine swim and added, 'I may not have much to offer, but everything I have or can do for you is yours. I must join Bruce for he has my parole. I must fight for him, even though the cause is futile. This is my country. I am Scottish and cannot ignore it. My brother has just been killed by the English and I have killed some of them trying to effect his escape. What future is there for me with the English? None. Well then, I must throw in my hand with the Scots and do my best for them. I want you to come with me, be my friend, my companion—my wife if you could bear to have it so—and if it is not too inconvenient. And if none of that is of use, then let me escort you to England to the court, where the king will put things right for you.' Finally, I said, 'I will do anything you want, Eleanor, but I would like to remain free.'

She laughed, loud and long and said, 'So freedom is important then? Are you not the man who thought freedom worthless besides peace and prosperity?' I was dumbfounded, as usual, by her. And a joyful feeling came upon me that brought tears to my eyes, and I stretched out my arms as if under forces beyond my control, and I enfolded her into myself and kissed her and went on kissing, until I got myself in a great tower of arousal and came up for air and caught my breath and cried out at the momentous thing between us, and she laughed and said how lucky we were to feel so, and grasped me and led me to her and so we joined and melted into each other and it was ecstasy, ecstasy! And the very earth shook beneath me, shook, as I mated with her, and the glory of it, the inexpressible sumptuousness of that place, that embrace, filled me with a delight as rare as the imagination dare fashion. It was like Paradise! Paradise!

She was soft and tasted of honey and I had never known anyone so beautiful, any experience so delightful. I felt as a man must feel who enters heaven, if there be any such place. Maybe heaven is an earthly place. If so, I knew it on that day and whatever should happen thereafter I knew no one could ever take it from me. I felt blessed, touched by God—if, after all, there is one. Then knew I what it was to be! To be alive was something wonderful and I cared nothing for the English who would be seeking to kill me. Had they come upon us then, I do believe I would have surrendered to them on the spot, so happy was I to be, to be with Eleanor, who was the whole of life to me. So grateful was I for what had passed between us.

Thus we spent some hours together, getting hungrier, until from a satchel she brought forth a loaf of bread and a haunch of cured beef. A nearby stream of pure water washed down our humble dinner and I declared it the finest I ever tasted, which made her laugh and disagree again. 'Well, I hope I enjoy better ones in future.'

The decision was difficult for her, I could see; what I could not see was that decisions would always be so, for her. 'You must know that I do not love you as you love me,' she said, quietly, 'but I think I could grow to love you.' We were sitting opposite, on two fallen tree trunks. Seeing my crest-fallen expression she added, 'But I must love you a bit. I would not have helped you escape otherwise.'

'Why did you do it? The risk! You could have been killed. You could yet be killed because of it. You may lose your English lands because of this.'

She looked at me sadly, regretfully. 'I know. I see that now. Maybe it was just a lark, something to amuse myself with. Partly that, I suppose. My life really is very boringly safe, you know. I crave excitement and am left in castles all the time while the men go adventuring. I should have been a boy, I think.'

I protested at all of this, of course, and received an admission of a kind. She said, 'I know you—I even know you well from all the talk about you over the years—far better than you know me. You don't know me at all. To you I am a mirage, a dream of your imagination, something very different from the reality. But knowing you as I do, knowing of your love for me, I could not just stand by and let you be killed. I had to help you escape. It is that simple, I think.'

'So it was not that you lusted after my body?' I tried to joke, though inside I felt diminished.

'Not really,' she said with a smile. 'I did lust after your body and the communion was worthwhile—though it was a bit quick. But it is just as I say. You were going to die without my aid. It was inevitable that I would help you.'

'Whatever the consequences?'

'Yes. It would be ignoble to count the cost.'

There was a hardness about her as she said this, which made me say, 'You are ruthless, then?' which made her reply, 'No, I don't calculate as you do, I follow my heart without thinking.' And there surely was one of these contradictions which make the human soul such a puzzle. How someone can be both deeply thoughtful and full of insight, the quality I value above all others, and yet at the same time either indecisive or subject to sudden actions on a whim. The first I knew of, because of her many disagreements with me, which were second nature to her—successful, I suppose because of her private studies and innate wit; the second I was to learn from experience.

How was it that she made up her mind to accompany me? I cannot tell, for it is beyond my power. All I know is that, fearing the appearance of pursuers, I grasped the bulwark of the cobble, hauled it upright and then began to push it to the water's edge. When I did, she joined me on the other side of the boat.

When it floated, I climbed in and sat down, steadying the cobble with the paddle. And there I waited for a while, and there she stood, holding onto the bulwark. Of course I begged her to join me. In vain could I get any response. Then, thinking she was determined to stay, which I could understand, for her situation without me was far safer, I made a move with the paddle and the boat began to leave the shore. At this, she leaped aboard just in time to avoid a drenching. I said nothing, for I was mystified. A few strokes later, when the ship was still close to the beach, I stopped and said, 'Do you want to return and go back?'

'I don't know,' she replied, and for a while I was content to sit while she made up her mind on the subject. When nothing further was said, I dug in the paddle again and moved off for the last time.

A hundred yards out, I said, 'I take it you have made up your mind?'

'It would seem so,' she said. 'I would not be here otherwise.' The first sign of reason in the process of her extraordinary decision making.

As the sea was calm, the journey to the mainland was easily accomplished. With the paddle, the cobble was propelled first to the northern point of the next island and then the mile or so to the mainland itself. Not a living soul did we see anywhere that day, until we beached the boat near Largs where there were fisher cottages by the shore. In one of these, we bought a meal and bed for the night.

The guid wife introduced herself as 'Mistress Jeenie,' which seemed a high title for one so commonplace, except that she was not. She must have been fifty, with great haunches of breast under a white shift and black hose in chipped and cracked wooden clogs. The face that sternly reviewed the world from beneath a straggling grey thatch was weather-beaten, as if she herself were accustomed to confront all the storms of the sea. A large ham fist, scarred by years of pulling on nets, seized my scholar's mitt and said, 'Ah see yur leddy's no merrit yit. Wull, she'll kin sleep unner the rafters and ye'll best bide doon here oan the kitchen flair,'—these deductions being the work of a moment, confronted with the pair of us.

The price having been agreed and that paid over by me, Jeenie was all smiles and told us 'to set doon the noo and hae a cuppy hoat ile,' which she brewed her self 'wi' her ain pickit herbs and sich' and 'swore on the banes o' the blessit Mary,' possessed the cure for all ills, natural and unnatural. After which, it was time for the exchange of news, common on such occasions, beginning with who we were and what about, which, having been explained after a fashion, produced the comment, 'Aye, Ah kent fine as soon as Ah set an ee upon ye, yes wur a perr that's no jist a perr, no yit oneywey. So yur oan yur wey tae jine the new king? Saint Andras, that's whaur he's gaed, tae haud a parlament.'

'Bit you're English, madeerie,' she said with surprise, after Eleanor had made some remark. 'Whatna pickle's this?'

'She'll be all right,' I announced, more for Eleanor's benefit than any other. 'She'll be with me. I am in the army—or I was till a few weeks ago,' I added foolishly. How is it that even great scholars are so easily rendered idiots by large-bottomed dames with nothing in their heads? Another mystery I had to consign to the growing list of imponderables. In truth, the world of folk has always been far less comprehensible than that of books.

Jeenie took a close look at Eleanor and sighed, 'Weel, Ah hope yer richt, ma boay. They Bruce brithers wis aye terrors wi' weemen, ye ken. Thur the talk o' the districk. Ah've heard tales wid mak yur een blush —an that wis afore they becam sae hecht and michty.'

In the next hour or so, we heard the full story of their lechery. How 'wan young wife doon the next bay hud been hingin' oot her waashin' whin the big yin cam by—that wid be Edwart—Ah wis in a cairt, passin' the hoose—an' the bugger hud her doon in nae time at aw in the grass. Aw Ah could see wis he's bare bum loupin' up an' doon.' She covered her eyes, then, as if overcome with ladylike delicacy and I guessed she was remembering the sight of him when he stood up afterwards. Oh, is it not a curse, this insight I value above every other thing?

Dinner was fish, fresh caught that morning, poached in 'ile' with more herbs and cream from the cow as a sauce, and vegetables from the garden; all consumed with enough ile to float it all the way up from the stomach and back where it came from. Mistress Jeenie was proud of her brew, that much was clear, and within the hour was snoring in the chair by the flickering flames of the fireside, rush-lights being in short supply in that house. Eleanor smiled at me and I guessed at her plan, but as soon as I moved towards her, the guidwife woke up with a start, 'Aye, Ah kent whit ye wid be uptae ma laddie,' which had me blushing protestations of innocence when all Eleanor could do was try, ineffectively, to stifle the laughter which burbled up within her.

Soon after, it was bed, a cold one for me rolled in a blanket on the floor, while my love scaled the ladder to the ramparts above, along with the mistress of the house. An hour later, when snoring again filled the dwelling, I heard a light footstep and then a muffled creak as a board moved. Above, a voice called out: 'Ah kin hear ye, ma laddie, jist you keep yer erse oan that flair.' The injustice of it! I huddled down in my blanket on the flagstones and hid my blushes from the darkened world.

Next day, we left early and began walking across country, an experience new to Eleanor, who soon tired of it, but when I suggested buying a horse for her, perversely, she refused, as if I had cast a slight upon her staying power, and so, hour after hour, we plodded along. In time, I came to see it as a test of some kind, not of her stamina but mine. By nightfall, we had stretched right across country, some way short of the River Forth, and as we subsided into the heather, footsore and weary, but neither willing to admit it, I said finally, 'That was foolish! We will walk less well tomorrow.'

'Not so,' said she, 'Now I know what you have in you, in this respect at least. This, I believe I can depend on in future. The intelligence is useful, you see.'

'And what else can you depend upon?' I said, naively.

'That you can shoot fair game from the back of a horse and have a head filled with useless knowledge.' Then, throwing up her head to laugh loudly in that warm rich mellow voice she had, 'and that you are too quick for a woman's needs.'

I reached for her in a rage of sudden desire, and caught her and fought her struggles for a time, until gradually we melted together again; and when it was over, by which time I was sweating and exhausted, she said, 'You are getting better, I think, but you must learn not to cheat, not to stop for a rest every few strokes. It is most frustrating.' After admonitions like these, sleep was a merciful release.

In this way, we proceeded to St Andrews, crossing the Forth on a ferry some way from Stirling which was still in English hands, and my education took on a new gloss, as I learned about how to please a woman, and I soon began to think myself quite the man of the world, who had a man's power of attraction over the female sex. If so, I was eventually to learn how inadequate mine was.

CHAPTER 10

The St Andrews Parliament

THE PARLIAMENT WAS HELD in a church and, being recognised as a comrade in arms, the sentries were happy to allow a scholar like myself to pass, once I had been divested of weapons which were collected at the door.

Bruce sat at the far end, on a throne of sorts on a raised platform, so that all present could see him. He wore a circlet of gold—all that was left of the crown jewels which had been stolen by old King Edward —which looked ridiculous, but performed some useful distinguishing function, I suppose. The treasury hardly existed, so there would be no money for the trappings of kingship. Besides, any money there was had to be spent on weapons, of which there were too few. His clothing was the best available in such a place, but not better than a wealthy English burgess: yellow surcoat bearing his own red lion, red silk padded jacket, yellow tights of lindsey-woolsey, and a new pair of black boots. Behind and around the walls were the guards; beside him, various clerics such as Baldred and the Chancellor, Bernard de Linton, in black robes; his brother Edward; Randolph, who had been promoted Earl of Moray; Keith, Boyd, Hay and the others all in coloured fustian or silk. Elsewhere, were the motley: sundry knights, squires, burgesses and scholars like myself in brown or black homespun.

I listened to the argument for a time. It was about the validity of Bruce's coronation. A document was to be written and sent to Rome to explain his position and demand recognition from the Pope. The argument was rubbish. Bruce, it was said, was the rightful king, not John Balliol, because Bruce was the fourth male in descent after the marriage of Isabella of Huntingdon, whereas John Balliol was the son of a man who had married the daughter of Margaret of Huntingdon. The inescapable fact is that both Balliol and Bruce lines were descended from daughters of David of Huntingdon by marriage to them. However, since Margaret was the elder daughter, her line took precedence. Thus John Balliol was rightfully King of Scots and since he had sworn fealty to King Edward, he could rightfully be deposed and banished by him, which event took place because Scotsmen could not or would not oppose it. If that were not enough, every Scotsman of note had agreed to accept the judgment of Edward Longshanks and with typical adherence to legality, he had decided the issue correctly.

I elbowed my way to the front and stated as much, but wasted my breath, soon being shouted down, for there was a demand to establish Bruce according to the law, which meant according to the custom and usages of the realm. None of it made any sense. Bruce was king, not according to the law but because many people wanted someone to lead them out of their morass after the exile of Balliol, and he was willing and able. Above all, he had established his ability in the position by winning several notable battles, crushing all resistance north of the Forth and, by these, shown that he was the only man who could lead the country forward out of English hands.

Eleven years were to pass before the force of my argument came to be accepted and formed the cornerstone of his royal house. Even then, a host of stupid men tried to derive his rights from primogeniture and the divine right of succession, all of which, since Balliol had submitted to Edward and been deposed, was irrelevant.

I wonder if Bruce saw the logic of my case. Certainly he was a shrewd and deep person, and may have seen it well enough. Maybe he was content to let his acolytes blunder about uselessly in false arguments, if only it kept them close to him. Perhaps that is what it takes to be a king: the effort of convincing them that the case already existed and could only be weakened by their wafflings was unnecessary; and maybe he knew that he gained something by their making efforts of their own in his support, even if they were futile and would be cast aside by the first papal legate to consider them seriously.

That was a difference between us, I have to admit, and it is important. I could not remain silent because the issue for me was truth, a commodity hard to come by, and all the more vital when it is seen clearly by a mind like mine and no other. Bruce's interest was not in truth, not then at least. It was in power, and he would do all that he could to maximise his own, even at the expense of the most lucid and convincing case available.

When the session broke up, I recovered my weapons and emerged into the tail-end of a sunny, blustery day, to find that Eleanor had vanished. Deciding to seek lodgings, which might have taken her off, there was, however, no sign of her an hour later, by which time I had established that there were none to be had, every available space having been occupied by burgesses from every corner of the realm, and soldiery, most of them under canvas. It was on the grass by the shore that I came upon her at last, shooting a match with some of the archers who were camped round about. She had been judged the best shot among a score, and a youth asked me what I thought of her achievement, not knowing my involvement.

I pointed out the obvious that shooting over a hundred yards might be entertaining, but it was no judge of an archer; and when Eleanor pressed me further, I explained that distance was essential, as was weight of shot, by which I meant how many shots could be fired in a short time, as well as concentration of shot, for no archer could expect to be successful with the first, and so a close group of shots around the target was what was most desired. These concepts emerged fully formed from my teeming brain, greatly to my delight, greater even than anything they represented as a fact or even my own skill in the activity itself.

Challenged further to shoot against Eleanor, I called for a test of distance first. To my great astonishment, and everyone else's, she shot an arrow 250 paces. Admittedly, it was with a following wind. For my own part, put on my mettle, I shot mine three hundred and forty, which all present accounted a miracle. But the real miracle was yet to occur, as I soon arranged.

I asked for a large target to be laid at three hundred yards distance, straight downwind, and when it was done, I fired ten arrows in quick succession, two of which scored a direct hit and two others were within a bow length. Even the other six were not four bow lengths away.

As we examined the result after a long walk across the hillocks, I turned to find the king standing beside me. 'What would it take to make a thousand like you?' he said to me with a smile.

'Pass a law forbidding the playing of gowf and making it every man's duty to fire a hundred bolts every day at targets, in competition.' There was loud and prolonged laughter from everyone around, especially from Edward de Bruce, that great blockhead, who enjoyed gowf as well as women and would no more conceive of giving up one than the other. And of course, nothing was done about it, then; but in a few years time, having understood me and my methods better, Bruce did pass such a law and while it lasted, it had a desirable effect. But the Scots are a stupid people at heart and soon reverted to gowf and other profitless sports, with the ill effects that we have fallen heir to since the Bruces departed this life. But I get ahead of myself.

Nothing would satisfy the king but that I should shoot against Eleanor again over the shorter distance; and over a hundred yards she was very accurate with one shot, but when asked for a fast, ten arrow volley, she had much to learn. At two hundred yards she was much worse, of course, and failed to hit the target at all. The wind was a genuine difficulty however, so there were mitigating circumstances. I put eight arrows quickly into the near target and hit the other with four, three others being close. 'The others are just as important,' I explained to the company, for the target can be expected to move during the shot which means it might be the shots that have missed here which would serve well enough in a fight.'

The king was sufficiently impressed by this reasoning and skill to invite us both to dine with him and sleep the night on the floor of the church with some others.

The meal was sumptuous as the provender of the town goes, though nothing like as good or plentiful as the food at the earl's table in Hereford. Bruce was warm and friendly, even kindly, when he heard about the death of my brother and how it took place, from Eleanor, who alone of the two of us had observed the proceedings. When she had told it, to my advantage, as I thought, he said to me, 'And can you be effective with the bow from the back of a horse, do you think?'

'If I have a good saddle and stirrups, a well-trained mount, and if the ground is right, yes. The accuracy is greatest when going forward, of course, and as one gets closer it increases. Ten arrows can be fired just before contact, so ten men can be shot down before the horse runs over them.'

Pressed further, I suggested that from a horse driving hard towards a troop of men in a bunch, a skilled archer could begin to fire from a hundred paces and loose off up to a score or more arrows in the time taken to cover the space. Most of these would cause some useful damage.

I think it was on the point of Bruce's tongue to re-appoint me commander of archers. Instead, he said, 'And what about your allegiance, now that you have found it necessary to kill a few Englishmen in your home town?'

'I accept you as the king and am glad this is so and will do what I can to help, but my view that this policy of independence is inevitably short-lived is unchanged. When the English are ready, they will invade this place and we must either destroy everything of value in front of them, or be killed and subjugated once again.'

'You don't think we can repel them, then?'

'Not if they deploy all their resources. Even today, after all your campaigning, they still hold many vital castles which all your best efforts have done nothing to relieve.'

'Was it not you who suggested that the policy of laying waste the land might induce them to leave us alone eventually?'

'It is only a short-term solution. Under a king like Edward Longshanks, one who will stop at nothing, we will be overrun by an army many times the size of ours.'

'You don't think a small army, well-trained and commanded, can defeat a larger?'

'Yes, you have done it already, often. But in time, when you are too old to lead and they have a strong king who will gather all his forces very carefully and supply them with foodstuffs and weapons from a fleet of ships, we must then lose the war. And if there is a pitched battle we must lose it right now. If they have five thousand archers and we have only five hundred; if they have three thousand cavalry and we have three hundred; if they have thirty thousand pikemen and we have three thousand—and all these numbers are a true estimate of the relative strengths of the armies at present—then, Sire, we must be defeated, and those who survive must either submit to English rule or lose their heads. And it is nothing new. It has been thus for centuries. Remember that Malcolm Canmore had to submit and pay his homage just to keep his head after he was captured. It is a question of numbers finally,' I told him. 'It is just a fact that there are more of them, the proportions are about ten to one. And there is nothing anyone can do about it.'

And that was why I was not re-appointed commander of the archers: I did not believe we could win, so it was felt, when the truth was that I did not believe we could win *in the long run*, a different matter altogether. But then, stupid men continually misunderstand how things are, other men's meanings, and make the wrong decisions.

When this was made clear, I asked the king to accept my homage just the same and said I would be available for any service he deemed necessary. This he agreed to speedily enough, and gave me a position in the archers, but I was to be responsible for training only. Eleanor, having lands in England, he would not allow to marry me unless she relinquished these first. But, as she had no particular desire for marriage, that proved to be no obstacle. I saw that confession would be a process full of penances for my sins, but there was nothing I could do about it. I had no hold over her and the king would not allow marriage even if she agreed. As I knew to my cost, in any case, it was unlikely that Eleanor would ever be able to make up her mind to marry anyone. Decisions about important things of that kind were beyond her. Yet, of course, I hoped that she would, for I loved her deeply, and no one could have taken more pride in her than me. Her undoubted success with the bow was a great delight and I suggested that she be allowed to join the company.

The king laughed and Eleanor looked coy, something I had never seen before. The others present thought it a great joke and said so, which she did not like.

'You might take a different view if you were under attack and needed her support,' I told them, angrily, like a lion defending a cub. 'There are not a score of archers in Scotland can shoot as well as her and with training she will be in the first six. My lords, you should not scoff but take every offer of help you can get, because, before long, you will have need of every hand that can wield a weapon. And if they are woman's hands, what does it signify? Even the women have a vested interest in winning. It might save them from being raped afterwards. Better they should die fighting than be deprived of the means of doing so and suffer for the failures of the menfolk.'

The King agreed, though Edward de Bruce deemed it a waste of a good wench. 'She'll be available for that purpose too, I warrant,' said the King, with a laugh, 'between battles.' This remark I was to remember some time later.

There being nothing much to claim my attention, I was able to immerse myself once again in scholarship, with the aid of a bookshop in the town, for though there is no university at St Andrews, there are churches, and elementary schools, convents, monasteries and small colleges of one kind and another, along with their associated clerics and dominies whose hunger for knowledge is almost as intense as my own. Eleanor accompanied me some of the time in these enjoyments, when not undergoing the training I set her on the grass, where the townsfolk played their games of gowf, that strange and futile pastime.

A round sphere of feathers and other paraphernalia, compressed together somehow, is hit with a stick, the object being to make it enter a hole some considerable distance away. This problem often requires many hits and the champion is he who takes least. So much I learned from my colleagues—the act being so odd and inferior to any other I might approve, that, of course, I did not deign to enquire of the players themselves. Some folk one simply does not associate with. Who knows what devils exercise control over their souls?

As you observe, I might dispute that there is anything resembling a God, if one means by it a divine creator, full of love—for so much in life refutes such a hypothesis—but devils? Life is full of them. Some men seem to be utterly controlled by them, the madness as plain as anything.

Once, walking to gather our flights of arrows from the target, we beheld the very earth itself thrown up out of the grass ahead, miraculously, so that some of the archers ran for the safe sanctuary of the nearest kirk. It was suggested by one who remained that perhaps contact was being made with Satan himself by digging into his demesne. On closer inspection, it turned out that one of the players had hit his sphere into a deep hole and the earth was raised many times only because his efforts to hit it out again towards the hole were ineffective, the slope being steep, or the player inept.

Evenings were spent in dancing and carousal but these were not for the likes of me. The music I enjoyed well enough but drink affected my wits. So I would slip off in search of candle, ink and parchment to explore my latest quaestiones. My fellows were not so loath, however. One evening, Left-eye drank a match against Shorty and fell down unconscious after fifteen tankards—of what I do not remember, ale probably. In the morning, he was stiff, lying where he had been left in the street outside. The chill or the poison in it had got to him or maybe he drowned in his own vomit, a happening all too common. We buried him with the usual crop of others the next day: some children, a few old people and some just full grown, seemingly hale and hearty, who had mysteriously given up their souls for some reason. There never ceased to be a great puzzle in all these unexplained dyings. Why some should live for ages, like myself, and others be cut off before their lives had hardly begun, is still most strange.

For a time then, all was peace while Parliament was in session, most days of which I omitted to attend because I had little sympathy with the goings on. Nights we spent, Eleanor and I, in the kirk until she, irritated by the lack of privacy and consequent inactivity, acquired a tent of sorts which became afterwards our sleeping bower.

One afternoon, Eleanor announced she was to go on the sea and asked me along. It was a strange sort of invitation, as if she would as well have gone alone. Maybe it was this that made me drop my quill and join her.

At the harbour we found Bruce, Gibby Hay and Eli boarding a skiff, watched by Girvin, like a small dog about to be left behind. Time and drink had done nothing for his appearance which was as unsavoury as ever. The plukes on his face were more prominent under that hot sun and the hairs that sprouted like cat's whiskers and the unkempt hair that stood up from his head because of the dirt and inhabitants within. Gibby swore at him to be off. Bruce studied the hang-dog expression and enquired: 'Why do you want to come?'

'Ah've niver been oan a boaat, Sire. Ah aye waanted tae gie it a go.' And when there was no response, he added, 'Aw gonny gie's a wee shoat, Sire? Wull ye?' Gibby asked if he could swim and when Girvin said he could, Bruce told him to come aboard.

And so we pushed the boat out and took up oars, which Girvin insisted on helping with until he caught a crab too many times, soaking the others and was demoted to the stern decking where he sat with his feet trailing in the water.

The weather was balmy and hot, after a day of high wind from the west and the sea was like glass, as we rowed further and further out, trawling lines for fish and occasionally catching them with lug worms for bait.

The skiff was about six yards from stem to stern, with freeboards a yard above the water and a mast in the centre. Eli and I sat in the bow, Bruce and Eleanor amidships and Gibby at the helm in front of Girvin. With four of us on the oars, we made good progress and soon were a league or more from the shore, the church spire reduced to a faint blur, far in our wake. Then, for a while, we slept or dozed, perhaps brought on by the sun and too many nights carousal or, in my case, scribing at my parchments.

What woke me was the swell. Waves had come from somewhere far

out to the east and begun to rock the boat. There was an uneasy still-
ness in the air and the seabirds which had followed us were nowhere to
be seen. Soon a wind blew up and the skiff pitched and tossed. Bruce
laughed and raised the sail and ordered Gibby to turn.

Before long, the canvas was tight as a drum and we sped back to the
land with the sea roaring in our ears, at either side, as if it were saying,
'I've got you now!'

At first the exhilaration gripped us. Then Bruce shouted above the
sound of the waves and the wind. 'Girvin's overboard!'

I turned to see a head bobbing at the tip of a wave and then he was
gone. In a moment, Bruce was over the side swimming in a powerful
side stroke, with every one of us shouting for him to come back. 'Leave
the wee bugger to swim!' screamed Gibby, above the howl of the storm,
as he tried to turn the boat; only to find the force too great, so that the
sail carried the skiff sideways and the mast tipped dangerously near
the water. Back on the wind came the reply: 'He can't swim.'

Again he tried to turn and succeeded only in flapping the sail, which
thundered back and forth, and then the wind caught us again and we
were diving madly shorewards as before. The wind was just too powerful to sail against. 'What can I do?' cried Gibby. 'Think, Bann!'

All I could suggest was to take the sail down and hang it from the
stern to act as a drogue. By the time we had done this, there was no
sign of the king and we were still flying for the beach, which seemed
much nearer. Finally, the keel grounded and we piled out, leaving the
skiff to be battered by the waves. And so, we four bedraggled souls,
soaked and frozen with salt spray, stood shivering on the strand looking eastwards, seeing nothing but white spume-tossed breakers.

The cold and wet drove us together and we cooried doon to watch,
with no feeling except the anticipation of disaster; but no one would
leave, and no one spoke except Gibby who was weeping silent tears.
'What will we do without him?' he muttered several times.

An hour we waited, and then another and there was not a sign of
him. Then, out of the dusk, far away to the south, I saw something
move out of the waves and began running, praying it was not just flot-
sam. And God be praised it was Bruce! Bruce lying in a stupor of frozen
exhaustion half in and half out of the waves which burst over him. His
right hand was holding onto something. It was hair! Girvin's hair! And
both were alive.

Sure enough, Girvin was unable to swim, would have drowned, and
Bruce had known it, seen the truth behind the lie.

The next morning, Bruce was as fit as ever and when Gibby berated
him for his folly, he replied, innocently. 'What else could I do? Why
would my countrymen fight for me, if I don't fight to save them?' After
that, not just Girvin, but everyone who knew of it, was as devoted a

follower as it is possible to imagine; for we knew we could all depend on our leader, even the humblest.

Not for several weeks, by which time we had moved off towards the west, did the full extent of the change in the company of archers become apparent to me. Then, waking up to the differences, I burst into the king's tent while he was at conference with his knights, past the guards, past everyone, ignoring the ongoing discussion and all civility, there to confront the king, who at that very moment was speaking to Jermyn Lindsay, the new commander of archers.

'Sire,' I blurted out, with black affronted rage, 'the archers are in decline as a fighting unit! Half of them have gone off to be pikemen or squires, the other half are in no training of any kind, because they are under no discipline, and the status of archer has been undermined, so that young men no longer clamour to enlist and struggle to reach the standards set! Why? Because there are no standards now! Any fool can join and think himself an archer if only he has a bow. This is a travesty of what it ought to be, of what it was so recently when I commanded. Sire, you must act now before it is too late! Already it is so! The company has shrunk to a mere eighty, of whom less than half are adequate. Sire! You will be facing five thousand Welsh and English archers one day soon. One flight of arrows from them is enough to annihilate the entire Scottish army!'

Bruce, whose anger had been blazing within, at my effrontery all the while, said nothing for a time, when I had finished, though the atmosphere in the tent was like a thunderstorm when everything around crackles with energy.

First there were shouts and protests from Lindsay and then Boyd, who disliked me, and even Keith, the King's Marischal, closely followed by blusters from Edward de Bruce that I be thrown out instantly and if no one else would perform the act he would undertake it himself, 'And damn me if I don't prick the bugger up the erse with my sword while I am about it!'

But the king signalled silence and asked Lindsay to comment. He said, 'What is this discipline he speaks of? What is the use of it? If the quivers are full, what need we of practice? Anyway, a good pike is worth two archers. It is right to let archers become pikemen when they are strong enough. And the men don't like training and discipline. How can I keep them happy with all that?'

When Boyd, and Cathcart, a young knight, shouted their agreement, the king called for silence. In a blaze of temper, I said, 'You, who agree with that, know nothing! One good archer with two score arrows is worth two score pikemen because from a distance, he can kill everyone of them. If you doubt it, pick out a score of your best pikemen and I will fight them from two hundred yards range. Before they get to me, I will kill them all! Go on,' I ordered Sir Robert Boyd, 'do it! And I *will* kill them! I promise you, and it will be worth the loss if it convinces you of the utter stupidity of your position.'

Snarling with anger, Boyd headed his bearded, round-shouldered giant's frame in the direction of the door, but halted and turned, uncertainly, for even he could see that I was right.

I said, 'Archers, not cavalry and not pikemen are the cream of the army—have got to be understood to be the cream—'

'Don't be daft!' said Edward de Bruce. 'What archer can stand against an armoured knight on an armoured percheron? And isn't that the way of chivalry?'

Very quietly, for he was the king's brother, even if he was a blockhead, I said, 'Climb onto your percheron, Sir Edward, and try and ride me down from two hundred yards and I will put ten arrows into your heart right through your boasted armour before you are even within a lance of me.'

There was another silence, for they could see that I was right again. The unbarbed, needle-sharp, steel-tipped arrows could cut through armour like a knife through butter—in the right hands.

'Now,' I said, defiantly, 'Now that you recognise these hard facts of life and death, perhaps you will allow me to do my best—and it will be the best I ever did, this I promise you—to build a company of archers strong enough to enable you to beat the English. And if you will not let me do this, you are lost and every life here is lost and every Scottish life out there is lost or in thrall to English domination'—pointing to the wide country beyond the tent. 'And for what? What is the point of fighting just to die, just to cause the deaths of those thousands out there? If that is inevitable, is it not better to do something else so that they might live?'

'Poppycock!' said Edward de Bruce, puffing up his red face like the brainless rooster he was. 'Archery is no way to fight a battle! There is such a thing as chivalry.'

'And defeat!' I replied. 'Rely on cavalry, no matter how well armoured, and you are all dead men. These five thousand English and Welsh archers will shoot you all flat before you reach them!'

There was a dead silence again.

I said, 'If you don't believe it, go and pick twenty fully armoured knights. Anyone you like! And have them attack me from two hundred yards, and I will *myself alone*, kill them all, every last one, with this bow and these arrows.'

Lindsay shouted, 'But Sire—'

'But nothing, numbskull!' I shouted at him, 'You have even stupidly reverted to the old Scottish bows!'

'But they are easier to pull!' said Lindsay, with surprise.

'Of course! And they do not penetrate armour nor do they fly the full distance! The six foot bows are hard to learn and harder still to operate really well, because they require so much more power. But—can you not see?—it is their very power which is the difference! That is why they can kill from a distance. Power, accuracy and concentration of shot—these are the criteria for judging archers. And you have failed this army, and this king and my country by your ignorance, and letting these vitally necessary perceptions drift on the wind, and all those fine men I trained with such difficulty, drift off to less important occupations.'

'Do you believe we can win?' said Bruce with clear, dark eyes, furrowed, diabolic pointed brows and a jawline like a steel trap.

'Without me and my ideas in control, you have no chance of winning a pitched battle. With me in command of the archers, we might just manage it.'

Boyd shouted, 'Ye canny, Sire. He's a fucken Englishman!'

'No,' I replied, 'I am a Scot, bred in the bone, but I am a realist. I use my head for thinking and not my fist or my balls'—looking at Edward de Bruce, that notorious lecher—'Chivalry is worthless if all it does is cause defeat. What we have to do is win a war, not just make a dance up and down a tournament rail. We are fighting for our lives and not just ours! Everyone else's out there!'

'But Sire,' said Sir Alan de Cathcart, 'Chivalry is what it is all about, isn't it? Don't we all believe that?' But there was the trace of a doubt in the voice of this young, slight figure, and I knew I was making an impression of sorts.

'Rubbish!' I shouted. 'Was it by chivalry that you won at Glentrool or Loudon? Of course not! If you had met the foe, lance to lance, as in a tourney, you would have been massacred! Because you don't have enough lances. They had twenty to our one! All we had were half-armed foot-soldiers. There is anyway, something deeply unchivalrous about an armoured knight attacking an unarmoured man on foot. But do you see the English knights dismounting and throwing away their armour to fight on an equal footing? Of course not! They are not chivalrous! Then forget this talk of chivalry for it is nothing but delusion and childish stupidity. There is only one thing to be done. Win by any means in our power, for if we lose, we lose our lives and our children's lives and our friends' lives and the life of every old person and simpleton in the realm, who does not understand and cannot defend himself if we fail to do it for him.'

The king told me to go and that he would consider what I had said. As I left, there was a loud hubbub behind me. Some of them, Boyd among them, wanted me hung from the nearest tree.

The decision was a long time coming; and what made it happen was that in 1310 King Edward II of England invaded Scotland. Like everyone else, I was involved in the systematic destruction of our countryside, burning every dwelling, every field that remained unharvested, and killing every animal that might be used to sustain the English, when they arrived. The smell in our nostrils for weeks was nauseous: the very heart of the country was burning to death and the lines of refugees, as they traipsed northwards, with their pitifully few movables, across the Forth and the Tay into the fastness of the highland wilderness or even as far as the islands like my own, was a sorry sight to every Scotsman worth a farthing. We were depriving our countrymen of their life's blood—the land and their homes and cattle—just to preserve the integrity of the government and the king, him most of all. I liked and admired Robert Bruce, but was he worth all this loss in those days? I was not so sure then.

I often wondered at the stupidity of my seniors in the army, all these knights and lords, some of whom had been at Oxford or Cambridge—Paris even, in one case, best place of all. Why could they not see what was immediately obvious to me? I suppose it was the training in logic I had received, which had made such an indelible impression upon me, and not upon them, because knowledge mattered little to them; drinking, gambling, wenching, tournaments and timewasting being their heart's desire; scholars they were not, despite their sojourn at university. To me, the truth was my God, what I sought above all things, and my extra studies at the feet of Hammond had amplified my vision, so that I saw with utter clarity what other men would not see by themselves if they looked for a century.

Was Bruce, too, like this? Woolly-minded? I think not, though mathematics had never been one of his strengths. And yet I think he knew, even then, that I was right. Maybe, seeing the opposition to my appointment—caused partly, one must admit, by the force and effectiveness of my very condemnation of their limited vision, which they resented—he decided to wait until time and the passage of events convinced some of my enemies that I was not such a bad fellow after all.

CHAPTER 11

Towards Acceptance by the Scots

FIRST, THERE WAS THE AFFAIR of the castle, I forget its name after all this time, for which act of remission there is a good reason soon to be told. Castles, then, were impossible to recapture, for we lacked the siege equipment and could not construct it without the skill or materials. This castle was by a river, like many, possessing high unscalable walls and towers as usual. After we had been camped across the river from it for a few days, I went for a walk along the river-bank and espied a grating, low down, at the foot of the wall, under water. It occurred to me, in one of these flashes of insight to which I am happily subject, that entry could be gained that way, if provided with tools for cutting through the iron bars.

A new man had joined the army, a Fleming, named Crabbe, an eager, energetic, skilful person, built like a whippet, who kept his hair cut short so that it stood up on end—because of the fleas and lice, which he detested, so he told me. Everyday he washed in some mixture of his own devising which kept him clean. To him I applied for tools to cut through grating. His small, two-wheeled cart was full of oddments: grinders, polishers, rasps, hammers, nails, pieces of metal and a small forge—everything required for improvising a thing of the kind I needed.

In a few hours, I was in possession of a small saw about a foot long with a narrow blade. Armed with it, I made my way to the king's tent where the usual discussion was going on about whether to starve the garrison, which we would not do because of the time required, or break in the gates, for which we had no adequate equipment, or move off to some more profitable activity, which was the inevitable consequence of such meetings.

I told the assembly what I proposed and big black-bearded Boyd laughed delightedly, declaring, 'Aye, let the English bugger crawl up the shite hole. Thull hang the fool fae the battlements.' But the king agreed to accompany me to view the point of entry, a task I insisted upon doing with him alone, as I did not wish a large group to be seen concentrating at the very place from which I must make my assault.

It was agreed that the plan be tried, that I would enter under cover of night, attempt to open the gate if I could, and that men would be waiting just beyond the drawbridge, until it fell down, when they would rush into the castle.

A few hours after full dark, leaving the sword and most of the quivers with Eleanor, I entered the water and began to swim slowly towards the far bank, to the grating. It took ages to saw through enough bars to effect an entry, and by then I was frozen, exhausted and disgusted by the stench from the pipe which was just wide enough for my shoulders. By arrangement, I then made the sound of a night owl and heard it returned, before ducking under water and entering the pipe, which broadened.

Inside, the stench was much worse, but the water level was below the roof and left an air space. Gingerly, I felt my way in the pitch darkness, bracing myself between the sides. Once, a sudden movement at my shoulder, announced the presence of a rat which squirmed past me, squeaking and squawking. Then, the light improved and, looking up I saw starlight, and another grating high up. The pipe had another leading into it from above and this one was much wider. The climb was difficult because the walls were so slippery, but, by bracing my back against one side, I was able to walk up the other side of the vertical shaft.

At the top, I carefully pushed up the grating, which was loose, crept out above it, and managed to replace it without much noise. I found myself beside a low circular stone parapet in the middle of a darkened courtyard, illuminated only by a few smoking rush-lights. For a while, I simply crouched where I was, listening to the sounds around me, trying to pinpoint the whereabouts of the guards. Then, a blaze of light shone out from a building, as a door opened, and a man came out. 'Come oun youse bastards!' he growled, and a moment later, ten men left the building to replace others at the walls, who soon retired to the same guardroom, muttering and complaining as they did so, at their cold vigil, and glad of respite.

Now I knew that two men were placed, one on either side of the drawbridge, and when the light from the door had shone, I could just see the windlasses for moving it and the portcullis. Somehow I would have to lower the one and raise the other and they would have to remain that way until my friends had time to get in.

But the serjeant had stopped at the door and looked in my direction. It was then I realised my teeth were chattering. He must have heard. I clamped them tight shut and put my hand on my mouth. In a little while, he seemed satisfied and entered the room, and the door slammed shut, leaving me in the dark again.

First I had to get close enough to shoot accurately, for the men were hard to see in the near pitch darkness. I took a dry string from a waterproof bag in my pocket and strung the bow. Then I loaded, holding the arrow at half-cock, and stood up silently. As quietly as possible, I began to approach the drawbridge until I could get a good sight of the guards there. A dim shape began to appear near a slot in the wall, but I could not fire yet until I had seen the other one and knew exactly where he was standing. Thus I continued my approach.

Treading with the delicacy of a sparrow and breathing as quietly as possible, I edged forward towards the man on the right. I knew I had to try and put him between me and the other man, wherever he was, so that his body would protect me from a snap shot from the man on the left.

I was twelve feet away when the man on the right turned and saw me. 'Wot's 'at fuckink smell?' he said, to no one in particular.

I stood petrified with fear and could feel the sweat, frozen though I was, run down my face. The sentry's crossbow was held upright with the quarrel protruding. 'That you, John?' he said.

'Yes,' I replied, out of a voice dry and cracked with fear, and continued my approach, walking now as if idling. Even then, I realised that my years in England were proving an advantage at last, for my accent would otherwise have given me away instantly. I had spent so many years in Cambridge, not all of it in the cloisters, that I could easily mimic the common accents.

'Fink they'll try anyfink on a noit like this, John?' he said, turning again to look through the slit at the starry sky.

'Naw,' I said, adopting a gruff voice.

When he began to turn towards me, I knew he had realised that I wasn't John. By then, I was five feet away from him. I lifted the bow and loosed the arrow. It caught him in the neck and went half through the other side, the point splitting on the stone. Thrown back against the wall, he dropped the bow, grabbed the arrow in both hands and slid down, making gurgling sounds for a moment, and then was still. I pulled another arrow from the quiver and loaded again.

The second man said, 'What's up?' and I knew without seeing that he was looking at me. Even now the bow would be pointed in my direction. But could he see me in the shadows?

'Nuffink,' I said.

I heard him move in the pitch dark and I tried to estimate his position exactly.

'That you, Josh?' he said. 'Christ what a focking smell!'

I fired at the voice. There was a screech as the arrow having hit him, went clean through and rattled the wall behind; then scuffling, as the man's arms vainly scraped at the wall to stay upright and then the sound of him falling, and the noise of legs twitching. It was horrible, and I listened within the gate area, with awful fascination, praying that others on the battlements would not hear.

Of course they did. There were footsteps above and a voice cried out, 'You orl right, Josh?'

'Course we's orl right,' I replied.

'Bleddy could noit,' he said, and then, blowing on his hands, he moved back to where he had been.

I waited awhile until things settled back into a somnolent state and then I took up the hammer lying beside the drawbridge windlass and hammered out the pin with one stroke. There was a roar of chains and wood creaking, as the entire bridge began to fall. I jumped away to the portcullis chain and began to rack up the windlass as fast as I could. The effort needed was immense.

Meanwhile, there were curses from above, sounds of men running, and a cry went up: 'Sound the alarm!' A horn was soon blown and feet were clumping down the stairs.

I left the windlass on the ratchet and hid in the shadows at the side of the great iron gate, with its fierce spikes at the foot. At least it was four feet above the earthen floor—enough for men to crawl underneath.

A man appeared carrying a sword and I shot him. He went down in a heap. A door opened and the courtyard was flooded with light. 'Wot's up fer Gord's sake?' said a rough voice, newly roused from sleep. Another man dashed down the stairs and said, 'The fuckin' bridge is down! Do somethin'! Rouse the men for Chrissake!'

They must have been asleep. How did they miss the noise?

The man in the doorway went inside and I heard him shout at the men but the second ran towards me and I saw him aim his longbow. 'Christ, here's the bastard!'

We both fired at the same time. The shock as the arrow hit my shoulder was tremendous. I had never been shot before. I was thrown backwards and landed in a heap on the earth, with my head right underneath the huge sharp spikes of the portcullis. As I looked up at it in the starlight, I knew that if it fell, it would turn me into a sieve, leaking blood from every aperture.

I could not move! Somehow the arrow had impaled me upon something. The hard earth itself! The arrow had gone right through with such force that it not only knocked me flat on my back it had buried itself in the ground! I knew then that I was going to die. In a moment or two, they would bring down the portcullis on top of me.

Frantically, I tugged at the arrow, struggling to free myself against the excruciating pain; and failed. It was barbed and I could not get free. I was done for and, knowing it, I passed out.

CHAPTER 12

A First Taste of Medicine

WHEN I AWOKE, AS IN DREAM filled with agony, it was to the shouts and cries of men killing, fleeing and dying, swords clashing on armour and other swords, the whirr of arrows and thuds as they found a mark. All around was chaos, and tumult, and once, a running foot stamped upon me and I myself cried out with the pain. It was then, I suppose, that my plight was noticed.

Torches appeared and faces, bearded and sweating, looked down upon me. A voice cried, 'Lift the portcullis!' It was Bruce, and he bent down to me, as the chain rattled and the awful apparition of the spikes rose out of sight into the dark recesses of the castle. Tenderly, he examined me and called for a hand-saw, like the one I had so carelessly thrown away. Miraculously, Crabbe had made another and it was used to saw off the fletching of the arrow. But though it was gently done, I cried out all the time during it, and wept floods of salt tears. Then it was off and I was lifted up, so that the arrow remaining buried in the ground, passed out of me or rather, I was removed from it.

By then, I had lost consciousness again, and came to in the hall of the castle, some time later, victory having been secured. Eleanor was by me, swabbing my filthy face. 'Wull huv tae dae the cautery, Rab,' said Gloag, with relish, and my heart missed a beat, for I knew my chances then were slim.

'I would prefer to do without,' I muttered.

'No,' said Bruce. 'You are too useful to lose. And you know that wounds like this do not mend unless they are treated. What do we have?'

'There's a cask of brandy, Sire,' said young Wullie, who had been rummaging among the castle stores.'

'Fetch it then, and we'll have a drink.'

And so I was sat up and forced to drink more than I ever drank before. They poured it down me, laughing at my discomfort, as they quaffed it down themselves, between times. 'Wull teach this bookish-bugger tae drink like Scotsmen,' said Boyd and for the first time I heard a touch of kindness in his voice and knew it for a small swing in the wind of his disapproval. Finally, when I was almost sick with drink,

I was lain down on my back, my bare back, for I had been stripped naked, at which Sir Edward de Bruce declared to Eleanor, 'By the Christ, ye'll get no' much satisfaction out of that!' which brought gales of laughter out of every drunken fool present, and quite woke me up, for the sheer embarrassment of it.

And then they did it. Poured a pint of the brandy into the wound in my shoulder. It burned all the way through and out in every direction, so that I thought I was aflame. And then I was truly aflame, for Gloag lighted the brandy with a taper and I shrieked and yelled with the heat and misery and bloody awfulness, as the brandy and every inch of the flesh in the hole between the two bones was burnt to a crisp. Of course I passed out again and I learned afterwards, that just for good measure, they had turned me over and repeated it from the other side.

When I woke up, it was full day, birds were singing and people were going about as if life had returned to normal. I made to speak and all I heard was a croak from my very parched throat. The stink of my burning flesh still pervaded the very air around me and my shoulder was blistered with the heat.

Then I slept awhile, and in the evening they came to see me and I woke up when someone slapped my face. 'He's alive, Rab. He's gonny live,' said Gloag's voice, a definite reluctance in it. Presently, studying my eyes, red-rimmed so they said I was, with brandy, I heard Gloag gloatingly remark. 'Yull soon be a drunken sot as weel's a spilt intileectual snoab.'

Bruce thanked me for my work, warmly, effusively even, and then made to leave to attend to any of the hundred matters that plagued him every day, but Eleanor stopped him. 'Well? Aren't you going to reward him for this? He killed three men at least and if it wasn't for him, you would not have taken the castle!'

Bruce turned to face her. 'What should I give him? I have no money to spare and no lands not already allocated. What reward do you suggest?'

'What reward would you like Bann?' said she.

'I don't know,' I replied.

'There, he doesn't know and I have nothing to give except my thanks. Some day, maybe, I will have something worth giving.'

'You could ennoble him. Make him a knight or something,' said Eleanor.

'How can I?' said Bruce. 'With his beliefs about our future?'

'That has nothing to do with it!' she shouted. 'You . . . you . . . are damned ungrateful!' and she stamped out in a rage, which some men thought funny.

I often wondered at this reply. I am not sure it was the real reason, though it may have been part of it. No, I think he despised base born folk like me, though a few of us had a genius of a kind, and were useful beyond other men. The only folk I ever saw him reward with great presents of lands and titles were the trusted few, Randolph, who was his nephew; his brother, whom he appointed Lord of Galloway and then Earl of Carrick; and Douglas, who was not a close relative, but I suppose had to get something: all the border marches, which was justified, for Douglas was a scourge to the English all his life. Myself, I still had hopes of something, some little thing, and I was not, in the end, disappointed. But for now, it was thanks and naught else.

I do not know why I cannot remember the name of that castle. And it irks me so! I cannot even remember where it is, so that I might go there and relive the moment. Maybe the knowledge was burnt out of me when my flesh caught fire. Or is it that one forgets whenever the body is penetrated by a dagger or quarrel? It is a great mystery to be set beside all the others. Maybe the spirits that supported these memories flew out of me when the hole was made by the arrow. I know not. I guess that the truth is somewhat more complicated.

Worst of all, there are of course so many other things that left me at that time, but since I do not remember them I have no idea what they are! A few of them are books, for I have sometimes since then opened a book I have no recollection of, only to find, once I am well ensconced, that it seems familiar, as if I have read it before. The loss of these memories is of course the greatest misery that ever befell me, for, to a mind like mine, the mind is everything, and when some of it is lost, it is as if part of my life is lost with it. Of course, I spoke of it afterwards with Eleanor and others occasionally, yet this was no help. Still I could not remember these things, as if the power to do so were beyond me, because of the nature of the experience. And though some men marvelled at my skill and bravery and success as they thought it, to me it was a matter for sorrow only, except perhaps for this: that I had the idea for entering the castle that way. I took pleasure in that mental event, more pleasure by far than in the action itself. For the success of it was luck, a mere routine of swimming and concealment and silence and waiting and shooting; and then my comrades arrived and I was out of it. But the loss of part of my mind, even if it was only a tiny part, was so depressing that I never liked to speak of the subject again and preferred ignorance to asking questions of those who knew. It is so embarrassing not to know what one should!

The wound was long in healing fully, but within a month I had picked up my bow and I began again to try to recover my skill. The old power was not there, of course, and this was a source of immense sadness, nay misery, yet I persevered, trained and trained for hours every day, and ate well and drank only good water and a little wine. And I devised exercises for increasing my strength, pushing myself off the ground with my hands many times, until the blood roared in my head; pulling myself up to a tree-branch; and exercises for suppleness, as stiffness had become a problem; and, every time I could, bathing in cold water; sea-water, preferably.

By and by, giving no let up, except on the sabbath, my strength improved until one day, Eleanor, who had deliberately shot against me and spurred me into a rage, every time, by her curses at my lost skill, suddenly smiled for the first time in months and said, 'I think it has returned, Bann.'

We had been doing the rounds as usual, of the various sorts of shooting I had devised. The air was still that day, and we fired a ranging shot apiece at full strength. For once, mine outshot hers. The next day I was further off yet and though there were days when I seemed to slip back, the gradual improvement continued, until I could again outshoot her by a full hundred yards. After that, accuracy was my main concern and finally, that most difficult quality of all: concentration of shot in quick time.

I soon had plenty of practice, for Edward II appeared over the horizon with an army as plentiful as fish in the sea. It was then that Bruce discovered that my exceptional numeracy had a useful corollary. Since I was a 'mathematical wizard' as he described it, estimating the numbers of troops was an elementary problem. All I had to do was divide up the army ahead into areas, compute the density of a small part and multiply up by the quotient of the whole area to the part.

If this sounds difficult, it is not. Often, the quaestio could be decided with a glance, for men march or ride in ranks which can be counted in a flash of the eye. Even when, on occasion, the force to be counted was a trapezium because of the terrain traversed, it was still elementary. I had merely to multiply the base by the median height, a triviality.

Of course, at first, Bruce did not believe my answers, but after he had set men to count them as they rode past—the work of hours and some danger, as they observed from hiding—he came to accept that my mental talents were capable of accurate estimation, in an instant, and without any danger whatever, for I could compute the numbers as well from afar as close to.

Then occurred the next step in my acceptance by the others. I formed the idea of attacking footmen on horseback, shooting them down quickly and then retiring out of danger. At first, I tried it myself alone, rode within a hundred yards of the English pikemen and then loosed off fifty arrows. As they were bunched, it was easy to hit them. In a single day, I shot off every single arrow I possessed and must have accounted for over two score men dead and many wounded. Then Eleanor, Eli, and others insisted on trying it; and for a few days we wrought havoc among their footsoldiers. Between our salvoes of arrows from the flanks, the scorched earth of the lands ahead, and the lack of intelligent will in their commanders, the English eventually retired, without any notable achievement and much loss. Of course they soon learned to take precautions against our sallies by stationing cavalry close to the foot-soldiers as protection, so that whenever we appeared they would run us down. Having superior horses, this was inevitable, if we got too close. But, for a time, serious damage was done among them; and the blow to their morale was deep and wounding. We were like wasps which flew out to sting and then vanished before retribution could be exacted. Their frustration was delightful to observe.

Of course it was not all plain sailing. Once, having made sure the enemy had no archers of their own in the vicinity as ever, our troop made the usual quick dart downhill to loose off many arrows fast, at long range, before riding back to safety. Eli's horse must have slipped and broken a fetlock during the return. Then, flat on the ground and unconscious, he was at the mercy of their cavalry who would always ride in pursuit. By the time we noticed his absence from the safety of the brow of the hill, it was all over. All we could see were the lances being driven in. He was a quiet, kindly person who just suffered bad luck.

When I asked Eleanor about her feelings on shooting down Englishmen, she said, 'It is not easy to explain. I have never really thought of myself as English but Norman, and since I suffered at the hands of my guardian, I owe them nothing. So why should it concern me?' And then she looked at me levelly, with those hazel-blue eyes that made mine swim and said, quietly, 'For some time now, I have considered myself a Scot and am proud to serve a king like Robert Bruce.' And my heart missed a beat, for I knew how attractive he was to women as well as to men. Bruce had only to lift his horn, for regiments of women to come running.

Later that year, Eleanor gave birth to a child and Bruce, who attended the christening, never mind that it was a fine little bastard, because of her inability to decide about marriage—apart from the king's continuing refusal to consent—seemed very pleased, in spite of the problem it presented, for she would now have a bairn at her apron strings and be less able to play her part as an archer. By then, there were but a hundred good archers and hardly any in training. In vain had I badgered the king to alter his policy, but pikemen were what he favoured above all at that time, because of the victory at Loudon.

At the celebration—a simple affair, because of the lack of decent dwellings to hold it and only ordinary food and drink—Bruce insisted on being godfather and asked her what she desired as a present. She replied, 'Make Bann commander of archers. Everyone knows he will do it best and that you must do this before long.'

'Why?' laughed the King.

I said, 'Because the English will be back one day in greater strength than ever. Do you think they will not learn from their recent experience?'

After some discussion, Bruce agreed; and so, at the end of 1310, I became what I should always have been: sole commander of archers, Lindsay, who was unsuited to archery, being seconded to cavalry duties, which he preferred, having the usual snobbish view of the gentry about the superiority of any form of chivalry.

I did not know how much time there was, but I could smell a pitched battle in the offing. It was inevitable, once the English conquered their internal dissension, for Piers Gaveston was causing great resentment among the English baronage. Also, we could not scorch the earth and run away for ever. If we did, we would all starve and they would catch us in some corner in the end, and either we would have to give homage or be killed as rebels, every one. Why? Because it had happened so often before and the pride of the English would demand requital, the more so since Scotland had so recently given itself up stupidly, voluntarily, to be a province of the larger country. In these circumstances, it was just a question of time before they returned with all their vast strength.

So I put my systems into practice again. Raised archery to the status of a science, demanding much training and constant improvement in every respect, weeded out the unsuitable and made the position of archer one to be striven for and not easily achieved.

Once again, youths were my raw material, and they began to come in to volunteer, in ones and twos, from every part of the realm. Every day there were lessons from me, demonstrations from picked groups, then supervised practice and, after a short rest, competitions. Before long, I was demanding useful gifts to be won as prizes. There was nothing I would not do to make the impulse to excellence among my young men as intense as could be. All this, while the army moved around the land on the king's business.

It was about this time that Gloag began to be plagued by his hobgoblin. Every time he climbed into his blanket before sleep, it was to discover a lump of shite, which announced its presence by its foul smell. Gloag was crazy with fury every time, and would run about the camp madly, blade in hand, screaming murder—which annoyed those anxious to get off to sleep and caused the rest to make things worse by catcalls of laughter, once the cause was understood.

Gloag tried everything to unmask the evildoer, even overcoming his natural enmity to call upon the services of Bess Morrison, who had knowledge of the wee folk of the forest; but she was unhelpful, declaring that it was unwise 'tae meddle wi' fairies in sich, in cased they took agin her tae'. In desperation, Gloag paid Sheugle to watch out for his bedroll, without success, for Sheugle could not watch it all the time. He even took to wearing it strapped to his back—which seemed to make things worse, for, magically, shite then appeared in it twice and three times a day.

Eventually, every one knew the culprit except Gloag: Jinky, the fat man with the irrepressible smile at all the vagaries of life, had been seen collecting shite. The problem remained unsolved by the Oxford scholar, to his utter humiliation at the laughter constantly rippling around him, until he paid Shorty to tell him. Jinky disappeared for a day or two and was black and blue when next we saw him. 'Why did ye tell oan him?' complained Torquil, 'Ye've spilt a guid joke.'

'A jaur ae whusky's better thin ony joke', said Shorty.

Late one evening, a troop of us returned to camp, Bruce at our head and I by his side as usual. As we came up over the last ridge, we heard it. Fighting. And in the gathering gloom, we saw the camp in uproar, two groups fighting across the glade made by the circle of tents.

Bruce spurred his horse and set off downhill across the intervening moorland like a bat out of hell, the rest of us following fast.

It was Boyd and Keith. Them and their forces were swording each other, hand to hand, even with daggers—any convenient weapon—a life or death struggle.

So it had come to this! Keith was a vain, undersized fellow who cared for his whiskers like a dandy; and the only thing he cared more for was his reputation. Well, Boyd cared nothing for anyone's self love and now the difference had shown itself at last.

I thought Bruce would halt and address them, but no. He rode them down, charged straight into the fighting line of them and burst through the centre, flailing right and left with the flat of the blade, shouting, 'Stop! Stop! Stop, you fools!' and when none did, he bawled: 'Scotland is lost! Scotland is lost!' and that did stop them, finally.

Off the mount he came and strode among them, punching heads as if they were bairns—as indeed they were at that moment. 'Stop and think, you madmen! Do you want to lose the country? After all this effort? After all these lives lost, would you throw it all away now on a whim? A harsh word? A trivial insult?' And that stopped it completely, for they began to see, had fallen under his spell, and even heard the anxiety, the fear and terror and real entreaty in that voice that was always so bold.

'Why do you kill each other? Why even consider such a disaster? Do I not need you all? Every last one of you? Have we so many men that we can afford to lose one in this stupid way? Of course not! Then mend your fences, forget your differences, and let no man leave this place until he has shaken the hand of all those with whom he fought this night.'

He had said it all, now; and no man could have said it any better. He needed us, everyone; Scotland needed us, every single one. The logic was incontrovertible, and heads that had been full of the wish to kill, bent down as man after man became aware of his sin and how he himself had put the very nation—that fragile thing Bruce and he and all of us had with so much difficulty put together again—in jeopardy, by mindless, childish, folly.

There was a long silence, and then Bruce went wearily away towards his tent. But just before it, he turned again to us all and said: 'My friends, I need all of you. Scotland needs all of you. And we need *you* to be friends with each other. Only if we combine fully against the English have we any hope of victory. You want to win, don't you? You want to live in freedom, don't you? Then combine, for freedom's sake. For Scotland's sake!'

And when he left, it was so, for in small groups men looked each other in the eye again as brothers and shook hands and then went off to sleep.

I have often pondered this happening. I know I could not have done it myself, nor any other man I know of. Only Bruce could have managed it. First it was the courage of the entry into the fight, which involved, by then, upwards of fifty men, all armed; then the energy of the intrusion, which took some aback; and then the force with which he pressed home his attack, knocking men down all about him, fearless of a blow in return, which was all too likely, for some would not have known who he was, in the gloom, and amid all that confusion. Never for an instant did he slacken his approach. He arrived among them like a storm, had the strength to carry on through it, and then, when he began to be heard, he found the words and the meaning and the emotion and the thing that was at stake was stated instantly, powerfully, in a way that no man could resist. It was a thing of the body, of the spirit and of the mind.

Of a certainty, there was no man alive who could deal with trouble as well as Robert Bruce. That was why he was our king. He earned the right every day of his life.

He was the commander because he commanded and everyone of us followed, because we could do no other. His self belief was absolute, his determination implacable, unstoppable, and he continually demanded higher and higher levels of maturity, responsibility, unity, which every man felt compelled to attempt, and blessed himself whenever he succeeded, which happened to all of us continually. Bruce made us into men who respected ourselves and our comrades. He made us into better people than we could ever have been alone. That was his gift, and Scotland's.

CHAPTER 13

Castles

IT WAS A TIME WHEN A METHOD had to be found for taking castles, for most were not like the last one, with a convenient sewer to climb up and open the gate from the inside. Stirling and Edinburgh were built upon unscalable crags, Perth and Berwick were defended by many soldiers on high ramparts, which could be supplied from the sea, and could not be starved out in a hundred years; and many lesser castles, like Rothesay, were no less impenetrable. Each had its own peculiar feature. Roxburgh, unapproachable without being seen, because of the steep bare hillsides around; and the fast rivers which bounded it on two sides.

The problem about how to recapture these fortresses was a constant worry, for as soon as we left, the English would re-emerge and continue, as before, to subjugate the local population. Until we retook every last one, the land would not be ours. And to think that they had all been voluntarily given over to the English, without a bolt fired!

But how was it to be done? No one could think of a way. If ladders were put up against the walls, they were thrown down by the defenders, which meant the climbers fell and were killed when they hit the ground. If many ladders were used at once, those that were not thrown down immediately, would soon be dealt with, for one man on the battlements could himself walk around and throw down every ladder that poked its head above the parapet, while others could shoot anyone in the act of climbing, roll boulders or pour boiling pitch down upon them.

The king and everyone else were so baffled by the problem that it seemed impossible of solution. Once or twice, burning the gate or drawbridge had seemed an answer, but the loss of life while this went on was too much to sustain; and, if the defenders were numerous, a tremendous hail of missiles came down on our heads for hours. Constructing a sow or protective covering under which the gate might be undermined was not much good either, as it was easily set on fire, killing all those within. But where there was a moat and drawbridge, even the gate solution was useless, for it could not be approached directly at all.

By this time we were, every last one of us, excommunicated by the order of Pope Clement V, at the behest of Edward II, whose emissaries had seduced the Pope to his side by presents, bribes and favours of various sorts. The effect on men and women brought up to fear hell-fire and damnation with all the manifold awfulness—so well expressed by Signore Dante Alighieri in the poem I grew to know well—was ominous, until the churchmen of our own land set their fears at rest by issuing a manifesto to the effect that Bruce had been chosen before God and man as rightful King of Scotland *ut deformata reformet, corrigendaque corriget et dirigat indirecta*—that he might reform what is deformed, correct what needs correction and straighten what had gone awry. And so the excommunication aided the cause by putting every man's eternity in jeopardy, for then, everyman had a tremendous vested interest in justifying Bruce and aiding his task, for if he lost, they lost their immortal souls.

For myself, the issue was of lesser importance, for the doubts engendered at Cambridge had become a conviction that, whatever other men believed, there was no hell but the one on earth, from which death would be deliverance. Of course I told no one, not even Eleanor, for I would have been detested of men and stripped of my power to do good for my country thereafter.

The raid into England was a case in point. To try to compel Edward II to agree a settled peace and recognise Bruce's autonomy, he led us across the border on two raids which became a pattern for the future. All that we had had to do to our own land in defence of it when the English invaded, we now did to theirs. Every farm and field was burnt, every horse, cow and property of interest, stolen. Anyone who resisted was killed.

There came a day when, at the king's side, we rode up to a farm worked by a man and his two adult sons. When the torch was thrown onto the thatch, they went for weapons and when the cattle were being driven off, one of the sons shot one of our men with a crossbow. 'Kill him,' said Bruce to me.

Kill a young man defending his property, which he has worked for years? It seemed so unfair! But when he lifted the reloaded bow to fire again, this time at Bruce, it was not so difficult. The arrow hit him between the eyes, travelled all the way through his head and pinned him to the barn door. And then his young wife came out and saw and screamed—a scream that will live within my own ears all the days of my life—and shouted abuse at me and shook her fist and wailed and tore her clothing. And I knew that I had killed someone who was loved truly, as I was not; and I was filled with self-loathing and jealousy for such a love.

Then, as Bruce turned in the saddle to look behind him, the father emerged with another bow and I shot him too; and the young woman lifted a pitchfork and ran at us, and her, too, I shot down; and she was thrown backwards with the force, and fell back upon the body of the father, the limbs of which were still twitching, and the blood surged out of the hole in her neck defiling her white linen dress.

I must have looked at Bruce as if my soul had flown out of me, for he reached over and laid his hand upon mine and said, 'Some bad things are necessary in war. We must harden our hearts.'

If he was severe on those who resisted or threatened us, Bruce was a man who kept his bargains, and when agreements were made to pay money into the treasury—with which we could purchase weapons from Ireland and the continent—for the sake of protection, whole districts were unmolested. Within the year, the entire north of England was in thrall to us, had supplied much property and money which, as Bruce pointed out, was only fair recompense for the raiding we ourselves had had to suffer or the scorched-earth policy we had been forced to carry out because of their raids.

In this, again, Bruce showed stature as a leader which few men would have been able to match; and yet it was necessary to be so cruel, for we had to give the English a taste of their own medicine. It was the only way to make them see that a negotiated independent settlement would be in their own best interests. The bully will always return for more easy victories, if he is not opposed vigorously and injured where it hurts most. So at least was the perceived strategy. As events were to show, it was not successful.

Far and wide we raged across England, and one day, I found myself on a headland below which a ship was passing. I had never seen one so large nor such a flag before. Dutch it may have been or Hanseatic, I know not, for sure; but I noticed something interesting: a boat was in the water beside it and men were climbing up the side on a ladder of some kind. And yet it was like no ladder I had seen before. It had rounded wooden rungs which were held together, not by long pieces of timber, but by ropes threaded through the wooden footboards. As I studied this, I had that strange feeling I am used to when a difficult mathematical or philosophical puzzle is about to be solved; but at the time I could not quite work it out fully. I just sensed I had seen something important.

Bruce was at his wine a few nights later, in front of a blazing fire, and round about were his commanders, myself among them, when the quaestio about castles was raised yet again. He had a genius for this kind of activity, shared, I am persuaded, by few other kings. It was not that he found the answers himself, rather that he drew them out of others like me. Where another king would have stolen the floor and held it, enjoying the sound of his own voice, Bruce let all men speak and listened intently, only occasionally interrupting to ask a question, or encourage a man with an idea to express it fully, so that others could grasp its full significance.

I was feeling particularly well that evening, as I had mated with Eleanor in the bushes only an hour before and she had seemed better pleased than usual, a soft sweetness in her at odds with her usual energy and strength. And for a while, I said nothing, until the king asked my opinion and Boyd guffawed in that raucous, unknightly way of his. 'Whit does that bugger know aboot castles? Books is his parish.'

Put on my mettle, I began to focus really hard and finding no immediate response to my search, I started to analyse the quaestio itself. 'The problem is the height of the wall,' I said. 'Hypothesis: there is no alternative but to use a ladder to climb up. Problem: the ladders just get thrown down. Solution: they must be made so that they cannot be thrown down.'

Boyd laughed again and irritated me to the bottom of my soul. I said, 'They are thrown down because they are so easy to throw down. Why is this? Because they project over the top. What if they were stopped short of the parapet? Would that help. Yes, men could at least climb up. But they would still be shot down or burnt with oil or knocked off with boulders.'

In the resulting silence, Bruce said, quietly, 'Well, what is the solution to that?'

'We must climb in the dark. Then they cannot see us on the ladders.'

In the fire-light I could see Bruce smile broadly. That too, was one of his strengths: he showed his pleasure and I felt warmed by it.

'But how can we attack in the dark?' said Randolph, testily, reclining on the grass nearby. 'How can we see to climb and fight at the top?'

'We must manage without seeing,' I said.

'But the noise made by the ladders going up the wall is deafening,' said Randolph. 'It would wake the entire castle. They would bring torches and see us then.'

'Then we must make ladders which are put up silently.'

But what kind of ladders would do that? It was then that the image of the ladder on the ship came into my mind and I sat up suddenly with a start. Bruce saw it and motioned for silence, so that I might again be heard. 'Instead of wooden sides, the ladder must have ropes.'

'But rope ladders make a noise against the wall too,' said Randolph, 'we've tried them. They are very difficult to climb because the rung is hard up against the stone.'

'Then we must have board rungs like on a ship's ladder. And the ropes will be threaded through holes in the ends.'

Randolph was suddenly scathing. 'And what, pray, will raise the ladder up the wall?' The critical quaestio which they had never been able to resolve.

I thought for a while and then gave up, for there seemed no answer. I rose and went to fetch some more wine and the talk continued around me as if, as ever, the problem had no solution; and then, just as I raised the goblet to my lips, it came to me, 'A single long pole which will be poked through a hole in the top rung and then lifted straight up! As the ladder is only of rope and a few wooden boards, one strong man should be able to erect it in an instant.'

There was a silence while men considered this. Then Boyd guffawed, as if the complexity of the idea rendered it ridiculous. But, undaunted, I continued my analysis. 'The pole will be slightly wider than the hole in the top rung but tapered at the top end so that only an inch will go through the hole there. And the pole will be a little higher than the height of the wall. About forty feet should do.'

'But what will keep the ladder at the top of the wall?' said Bruce.

'A couple of metal irons, one at each end of the top rung, shaped to fit the battlement. These will take hold of the top of the parapet.'

'But they'll kin throw doon the iron brackets!' said Boyd.

'No,' I said, 'with men on the ladder, the iron will be impossible to throw off. Their weight will pull the brackets down tight on the parapet.'

Randolph was still unhappy. 'But what about the noise of the iron brackets on the stone?'

'We must wrap rags around the brackets so they don't clink,' I replied, 'and they must be just the right shape for the top of the wall.'

'But what about the pole?' said Gibbie Hay, who had not understood either.

'Once the brackets are in place on the parapet, the pole will be quietly pulled free of the hole in the top rung and laid down flat on the ground. Then we climb up.'

This was how we won many of the castles. Crabbe made a pilot version which was soon modified because of the weight: light, thin, round rungs were easier to carry. Each rung had a small hole at either end, through which a rope was fed. A knot was tied on either side of the rung to keep them in place. The rungs were kept off the wall by a few horizontals at right angles, fastened to the rungs and projecting inwards. This meant that only at three or four places was there any contact with the wall and it was limited to the small round end of a horizontal, also bound in rags to minimise the noise of slipping. We tried it out on the next castle we attacked. Rothesay.

With characteristic skill, Bruce sent Sir Robert Boyd to do the job and, because I was disliked by him so much, appointed me second in command, for, knowing the place and castle as I did, my advice would be invaluable; and being thrown together, when each must help the other, the rift between us must either fracture or mend. Of course he said nothing about this; and at first I did not realise it. Only later, did I understand the sense in it.

At first, things were difficult, for Boyd, though energetic, was a clumsy, blundering creature as well as a coarse and stupid one. But I managed to prevail upon him to start with, about the necessity of concealing our approach, for the sake of surprise. As darkness fell, our four ships set off from the mainland, some way south of Inverkip, and landed a while later in the very wood between Craigmore and Kilchattan from which Eleanor and I had set off during our escape. Once disembarked, I led the men up the hill through the forest and had not gone a hundred yards before Boyd came puffing up after me, bellowing that we should go by the track along the beach. But I insisted that any watchers would lie in wait at the shore and we must first journey inland to outwit them.

The sky was cloudless and travelling easy, in spite of the two ladders that some of the men had to carry. Soon, we were on the hill to the east of the castle, looking down upon its gaunt eminence above the moat, silver-gleaming in the moonlight.

There, Boyd proposed to rest awhile and eat, against my wishes, for I feared the smoke from the cooking fires would be seen against the night sky. Having eaten and drunk his fill, Boyd then wanted a woman and went in search of Bess Morrison, who was of our party, but he arrived just after Girvin, who had somehow persuaded her to yield up her charms even to him, perhaps for a coin. 'Git aff ya wee bastart!' he roared and pulled the ears of the stocky dwarf, just beginning to shudder with his evacuation. A fight followed, an unequal scuffle of exchanged blows which mostly missed in the dark, during which Girvin ran between Boyd's huge tree-trunk legs and escaped to the rear, before turning and stabbing him in the arse with a small dagger, which enraged our leader mightily, so that he shouted and stamped the ground like a bull and I feared our presence would be announced to the English in the castle below. To escape, Girvin disappeared into the woods and we saw him no more until after the attack had been carried out; a lesson to me about the restraint necessary in commanders, if they are to retain the use of their troops.

Deprived of his short adversary, Boyd soon forgot Bess Morrison and fell asleep. I was half-minded to proceed without him, a failure of decision I was to regret. The men slept on the slope among the trees, myself, I am ashamed to say, among them.

It was Eleanor who woke us, tipping a pot of spring water over my face and sprinkling others. Already, the sky had lightened and I was eager to be off, but Boyd was grumpy and wanted his porridge. So we had to wait again. A full hour passed before we were in position at the edge of the moat on the south side, as far from the main garrison as possible, who dwelt in the tower at the drawbridge.

The water was freezing as we entered, Eleanor and I, swimming, each with an end of a rope ladder. At the far bank, we held each ladder until the men had used them to cross over, pulling themselves hand over hand, with legs that could not swim dangling uselessly, and, I am afraid, making more noise than was desirable, even without armour, which would have made crossing the water more dangerous. When thirty had crossed, the ladders were pulled over, we ascended the steep bank, and I put the end of the long pole we had brought through the hole in the topmost wooden rung. In a moment, the pole was vertical and the rope ladder rose with it into the starlit sky. As Eleanor knew the shape of the battlement, the metal bracket at the top would fit the parapet well enough, but I lacked the skill for manoeuvring it into position. In spite of the rags, it fell with a clunk. Around me, in the dark, men seemed to stop breathing.

Above, in a tower, I heard a voice say, 'Whit the fuck's 'at?' A Scotsman! Like so many who had sold themselves to the English. Then I thought of myself and smiled and, dimly, saw the shape of Eleanor's fine teeth as she shared the joke, knowing what had passed through my mind. Her ladder was not yet erected. I took the pole, put the end into the hole and raised the ladder in one movement and then, with more skill now, succeeded in securing the bracket on the top of the parapet without so much as a sound. 'Come oan!' said Boyd, when he saw the ladders in place. 'No,' I whispered. 'They don't know we are here. Wait. Wait until things settle.'

Boyd would have none of it. The cold immersion had wakened him and he would be at the task now, against all sense. Up he went and I felt obliged to follow. He was not half way up before there were shouts. The sentry had moved out of the tower to investigate and was standing right above us. 'Raise the alarm! Christ, thur here!' A horn blew from the far side of the castle and there was the clank of armour and the sounds of weapons and doors opening onto the castle yard—all this, as we ascended into the rocky heights of the battlement.

'Puush the ladder doon aff the wa'!' I heard someone say, and another, 'Ah canny! Ah canny fun' the tap o' it!' Arrows whistled past my ears. Below, I heard screams, and after them, thumps, as bodies hit the ground under my feet. And though the terror rose in my veins at the eerie height I might soon fall, with a lance through me, I smiled at the success of the idea of the ladder.

Shouts and curses followed, as Boyd fell onto the battlement among the watchers, scattering them under his bulk, so that when I arrived, they were still asprawl, the two guards and Boyd, panting at the effort of rising. In the moonlight the scene was clear enough. From the parapet,

I shot one and then the other in quick succession, and then jumped down as a flight of arrows from the courtyard just missed and splintered on the stone.

Men were running along the battlement towards me, as well as firing from the doorway of the great keep and across the yard from other places, some of them high up on towers, built higher than the battlement, by design, to deal with an investment of this sort. The light was coming and I could make out shapes much better. I began to fire at them and was soon joined by Eleanor at the same task. Boyd was still down, groaning with some wound, but there was nothing to be done but defend our position until reinforcements arrived, which they soon did, the dribble becoming a tide of men, swirling in both directions away from us towards the sound of steel on steel and screams as men were sworded or died. But it was close, all too close, lives had been lost, were being lost all around, and all because of starting too late, making too much noise and advancing too fast.

Later, the drawbridge fell with a clatter and the rest of the force rushed across the moat into the castle, shouting so loudly that some defenders were demoralised and threw down their arms. The English had still to be got out of the keep and that took a while as the winding stair was fought up over the bodies of those who had fallen beforehand. Then arrows were most useful as ever, and I fired my share again, aiming with precision at the figures crouching above, which came into view occasionally to see what we were about. Each time this happened, I struck.

When it was all over, the proud serjeant and most of his men dead, I stopped to wipe the sweat off my face, and noticed that Eleanor was nowhere to be seen. I found her at the wall we had climbed, lying near Boyd, with an arrow in the mouth and another in the chest, high up. She was unconscious. I cursed and swore and wept and looked down at her and fidgeted with frustration, stamping up and down and looking again at wounds I knew to be lethal. And I did not dare grab her, as I wished, for fear of the pain it would cause.

I shouted at myself to be calm and, with utmost gentleness, gathered her in my arms and brought her to the great hall in the keep, laid her on a table and began to examine her. And there was no physician, Bute never did have a physician. Anything that could be done, I must do myself. And medicine was a subject not much in evidence at Cambridge and not well understood anyway, so I had never attended any lectures on it.

Two front teeth were smashed and that would help, I realised, for some of the force would have been spent on that. But the arrow-head was deep embedded in the flesh at the back of the mouth and a trickle of blood fell down her throat from the wound. When the arrow was removed, I knew that trickle would become a flood. Somehow, I had to prevent this. The arrow in her chest I did not concern myself with. I knew instinctively that its removal was impossible without killing her.

In a feverish panic, I wondered what to do. Around me, men were celebrating with jugs of ale or wine from the castle cellar, or tormenting prisoners with knife-points or remarks about their masculinity, as their clothes were cut off and they were stripped naked. The laughter and cruelty were bestial and I could stand no more of it.

I shouted—screamed, more like—and demanded to be left in peace to attend the wounds on my love. Mercifully, they left me, to carry on with their revels elsewhere. My final demand was that all our wounded be fetched to the hall.

The problem of what to do about Eleanor was as difficult as any I had ever faced. I soon had one useful idea. It must be best to have her stand up, and since she could not stand up, she must be forced to hang with her head as high as possible. For I remembered that when I had a wound in my arm, the blood flowed more freely when the arm was held low down, but when I held it up high, the flow slackened off so much that it stopped altogether. With this idea alone, I called for rope, and when it came, I hung Eleanor from the rafters by the armpits, and because her head rolled to one side, I ordered Sheugle, one of the archers, to keep it upright. He was worried, for he admired Eleanor as most of the men did. 'Ye should get a leech, Bann,' he said.

'There's none here. I must be the leech myself.'

Eleanor's pallor was ashen with exhaustion and loss of blood, yet I knew the loss would soon increase. The difficulty was how to cauterise the wound once the arrow was out. I thought of a branding iron but could not know how far in to put it. The danger was in burning more flesh than needed and causing a mortal injury. Of course it was a waste of time, for she would die of the other wound, but I had to try something and chose to start on the lesser problem.

I felt the back of my throat and realised how hard it was. Maybe, just maybe, the arrow had not gone in very far because of the hard bone that surely lay behind that flesh. It was then that Eleanor opened her eyes. They were filled with panic and shock and she tried to speak and uttered only foolish noises. I spoke gently to her, assuring her that all would be well, and held her hands when she tried to reach for the arrow in the mouth which would be uncomfortable. Then I sent for drink and poured a goblet of whisky down her throat, at which she struggled and protested, in vain, as Sheugle grabbed her.

After another dose of whisky, she passed out and I called up others to help, fat, dark-haired Jinky among them. Carefully, I explained the problem and what I had to do. When the goblet was filled again, I pulled hard on the arrow and it came out. Then I pressed my thumb on the hole and told the others to heave her upside down. Next, Sheugle poured the whisky around my thumb and I let go so that it entered the bloody hole. I stuffed a rag over her throat and tongue and tried to light the wound and failed utterly. Then Eleanor woke and started kicking and the men held her fast. I put more spirits into the wound and applied a taper to it again. This time, a blue flame appeared and she tried to scream and could not, for we had her mouth wide open and her tongue clamped.

The flame died quickly, and I pulled out the rag. She gasped for breath and then seemed to quieten, and I realised she had been unable to breathe. A last dose of whisky was poured everywhere and then I had her laid flat on a fleece on the flagstones near the fire, with a blanket over her. I pushed her head right back and held her mouth wide open. The wound had stopped bleeding.

But the wound in the chest! What to do about that? I was standing looking at it, wondering what to do, when Crabbe appeared at my side. 'Yull nay save yon lassie, Maister Bannatyne,' he said in his guttural-sounding Scots. 'Ye maun aid they ithers and lee hur alane.'

'I have to try! The arrow must come out!'

Crabbe replied, 'Aye, weel, whin it dis, it ull damn near bring the hert oot wi' it! Aw they Inglish yases barbs.'

Which set me thinking profitably, for now the problem had been clearly stated. This arrow was in deep and the barb would tear out the flesh when it was drawn.

'We'll have to think of a way of drawing it without pulling the flesh.'

'Bit ye canny! How kin ye pull oot a barb withoot drawin' aw the flesh roon aboot? It canny be done!'

Which was a gauntlet thrown at the door of my brains. I called for pen, ink and parchment and when they came, I drew the shape of the arrow-head with the barb and began to consider how to avoid the tearing that withdrawal would entail. No solution came to mind and I wept tears of frustration at the figure lying on the floor with the arrow protruding from her chest. There was nothing further I could do for her.

Boyd, who had watched these proceedings uncomplaining, was next. He had fractured the upper arm, the absence of chain mail having provoked injuries unusual for him, even though the sword had struck him with the flat of the blade. Having filled him with whisky, with tears still in my eyes, I fashioned some rude splints, heaved on the bones to set them in place, and bound up the arms. A bone between the shoulder and the neck on the other side had been broken also. All I could think of to do was draw the bones into the natural position, as before, and bind them up with bits of cloth.

When I had done what I could for all the wounded, ours and theirs,

I went outside into the yard to the cool of the morning, bleeding inwardly in my soul, for I knew that Eleanor, my beloved, must soon die.

All around was mayhem, bodies strewn everywhere, stinking with urine and filth and already assaulted by swarms of flies. A scream rent the air and drew me across to a wooden lean-to by the wall. Inside, a man—Malky, with whom I had formed a kind of friendship, his face and clothing black with filth from the moat—was just standing up, a half-erect dripping penis protruding from his breeches. On the earthen floor, the bare backside of another I recognised as Shorty—from the narrow arse, long thin legs and back—began to ride some figure underneath. In revulsion, I shouted at him to stop. 'Get out! Get off!' and I reached down for the man, but his passion was urgent and he swept me away with one long stringy arm. Then I saw the woman. It was my mother! I kicked him hard in the side of the face and he fell off, I drew my dagger and threatened to separate him from his precious part; and the rest with instant disembowelling; and cursed and swore blasphemies of a kind that never crossed my lips till then.

My mother lay on her back, opened like a flower, red, raw and defenceless in a dark shift, all but torn off. Her hair was lank and grey, her face gaunt with exhaustion and fear and sweat, and when she opened her blue eyes and saw mine, she hid her face in her hands, curled into a ball and screamed again and wept.

I picked her up in my arms and walked across the yard with her, past the men who still stood about as if, even now, I might relent and give her up to them. One tapped me on the shoulder and I turned to see Right-eye. 'Whit the fuck's wrang wi ye, Bann?' he shouted indignantly. 'It's jist a fucken wummin, fur Christ's sake!' He reeked of whisky and stank of blood and other folk's excrement, in which he must have rolled during the struggle fought around bodies which had evacuated after death.

Speechless with shock and revulsion, I made to move on and felt my gambeson pulled from behind. I turned and kicked him full in the crotch and he went down on one knee, yelling: 'Yur a fucken English bastart, richt enough!'

Over the drawbridge we went, my mother and I, and down the hill to the shore. At the water's edge, I did not stop, but continued into the sea until I was up to my waist. Then I let her slip into the water and heard her cry out as the salt bit into her exposed soreness. She bent down and cleaned herself and I turned away and walked inward again.

In a little while, I went back and found her crouched in the water, only her head visible, crooning an old love song so piteously it wrenched my very soul, made me feel as if for the first time what I owed her, what she was to me, what, even now, I cannot put into words, for the bond is beyond expression. I walked out to her and raised her up and held her close to me and looked into the blue eyes that studied me so intently, as if I might be an enemy, intending assault, and then I said, 'It's wonderful to see you again, mother,' and her eyes filled with tears and she hung on my shoulder, and I knew it was going to be all right.

We walked home together, hand in hand, all the way to Ardmaleish, and I put her to bed there in the kitchen and lit a fire and scavenged for food and took her some. All that day and night, I stayed with her, and ministered to her and clasped the sorrow of it all to my heart, sitting beside her bed on a stool, as I used to as a boy. And I told her my doings and about Eleanor, whom I loved and made love to, but who did not love me. And the child, Alexander, who was with a woman in St Andrews. Then I told her of the wounds and my feeble attempt to mend one and that the other was mortal; how she would die soon if not already, and my mother wept tears for my sorrow and we held each other for a while, she in the bed and me on the stool beside it, until, at length, she sat up, wide-eyed, and said, 'John, you must go to her! She needs you!'

'But what can I do?' I cried. 'She is beyond saving! The arrow is near the heart. It cannot be pulled out without killing her.'

My mother seized my arm and pulled my head down and stared into my eyes. 'John,' she said, earnestly, 'you can mend it. I know you can. You can do anything you put your mind to. It has always been so.'

I got up and paced the floor with so much pent-up anger and frustration, I felt I would burst with the force of it, protesting at this unwarranted confidence in my poor abilities, but my mother insisted. 'You just go to her now, John, and you will think of something. I know it. Go now.'

And in no very good spirits, I went. The road was dark, except for the moon which shone between high clouds, and I walked the miles into the town, past the houses at Kames and the fields with cattle standing stolidly asleep or lying down, mindless of everything but the loss of my love.

After a while, as if a spirit of magic clasped me, I looked up and saw the stars glinting and marvelled at their beauty and the wonder of their meaning. How far away they looked, and how odd the shapes they made. There is a science there somewhere, I said to myself, and promised that one day, if God willed, I would myself investigate these heavenly bodies. What were they and what did they mean? Somehow, my mind relaxed at these ideas and thus unencumbered by grief and thoughts of impotence—the intellectual variety, so much worse than any physical—my muse came down to me and delivered me of an idea which near stopped my heart with its power.

The sharp ends of the barbs were the difficulty. It was these which would prevent the easy withdrawal of the arrow. Therefore, they must be prevented from tearing the flesh, for the one *sine qua non* was that the arrow must be withdrawn through the same hole, because her heart lay beneath.

But how to prevent the sharp ends from catching? And then, oh glory! I did see at last! I must introduce things to the wound to mask the sharp ends. And I thought again of the shape I had drawn on the parchment and saw it for what it was: a plane figure, a two dimensional figure; and I imagined a pair of tweezers inserted into the wound which covered the sharp ends and saw that they could draw the arrow out. But there was the arrow itself, which would prevent tweezers being inserted. Worse, both probes would have to be inserted simultaneously, an act of impossible dexterity; for, if one was in, it would move about while the other was fitted, causing great pain.

This too, I saw in my mind's eye, and the solution, the only possible one, occurred to me. A pair of thin-shanked tiny spoons, each carefully inserted and fitted over the sharp end of the barb and done separately, which was all that was possible, and afterwards tied to the arrow, while the other was done, and then spoons, shanks and arrow could be withdrawn together. Since the barb had entered, the hole would be wide enough to permit its withdrawal. Any little extra width, due to the spoon's thickness, would be accepted by the surrounding flesh which could be eased back for the purpose.

I began to run towards the town, past sleeping cottages and tree trunks waving cheerfully in the warm night breeze.

But was she still alive?

I found she was, breathing quietly and asleep still, with whisky and exhaustion and loss of blood and much earlier pain. Fascinated by the problem, I took a knife and carefully cut off her tunic around the wound, exposing the once fair breast, now defiled by a yard-long arrow which had sunk in deep, oh deep! When I saw how it was, I turned away and nearly fainted with the sheer awfulness of it.

Crabbe heated up his forge and made a pair of long-handled tiny spoons with small holes in the shanks for ease of tying and when they had cooled and the light was good, I set to, with men holding her down on the table of the great hall, Jinky, Torquil, Tam Anderson and Sheugle.

Of course, as soon as I inserted my first spoon, she woke, shrieking. Then, mercifully, she passed out and I tied the shank to the arrow with twine. I pushed the other in and manipulated it around the flesh until it was where I wanted it, masking the barb, and tied this shank to the arrow also, tightly now, trying to bend the barbs inwards to make release easier; winding the twine around the spoon shanks, closer and closer to the wound, so that the three things: spoons and arrow, became as one. I poured some whisky in and saw her wince, even in sleep, then she woke and tried to sit up, screaming—a sound that threatened to unman me by its very fright. Then, exhausted, unconscious, she fell back again under the weight of hands pressing her down.

Gradually, I began to ease the head out, still attached to the arrow, thankful that it had been left entire, for ease of grasp. It came out, slowly, the spoons pushing the flesh to each side, preventing the barbs catching and at last it emerged with a sucking sound.

I sighed with relief, for I knew that little extra damage had been done. There was blood of course, a lot of it, seeping out of the hole. Whisky and flame were applied and the blood stopped coming, congealing in a dark, solid mass about the wound. Even as I watched, the hole began to close, and I thought of leaving it open as I had seen surgeons do, applying caustic to keep it so; and rejected the idea. What could be better than that the wound should be allowed to close, given that I had tried to cleanse it? Anyway, I had no caustic.

And then it was but to wait, and I do believe the entire force of men went about the castle on tip-toe, in respect and reverence for the attempt which had just been made to save a life. Food was brought to me, but I could eat nothing. For a long while, I stood above Eleanor's dormant form like a man awaiting execution. Then I would walk about the room, returning every few minutes in the hope of some sign of life, but there was none. She lay in a stupor, hardly breathing, on a bloody fleece near a warming fire, which I kept going all night, the wound open to the air, as I judged best.

Sometime during the night I must have fallen asleep in the seat I had drawn up by her. In the morning, when I was wakened by the cockerels, there was no change in her. Demented by the strain and effort, I walked outside to the well, drew a bucket and poured it over myself and then thought better of it; and crossed the drawbridge and ambled down to the beach and straight into the sea, swimming out some way.

When I returned, the men asked if the castle walls should be torn down as planned and I said no. There would be no loud noises until we knew Eleanor's fate. The entire place and the town too, came to a standstill. Small groups of people and soldiers met in groups and spoke quietly, but no more. No work was done and no one felt like celebrating now, for it was known that the woman who had crossed the moat, climbed the wall and held off the sentries till the men climbed up, had been gravely wounded and could not live. And that everything else must wait until she had met her maker.

All the others not already dead when I began to treat them were still alive and conscious. I gave them food and drink and they smiled and spoke their thanks to me for my work. One of the Andersons was there, with a slashed face which would never endear him to women again. And many another I never knew the name of, or time has erased from memory.

I was sitting in the great hall, at a window, remembering the time I had spent in that very place as guest of the Cressinghams and how Eleanor had looked then, how virginal, how lovely, how full of the joy of life, when a small sound came to me, so that I thought it a rat which had been attracted by the blood, and I turned to deal with it. Her eyes were wide open and they looked straight at me, and I thought at first it was a mirage, the ghost of her soul, about to take wing. But no! She was awake, better still, she was alive! I knelt beside her and kissed her cheek and uttered prayers to a God I had rejected long since. Speak I could not, for tears, which fell as large as hailstones.

'You have saved my life then, Bann?' she said, in a small surprised parched croak of a voice. But there were no words for what I felt. Instead, tears dropping on her bare breast, I silently clasped her hand and squeezed gently.

'You look tired,' she said, 'you should sleep, my love.' And I never knew such happiness, for she had never used that word to me before. I felt blessed. I felt as a man feels when he is loved truly for the very first time. What a miracle it is; what a consummation of being, to be so valued.

I gave her water to drink and then a little meat and bread, but the wounds were sore and she would take little. Then she slept again and I watched over her, until I, too, fell asleep.

Much later, a messenger came to tell me I was wanted at the gate and when I got there, I found my mother, dressed all in white, seated on a cart on the track just beyond the drawbridge. She was fearful of the men in the castle and would come no further, but she had come to take me home, she said; and when I told her Eleanor still lived and seemed better, her face lit up and she said, 'I knew it! I just knew you could find the go of it.'

A stretcher of cloth between two lengths of wood was made and the men helped me move Eleanor to the cart. Then we set off, the three of us, for Ardmaleish, and there we put her to bed beside the fire where, so recently, my mother had held me and insisted I could save her.

There then began a blessed time, a time I cannot think of but with tears in my eyes at such a quantity of pleasure, for here at last, Eleanor was truly my own and it was my privilege to help her and feed her and entertain her, aided and abetted by my mother who soon struck up a bond of friendship with her. I forgot the castle and my archers, knew I should return and see to their needs and command them as commanders are meant to do, instead of wallowing in my home like the schoolboy I used to be; but my mind was enraptured, absorbed utterly in my love, and I put duty out of mind.

After a few days, Eleanor was much better and insisted upon rising. With my support, she walked slowly around outside, where she saw the farm buildings, the fields and the views across the channel to the heather-clad hills of Argyll. Then, being tired and stiff from her wounds, we sat quietly together on a fallen tree-trunk, like an old married couple holding hands in the heat of the sun, listening to the cries of the gannets which whirled in the air and dived, every so often, in pursuit of fish.

Gradually, her fragility disappeared and longer journeys were undertaken, until one day, we set off for the beach itself; and nothing would do but that she would swim, so we stripped off and bathed and both knew it was good, for the clean salt water would heal her wounds as nothing else; and for an hour in the warm sunshine we gambolled in the clear cold water and minded it not, for the pleasure of each other's company.

Each day was a new magic, full of high thoughts and deep feelings; walks to the north end of the island were soon possible and up onto the hills behind; even into Kames, but no further: the castle and the town were out of mind. We had eyes and ears only for ourselves and walked everywhere, arms clasped around the other as if afraid to let go. Then there was the work of the farm to do, which my mother soon reminded me of; and so we would collect eggs and I would dig an ever-increasing patch for vegetables and, in the evenings, push out the boat and fish with handlines for the supper, returning with a pail-full when the boat should have been filled, if we had not been so engrossed in each other. Until, one day, hooves clattering in the yard announced a rider. It was Boyd. He took off his helm respectfully, stooped his tall presence and entered the house, sitting down where my mother bade him by the fire.

'Weel, yer no jist a deed rat efter aw,' he said, in his gruff way. 'Ye hae a wey wi' chirugery, Bann. Bae Christ, maist ae they sodjers is alive, ye ken. Ye pit thaim thegither jist brawly.'

'And yourself?' I said.

'Ah'm fine tae. The airm's no jist whit it wis, ye ken, bit it'll dae the noo; and the shou'der's mendin'. An' there's the lassie tae!'—Seeing her as she appeared in the kitchen—'Weel, begod, Ah thocht ye wis fur the hole in the grun.' And for the first time, I saw something approaching a grin bestride his black potholed whiskered cheeks.

'I had a good physician,' said Eleanor, smiling at me.

'Aye, so ye did, tae, Ah canny git ower it. Ah seen the hale jingbang. Ye wudnay credit whit he did tae ye,' and so began a long rambunctious and not very accurate account of the treatment that had saved her life. Finally, he said to me, 'Ye ken ye desertet yer command?' And when I agreed and pleaded extenuating circumstances, he concluded, 'Weel, wull say naething aboot it. Ah've taen care o' the castle wa's. As mich as Ah kin, oneywey. If the English tak it again thull be herd pressed tae rouse up aw they big stanes we flung doon. Jist you twa stey here awhile and ye kin folly us whin yer ower yer hurts.'

And so the command left the island to return to the king's service, leaving us to our own devices. I borrowed a stallion and ploughed a field with it, back and forth, for two days, till the soil was like fine sand; but where was there seed? I reckoned without my resourceful mother. She had hidden a bag-full in a secret place and armed with it, Eleanor and I soon travelled the length and breadth, broadcasting and sowing.

People came to visit and things were exchanged, for now that the English were thrown out the spirit of community re-asserted itself. Sadly, a few folk considered to have fraternised with English had been stripped and beaten, even killed in one case, but my mother was spared such excesses, because her son had been involved in the fight. This became clear at market day, when we hitched up the pony and jour-neyed in the cart to town. There, beside the mercat cross, we stood, the three of us, remembering my brother, Eck who died so bravely, when a high-pitched voice piped up: 'Do ye no' ken yer auld dominie, noo yer sich a swank?'

It was Weasel Wullie, he of the long body and short legs whom time had given a tonsured head, except the surrounding thatch had become sparse and white. Leaving Eleanor and my mother to barter for these things that women so desire, I joined him in the tavern and drank some ale. When all my doings had been related, he eyed me quizzically, and said, 'Weel, yeer a wheen chinged fae that young stupat I mind seein' wi' aw they English.'

I blushed at the memory. How could I forget what I once had been, my Englishness and my snobbery, afraid to reveal my peasant connexions? 'I'm older now,' I said, 'and maybe wiser.'

'Aye,' he agreed, fingering the lump on the top of his egg-shaped pate, 'Ye wur aye that. But hiv ye learned yer lesson? Aboot Scotland? Or are ye jist as sure that we should gie in and become English?'

I was on a stool crouched over a tankard, and he in a window seat. My head rose and flew back as if he had struck me, as he had, and knew it. 'Aye,' he said, 'so that's how it is, then?' I had nothing to say. My old schoolmaster had discomfited me yet again, even after so many years of study and experience of a kind he could hardly appreciate.

'We can't win in the long run,' I forced myself to say, and even as I spoke, I realised that the conversation was being overheard by the entire contents of the room, eager, every one, to renew acquaintance with the boy from Bute who had attended the University of Cambridge and known Robert Bruce, the King.

'Weel, whit wur ye daein' fechtin' fur the Scoats?'

'They killed my brother. What else could I do?'

'Ye coulda gin doon tae England again and focht fur thaim.'

'I was under parole to Bruce.' But I knew it was not that, not that essentially; for that was only an excuse. In a dazzling moment of insight, I saw I had been living an illusion. No, it was not that. With amazement in my voice, I heard myself say, 'I was born here. I am a Scot. How could I fight for anyone else?' And that was the plain truth of it. No matter that the cause was ultimately fruitless, as I could well see, even then, it was one I was compelled by birth and upbringing to defend and uphold as best I could, even unto death. And this more I saw, sitting there in that dusty tavern reeking of beer and spirits, with the morning sunbeams dividing the dark interior like parchment lances, not for all the paroles in Christendom, not even at the cost of my life, could I fight again for England against my fellow Scots.

'Weel, ye micht no' be an Englishman, ma laddie, bit ye sound like wan efter aw that time yuv spent there.' He looked at me for a moment stiffly, fiercely even, and then held out his claw-like hand. 'I'm richt gled tae see ye back, son. Ye did richt weel when yer brither wis hangit. Ah saw the hale thing. An' a praised the guid Goad whin ye won oota yon dungeon. How the hell did ye manage thon?'

And I had to tell him, for the Cressinghams had kept the event secret, Eleanor being one of them, as it were, and, being considered English, might have been conceived to have played traitor; an office inconvenient to a small force in an alien land, lest others were encouraged by it. Around me, I heard a fascinated silence, punctuated only by the occasional sough of ale or the gasp as the stronger stuff was thrown down and the goblet laid to rest on the counter for more.

When I had finished, they were all around me, reminding me of names long forgotten and full of questions about university and London and the Palace of Westminster; and King Edward and Robert Bruce and Douglas and all the others whose doings were an ornament to the realm. And no drink could I purchase. In the manner of men starved of news and heroic deeds, after so many fruitless years of foreign domination, I was a celebrity, and it was every man's desire to set drink before me so as to be able to boast in days to come how he had done so and thereby become my friend.

If my new found splendour in the company of my islesmen did not go to my head, the drink did. After countless ales and drams my head spun and I felt my stomach begin the agonies of complaint at the infusion of so much poison. Fortunately, I was rescued by Eleanor, until, seeing her, a fresh bevy of questions volleyed forth, this time in her direction, mostly for confirmation of my extraordinary tales. And she settled all, to universal amazement, that I had indeed seen both Longshanks and Bruce, argued to some purpose with both, saved Bruce's life—which modesty compels me to doubt—and that I was the finest archer in the country, which prompted one wag to ask, 'And whit country wid that be, mistress?' To which Eleanor, undaunted, replied, 'Yours and mine, both,' which had them smacking their thighs and laughing at the joke.

'Bit, lassie, yull no kin gae back doon there noo?' said one.

'Why not?' said she. 'If I got the right kind of offer. From an earl, say, with much land and a fine table. Think how well I could live, dressed in silks and satins, waited upon, hand and foot. Instead of which I am condemned to this poor peasant here, who can't even buy me a drink.'

In a moment, a dozen drams were being ordered for her from every boozer present, but she laughed and said if she agreed she would never get me home, and by the looks of things I would be sleeping where I sat till the morrow. And so, I fearing further damage to my newly acquired esteem, and she, to my bodily function, we agreed on one thing: we left.

The lyrical period continued for a time until, one day, a boat beached at Ardmaleish with a messenger bearing a letter from the king: a summons to us both to rejoin the army.

The shock was instant, our small world of loving domesticity shattered. Eleanor was not yet returned to full health—had not lifted a bow—and probably could not, because of the ruptured muscles, which would require the most careful and diligent exercise, if she were ever to recover her skill as an archer. And yet we were summoned by the king. And the boat was waiting, the messenger at the door, prepared to carry us off to the mainland.

Thus, we packed our few belongings, said goodbye to my mother, and departed, waving to the taut figure on the hill with grey hair blowing in the breeze, as the ship sped eastwards to Inverkip where we could disembark and head for Perth, which the army had beseiged.

CHAPTER 14

The Siege of Perth, 1313

NEVER WAS A TOWN BETTER DEFENDED. High walls and towers surrounded it completely, as usual, but the River Tay, which flowed down one side, had been diverted to circumscribe it, forming a deep moat impassable to troops, which must be bridged before an attack could begin; and then only at great loss of life, from the defenders on the town walls, who could fire down a hail of arrows and spears with impunity from the battlements. The position looked hopeless and every effort had failed, which was one reason Bruce had requested our presence. He was a man who would try everything in such an extremity.

The success at Rothesay could not be repeated so easily, because of the impassability of this moat and the number and readiness of the defenders, who were on constant alert. I listened to the reports of the activities so far, trying to see a solution, and, to Bruce's displeasure, had nothing worthwhile to communicate. I found myself in the position of one who is brought from afar, at some trouble, to perform a miracle, and cannot—a grave disappointment to one and all.

And so, rather than give up and admit defeat, another assault was ordered for that night, hoping to get the bridges across and scale the walls before enough defenders appeared at that spot. But the outcome was the usual disaster. Bridging the moat, even at the narrowest part— at least twelve yards—required a lot of wood and effort and much unwelcome noise. By the time the ladders were across, sentries had raised the alarm, and scores of men came running to the battlement to shoot down upon the climbers, who soon fell, shot down with a withering hail of steel-tipped arrows. And the reinforcements would not go out on the bridges to be shot down in their turn, as their officers commanded. Mutiny was in the air.

Then Bruce announced himself and said he would not have his good men wasted, so the thing was called off. By dawn, the bridges had been set on fire and burnt and any wounded still lying about below the walls had been shot dead while trying to crawl away.

At the council, in the king's tent, many were for leaving, the task being impossible. One fool suggested sitting them out until they starved, but was quickly routed, for had not the town just recently been supplied through the water-gate from the ocean by an English ship, easily navigating the river from Dundee? I listened while these opinions were expressed until, finally, the king's eye alighted on me.

Outside, a sharp January frost lay hard upon the ground and we huddled inside around a blazing fire, smoke from which escaped out of a vent in the tent roof. There were about a dozen of us, in mail or gambesons over stained tight breeches, all wrapped up in full-length cloaks or plaids. Bruce wore the same brown homespun as the rest of us but stood out because of his height and presence and dark-eyed looks. When he plied me with quaestiones like this, he would raise his eyebrows till they were like arrow points, giving him a diabolic air in that small world of shadows.

'We succeeded at Rothesay,' I said, 'because it is a small castle and we managed without armour because it had few men and we could swim across. Perth is different. It is a town, with five hundred men-at-arms inside and a moat which is far wider.'

I paused to think and, as no one around said anything, continued, 'Bridging the moat is no good. There is too much noise. That means we must swim across.'

'Who can swim in armour?' said Randolph, derisively. 'And what good is it if we get across without armour? How can we fight in the town against so many men in armour when we have none ourselves?'

I thought for a while, in the resulting silence, and when others would speak, Bruce held up his hand to give me time. 'Some at least must swim,' I said, and then I had a dazzling idea, '—unless there is a place where we can walk across. A place where the moat is shallow enough for an armoured man to walk over, with his head above the surface.'

'There is no such place!' said Douglas.

'How do you know?' I replied. 'Have you tried it everywhere?' There was confusion then, as my quaestio bit deep. I said, 'Even if there is no place, the shallowest part must be found, for that is where the moat may be crossed, as we must do, for there is no other way.'

Young Walter Stewart said, 'What if there is no shallow part we can ford? It can't be done this way.'

'In that case,' I said, 'we must dam the river where it enters the moat, so that the water-level is reduced. Then we can definitely cross there.'

And so a search was made, covertly, by a few men in the dark of night, who set off swimming from one end of the moat to the other, a painful experience in the depths of winter, trying to touch down every so often to determine where any shallow points were located.

After a few nights of trial and error, it became clear that there was a shallow point which might be forded by a man in armour, if he were tall enough. Thus, there was no need to reduce the water level. Unfortunately, the moat was twenty-five yards wide at that place, which was a long way to walk in the dark with water up to the neck.

The final idea in the plan was supplied by Bruce himself, who was a great student of other people's military exploits. He remembered the tale of the Trojan Horse left by the Greeks outside the fort, before they set sail, pretending to give up their siege. Of course, the people of Perth would not fall for any such stratagem, some of whom must know the story too. And yet, unless we took the town, give up we must. This at least might help by lulling the defenders into a false sense of security.

So the next day, derided by cat-calls from the battlements, we folded our tents and set off for the north, behaving as would defeated besiegers, with heads held low; and thus we travelled for a few days. Then, having rested a few more, we turned in our tracks and within half a day's journey of Perth, a small assault party went on ahead with nothing but the essential materials for the attack.

At four of the clock on a dark, freezing January morning in 1313, Bruce himself, mailed from head to foot ready for fierce battle, set off into the moat at the place we had discovered, carrying, along with a sword, the long pole for raising the ladders. These were borne by others following behind, myself among them.

Bruce raised the first ladder and I the second, using the same pole, all in silent haste, lest we be spotted, but the rags binding the iron brackets fell into place without a murmur and the ascent began, slowly and carefully, to minimise the noise. And we climbed up without incident, finding no guards on duty at that place. Surprise was complete. A young French knight named Le Bel, who was with us, afterwards expressed astonishment that the king himself had led the attack in person. Where he came from, everyone of importance stayed well away from the point of conflict, only arriving after the fight was over, to claim the credit.

Men were soon swarming up the wall and spreading out along it, directed by Bruce. In an hour, half our army had climbed into the town, the gates were captured in silence and thrown open for the rest to enter. The remainder was a mopping-up operation of house to house fighting, and some of it was fierce; a messy business of butchery of folk, some hardly out of bed, houses being searched and all males summarily removed to join the queues of prisoners who came to line the market square. By dawn, it was mostly over, a few buildings only, remaining to be stormed. In the square, the atmosphere was full of triumph on the part of ourselves, for what could be more rewarding than to prevail in such intelligent and daring fashion, after so many weeks of failure and so many good men lost?—And utter dismay on the part of the townspeople, who, having caused us so much trouble and loss of life, feared the worst.

Bruce stood at the head of a stair up to the door of the town hall, with myself at his side, bow at the ready, in case of difficulty. The burgesses were brought forward and Bruce called out to the English to go to the left and the Scots to the right, for many people in the town were English, having settled there over a dozen years before, when Edward Longshanks had taken the place, along with the realm and every castle, almost without response. Now these English merchants were quaking in their shoes, and to a man, beseeched Bruce to spare their lives for all the money in their possession.—At which Bruce laughed, not unkindly. 'Your possessions are mine already, it seems, without your gift. The issue is your lives.'

I have often wondered since how many Englishmen pretended to be Scots, in the belief that they would then be spared. Until the outcome was decided, none of the Scots would tell on Englishmen who claimed to be what they were not. Anyway it did not matter after all, for Bruce ordered the Scots burgesses to be slain. The English ones, those who had courageously admitted their true nationality, he set free.

There was wisdom in this, for henceforth, any Englishmen in a Scottish castle would be encouraged to give up, if besieged, and any Scots would think twice about remaining if a besieging force came close. And then, the castle would be controlled by Englishmen, so that issue was decided to best advantage, from our point of view.

Days of carousal followed, of course, and then the walls were torn down, as far as practicable, to prevent the English reinstating the defences on a future occasion. It must have been then that Torquil deserted. Much later, I heard he had taken up with a wench who would stay with him only if he remained in her city.

When all was set to rights, the army headed south to Galloway, to see if this new-found skill at recapturing castles could be applied in that intractable quarter. On the way, I began to chivvy Eleanor about archery, and soon she joined me at practice with all the young men, properly registered and apprenticed, for a good number joined us at Perth and were admitted, after swearing allegiance to the King.

There was a vulnerability about her now, which was new, as if the imminence of death had intimated a mortality she had never before imagined. The disfigurement was slight: a pair of rotting stumps where there had been two fine, large teeth, only visible when she smiled; and the wound in the mouth had healed well and gave no trouble when eating and drinking, providing the food was not too hot, when she would complain. The chest wound became a bright pink scar, riddled everywhere around and especially below with marks where, I suppose, blood flowed into surrounding tissue. In time, these disappeared, leaving only a pale pink mark where the arrow had entered the breast, a trifle less substantial after the ill treatment, which displeased her mightily, when she saw it one day in a looking-glass. She sat down and wept, and said, 'I am not the same woman! I am defiled!'

'Yes, you are not the same; no, you are not defiled. You are different; and it is a great improvement. You now know what a battlefield wound is like and will duck your head more quickly in future, when arrows come whistling by. And the wound is a great enhancement. Any man can go to bed with a woman, but what man can bed a woman who has played a heroic part in a siege, and survived a lethal wound like that? My dear, you are a walking miracle! A living testament to my chirugical skill,' and I laughed long and loud at her woebegone expression, for she wanted to believe my every argument and could not quite manage it. But, I spoke too soon and too loudly, for Bruce joined us and, overhearing, referred to my success at saving lives, which Boyd and others had boasted of.

'You must put these gifts to work for us,' he said, and in this way I came to the proper study of medicine; and even grew to enjoy it, as I enjoyed most of the universe of knowledge.

I sent everywhere in the realm for copies of the latest medical textbooks and immersed myself in everything from the works of the ancients like Hippocrates and Galen to Avicenna and John Gaddesden, who was about the same age as myself but died sooner of plague in 1349. His *Rosa Anglica* was sound, I thought at first, except for some miraculous claims of having cured kidney stones by scarabs and grasshoppers —incredible!

Best of all was the work of Henri de Mondeville, educated at Montpellier, who differed markedly from every other in treating wounds by closing them with sutures, rather than the method current everywhere else: keeping them open by the use of caustic, which was less effective and provoked awful scarring.

Provided the wound is clean, it can and should be closed up, it seems to me, for then it will heal quickly, the edges joining and binding together as desired, to keep out any evil humours that might otherwise invade it. Time has justified this, I think, for many wounds have I treated, often successfully; failures being due to the impossibility of cleansing and, perhaps, evil humours in the twine used for stitching. I never have found any sure way to cauterise the suture, which cannot be set on fire or it burns to nothing and is useless, nor does dousing it with whisky or brandy serve in every case. Thus is it, that the suture sometimes conveys the infection which kills the patient, in my view. Even so, suturing is successful in many cases.

The best method I have discovered consists in boiling the suture in whisky or brandy for some time before use; but the evaporation of the spirit has the unfortunate effect of rendering the chirugeon quite drunk by the time he begins to sew, which makes his hand less steady and his eye less sure.

As well as commander of archers, then, which title I still held, in spite of deserting my post for the sake of mother and lover, I was applied to for medical treatment. At first, I resented the intrusion into my own practice with the bow, but I became so interested in the problems that were presented to me, and received such a powerful satisfaction when I happened to solve them, that I counted myself blessed by this new appointment. Now, as never before, there was always something deep and challenging to exercise my mind, which pleased me greatly and saved me from the boredom and mental disintegration so many other men suffer while travelling with an army at war.

I have lived a very long life, far longer than most, and I do not put it down to carefulness with money, keeping my head down in a fight, or refusing to bandy words with my spouse—which, indeed, I never had properly—or declining liquor, sex or immoderation in eating, all of which I enjoyed to the full when opportunity presented. I was even careless of myself much of the time, running into battle rather than fleeing, which might be thought the way to preserve life. No, I think it was the joy of invention which gave me long life, for, you see, it is such a pure delight to think of some new idea, to conjure it, as if by magic, out of thin air, and then, behold, it is! Capable of application and sometimes of great good in saving lives. What delight then! So many instances of delight make for a happy existence and these for longevity, so at least I theorise. Of course most of it is luck, pure and simple.

But the domain of ideas never ceased to be general for me, though many of mine were medical henceforth.

One night, around the camp-fire, the old argument about the comparative value of archer and armoured knight came up again. Douglas challenged me, half in fun, I think now, to say how many armoured men with swords I could dispatch in an enclosed space before I were myself cut down. I thought for a moment and replied, 'At least three.'

The resulting laughter was boundless, as if I had cracked a great joke, but when I remained unmoved by it all, Bruce insisted I explain myself. 'Providing they are all at one end of the room and I at the other, with a little practice and maybe none at all, I could kill three at once,' I said. Nothing would do but that I should instantly be put to the test by men who wished to wager on the outcome. Randolph would have it impossible and Douglas, who always took the other part, that I could do it. But who would volunteer to be killed, in case I succeeded against most predictions?

The difficulty was resolved by having three men hold up thick planks of wood to protect themselves. There they stood about ten feet away, swords in hand. I loaded three arrows, gripped the ends in the three spaces between the fingers of the right hand, turned the bow horizontal, pulled and loosed in one continuous rapid movement. All three buried themselves in the wooden boards, and even came out at the other side, to the confusion and shrieks of my opponents. Great shouts greeted this feat and those who lost wagers thought themselves well served by the lesson.

I did not tell them I could manage four arrows, for, as anyone knows, five fingers provide four spaces in all. This secret I kept to myself, instinctively realising that it gave me an edge over every other person present, who might have expected to have discovered my limits.

Southward to Galloway we travelled, some of us on horseback, many more on foot. There we took Dumfries Castle and with it, Dungal MacDowall, who had captured Alexander and Thomas de Bruce and handed them over to be executed. Yet, the king did not seem angry with this man, who had even chased Bruce himself about the Carrick Hills soon after his return from hiding in the western sea.

No, with perfectly accurate moral calculation, Bruce decided that MacDowall had simply responded to the loyalties he had recently sworn to the King of England. Since he had not sworn allegiance to Bruce, he could hardly be blamed for acting in his own interest. After giving surety of his good conduct in future, and not taking up arms against us again, he was released, to seek sanctuary across the border, in the country of his preference.

This castle yielded easily enough, as did Rushen, on the Isle of Man, which we took soon after, so I do not dwell on them. Except that we once again captured MacDowall, who had no sooner fled across the border than he rejoined the English. Here again, Bruce was forgiving, recognising that MacDowall could not have been expected to know that we were going to attack the very castle in which he had so recently found a position. Given that Bruce had no reason to love and many to hate MacDowall, his mercifulness a second time was exceptional.

Not all castles were so easy, especially those like Edinburgh and Stirling which were perched high on towering precipices of rock. Against these, our ladders were useless, for they could not be got to the top of the rock, still less, raised up the wall, for lack of a place to stand while lifting the pole. Nor had we the means available to Edward Longshanks, who succeeded in taking Stirling himself with the aid of very remarkable, very heavy, machinery, such as the War Wolf, which tossed enormous boulders at the wall and over it, destroying everything in its path. No Scot understood this, could operate it, or had the materials or skill for making one.

And so, when Sir Edward de Bruce was ordered to lay siege to Stirling by his brother, he made little impression. All efforts to climb the rock were frustrated even before the arrows fell like hail upon the attacking Scots, and, as there seemed to be a ready supply of provisions, starving the garrison would take months. There then took place one of our greatest mistakes, a disaster brought about by the impatience of Edward de Bruce.

Seeing his enemy's discomfort, knowing his character, and because supplies were low in the castle which could not last out very long, Sir Philip de Mowbray, the castle governor, asked to speak to him one day and when they did, offered a truce for a year. If in that time the castle were not relieved by the English, he would agree to yield it up without further conflict.

Sir Edward was delighted, for it would save him the trouble of sitting there all winter in the freezing cold, waiting for a change in his fortune. And so he agreed. The date was June 24th 1313. The date the castle was to be handed over was therefore June 24th 1314, a fateful day.

When the news was brought to the king, he was as angry as I ever saw him. We all realised that an English army must come before then and take the castle, for chivalry demanded it. If they did not come, they would lose an important castle—the one guarding the road to the north—without a bolt fired. A gross dereliction and blight on their honour, that would be. Thus was it, that everyone in the camp that night mourned their freedom, for a pitched battle would have to be fought by a definite day, a year hence. Knowing this, the English could be expected to prepare long in advance and send the most powerful army at their disposal. The prospect was frightening, and not a man did not recognise it, except Sir Edward de Bruce himself, who said to the king when berated for his stupidity, 'Ye'll manage fine, Robert. Have ye not beaten them all up to now?'

Everyone knew Bruce had lost at Methven and that the only battle against English troops had been won by Bruce having choice of the ground, for Loudon was exceptionally favourable to our forces. But Stirling was chosen for us; and that was where the problem resided.

The king and I began to speak of it almost immediately and continued to ruminate over it during the entire year, even visiting the place specially to consider what might be done.

Berwick, too, was an impenetrable fortress, which resisted all our efforts for years, partly because it was supplied from the sea—which made starving the garrison futile—and the number and quality of the defences and defenders. Once, a near success was recorded, but a barking dog woke the guard who easily repelled the invaders. In time, we did manage it, but it took many lives lost and was the last place to fall to us. Young Walter Stewart was our first governor there.

Roxburgh was very different. Sited on a high place between two rivers, the Tweed and the Teviot, every tree around for miles having been cut down, any attackers could be spotted very easily. James Douglas captured it at last. He waited until a fresh supply of wine, ale and foodstuffs had arrived by sea and up the river from England, studiously allowing these to pass unmolested. Then, when many of the the garrison had drunk themselves to sleep, he approached the castle in the gathering gloom, having first disguised his leading men as cattle, skinning some for the hides, as an aid to concealment.

A guard who saw them crossing the Teviot and apparently grazing just below the walls, commented—it seems very funny now—that Douglas, who was known to be in the vicinity, would soon add these to his collection, but no further interest was shown. The ladders were raised, the wall scaled and the castle taken.

Apart from Stirling, which we had agreed not to attack, all that now remained of major fortresses were the castles of Berwick, Bothwell and Edinburgh; Linlithgow having been taken by a local man, William Bunnock, with the aid of a few friends, acting on his own initiative, a deed that moved me to tears by its courage and daring. Bunnock stopped a hay-cart in the entrance, so that the portcullis could not be lowered and out from hiding sprang his followers to stoop under it, around the sides, rush the interior and capture the inhabitants. Simple but effective.

If a few ordinary, untrained Scotsmen could rise up like this, then I, and every other able-bodied member of the nation, had a moral duty to confront the English wherever they appeared among us and turn them out. I began to think that the numbers of lives lost already and the vigorous desires of the ordinary folk for independence, might be no insignificant argument in its favour.

Learning of Douglas's success with Roxburgh made Randolph anxious to emulate the achievement, and he was lucky. He discovered a man living in Edinburgh, named William Francis, who had been brought up in the castle and, as a youth with a lady friend in the town, had found for himself a way down the castle rock, so that, when the gates were locked for the night, he could spirit himself down the wall, where it was lowest; and then, by a devious route, descend to the ground far below and meet his lady at her house. Early in the morning, before dawn, he would return by the same method and escape the disapproval of his parents.

I have often wondered how an austere, knightly fellow, like Randolph came by such intelligence. He was not the kind of man to wassail away nights in the tavern, where he might have heard it. Somehow he sought out Francis, who agreed to lead a force up the rock. As they approached, a guard shouted out: 'I can see you down there,' but, over-confident, he took no action and soon departed. After raising a single small ladder, the ascent was made and the castle soon fell, after some bloodshed.

Apart from Bothwell, which was an impregnable closed stone fortress of great height, that no ladder could penetrate, and Berwick, that left only Stirling, and for the battle to save it we began to prepare in earnest.

CHAPTER 15

Preparations for a Great Battle

AS FAR AS BRUCE WAS CONCERNED it was a case for pikemen. To my mind, something else was needed: archers; for we would face thousands of them and must expect to be shot flat with arrows, before anything else took place.

Of all the things I ever did—all the books I ever wrote and the lives I saved by medicine—my part in the strategy of this battle is by far the most notable achievement. After Edinburgh fell to us, we used the last three months available for recruitment, training and deployment. There were many discussions about what we should do, but gradually the options open to us became clearer, as the fateful day approached.

At Courtrai, in Flanders, in 1302, an army of Flemings armed with pikes had stood off the assaults of the entire French cavalry—a fact those of us who had been at Cambridge were well aware of, for Flemings had afterwards attended the university and the matter had been boasted about across high table and low. In Bruce's mind, then, there had come to rest a kind of theorem that resolute pikemen would see off cavalry. I knew it was not so, that there were other factors, and one night the quaestio came to a head between us.

'There are too many of them,' I said. We were sitting cross-legged in his tent together, with a large sheet of parchment I had drawn out between us, showing the various approaches to Stirling in a picture, like a map of the area. 'They can call up men from every English and Welsh county—from Ireland and Gascony and Ponthieu. They will even come from Savoy, where the king's aunt and uncles live. That is a measure of the difficulty, Sire, he is related to half the nations of Europe, each of which will send a contingent of experts, the best in their land. Why? Because of the glory, and driven by chivalry. They may even win lands and titles. They will all want to play their part. For them it will be an adventure.'

'Then some of them should fight for us,' said Bruce, explosively, and thereafter broke out laughing. 'There is more glory to be had defending the weak.' That was one of his endearing characteristics: he would find something to laugh at even when the danger was fiercest.

'But they have the rights of it, Sire, legally; and Longshanks was a stickler for legality.'

'Are *you* saying I have no right to be the king?' the quaestio was full of menace and I knew it irked him deeply.

'No, Sire. You took this realm by force of arms with the consent and help of its people, when the rightful king had been deposed and the overlord was doing great harm to us all. In such cases, legality counts for nothing. A mistake was made. In swearing homage to a foreign king and giving up our castles. A grievous error, in which your own grandfather played his part because he expected to gain a kingdom by it, and could not unless he agreed to be Edward's vassal, which he was already for the sake of his English lands. All that is over and done with.'

He eyed me sternly, grimly, as if my views were unwelcome, but then his expression softened and he said, 'There is no malice in you, Bann, I see that. You are just a fellow who cannot tell a lie, who must state boldly what a lot of other men could never say for fear of the consequences.' He poured out goblets of wine and added, 'At least I always get the truth from you and that is invaluable. It hurts, of course, but it is the only way to manage this. Illusion is the road to the grave.'

There was a sadness about him that night, which told me he did not believe in our ultimate victory any more than I did. The map showed the castle with the River Forth winding eastwards to the sea. To the south were the woods of the New Park and, to the west, more woods and fields all the way to Glasgow. The Roman Road from Stirling ran east, straight across the Bannock Burn, all the way to Edinburgh, from which the English must come, for they would assemble at Berwick, as usual, and travel up the coast through Lothian, which was still half English anyway, as it had been for many years.

As he looked at the map, I looked at him and he seemed aged, harsh lines creasing the sunburnt face and, since his brother's news about the pitched battle which must be fought soon, his hair had turned grey in a few months.

He said, 'We must station ourselves across the Roman Road between them and the castle, except for one division which must lie back here, at the church, in case a flying column goes around to the north, for there is another way across the Bannock Burn just here. And we'll dig pits like at Loudon and put down calthrops to spike their cavalry.'

'And then what?' I said.

He looked at me wanly, as if I had just pierced his defences with one of my arrows. 'Then we wait for them to come.'

'How many men will we have, do you think?'

'If Angus Ogg brings his Islesmen? Maybe twelve thousand pikemen.'

'You are dreaming, Sire. Angus Ogg has but two thousand, if that. Randolph has barely a thousand, Douglas and Edward have two thousand each and you, Sire, have another two thousand. That makes nine thousand at the outside. They will have double that. Then there are their archers. They will have at least three, maybe four thousand. With the best will in the world I will not have more than several hundred. I say nothing of cavalry. As you know, that is their greatest strength, while we have hardly any. I would expect them to put at least three to four thousand knights, squires and mounted men-at-arms in the field; and they will all be fully armoured, unlike any of us. Even the horses will be armoured.'

Bruce was startled by these figures, for at all times he projected and promoted an overwhelming confidence. Sometimes, this was dangerous, as now; and it was my unhappy task to reveal this to him. He rose, looked at the walls of the tent, and ushered me outside, 'We will take a bow each and hunt for the pot,' he said.

Not till we were well out of earshot, did the conversation resume. 'Walls have ears, Bann. What you say may be true, but it is no help if it undermines the morale of the army.' He was right, of course. These harsh realities I was forced to confront were not suitable fare for lesser minds, whose courage must be kept hot for the battle to come. Leaving them in ignorance was the best way to manage that.

'What do you intend to do?' I said.

'I do not know for sure. I only know we must be there in as much strength as we can muster. We may be able to halt them for a time, but I expect we will have to march away eventually, if only to save the army.'

'They will pursue us, then, and that will be the end of everything. You know how easy it is for charging cavalry to deal with fleeing footsoldiers.'

'Yes,' he admitted, and seemed to age another full year before my very eyes, as he did so, 'we would have to scatter and hide in woods where they cannot follow. Thank God there are enough of these.'

'Not around Stirling, Sire. It's a flat plain. It would take a day at least to march them into the kind of wild country where concealment and escape might be possible.'

Bruce turned to look at me and his eyes lit up. He said, 'I feel confident somehow, even though it looks impossible. I can't explain it. I know it is against all reason—you are just the man to see that—and yet it is so. We have done so well up to now. Is it all to be lost in a single day outside Stirling?'

But I was not alone in having doubts. That night, by the camp-fire, Douglas and Randolph, Keith, Boyd, Hay and Edward de Bruce, joined us at wine, and the king gave me a look which I knew meant: be careful what you say.

Randolph began it innocently enough. 'How are we going to fight, uncle?' he said.

'In shiltrons, as usual, but each commander will be on foot.'

'How can that work?' replied Randolph. 'Are we not better on a horse, where we can see what is going on?'

'Not if you are shot down by an archer,' said Bruce. 'You are safer on foot. They won't see you so easily. Anyway, the men fight better when we fight among them at their head. A banner held up behind each commander will show where he is going, so that others may follow.'

Hay said, 'How do we get all these men of ours, who are on foot, away afterwards?' And there was a sudden hush, for he had spoken what was in every man's mind.

Bruce said, 'If we depart, we must do so at night so that we cannot be pursued, even by cavalry.' No one said anything for a while, and Bruce saw that heads had drooped at the implication that we could not succeed. For once he was at a loss and I knew he feared to ask my opinion. And yet he did, for courage became him; he was a man who could face anything, and in this case, as so often, his fearless attitude brought good results.

It was then—perhaps because of my acute awareness of the difficulties—that I really began to think deeply about the battle and how to resolve them, as if waking from a sleep. I unrolled the parchment with the map drawn upon it, plunked down some goblets to prevent it rolling up again, and began to ruminate aloud, analysing, as was my habit. 'We agree they must come from Edinburgh. That means they must cross the Bannock Burn. Well, we must meet them on the other side, otherwise there is no point in being there at all. I wonder what will happen?'

And I began to see what must happen, given the ground and the nature of the enemy. 'Their cavalry will be in the van, as usual, they being quicker. So they will rush down upon the pikemen and some horses will fall in the pits and be spiked by the calthrops, but many will pass on to the lines of pikes. The quaestio is: will they hold?'

'They held at Courtrai,' said Bruce. 'We tried it at Loudon and it worked for us there.'

'There were very few cavalry there,' I said, 'and the place was narrow. Here there is a lot of ground for them to manoeuvre.' As no one said anything to contradict me, I continued my analysis and tried to imagine what might happen. 'If we can hold them, they will draw off. They will be unable to draw back for the press of men behind, so they must draw to one side or the other. On their left are the woods of the New Park. Well then, horsemen cannot deploy among trees, as we all know, for they have no room to turn and have to turn continually; and overhead branches are dangerous. It follows that they will move to their right onto the plain, which stretches all the way to the river in the north.'

The silence was awesome, for here was I unravelling the probable course of the very action which we had all been worrying over for months, mostly without requital.

Every head was stooped over the parchment which could be seen in the fire-light.

Keith said, 'And whit if they dae gang in the woods? They micht ootflank us.'

'They can't move fast in the woods,' I said. 'So if they go there, we have them; for we can run in among the trees and knock them down as they come through. But they won't go into the woods. Why would they, when there is so much open ground on their right?'

I moved my finger over the map, showing where the English cavalry must concentrate. And then I noticed an interesting thing. The streams. The Pelstream to the north west and the Bannock Burn to the south east of the plain. These, as I well knew, were deep and muddy obstacles to heavily-armoured percherons. 'These streams are the key!' I announced.

'Why?' said Bruce, smiling at my new-found enthusiasm.

'Because if an army gets between them it may have difficulty getting across them. And look at what lies behind, to the north! The river, and all these pools of water and marshes in front of it. Once jammed into the space between the streams, they will be unable to get out at the back, because of the marshes. It follows that they must come out of the plain.'

But that night, inspiration deserted me. It was not until much later that the full conclusion of my premises became clear. Instead, I contented myself by turning my attention to the English pikemen. 'They will come last of all and so there will be no space for them to occupy in the plain between the streams, for the cavalry would never allow them to go in front of them. These English knights regard themselves as semi-divine beings, far superior to anyone else. And they lust for glory—many of them will have volunteered for that reason alone, without need to serve, or pay for so doing. That means they will want to have first crack at us.'

'Well, where do you think the foot will go?' said Bruce.

'They will stay on the other side of the Bannock Burn, for there is nowhere left to go! They will even go down as far as the river, until the marshes become too obnoxious. They will want water after a march like that, all the way from Edinburgh.'

'All that seems reasonable,' said Douglas, 'I just hope they do as they are told.'

Loud laughter greeted the idea that they might respond to my orders, for I was known to be the quietest commander present, one who rarely saw the point of raising his voice.

Randolph said, 'Maybe they'll just cross the Bannock Burn and carry straight on to Stirling Castle.'

'They must be stopped,' said Bruce. 'Your folk will stand between them and the castle, in case they try and round the flank.'

'I claim that task,' said Edward de Bruce.

'No,' said his brother. 'You lead the left wing. The whole of the left of the road is your responsibility.'

I scribed the names of the divisions, where they would stand, made marks for calthrops and pits, and drew the approaching English cavalry, showing it in a large curved arrowhead which burst against the lines of the Bruces and then moved down right to the north to fill the plain between the burns. 'That's how it will be,' I said, calmly, and some laughed, but less surely now, for as anyone could see, there was no other possibility, if indeed they came, as we knew they must.

'What about their archers?' said Bruce, quietly, once the laughter had died down, a most daring remark, and one he felt able to make only because everything had gone so swimmingly already.

'They will either come right across the front of the cavalry and take up position on our left above the Pelstream, or they will remain on the south side of the Bannock Burn. It hardly matters.'

'How no?' said Boyd, who never understood anything quickly.

'Because they will come in such numbers that they can slaughter us all by themselves, without moving a foot.'

'Oh, come now!' said Bruce. 'They don't have the range to cover the plain. They might be out of it altogether.'

'Many will be able to shoot two hundred and fifty yards, some of them, three hundred, I would guess. That means wherever they are sited, they can demolish that side of our army nearest them.'

In the resulting ominous silence, I began to wonder what the ranges were exactly, and said to Bruce. 'How far is it from the end of the Pelstream to the Bannock Burn?'

'I made it seven hundred and seventy seven paces.' How like Bruce to take the trouble to count out that distance and remember the answer. It showed how eager he was to win: nothing would daunt him and he would do anything to succeed. I, of course, had been so bored by the prospect of marching so far, counting, one by one—a vile tedious process to a mind like mine, used to range far and wide at speed, that I had not taken the trouble. And so I did not know what he did.

I gasped at the mathematical mystery of it: all these improbable sevens! It was a figure that rolled round and round in my brain that night as I tried to sleep, for there was something important there. I could feel it, sense it, in the deep recesses of the part of my mind where mathematics was located; but some time was to elapse before its significance became clear. Waking, I thought of the number; sleeping I dreamed about it; for weeks it tormented me and finally, in a blaze of the most wonderful illumination of insight, I saw what it meant.

Until then, I bustled about my business as did everyone else, full of hope, full of brave confidence, full of ploys whereby I could add some small but significant fragment to the total effort; but inwardly, secretly, silently, shaking in my shoes at the certainty of inglorious defeat and imminent death, not only for myself, but all my friends and relatives and every person of consequence in the land. Their deaths seemed as inevitable as the very battle itself, in spite of the hope and prayers of the entire realm, which had grown to hate the English with a venom and viciousness it was a hardship even to contemplate.

It was indeed a strange time to be alive, faced with such a death. As I went about I would suddenly be stopped in my tracks by the awful prospect, seeing in my mind as if it were actually happening, the press of English pikemen surround me and feel the first prick as the steel went into me; or the high flight of arrows which would rain upon us and penetrate eye, cheek, mouth, breast, leg, arm—it was of no consequence; terrible it would be, wherever they hit, for I remembered the terrible pain and suffering of my own wound.

Mostly my days were spent with archers. These I cosseted and nourished and trained and shouted at and educated in all I thought important, angrily speaking to them as if they were children and working myself up to a fine pitch of temper at their incompetence, and how they would be shot flat by one well-directed volley from the invading force of Welsh and English bowmen. But I did work them all, how I worked them! Every man-jack was required to fire off a thousand arrows a day—as a minimum requirement. Some, I knew would go on firing after the light failed, so eager were they to meet the standards I set. But I went beyond men.

Eleanor's presence gave me the idea of employing other women and, before long, I had collected a motley group of earnest maidens whom I tried my best to teach, in a short time, to learn the greatest military skill of them all. Of course, there were problems. Other commanders objected that women in the ranks would undermine the efficiency of the hardened male characters. When Bruce raised the issue at a meeting, I said, 'We don't have enough archers. What else would you have me do? I have found fifty females with the strength and courage to fight alongside the men. Why would I do without them? Fifty might make all the difference.'

Of course, these differences were minimised as far as possible. I ordered every woman's hair cropped so that they looked like men; and they wore aketons and tunics like the men. I even insisted upon steel helmets for my archers as well as a targe to hold up when the enemy flights of arrows came over. All these my women had too, just like the men, and some, it must be admitted, were better than the men. Bigger and stronger and no less agile or clear-eyed. Using women was a revelation to me, which I am proud of. They were very accurate over a short distance and, in time, could attain the same sort of range as the men, by developing the necessary muscles.

Recruitment was inevitable, for every time a woman observed Eleanor among the archers, she would realise that here was something she might reasonably expect to do herself. In this way, as the army travelled around the country, I collected over a hundred female aspirants, all of whom got the chance to be in my company.

For many weeks around Stirling, the very air sang with the sound of hammer on anvil, as the smiths struggled to manufacture steel hats, breastplates, shoulder plates, pike-tips and arrow-heads. And hardly a bird of any description could be found, every one having been killed for the feathers wherewith to fashion arrows. But none of the trees of the New Park were touched, on the king's orders, for these were essential if the enemy were to be forced to occupy the plain between the streams and the river.

Pits were dug between the Bannock Burn and the point of contact, in a line across the Roman Road, and calthrops laid down. On the hill behind, the shiltrons practised until they moved as one, following the commander's banner, obedient and instant in response. Worst among our troops were the kilted highlanders from beyond the Forth. Many hardly spoke the language, so orders had to be translated into Gaelic by their leaders; and they were unused to the discipline that would be necessary here and which Bruce, grim-faced, was determined to instil.

Once, after several quick movements at his command, a group of three men were seen to be dilatory, every time: casual about taking their places. Bruce held up his hand for everything to stop and approached the men. In a loud carrying voice, he said, 'We are fighting for our lives, you men! And we need your aid! We cannot do without it! I need you to move fast! And together, and as if you are eager to get to grips with the enemy. We—the rest of us—are doing our best for you and your loved ones. Will you do your best for us and ours?'

A hush descended upon the shiltron and every eye turned upon the men who had failed to run at the command into position. And the heads of the three men wilted under the angry glares of the rest. There was no more trouble from that quarter thereafter. Thus, where other leaders might have put the backsliders to the sword as an example— one even, that was well-deserved—Bruce gently shamed them into compliance. The shame was induced by the stares of the men who were willing, active and obedient; and the rebuke was effective for many reasons.

Bruce was doing ten times the work of everyone else. He hardly ever sat down, he fought on foot among them; and where he went, they followed at the run, once they understood the vital necessity of it. Explanations of what he was attempting were frequent, so that every man understood the part he, as an individual, had to play. And all men raised their heads as men should, who face the greatest test of their lives. Bruce was like a beacon to us, a flame we wished to follow, for we knew his earnestness and above all his generosity, even his love of each one of us. If a man would take an accidental wound or suffer a muscle-wrenching fall, Bruce was first to tend him, like a broody hen with a damaged chick. And the men felt blessed by his care of them. It was a kind of miracle. .

I see now, that was where I failed as a commander. I never loved the men enough. Probably, I had too much awareness of my intellectual superiority, and showed it, so that they held me in awe for my skill but not in love. Bruce they loved, most of them. He was the best man, the most complete man and soldier on the field and everyone could see it plainly. But it was his fascinated concern for the troops, every one, that was the basis of his leadership.

I suppose it might not have been utterly genuine; that he knew that, without their regard, he could not hold the kingdom, which he had so recently taken at his own instigation, his own need. So how could he hold the realm when he lacked any divine right—despite stupid men among us, thinking he had such right—without pandering to the people? And yet, had this been so, I think it would have shown through. The truth is that he was a very good man and he really did care for the men. It is easily shown by the fact that he cared for everyone, even his enemies, to whom he was invariably generous. That is the clinching argument. And when some among us hated and detested the English and would have subjected them to every kind of indignity, Bruce would have none of it and would not even sanction it. You see, he was a very fine human being and understood that to remain so, he must ever behave as one.

Of course he could lose his temper. When he did, the earth shook. The offender was reduced to a quivering wreck by his bolts of rebuke. But afterwards, when tempers had cooled, Bruce would go to see the man and take him off on his own and talk gently and make him understand his error, and how he could do better in future and that he, Bruce, knew and expected and hoped and prayed that the man would not let down himself or his country. And the man would feel himself blessed at such personal attention, for all knew how much—what a vast load —his poor shoulders had to bear, and would himself pray thereafter that he would not let down Bruce himself, without that ever being an issue stated by the king.

And so the preparations went on for weeks and some of them were self-destructive, as our cavalry rode south, burning grass, barley, oats, crops of kail and beans, farms and cottages, until the sky was black with smoke. Every movable article was taken and every useful animal driven northwards beyond the limit of our army. Then, at Douglas's suggestion, I was ordered to ride with him to estimate the forces we would soon have to confront. For a day or two, we rode up and down the hills observing the invading army, which had set off from Berwick, having assembled there as expected.

With us, were about seventy men, a necessary protection, in case of scouts or pursuit by young English knights anxious to make a name for themselves; a thing to be feared, given the quality of their horse-flesh.

I was lying on the west side of a ridge, one evening, counting them, when I first became aware that Douglas had grave doubts about the outcome and thought the wisest course would be to scatter our forces and disperse to the far corners of the various wildernesses of the realm, without ever giving battle.

'Except that when we came out of hiding,' I told him, 'every castle would be in English hands again, and the common people would be commanded and abused again and degraded by the English left in control.' How I had changed! Once, I desired nothing except to be part of the great commonwealth of England, with all its advantages of good law, efficient administration, good living and high scholarship, that above all, I admit, for that was my natural bent.

When I said as much to Douglas, he replied, 'What else can we do, Bann? You know perfectly well that our pikemen are no match for their cavalry. Look at the number of them! How many are there?'

'I have seen three thousand, so far,' I said.

'Well how can our six thousand pikemen stand against three thousand heavily armoured cavalry?'

And there was nothing I could say in answer, for the thing was impossible. It was obvious that one knight on horseback would easily trample down two men in his path; and all the more easily, if the men were bunched together in a shiltron. A great gloom descended upon us both and not another word was said on the subject, as we returned to the others, or when we sat round the camp-fire that night, or even during the whole of the next day, as we rode along the far western flank of the advancing army, myself stopping from time to time to make notes on parchment, about the details of what I had seen.

Once or twice, I saw Douglas look grimly at the multitude of brightly coloured banners, surcoats of diverse patterns, coats of mail and shining breastplates and then turn to me, directing an agonised glance, as if to beseech me to remove his dilemma by answering his unanswerable quaestio; but I said nothing; there was nothing useful I could say; and I felt strangely guilty, as if I had failed him and everyone else of the command by my failure of insight, the one thing of mine I prized above every other.

This I understood far better than they ever would. To them it was magic, to a few, a black art, which might in other circumstances bring about my death for witchcraft; but I knew it clearly for what it was: a power of perception, depending upon vast numbers of similar problems solved in the past, and great acres of parchment knowledge gleaned from libraries, and the self-invented concepts of the nature of mind itself, which made the use of my own all the more easy. And logic. And the ruthless application of all in the cause of truth.

Back at Stirling, a day or so later, Bruce soon became aware of Douglas's depression—unaltered by the arrival of Angus Ogg with his Islesmen, during our expedition—and sensed it among the riders who had accompanied us, even though they were ordered to say nothing of what they had seen. That evening, after supper, Bruce took five or six of us off up the Coxet hill some way, out of earshot of everyone, and began a private discussion, when I must reveal the true extent of the force about to meet us here in a few days.

We sat together around Bruce who alone stood up to see better, on the topmost slope overlooking the plain which stretched all the way to the black waters of the River Forth, which wound in snake-like coils across the north edge towards the widening estuary, heading for the eastern sea.

I said, 'The baggage train is twenty miles long and they are supplied also by a fleet of ships which sail off-shore and land stores on demand. I counted 400 archers under the Earl of Pembroke, mainly Welsh, then; and English archers under several banners, small groups from most of the north and midland counties of England. 270 from Cheshire, 390 from Staffordshire and 320 from Derbyshire; 270 from Lincoln, 180 from Rutland, 246 from Sherwood, 184 from Norfolk, 350 from Lancaster, 500 from Yorkshire and 200 each from Cumberland and Northumberland. That makes around 3,700 archers in all; and there may be more on the way, for I think more may yet appear late and there is time to catch up, especially if they come on horseback, and the army wastes time in Edinburgh.

'The foot soldiers cannot catch up. So the number I counted is the limit we shall face. 17,000 in all. The cavalry are more difficult to count as they ride in no set order. I saw three thousand English cavalry composed of knights, squires and men-at-arms, most well-armoured and on fully armoured percherons. But there are at least three hundred other heavy cavalry from other nations: some from Ireland, with Sir Richard de Burgh, earl of Ulster—your father in law, Sire—many from

France, some from Austria, others from Alsace, Italy, Switzerland, Prussia and even Spain, where Edward has relatives. The Swizers look like mercenaries, hired for the purpose; many others are doubtless volunteers, there for the glory. I would expect more cavalry to be on the way and that they will catch up with the foot, for whom the army must wait.'

'That makes 24,000 all told, then,' said Douglas, mournfully. 'What are we going to do, Sire?'

Bruce looked grim, and sat down on the grass as if further movement was a waste of effort in the face of such enormous odds. Without waiting for another word, I pulled myself a stem of grass and began twirling it between thumb and forefinger, looking out across the sloping plain to the river whose giant curves twisted and turned in the distance. To the west, half hidden in a summer haze, lay the castle, impregnable as ever on its rocky hilltop, and about to fall into English hands by the appointed day, only three days hence. 'What do you advise?' said Bruce.

One by one we spoke. Randolph was for a token battle, for the sake of chivalry and dispersal at nightfall. 'Where to?' said Bruce.

'Anywhere but east and south, where the English are. To Ross and Argyll and Orkney and the Hebrides even. Maybe to Ireland or France.'

'Give up the kingdom, then?' said Bruce.

'No. When they leave, we return,' answered Randolph.

Bruce said, 'But they will leave men behind, to tax the people and man the castles and to govern. What about them?'

I sensed Randolph knew this all along; he just had no ideas. He said: 'We go for them when the army leaves and it is possible.'

Boyd was for fighting. No enemy was too great for him; he had not the imagination to see what must transpire when we were faced with odds of three to one.

It was then that Douglas said something useful. 'Sire', he said, 'their cavalry will run down our pikemen. There are nearly 4,000 of them, and each is fully armoured. How can our 9,000 men stand against them? If they run at us, they must succeed! For how can we stop them? They will run at us and knock us all down like skittles.'

The silence was oppressive. There was nothing to say. Our predicament was impossible of resolution. Our pikemen would be mown down like blades of grass under those thundering hooves. It was as clear as one of Euclid's theorems with QED at the end. I lay in the grass, chewing the stem, afraid to look at the others who looked in several directions, each to his own, to avoid seeing another terror-stricken face.

'Bann?' said Bruce at last, the quaestio I had been awaiting, uncertainly, unhappily, but knew to be inevitable.

As I looked out northwards, across the church down in the valley, between the town and the Bannock Burn, beyond the triangular plain in the distance, and across the marshes and pools of water all the way to the river, curling like some black serpent in the background, my eye fell again on the streams: the Pelstream on my left and the Bannock Burn on my right, which defined the triangular plain where the English cavalry must bivouac, joining up at the apex. In the heat of summer, I felt suddenly lazy and my mind drifted off to observe a hawk rising in the clear blue air. How fine and noble it seemed. For the moment, all depressing thoughts of the steel entering my belly departed, and my soul seemed to soar like the bird.

Then I remembered the distance between the streams: 777 paces; and wondered how far that was in cloth yards, and could not think of an answer.

I tried to picture in my mind's eye again what would take place when the English arrived. Immediate contact with our pits and calthrops, and then—those that came on, as many would—with the bristling pikes of our tiny shiltrons, oh so small they would seem, packed tightly as they would be. And then I shut my eyes and prayed, prayed as never before in all my life, prayed that the advancing cavalry would be stopped by our brave pikemen and be driven-off. Down to their right, they would go, towards the river; down between the streams they would go, and pitch their tents for the night, while the rest of the army came up and bivouacked.

I grew tired, suddenly, trying to imagine how it would be, the awfulness of it, the inevitability of defeat, crushing disaster, making it more difficult to concentrate on the matter in hand.

Then this I saw. The cavalry would fill the triangular plain between the streams, this being the best spot, one ideal for cavalry; and I remembered that the archers would come next across the front but be moved on by the knights who would want a clear field between them and us, for they were here for glory and knew themselves invincible. And there was no place for the foot, who would have to bivouac before the Bannock Burn and would gravitate all the way to the river. That was how I saw it, and, for a moment, I contemplated the dispositions as if it were a map in my mind. Then I yawned at the effort and lack of sleep and rose to fetch the parchment, which I found nearby, in a leather bag.

I unrolled it and held it down with stones and then took quill and inkwell from the bag and began to look again at the marks showing where the enemy would be. The others came to me and bent their heads above my work, as I scratched a few finishing touches. I said, finally, 'Well, that is what I foresee. Their cavalry is here and they will occupy that flattish area and it has a frontage of 777 paces, as we know.'

And no one said anything; and I knew that it was still up to me, this analysis. I felt suddenly guilty again, as if I had been expected to perform again and failed again; and nearly wept at the injustice of it. Why me? Why must I be blamed for this, I said to myself? And then I looked down at our army, resting among their cooking fires on that summer day, and knew that a catastrophe must be prevented; and when I turned again to look at the plain, turning my head slowly in the fine Scottish air on that hilltop, with the scent of smoke in my nostrils, it was there! The idea that would win the battle was present in my mind at last! I leaped up and raised my hands towards the heavens for very ecstasy! I had found it!

'What is it?' cried Bruce, also springing up.

'I have it! I have it at last! Look!' I shouted, pointing futilely at the plain below, and then bent over the parchment again and tried to draw with my quill. 'We must attack! We must advance to the line between the streams in a straight line, so that we fill the space!'

Douglas roared, 'Leave our prepared positions? Never!'

'We must!' I insisted, failing to mark the parchment, for there was no ink on the quill. I stuck the quill into the inkwell and tried again without result. It was dry! Dried in the summer sunshine. Just when I most needed it, I had run out of ink! The nearest supply was far away in the camp. I took my dagger and cut my left arm and when the blood flowed I dipped the quill and drew arrows on the parchment where the four shiltrons must go: all of them, to fill the space between the streams! And dipped again and again and coloured the thin red line across the plain which hemmed in the enemy.

When I had finished, Boyd, who had been thunderstruck at the use of my own blood, was all attention but could not understand. 'Attack armourt cavalry wi' men on foot? Yer daft, Bann!'

'They'll jist run ower the tap ae us!' declared Keith.

With every eye upon me, I pronounced the vital insight that won the battle: 'Not if they can't get up speed!'

Boyd snorted and stamped his feet in frustration, Keith stood pulling at his whiskers, puzzling over my meaning, Randolph looked as if he had solidified to the spot and Douglas was suddenly alert, the light of hope shining in his eyes. Bruce's grim, set face, broke into a smile, and he said, 'Go on!'

'We must move forward and pen them into the triangular plain between the burns.'

'And whit then?' said Keith. 'They'll just ride us aw doon, trample us intae the grun!'

'No,' I said. 'We will hold them!'

Douglas stooped over the parchment punching his finger at it. 'You mean get up right close, don't you? Then they havenay the space to get started?'

'Yes, the closer we get to them, the worse it is for them and the better for us.'

'Ah canny see it!' said Boyd. 'We canny jist merch up tae thaim and cry: *Guid day surs, wull ye fuck aff back doon tae Ingland!*'

Everyone fell about laughing, except Boyd, who stood like the rock he was, unmoved by time or tide, still less, the intelligent affairs of men.

I said, 'Imagine that our lines of pikes have got to within twenty yards of their horselines. Then they mount their beasts and then they charge. How fast will they be going when they hit us?'

'Christ, Ah dinnay ken,' said Boyd.

'Hardly oot of a trot,' said Keith.

'Aye, that's it! That's it!' shouted Randolph and Douglas together, and Bruce, looking grim again, but happy, announced in that measured way of his, 'So it is, by the great God! They will maybe knock down some of our front rank, but they won't be able to break through.'

Then it was that the number 777 became vital. I said, 'Premise: one yard is more than one pace. Then the distance between the streams is about 700 yards. That means 700 men standing shoulder to shoulder, a little between each for ease of manoeuvre. We have 9,000 pikemen. That means 13 men deep.' And I laughed for pure joy! It was enough! We had men enough! No charge of knights would be able to break through 13 lines of men, shoulder to shoulder. 'That is it!' I shouted. 'We have them!'

The next half hour was taken up with convincing Boyd and Keith and refining the plan: which shiltrons would move where and how they would be arrayed to meet that first charge, for everything depended on it.

'It turns on how close to them we can get,' said Bruce, with excitement. 'We must be as close as possible. We will eat our porridge before dawn and march into position before they can do anything to prevent us. Then we wait for them to come to us.'

'Aye, but how will we wait,' said Randolph. 'How do we meet the charge?'

Bruce said, 'The front two ranks will kneel down with their pikes up at an angle, the back ends stuck hard into the ground to stop the horse when it comes forward, as we agreed. Ye take yer dagger and cut a hole in the earth for the end. The next two ranks will stand up with their pikes stuck into the ground as well, but their pikes will stick out between the shoulders of the men in front. Then the nine ranks behind will stand with their pikes level, each man's pike between the heads of the men in front and the end of the pike at his chest to take the pressure, when the horse runs in.'

'And after the charge is stopped?' said Randolph.

Douglas said, 'The horses will rear up and our front rank can spear the horse in the belly. When it falls, the knight will fall down and we lift his visor and chap doon wi' a hatchet.'

'Aye,' said Boyd, a grim satisfaction crossing his hairy pockmarked face at last. He fancied the hatchet idea more than any other.

As the general rejoicing cooled, Randolph, wary as ever, said, 'What happens next?' And when we looked at him, he added, 'I mean, once we have stood up to their charge and held them, what then?'

Every eye turned back upon me and I said, 'We must simply stand our ground until they weary of throwing themselves at us.'

'And then?' said Bruce.

'They will want to leave and we will help them to.'

Boyd roared gruffly and slapped me on the back. 'Now yer talkin' Bann. Wull mak' a man o' ye yit!'

'Where will they go?' said Randolph. 'I can't see it.'

'They will try to cross the streams but they will soon be muddy and impassable. Look at them! How deep and muddy they are already. In fact, we would do well to go down there and make them muddier still, by running our horses over the entire area!'

'And if they canny get oot that wey, whit then?' said Keith.

'They will move backwards into the marshes towards the river. And we will help them.'

'Bit how?' said Boyd, scratching his balding head.

'By pushing them in with our pikes!'

The king took control again and ordered every one of us to report that night for one of his celebrated carousals, everything having been decided right royally, adding, 'Say nothing of our tactics to anyone. Just go about knowing we are going to win. That will be enough for now.'

It was then that Douglas threw a lance into the thick of my construction. 'What if they arrive in the morn? They won't need to take up position in the plain. They'll just ride us all doon.'

In the hush that descended, I thought again. 'They can't arrive until the 23rd. They are not all in Edinburgh yet. That means they must travel here from Edinburgh and that will take the cavalry most of the day. So they will arrive in the late afternoon, the foot being some distance behind. If we can hold off their advance guard in the afternoon, they will draw off to the plain as I suggested.'

Bruce said to me, 'Well if they come early and look like fighting all day, piling everything in behind the advance guard, we'll send you down there to tell them to call a halt and bivouac for the night in the nice flat space we have left them.' The explosion of laughter which could be heard, and the smiles of every one of us as we strolled down the hill with happy, gleaming faces, did wonders for the morale of the army, who looked at us with renewed hope themselves, as we walked among them again.

Of course it was not going to be quite as simple as that and meetings in the last few days raised quaestiones of many kinds.

It began with Boyd who demanded archers to accompany Douglas's shiltron, in which he was to fight. Traditionally, Scottish archers fought between the shiltrons, often in front. I was having none of it and Bruce arrived in the nick of time to prevent a fight between the two of us, Boyd having drawn his sword, so angry was he at my stubborn refusal to divide my command.

'Sire,' I said, 'the archers must fight behind the pikemen and they must remain as a single unit, able to direct fire wherever it is needed.' Out came the parchment map and I bent over it explaining that the archers must be free to range along the entire rear of the line of pikes. 'That way, we can move to the left to deal with their archers, who will be on their right, or go to our right flank at the Bannock Burn, to repel their footsoldiers, who may try to outflank us. Sire, if they cross the Bannockburn in numbers, our plans are useless. They must be kept out of it.'

'But, Sire,' said Boyd, 'Wuv aye hud oor airchers at the front! They kin shoot doon thur cavalry afore they git tae us.'

'Then they will be trampled down,' I shouted, 'for there will be nowhere to go out of the way. And what use will a lot of dead archers be then?'

'They kin melt intae the ranks of pikemen,' said Boyd. 'The wey they aye dae.'

'The way we always lost, you mean, fool!' I said. 'As soon as they melt into the ranks of pikes, these will be broken down by the cavalry! That's what this is all about. Standing fast against the cavalry. Penning them into that space where they can't manoeuvre. There must be no talk of melting archers in amongst pikemen. The pikemen must present a solid and impenetrable wall.'

Bickering from the others took place for a while, until I asked where the cavalry were to be deployed? Douglas thought behind us, and I agreed. 'They may be needed to ride down their advancing pikemen as they cross the Bannock Burn. If we archers cannot deal with them, our cavalry must ride them down and shove them into the Burn.'

'And if there is no need for that,' said Bruce, 'our cavalry must attack their archers.'

And that was the strategy fully worked out. Our cavalry and archers must prevent them outflanking us. Once this was made clear, Bruce threw back his grey head and laughed and laughed, and when he stopped finally, he said, 'I just wonder if they will be as obliging as Bann thinks.' And, of course, the rest of us joined in the laughter. Predicting the actions of one man was hard enough, but an army? Under the King of England? The entire exercise did seem ridiculous all of a sudden.

As he left us to attend to other things, Bruce turned and smiled at me. 'On pain of death, do you swear that everything will be as you prophesy?'

I laughed and said, 'On pain of death, I swear that it will not!'

'Then whit hiv we been speakin' aboot aw this time?' said Boyd, scratching his balding head.

'Speculating,' I said, 'What else can we do?'

'But Bann,' said Randolph, explosively, 'what makes you think the English cavalry will let our pikemen walk right up to within twenty yards of them?'

There was a hush around me and I used it to think. 'I don't know about twenty yards, but if we are up early before these lazy English knights have breakfasted, they will definitely let us get close. Why? Because they think they have a divine right to win and they think they will knock us all down flat themselves, without benefit of archers or pikes. Most of all, because they will be surprised, because no one ever did this before. That's why they will let it happen! The few that can think will just believe we are saving them the trouble of riding after us. That's how arrogant they are. Believe me, I know them!'

Next day, they came.

CHAPTER 16

Bannockburn, 1314

I WAS IN THE KING'S TENT sharing his breakfast of porridge and a haunch of fine cow meat, when the sound of hooves approaching rent the air. Moments later, a young knight came tumbling in amongst us—Douglas, Randolph, Edward de Bruce and me—falling in a heap at the feet of the king, which caused Edward to exclaim: 'Kick this bugger out!' But Bruce would have none of such ungenerousness on such a day.

'No,' quoth he, 'he is young and the energy of youth is in his step. We have need of it and should not complain of his shortcomings if he is over zealous,' and we all laughed.

The youth got to his feet, dusted himself down, took off his helm, and declared, 'Sire, they are here.'

'Who are here?' said Bruce.

'Sire, the English!' shouted the youth.

'I'm not deaf, Sir,' said Bruce. 'Now would you say what you have to say and then begone about your business. I have my breakfast to eat.'

'Sire! There are thousands of them!'

Bruce laid down knife and meat and replied, 'We expect that.'

'But . . . but . . . but Sire, what are we gonny do?'

Bruce smiled and said, 'I am going to finish my breakfast.'

The youth was flummoxed, like a calf springing every which way, not knowing its direction. 'But . . . but . . . Sire, there's so many of them!'

'All the more for you and me, then, eh, boy?'

The youth's mouth dropped open and he said, with evident surprise, 'That's a good thing, isn't it, Sire? I mean it would never do if there wasnay enough tae go roon, would it?'

Bruce laughed. 'No indeed, son. There's plenty for you and plenty for me and my friends here. So we are well content.'

The boy sighed with relief. 'Oh that's good, Sire. I'm richt gled yer pleased. I thocht ye should know.' When Bruce invited him to leave, he did so with obvious relief at having given his news and been well-received.

The youth was Sir William Vieuxpoint. He was killed the next day.

By midday, the advancing army could be heard in the distance, the sound carrying across the rolling hills to the east. Then the first riders came into view, silver helmets gleaming with feathered plumes of white and red and blue and green; surplices, of many colours and patterns, many with the red cross on the white ground but regiments of others, and mail which jinked merrily and shone in the sunshine; and tall banners rippling, full of design and colour and richness and artistic splendour.

'By God, are they not a pretty sight!' said Edward de Bruce, scornfully, as if they were but children dressed for a fancy dress party. And some of our men laughed; but the king's brother had the daring of the strong and mindless, who had never known defeat. Many of us knew better and our imaginations could easily envisage what close contact would mean with such an astronomical number of weapons.

It was then that Bruce mounted a pony and rode off to take a better look at how our own lines appeared, though in truth, there was not much to alter. Edward de Bruce's men were lined up in a rectangle, roughly 200 long by ten deep, on the north side of the Roman Road. Next to these, were the lines of Robert Bruce's shiltron stretched out southwards in the other direction. In this way, we had blocked off the approach to the castle. However, down in the valley was another route with a ford over the Bannock Burn to make it practicable. Randolph's shiltron, which was stationed some way behind and north of us near the church, was to prevent a flying column outflanking us and raising the siege.

The king was hardly ready for battle yet. He wore no armour and carried the short axe he liked, but he did have the gold circlet to distinguish him. As he lifted himself up in the stirrups to see us all better, there was the sound of hoofbeats.

At first, no one paid any attention. The men of the two shiltrons had been standing at the ready for over an hour, and every man had begun to appreciate just what an enormous task faced us, for over a distant hilltop appeared soldiers by the thousand, the noise of their marching feet carrying all the way to us in the still summer air. The entire hill from end to end was carpeted with tiny figures, each with his coloured surcoat, white mainly, with a red cross on the breast, crossbows and pikes held above shoulders, longbows slung on the back. And they rippled onwards, relentlessly, like a deadly tide, covering all the land ahead of us, and our own men were gradually unmanned by it.

Here was the difficult time, the waiting, when the full force of the enemy became manifest in all its dangerous presence. This was no paper game, no talk around a camp-fire about English might, this was the real thing, the very thing itself. Down hill, came the cavalry banners of the knights bannerets in the van and pennants of lesser knights behind them. And then every eye sought out the source of the hoofbeats, for they seemed closer and we saw that one of the knights from the van had detached himself and was heading on a huge, fully-armoured percheron, at full speed towards the figure of Bruce, and was not a hundred and fifty yards away.

Men shouted to him to return to the safety of his own lines and he turned in the saddle to view the danger, and saw the knight, the visor down, the white plume spreading back in the breeze like a bird; ahead of him, the drooping lance, as he took aim at our Bruce, the best loved man in the army. And everyone gasped for very amazement and sorrow, as the king turned his pony and rode out to meet the advancing knight. And he went carefully, in no particular hurry; haste was all on the part of the challenger.

Silence descended upon us like a cloak, as men stood motionless, afraid to breathe, lest it affect the outcome by distracting our man.

And then, in a great rhythm of rushing, sweating, clattering horsemanship, the Englishman was there, right there, at Bruce, and the lance was pointing at his unprotected chest and it was as if no one would breathe again, and some men averted their eyes at the utter certainty of catastrophe. And then an astonishing event took place.

Bruce swung the little pony to one side and the lance swept past him, he raised himself to the limit of his stirrups and, as the percheron flew by, Bruce's axe smashed down upon the white-plumed helmet of the stooped figure and they parted, Bruce circling around to return to us. But the English knight had fallen and was being dragged along the grass by his stirrup towards our lines.

Around me, amid the collective sigh of amazement, the earth seemed to quiver, as every man shook in his shoes at the escape and then, the sight of the fallen knight, degraded, with the axehead still sticking out of the helm, brought understanding, and in one tumultuous shout of triumph we broadcast our delight. It was a miracle, like the parting of the Red Sea! Waves of cheering surged within our ranks, which waved like stalks of barley in a divine wind, resounding everywhere about us.

The advancing English cavalry halted and seemed cast down by the event, as if it were an omen. Then they came on, spurred on by bannerets, and they hit the calthrops and some went down, and hooves landed in half-yard deep pits, each with a sharp stake in the centre, lightly covered with reeds, and more went down, and horses tried to rise and could not, and some stumbled crookedly back the way they had come, except that they were then ridden down by others coming from behind. But there were contacts, and soon our men were in action, fending off mounted knights, squires and men-at-arms, with their pikes, pricking horses in the belly as they ploughed into our massed ranks and reared above us, and when the horsemen fell, our wee Scotsmen ran out, lifted up the visor and smashed down with the little hatchet every man carried.

It went on for some time and Bruce, who had returned to his tent, watched with me and a few other commanders. 'Sire, thet wis a bliddy daft thing tae dae,' said Gloag angrily, fussing over his chick. 'Ye coulda goat kilt. Ye hivny even airmour nor lance.'

'It was braw, Sire,' said Keith. 'The baist thing ye coulda done!'

'Well, I lost my best axe,' said Bruce, ruefully. 'I could have done with that too.' The axe did not remain lost for long. The iron head was removed from the skull of the knight, Sir Humphrey de Bohun, before his corpse was sent back with a slap on the back of his horse, and was soon fitted to a new wooden shaft.

Both shiltrons were in action by this time and, behind them, I ordered our archers to fire carefully into the advancing reinforcements, at a range of 150 yards from us. Then flight after flight went off and the sound of the volleys made Englishmen look skywards and raise shields to stop the falling bolts which cut through everything, shields, armour, helmets and all—for nothing could stop a needle-pointed steel tipped yard long arrow over that range—if it was well directed. But after several flights, I called a halt, for I wished to conserve arrows, always a scarce commodity when you most need them, even though I had myself bullied and plagued every fletcher in the area for weeks to make more and more.

Fighting was greatest around Edward Bruce's shiltron where the advancing cavalry were naturally driven by the slope and the pressure ahead, but they stood firm.

Then, nearby, I heard Bruce say to Randolph, 'Look yonder! That's Clifford and Beaumont running for the castle across the ford. A chaplet's fallen from your brow!'

Randolph ran, mounted and rode off to command his shiltron; to prevent the seige being raised before we had properly come to grips with the enemy.

By great good fortune, Clifford saw Randolph approach and elected to wait for his command to make their defence—the one act of chivalry and the first tactical mistake the English made all day. The shiltron were allowed to block the path and the knights began to charge at them, and for a while the massed pikemen from Moray could not be seen for the press of armour and lances surrounding them from all sides. Douglas asked to go to their aid and Bruce refused. 'Everyone must stand his own ground now,' he said.

Silently we watched and it seemed that the battle there was lost, for we could see our lightly armed men being pricked and fall down to be trampled underfoot as horse after horse ploughed in amongst them; and Douglas, in desperation that a defeat here would raise the siege and win the battle, demanded again to be allowed to help. This time the king reluctantly agreed.

So Douglas mounted and left to rejoin his men and they ran off towards the sound of the battle behind us. But the advance slowed; for some reason Douglas would not proceed; and then, across the green hill, came sounds of cheering and the sight of Clifford and Beaumont's cavalry retreating down to the very plain we had planned for; and what had been 800 mounted knights, squires and men-at-arms was now reduced by a third. Behind them, a great mass of fallen horses obscured Randolph's shiltron where Englishmen were speared or captured for ransom.

Bruce smiled and said, 'Douglas held back because he could see he was not needed. He left all the glory to Randolph.'

Cavalry continued to attack the Bruce shiltrons and archers began to send down volleys of arrows upon our men there, but they must have feared to kill their own knights in contact, for that quickly stopped. Eventually, after a bruising struggle of an hour or two, they drew off to lick their wounds and consider the issue more carefully. Just as I foresaw, they too, headed for the triangular plain, following Clifford and Beaumont like sheep into a fold.

Afterwards, the entire English army gradually assembled, the archers next, followed by the slower pikemen who wore mailed hauberks and wielded heavy pikes above their shoulders. Seeing the difficulty faced by the cavalry, the archers stopped short of the Bannock Burn and marched along the banks down towards the river, followed by the foot soldiers, until by nightfall, the entire area below and to the east was packed with English, Welsh, Irish, many from the continent, and even some Scots, the Balliol clan, mostly.

All night, we watched their camp-fires. Everything I had predicted had come to pass except that the archers had not crossed the plain, they had taken the easier route. During the night, they crossed the plain behind the cavalry and by morning we saw them on a mound just west of the Pelstream, where I expected them all along.

Before then, when it was clear that the English would not fight any more that day, Bruce addressed the men, going from shiltron to shiltron, shaking a hand here and having a word there, before speaking to the whole group, and it was a model of what a man might say at such a time. Certainly, I never heard it done better.

He spoke of the reason for the battle. How King Edward had un-justly taken advantage of the Scottish people when there was a hiatus in the inheritance which he was asked to resolve. And this was true, and I was glad he did not spread the same lies as so many, that Edward was not rightful overlord. Then he spoke of how the period of English domination had been cruel and wicked and unchristian, with many folk being abused or killed, treated as so many slaves of a conquered nation, so that no Scotsman had been able to hold up his head without losing it. And how we had won back the country, castle by castle and now had to fight again, not just for Stirling, but for the very realm itself.

If we lost, he told us, the English would hunt us down and kill us all and kill our children and rape our womenfolk and Scotland would revert to a province of England again, which no self respecting Scot could stomach. Well then, we must fight, and the plan was good and he was confident of victory. But if any man wanted to leave now, he was free to do so. Yes, there were many English out there, but he was staying. 'Who will stay and fight with me?' he asked them, and with one accord, a great shout went up and every man vowed to remain and fight. And die for his country if need be.

I never saw, nor ever hope to see, a more wonderful response to a speech. I wept at it, as many a man around me did. And were we not blessed? Blessed to have such a commander as this, who had single-handed shown every man in both armies the way these things should be done. It makes my blood run strong again in these old veins just to remember how it felt that evening, as Bruce told us we had fought well and could leave without rancour if it was our will. Yet, I think if any man had taken the offer, he would have suffered the hard looks of his fellows for all time to come; and in his soul would have known himself a poor sort of person.

I suppose Bruce knew there was no question of anyone leaving after that. Maybe it was part of his calculation, for he knew men, as few men ever did. The offer made every man see very clearly that he did not wish to leave, that he wanted to stay and fight—even if he died of it. That was the miracle Bruce performed: ordinary men and cowards, which most of us are at times, were transformed in a moment, into the bravest of brave men, who would fight with all their power until they were cut down or the energy was burned out of them by exhaustion.

Every head lifted proudly as its owner counted himself among the blessed, every heart beat a little faster, every sinew tensed as if for combat. We were all of us suddenly ready for anything. Our leader had shown himself to be courageous, almost beyond belief, skilful as few men ever could be, and if he was staying and he was confident— and he was truly! The message shone out of him—then so were all of us.

And some of us would die, we knew that, for Bruce said so and spared us the lies lesser men would have told. But the dependents of those who died would be cared for, we were assured, and any who had committed crimes would be pardoned, for what was at stake was the integrity of the Scottish nation itself and nothing was more important to a Scot and everything could be forgiven anyone who did his best to help.

Every person in my company I inspected, and made sure he had enough arrows for the forthcoming battle. Many, we got back from the enemy, who had fired their share, but some we collected where we had shot them, going out in the dark to the places where our targets had been that afternoon. The English, I knew, carried a couple of dozen each. My folk carried at least twice that number, and some, like me, could hardly walk for the quantity of arrows we wanted to have at the ready. At Bruce's order, a strong guard was placed at the bridge over the Bannock Burn and on our side of the ford, for it was vital to our plan to keep the sheepfold bolted, so that the sheep did not escape before we got at them. Holding those crossing points was going to be a hard task but one I intended to see to myself.

That evening, I was present in Bruce's tent when Gloag appeared out of the darkness to announce that the Dewar of the Maine wished to see him. Into the tent he came, an ancient tall man in rags with a very shaggy white head and beard, carrying a wooden box. 'Ah brocht the relic, Sire.'

'Relic? What relic?' said Bruce.

'St Fillan's thigh bane! De ye no' mind? Ye saw it at Glendochart afore ye wur turned back at Dalrigh bae the MacDougalls.'

This must have been after the battle of Methven, when Bruce and his followers had to flee west. After being stopped at Dalrigh, trying to find a way to the western islands, Bruce had sent the women off to the north in the care of his other brother Nigel, who was captured at Kildrummy and killed at Aberdeen by order of the very king on the other side of the field, then Prince of Wales.

Bruce explained that he had met the Dewar at that time and that his office as Dewar of the Maine was to keep safe the saint's relic and bring it for good luck to battles like the present. While Bruce talked, The Dewar drew himself up to his shambling height and then, the effort of remaining there being evidently difficult, slouched down again.

'A dram for my friend,' said Bruce, to Gloag, realising the man's need. Then, 'So what do I have to do?'

The Dewar took the goblet, flushed it down, smacked his lips and replied, 'Ye could say a prayer ower it, Sire.'

'Right then,' said Bruce, coming over to him. 'Open it up.'

The Dewar seemed to back away, as if that was not what he had in mind, tripped, drunkenly, and the sacred box fell to the earthen floor and sprung open revealing a long grey bone. 'Ma Goad! Ma Goad!' said The Dewar, astonished.

'Whit's wrang wi' ye?' said Gloag.

'It . . . it's here! The bane's here!'

We were mystified. 'But it's supposed to be here,' said Bruce. 'That's why you came. To bring it to me.'

The Dewar's eyes blinked. 'Bit Ah didnay! Ah left it back hame in case they Inglish got holt ae it!'

There was a puzzled silence. And then The Dewar announced, 'It's a meeracle! A meeracle! De ye no' see? Ah left it back hame and it's fun it's wey here aw bae itsel'! It's a guid omen! A guid omen, Sire!'

Without anyone telling him, Gloag poured out a huge dram to The Dewar, who sank it down in one and smacked his lips again. Bruce knelt by the thigh bone and muttered a prayer for victory. Then, hardly able to walk, the shuffling, ragged giant was led out by Gloag, who winked knowingly.

Bruce and I looked at one another and laughed. 'He was too drunk to realise he had taken it,' I said.

'It will do no harm around the camp, tonight,' said Bruce. 'He is right. It is a good omen.'

Eleanor, who had taken unofficial command of the women, who followed her naturally, was strangely subdued that night, in the small tent we shared. I never knew her so loving and so womanly. Tears are in my eyes as I remember how it was. We made love slowly, quietly, early in the morning, with the sounds of men and a few women all around us, for few slept that fateful night. Then, in the light of the candle, we looked at each other, and I can see again, as if it were yesterday, the auburn hair, close-cropped, and the freckled face and the gap in the front teeth into which I put my finger and smiled, and she smiled too, for she knew how I loved that omission, for I remembered, every time, the day when I saved her life; and to save a life such as this was very heaven!

The flesh of her was all lean muscle, curving below my caress with lines more lovely than anything in nature; and there was the pink mark on the white breast where the arrow had entered and been drawn after so much worry and fright and thought and careful work. I fingered the scar, which was not quite round, a strange rough-edged figure it made; but I felt deeply that it was my own and I loved everything about it. After I had bent to kiss it for the hundredth time, she said, 'I love you, Bann, you are the cleverest, finest man I ever knew.'

I smiled and said, 'What about Bruce?'

'He's not as clever as you, and you know it.'

'But he is a finer man, and you know that.'

'A rare man, certainly, but you are my man, you are the man for me.'

I think I wept then, upon her naked outstretched body. Then she said an odd thing, 'Do you hate the English, Bann?' There was a puzzled look about her, one of vulnerability and confusion, as if things must be settled now.

'No,' I said, knowing she had no love for them. 'Most of them are just following orders. How can you hate a man for that? They are ordinary men like me; and some are even good men.'

'Then what are we fighting about? Why are they here in Scotland?'

'They are here because they think they have a right to this place. They think that because, twenty years ago, the great lords of this realm paid homage to King Edward, that made him overlord of Scotland. His son is here to claim the same right.'

'But why did they give the kingdom away?'

'Greed. Each great lord thought to be King of Scots and knew he could not be without Edward's approval. But they were right to ask him to arbitrate, for Edward was used to that very duty and the very best person to decide—or so it seemed at the time.'

'So if they had not agreed that he was feudal overlord and had not given up the castles, there would be no battle tomorrow?'

'No,' I said. 'The King of Scots has been a feudal underling of the King of England for generations and if any King of Scots refuses homage he will be attacked by the English and forced to submit.'

'Except this one.'

'Except this one.'

I suppose we must have slept a little but, before dawn, the camp was astir, as porridge was cooked and any other food consumed, without thought of the future.

Afterwards, I left the tent and went to Bruce's side, where he announced he would take the time to speak to every man again. And when I protested that we must use the darkness before the dawn to take up our positions, he gently silenced me. 'No, Bann, I think not. The English will be in no hurry, so we need not hurry. Our men have had the night to wonder and to wait in fear, and some will have daggers in their bowels before the fight even begins. No, I will rouse up their blood; put the daggers in their hands.'

So once again he took the time and trouble to go round the shiltrons and speak in a loud carrying voice to every man, and once again it worked. After explaining the tactics, which were well received, he told them that of course it was natural to be worried about what was soon to happen, but the English would have seen how futile it is to run their chargers at our pikes. Many a man will have dreamed of dying with a Scots spear in his belly, or a hatchet in his face. And they had no business here. Most were conscripts, called up because each knight and village owed so many men by feudal law. Thus they were not here by choice, as we were. What did it matter to most of those men whether Scotland was an independent nation or not?

Now that was most important, for every man present wanted the freedom of Scotland—for himself and his relatives and descendants—more than his own life. It was a fact, said Bruce, or why were they still here, when they could so easily have left the field and gone home?

In the silence which followed, he eyed us bravely, boldly, with cheeks hard-set into lines of grim determination, and said, 'Those who now wish to leave, may go, and no hard feelings.' And no one moved. The air seemed to stand still, as if the very world waited with baited breath, and I have often recognised since, that if any man had got up to leave, a mass exodus might have ensued. It was a very daring stroke; all the more, for having been done already the previous night.

But no one moved. Then Bruce called out a second time: 'Who will stay and fight with me?' And with one accord, every man was on his feet cheering, shouting, 'Me! Me! . . . Me!' Then the horn blew the call to move and the shiltron, as one man, ran to where everyman knew it was supposed to be, and it was done in silence and when they reached the place, they joined up with Edward de Bruce's which was on the extreme right and Douglas's border men, who were on the left. Beyond, were the men of Randolph's shiltron. All of it in silence, except for shuffling, while the front line was straightened, as they had often practised.

That was Bruce's gift, you see. He gave everyone a choice and men drew courage from making it themselves. But the greatest courage was in giving it to them at all in such a place at such a dangerous time; and the greatest gift of all being so loved and admired that the choice was so easily made. In truth, there was no choice, but it felt as if there were and as if we had gained in stature by making it for ourselves. Men everywhere around stood suddenly taller than they had ever been before and eyed their comrades with eyes of steel and high endeavour and gigantic confidence which we sensed in the deliberate steps we took.

Then the slow advance began; and as soon as the line closed-off the escape from the triangular plain, we who understood the full details of the plan in all its wondrous inevitability, smiled, for the battle was as good as over. And then, a few yards on, old doubt struck: would it be enough? What were my parchment maps and imaginative creations worth now? Did these speculations bear any relation to this harsh reality? A hundred yards from the English horselines, where men still stood around blinking sleep from their eyes and had not yet mounted, many of them, the horn sounded and our front lines knelt down, pikes at the ready. Then we all knelt, as Maurice, Abbot of Inchaffray, in a white surplice, went out in front with another reliquary and led us in prayer and every man made the sign of the cross, myself included, even though I had little faith. For the first time in my life I felt part of the community and I was glad to do as they did.

When the Abbot returned through the ranks, we started up again for a few yards more, and I heard myself pray for more yards yet, but Bruce soon judged the space close enough for our purpose. About sixty yards away, he ordered the front to kneel and the second pair of lines to do likewise, every other line pressing in from behind. There we would stay, there we would take their charge, and there many of us would soon die.

I led my archers to our right flank behind Edward de Bruce's men and stuck my first flight of arrows in the earth at my feet for ease of access, surveying the lines of my command around me, nodding to a man here or a woman there. Eleanor, I could not see, but knew she would be with the women, encouraging and leading them.

I looked to right and left and far ahead. Everywhere the ground was filled with silent English troops, a vast number, each with his lance or bow or sword or pike.

There was a hush in the Scottish lines then, as men prepared themselves. I felt as if I were about to be executed in the next few moments; for how could any of us live, confronted by such a tremendous horde? And for a little, my body trembled with nervousness. I had a sudden desire to evacuate my bowels and yet, somehow, it never happened. Around me were ranks of Scots men and women, and I was lifted up by their presence, so that I stood tall and straight. Who among us could show fear in such a place at such a time? It was unthinkable! I would rather have been struck dead instantly instead!

To the front, waved the bright Bruce banner of the red lion on its field of gold, and it comforted me to see it, standing in the van, so proudly, for Bruce was a beacon—a talisman, even—to us all. I considered the extent of my life and wondered at it, whether it had been of value; and this I saw: that if I were killed that day in that place, I had at least done the right thing. Then, *since I would* be killed there in that place, was it not just as well to fight bravely, with every atom of my being, and cause as much carnage among the enemy as possible? And so, recognising the *certainty* of my own death, I made up my mind to go out in as much style and to as much effect as my poor skills would allow. Since these were my last moments on earth, they would be my very best ever!

From that point on, I ceased to be a trouble to myself; set about my task with cool calculation and, it must be said, a certain amount of cold rage too; for what were these interlopers doing on my turf? By God, I would turf them out!

It began slowly, as if the English had been mesmerised by our initiative. Horses were mounted, aided by squires, who also mounted afterwards, and once the whole division in front was mounted, they gradually set off, as if on the fox hunt they expected, two lines of them only, for the others took more time to start, waiting for space in front in which to move. And by the time they did, the front two lines of cavalry had ploughed deep into our pikes, amid a great roar of spirit from our men and shouts from the horsemen, but our lines, though dented and shoved back upon themselves, held steadfast, and horses were surrounded and reared and were piked in the belly, and the knights fell down, having killed or wounded only a few of our number by trampling or with the lance, and were themselves killed where they lay, by wee Scotsmen who lifted visors and chopped down with hatchets severing chin from nose, cutting through teeth into bone making a gaping, gory hole of what had once been a mouth; blood flowing down the throat to drown him in a few minutes of futile, quivering limbs. The noise was deafening, frightening—of screaming and shouting and horses neighing in terror and the clash and clang of weapons.

Then the next few lines arrived and could not get to ours for the bodies of horses and knights already dead or dying at the front of our fortress of pikes. So they milled about or jumped over the obstacles to get at us and were treated to the same inevitable fate. And so it went on for a time, as horses and men piled up before our front line, and all because no Englishman could bear to think himself a coward or would be seen to hold back, and so the stupid and unavailing attacks continued. There was great shouting and screams as men stabbed each other and died.

The English pikemen came up the sides of the Bannock Burn and some tore off the door of a cottage and used it to help bridge the current. Across they poured and we shot them down as they did so. Others crossed at the ford and we shot them too, and more went behind us, all the way to the bridge itself, and were met with a hail of our arrows.

Arrows began to fly among our pikemen, on our left, as their archers stationed on the mound west of the Pelstream attacked and our men fell, but Englishmen fell too, for footsoldiers had scrambled through the advancing cavalry and attacked our line and even their mounted knights were hit by arrows seeking Scots billets.

Robert Bruce was nowhere to be seen, except for the red and yellow lion banner which still waved proudly in the centre. There was no hope of orders from that quarter; he was where he had to be, in the thick of the fight, at its very apex.

It was then that I divided my command as I always knew in my heart I might have to, though I hated the idea. Leaving five squadrons to deal with attempts to outflank us on our right, I led the rest across the back of the field to within long range of the Pelstream mound, and there laid down as rapid a fire as I ever dreamed, man after man, standing beside me, knowing without my saying, exactly what to do, as we had practised so many times. Ten arrow flights I fired and saw them concentrate in the middle of their archers and for every one of mine were three hundred others. In a few minutes, I had fired off thirty arrows and all my company, the same or similar.

The effect was devastating. Thousands of arrows rained down upon them and the sound of it was like hailstones in a storm of unimaginable violence. When it was over, their archers were finished, spreadeagled on the ground, many of them, with here and there a hand or an arm still moving, but the very earth of that mound was carpeted with dying men, who screamed and twitched and then were still; others behind them preferring to move off towards the Forth, out of range of our withering fire. Around me my own men lay dying in droves, for we had taken our share of arrows, but the destruction was nothing to theirs. We had been firing with better accuracy at long range with concentration. Above all, we had got in first and that was the real key to our success.

Keith set off then, for the danger to our right flank was now ended too, and he led his small division of horsemen down the west side of the Pelstream to chase the archers still left alive into the marshes and on into the great black river itself. It was well done and well timed, for his horsemen wore no armour, nor his horses, and had we not cut down the English archers before they rode, our cavalry must have been shot flat in a single volley from the mound. So Keith had a clear field to run at them and hardly a score did not make the full distance. Once there, they roamed the area, pricking the archers with their lances and swords until the mud became too thick for good progress.

Trumpet calls announced the King of England leaving the field; and with a large troop of riders for protection, the three-lion banner crossed the Pelstream in a flurry of mud and made the other side. Some were not so lucky. The last of the departing group got stuck and one or two collapsed into it, as horses slipped and fell. By this time, Keith's force was far into the marshes and too hot in pursuit of archers to turn and follow.

Towards the castle rode King Edward's party. Among the front line pikemen, pandemonium reigned. Englishmen shouted to their colleagues behind to attack with all their power, but everyone on the field was affected by the retreat of the great King of England. A voice—Bruce's—shouted out above the babble, 'On them, now! They flee!' And every Scot shouted and leaped forward, over the backs of dead and dying horses, and over the bodies of knights and squires and men-at-arms, mounted once, now supine or hemmed in on every side and pressed by an invincible wall of steel pikes which advanced upon them remorselessly. Back and back went the English, a great struggling press of men, unable to manoeuvre, forced further backwards with every passing second.

I thought about a volley of arrows into the midst of the main body and looked around at our supplies. Many still had a dozen or more. I ordered five arrows each to be fired together, increasing the range from 100 yards to 200, directed down into the apex of the triangle and called the pulls. Nothing did we see, for it was too far into that great press of chaos, but the sound came back to us as they hit, slaughtering all in the way.

After that there was not much to do, and I turned to see the rest of my command on the far right and found they had been pressed hard from the bridge and ford by men-at-arms on foot, attempting to out-flank and enfilade our right. I called the company to go to the bridge and the ford to deal with this menace.

As we approached, the fighting intensified, archers shooting at point blank range, as swordsmen in white surplices with the red crosses on the breast came running in with crimson blades, hacking this way and then the other. And when the arrows were gone, it was down with the bow and out with the sword.

In the midst of it, there were shouts from the centre, far down into the plain, now, and, over the burn, the enemy began to leave in great numbers, as the press of Scottish pikes drove them back to the marshes and the Forth; and the inevitability of defeat became clear. On our side of the burn, we were fighting five hundred strong men with barely two hundred archers remaining, most having shot off every arrow in the quiver, and now reduced to sword-play. It was hot work and exhaust-ing and frightening and every moment another of my men would go down with a sword cut or thrust; but the field was changing fast, as Englishmen sped in all directions, some west over the Pelstream, the great majority east to Edinburgh; and, beyond the ever diminishing lines of pikes which had bunched in the apex of the triangular plain, a great horde of Englishmen, mounted and on foot, and weighed down with armour, were being pressed into the swamps and far, far into the mire, all the way to the black river which swirled menacingly behind them.

I picked up a stray arrow, fitted it to the bow of its dead owner, then found another and fitted it too and shouted. 'It's finished, Englishmen! Lay down your arms and your lives will be spared.'

Ahead, two men moved in on me and I shot both simultaneously at close range. I had nothing left to fire and Englishmen were eyeing me, to see what I would do next. I drew the dagger and made as if to fit it to the bow, pretending it was an arrow, and pulled it back half cock. 'Lay down your arms!' I demanded, menacing with the bow and the dagger held as if it were an arrow. Some looked around and saw the departing hordes and the thousands trapped in the swamps in front of the river. 'Lay down your arms and you will be spared!' I shouted.

One looked at another and laid down his sword. Then another

followed suit and in a minute or so, the two hundred men still facing us had let fall their weapons. Around me were fewer than three score Scots, without an arrow between them, clutching swords or daggers or standing with bows unstrung because they had nothing left to fire and only the bow itself to use as a quarter staff.

I ordered the enemy to walk up the slope a bit and then told my men to collect their weapons. When it was over, the Englishmen sat down at my command and my men stood guard over them, while a score of others went in search of loose arrows in the ground and bodies of the men around the ford and the bridge.

It was a worrying time, as we waited, guarding ineffectively so many of the enemy, their own weapons so close to hand. In a little while, my men returned with arrows in plenty and we armed ourselves and were safe.

By now, Englishmen had been driven into the river where many drowned, though many others had already drowned in the burns and the swamps. The east of the Bannock Burn was a confused mass of flee-ing Englishmen, thousand upon thousand of them; and if we had had the arrows, we could have shot them all down in volley after volley. It was not to be. The few arrows collected must be kept to guard the prisoners, for that was the new danger: so many were surrendering that they could not easily be guarded.

On the west side of the Pelstream, the remaining archers were leaving the field behind a blue and white banner with red martlets I recognised as belonging to Aymer de Valence, Earl of Pembroke; Keith's cavalry having scattered among the marshes in pursuit of stragglers and all the way up the river bank towards the bridge across the Forth itself, far to the north west. As we watched over our captives, many Welsh archers headed due west for Stirling castle and were soon out of sight. Others were not so lucky, because not so well led. By dusk, there was a great number of English footsoldiers milling around below the castle walls, but the governor, Sir Philip de Mowbray, would not admit them, saying, as he had done to the King of England not long before, that since the battle was lost, he must now yield up the castle, so any who were admitted would become prisoner.

Accompanied by a large troop of knights, King Edward was long gone, and Sir James Douglas was sent after him, but with only sixty men—all Bruce could spare, for a similar troop was sent east under his brother to chase the Earl of Hereford. That was all that was left of our cavalry, many of whom had sunk in the marsh or been cut down by desperate fleeing men. Before dark, the plain was nearly empty of living beings.

Only the dead remained and the scavengers from the town who had come to pick their belongings. Our prisoners were taken from us into custody to be confined in a great pen below the castle heights, under close guard.

Around me was great euphoria, shouts of delight, and strong men wept tears of pleasure, knelt down and gave thanks to their God. It was a happy time! We looked at one another as if we were ourselves had become gods; and then, being but men, exhausted after so much effort and excitement following so little sleep, we sat down, and some of us promptly fell unconscious; and those who did not, laughed and laughed that on such a day—the greatest day of our lives—these could only sleep.

But the sounds were not only of gladness and snores; there were moans and screams and the small movements in corpses that proclaimed the presence of life.

I rose, called for a tent and, on a trestle table, I began to attend the wounded.

I laboured all the rest of that day, and when darkness fell, by rush-light, doing what I could with the small skills I had learned. Arrow-heads were becoming a speciality and I had understood that the best method was to insert a tube over the fletch of the arrow which could be moved into the wound around the barbs, which the English always used, given our lack of armour, making withdrawal easy, by protecting the tissues from their skewed steel points. For many hours I worked on, mostly on men I did not know. Once I came across the last surviving Anderson. A lance had pierced his chest, leaving a raw seeping wound from which bubbles appeared. His breathing was difficult and the pain very bad. There was nothing much I could do, for cautery would kill him and even spirits poured into so deep a wound were unlikely to help. Anyway, by then there were no spirits, all having been drunk or set on fire in other wounds. Several times I felt giddy but carried on, even with English; until, suddenly, I fell down exhausted and slept where I lay, face down on the earthen floor.

When I awoke in the dawn, it was to find scores of others ready for me to deal with. After mending all those with some hope, the rest were brought and laid on my trestle. The very last of these was covered in blood from the neck up, after a fierce sword wound, and the face was unrecognisable, having been smashed in by blows of the blade which had sheared off eyebrows amd nose. I began to clean the gaping wound, thinking that there must still be life there or they would not have brought such a badly injured man to me. Then I looked elsewhere and found an arrow in the ribs, the shaft having broken off. I stripped the body and found it was a woman, and when my eye took in the left breast, and saw the mark there, I knew for the first time who this was. A great scream came out of me, and I stood for a while motionless, almost senseless with loss.

And I knew I could do nothing to help, for not only was the face smashed to pulp so that eyes, nose and teeth, even, no longer existed, but the lower right chest was deeply skewered, so that the arrow-head protruded from the back. I wept aloud and swore and cursed, and then heard her cry to me, like a stricken animal, in the deep recesses of that broken face, and I knelt beside her and murmured words of comfort, anything that came to mind; how I loved her and admired her and coveted her love of me. And in the midst of it all, I realised that she had left me; and when I did, I lay across her body, protesting loudly at the deadly injustice of it all. And I stood up and cursed God! And swore and became mad with indignation that I had lost the woman I loved and who had only recently come to love me. And for a time, I was like a madman and would talk to no one, eat nothing, and did nothing but sit in silent contemplation of my lost love, inwardly raging and beyond relief.

Sheugle it was who comforted me, now, but I would listen to nothing until Boyd appeared. 'So she's deed, eh? Efter aw? It's a sair fecht! And you that saved her the last time.'

I became aware that he was standing before me and wondered at it, out of my trance of desolation, and I looked up. I never saw him with a look of sympathy before and it was something new. He seemed unsure of himself, for once, and said 'Do ye no' think she's ower fat, the lassie?'

I could not understand him. 'Fat? What do you mean, fat?' I said, angrily, as if he had insulted my beloved.

'Is she no' huvin' a bairn? Mibbe ye could tak' it oot.'

And so she was! And I had never noticed. I rose and charged back into the tent and tore the shift off the body and took a knife and cut and then cut again, deeper and deeper and the blood did not spurt out, but oozed, for she was dead, and there, there, deep inside her, lay the foetus, the small shrivelled up animal! And I cut the chord and tied it off and held up the object and moved it back and forth to see if it had life and a cry, a feeble, pitiful sound, escaped from it and I raised my eyes to heaven and gave thanks to the void.

Bess Morrison soon appeared with a few women and took charge. One of them, who was carrying milk, had just lost her own. So she fed it and clothing was found and it was soon swaddled in a blanket, being nursed.

'Ye see,' said Gloag, triumphantly as ever, prancing into the tent with outstretched forefinger and that delicate chicken-leg way of walking he had, 'there is a God! And he hus jist smilt on you! So ye're no sae cliver efter aw! Ye don't ken everythin'!' I ignored him on this occasion, stood gazing down at the infant sucking on the breast, astonished.

'Here, tak' a slug ae this!' ordered Boyd, handing me a jug, 'ye'll need tae think ae a name.'

'Ye should cry it Bannockburn, efter the battle,' said Gloag, confidently.

'Whit kin a name's that fur a baaby?' said Boyd. 'Whit aboot Robert?'

Gloag looked down at the child and laughed. 'Robert? De ye no' ken it's a lassie?'

'Eleanor, then,' I decided.

Drink I would not, not even if I had just become a father, for the cost was too great. I sat me down on the ground and sobbed and there they left me, for there was nothing they could do about it.

CHAPTER 17

Aftermath

AROUND ME, AS I NOW KNOW, all was jubilation, every Scots man and woman was drunk for days, not on wine or ale or whisky but freedom, the most intoxicating spirit of all, especially after such an awful prospect and hard-won contest.

Archdeacon Barbour was wrong about so many things, you see. He did not understand the battle, not only because he was not present, but because he had not the wit to ask the right questions of those who were. He had no military training and so his efforts to write a soothfast account were in vain. His omits all mention of archers, my archers, and how they saved the right flank, which threatened to cave in and, if it had, all our pikemen would have been taken in the rear and killed easily, for ours did not possess the mailed coats of so many English. And it was my archers who dealt such a stunning blow to the Welsh and English on the Pelstream mound. How else were Keith's cavalry free to travel a full half mile, unprotected by armour—horse or man— and get to grips with them, without being shot flat in the process? One arrow each from that vast number of enemy archers would have killed every one before they got close.

No, Barbour's poem is a travesty of justice. And its effects upon the future of our country, because of this failure to appreciate the advantages of archery over every other military arm, were to last all the years of my life, cause much needless bloodshed and the actual loss of the country too many times to remember.

All Barbour wanted was to beatify the image of Robert Bruce for the sake of his admiring relatives who were nothing much by comparison and too little compared to their English counterparts. And so he built up Bruce and understood nothing of the battle and all the advances we had discovered by 1314, in how to defend ourselves and even win pitched battles, were lost.

John Barbour did not have any idea where the battle was fought— about the significance of the two streams, which made a natural killing ground for cavalry who were sent there inevitably, or the marshes and the river behind, into which they were driven. Nor did he understand the idea of marching unarmoured footsoldiers as close as possible to the English cavalry lines so that they could not get up speed and, therefore, could not break through our unarmoured lines and were engulfed and fell down and killed with hatchets.

Of course his poem is inconsistent: he says 30,000 Scots defeat 100,000 English. What rubbish! Even if you add up the numbers he gives for the shiltrons you could hardly get 5,000 Scots in total.

I do not know what to do about this true account of my own. Honour demands that the truth be told; that the part of the archers be preserved for posterity—that my part in it too, be remembered, this I admit. And why not? These mental events that were so important should be celebrated as a spur to others who follow, when it comes their turn to act in defence of the realm. For it is by intelligence that these things are done best, and the branch of it I call insight. And if no one in the future knows of this, how will the quality be preserved? How else can it be inculcated, held up as a light for others to be guided by?

After Bannockburn, Bruce did recognise the importance of archery, as never before, of course; and laid down ordinances that gowf was to be banned so that archery could become the national sport, but this only lasted a few years and ceased to be insisted upon when he became ill, as he often was during the last ten years of his reign. And because archery was never celebrated as it should have been, it fell into decline along with the other things we had discovered. Scotsmen were ever self-willed and soon reverted to gowf, which they preferred to archery.

Perhaps if Bruce had ennobled me, as Eleanor wanted, I might have been able to keep these things alive and add to them—found a university in Scotland to encourage all these things of the mind I value so much, as well as the military ones which matter for the defence of the realm and are dependent upon them. But Bruce was not generous with land or titles and he despised peasants like myself. So only Randolph and Douglas received the laurels and the power which comes from controlling so much territory. Anyway, what use were lands and titles to me? My interests were in scholarship, my territory the scriptorium not the battle-field. I never fought again nor had to fight; and spent my days deep in books, and the only tasks I carried out were medical ones, for of course my skill in materia medica improved with study and experience.

For the sake of my father and mother, I agreed to accept the lands at Ardmaleish on Bute, which we had farmed as villeins for the current lords, whoever they were at the time, the Stewarts, latterly. Now they were to be our own in perpetuity. I suppose I could have asked for more, but, as you can see, it was not my style, not my way. I might take money for copying a manuscript or even saving a life, for these were my trade, as it were, the means whereby I lived—though, God knows, I have been slow to accept coin for medicine, when the man whose life I saved is so defenceless. But take money from a friend? Or titles or honours or lands for my part in the defence of the realm? I was not a mercenary, but a volunteer. I did what I could not avoid doing.

Now that I am so poor, and old and defenceless, for my life is at the whim of careless kings and their lackeys, like Archdeacon Barbour, who have forgotten or chosen to forget my own important role, I expect that more money for food and comforts would be appreciated, but I do not regret the lack of honours. What would I have done with a title and lands to administer and defend? A confounded bore these would have been, taking me away from the library and the studies which have absorbed me since. Only clever bookish men will understand the sense of this position; none of the common sort with the usual love of fame and lucre ever will.

The only value of fame is that, by it, one may do much good. Apart from this, it is a hateful thing, for one is recognised everywhere and beset by fools who would climb upon the back of it and, by their very contiguity, not only taint the reputation, but hinder the real development still to take place and the efforts necessary to make it so.

I do not know if this will ever be read, I only know it cannot be read now, for if it is, because it presents a less praiseworthy picture of Robert Bruce, it would be destroyed and me, its poor author, with it; for I am so old a puff of wind would blow me over. Barbour's fault is in exalting Bruce without explaining either the battle or his contribution, which was phenomenal, critical. But he was not God, he was not a master of the mind. Others did that for him. And if he had had the kind of mind that could do it, he would not have been the leader he was. For the mind only functions on a constant diet of truth, while the leader must be able to tell lies to preserve the morale of the men and do many other foul things no intellectual, with the appropriate integrity, could stomach.

I do not fear death as much as most, for I see it as a beginning of nothingness rather than a journey into hell or heaven. And yet I do enjoy to be, to think, and the pleasure of the fruits of thought. So I will keep my old bones in being until they give out finally, if I can. Then I shall tell my servant Sheugle, who was a mason before he grew too old for the rigours of that life, to find some safe place where my manuscript with its unwelcome intelligence can be deposited for a later age; when, perhaps, it will be possible for men to face the truth about themselves and their ancestors bravely, as good men should, without fear or favour and prevarication. Only by attending to the truth, in the cold light of day, can men improve upon themselves. Convenient lies, confused thoughts and inconsistency of mind only promote disaster. Lucidity and light are everything men should aspire to, in telling their story.

Another thing I see is that Bruce and his nobles had no idea of the great role I played that day. How could they? When they were at the front, in the thick of the battle, when all my work was at the rear, one side and then the other; and so few of my command survived to make a fuss about it. So I do not blame Bruce for his faint praise of my conduct. Anyway, I am better off without it.

After the battle? There was much clearing up to do, bodies to bury, weapons and booty to collect, prisoners to guard for ransom and a great deal of celebration which took a lot of recovering from; but did not trouble me.

A few hours after the child had been found, I was wandering off by myself in a state between exhaustion and misery, when, down by the Bannock Burn, in a hollow, out of sight, I came across a man in congress with a woman. He was kneeling and held her in his arms, thrusting into her, calling out as he did so; an act that was being repeated elsewhere, I suppose, around the place, now that danger was at an end. Countless children must have been sired that day of all days.

Resolving to keep out of the way, I crossed over by the bridge and strolled off eastward and then, hearing a shout, I turned and looked back.

'John!' I heard. Who would call me by that name? None but my father. And so I went back and made my way down to them. 'Can ye help her, John?' he said, through tears. 'You're clever wi' medicine they say. So wull ye fucken help her!'

The voice was anguished, fearful. I had never heard my father swear before and was shocked by it. Time had altered him, aged him, coarsened him even, I could see. He had been knocked about a bit, like many of us, collecting bruises and scars; and bore a respectable amount of blood on his clothing, his own or someone else's. Otherwise he seemed well enough.

The woman's eyes were open but unmoving and I soon knew that she was quite dead and had been dead for some time. I stooped and closed them. 'There is nothing I can do,' I said.

He wept and buried his face in her breast, crying and screaming to God. As I walked off, I saw that she had a hole in the back of her head as if it had been sheered off with a sword, and the back of her was awash in her blood. My father was unaware of it, apparently; had blocked it out of his mind in some way.

I remember nothing much else for days. I know not why. Maybe it was being too much in the way of horrors, in the battle, in the tent, where I fruitlessly tried to mend the wounded, and then watching Eleanor, my love, dying in such awful, such piteous circumstances; mutilating the very body I had loved so often and so much, for the sake of the child; and then seeing my father like that with his woman, shagging her when she was dead. The betrayal of my mother was nauseous; and yet my mind knew that it was nothing my mother had not done herself, even, that she would have understood. It was something stronger than the mind; a hot revulsion of the spirit.

My latest memory of that time is of wandering among piles of dead men and horses, on which crows feasted, and tinkers picked about for clothing and weapons—that too was nauseous, inhuman, and yet all too human. I saw the Cressinghams, father and son, these two who had once fought over Eleanor, lying side by side, as if they had made up their differences after her escape. Sir Hubert I recognised from his colours, the face having been smashed in with a hatchet, like so many fine English knights. Richard lay with his blue eyes gazing upwards at the sky above, cloudless in the heat of summer. Two arrows pierced him, one in the neck, the other in the ribs, the fletches close in to the body, which must have been impaled on the hard ground beneath. And though they had strutted their stuff over my island folk and my family, I had no feeling for them but utmost sorrow. I felt as if the shafts were my own; and certainly they were, at least in part, for I had given the order which fired them. There was some deep mystery here, in the deaths of these men, whom I had once sought to impress and called my friends. It made no sense whatever, and the lack of any, I suppose, took me into some inner part of myself, where I was for a time content to meditate in silence.

What I next remember begins from waking up one morning in a cell at Cambuskenneth, the abbey on the far side of the Forth. They told me I had been picked up and taken there, wandering the field, exhausted, like a man half dead with horror; and that I had slept for two days. But I was not myself for a long time. The abbey did not help my recovery, for it was littered with corpses. The young Duke of Atholl, terrified by the numbers of approaching English, had turned traitor and attacked the small Scots force quartered there, butchering them to a man. The stench of so much flesh rotting in the sunshine hung everywhere for many days.

Once, Bruce came to tell me what had been arranged, but I merely listened and said little, hardly comprehending, too lacking in motive even to greet him or respond.

The child had been taken by my father to Bute, along with the other at St Andrews and there they would be brought up by him and my mother, for now, at least, until I came to my senses. Though the lands at Ardmaleish were gifted to us for our part in the battle, I had no wish to go there, so long as my father was there. I suppose it is this knowledge that all the way through this narrative has kept me from mention of his name.

Him I thought a traitor to my mother and me, even if, for so long, it had been me who had been the traitor, not only to him, but to my country. And so I chose to spend the next several years in monastic surroundings and gradually recovered from the horrors. I immersed myself in books and writings of my own and I helped with the bees and the fishings and the garden, and grew to love the peace and the solitude, though I came no nearer to God by it.

And so I missed the adventure in Ireland, when the Bruces led an army around it, Edward de Bruce having been crowned High King of Ireland, at the invitation of some Irish lords, who wished to profit from our experience and free themselves from English dominion; and I am glad I did. For the rain fell that year as never before, the crops were ruined and the Scottish army was defeated by disease, starvation and the unreliability of those they went to help. Once, briefly, they were only a few miles from Dublin and could have walked in and taken it. For some reason they did not and the effect was disastrous, for it allowed the English there to regroup and collect another army of mainly Irish, and attack our force.

When I heard that Sir Edward de Bruce had been killed it was no surprise to any who knew him. He had divided his army and led half against odds of twenty to one, which, even for a Scot, in those days, was too much.

The next ten years were peaceful enough on the whole, except for the odd foray by the English across our border when everything had to be burnt again and our army retreated to avoid another pitched battle, and by us in return. Bruce was old by then, a balding, white-headed fellow without his front teeth, which he had got knocked out in Ireland. Much of his later years were spent trying to secure a treaty of independent sovereignty with the English and he did in the end succeed in this, but it was fruitless, as I knew all along it would be.

What really aged Bruce were two things. The conspiracy in 1320, when the remains of the Balliol party tried to usurp the throne by murdering him, which, given all he had achieved for Scotland, was as poor a reward as could be imagined. These five years were glorious, you see. There never had been such a period of peace and it was caused by the success at Bannockburn and the confidence it gave us. For once, Scotland was rich on the captured baggage of the English and numerous ransoms for their great men. In that brief period, no English force, be it ever so large in numbers or arms, felt safe against us. And so, that men who had sworn allegiance to him should now conspire against him, was deeply hurtful to Robert Bruce.

Why did they do it? His illness, I expect, and their own ambition. They were stupid people and they misunderstood their situation. If they had succeeded, no good would have come of it. Scotland would have risen up like one man against them and struck them down, for, to almost every other Scots person, Bruce was revered as if he were a god. They were Balliol men, of course, there was that too.

The other ageing thing was this illness, which returned more and more often, something like the plague, which years ago, 1350 or thereabouts, swept through the land like a wind. His skin seemed to burn up and discolour and he would grow weak as a kitten for weeks on end. Then he would recover for a time and then it would all happen as before. Leprosy, some thought it; but I never did. I do not know what caused it, whether it had a cause, even. Bruce, I observed closely at this time for a while, as I had been called particularly to help, my medical skill being better regarded than it deserved. But I could not fathom either what caused his lapses or his temporary recoveries. Maybe it was his diet. He was not a man to eat vegetables or fish, unless there was nothing else. It was his only peculiarity, caused by pride, I expect; and in his later years he had no need of such, for meat was plentiful.

His last years were spent mainly at the house in the country he built by the river at Cardross near Dumbarton, where he interested himself in ship design, for he saw the importance of swift movement in force by sea, with a nation of islands so widely scattered as ours. It was a fine house, one of the first to have glass windows installed here. When he died, it was as if the nation he had fashioned died with him. He had ordered his heart cut out and taken to the Holy Land, for he had long wanted to take part in a crusade, but Douglas, who was entrusted with it, stopped at Granada in southern Spain, and finding a good battle of Christians against the Moors could not resist the challenge. The Moors feigned retreat and Douglas with a few others set off in hot pursuit. But the infidels turned their horses, and, outnumbering them, soon killed the Scottish troop. The heart was brought back in its casket and buried at Melrose, the body having already been interred at Dunfermline.

I saw him a few times, in those last years, for I was eventually called to the court and sent on an embassy to Avignon, where the new Pope had taken up residence, to argue the case for Scottish Independence with the papacy. The English hotly contested this, of course, and used bribes of money and favours to secure their advantage.

Yet, in the end, we prevailed; and I even had a hand in that too. A letter was written explaining the part Bruce had played in releasing Scotland from the dominion of the English and how we Scotsmen would never submit to English rule so long as there were a hundred of us left alive—even if Bruce himself should demand it. Then we would expel him! That was the clinching point. Independence came before everything.

Of course, I never ever believed it possible or long lasting, not even then, when we had won it by force of arms with Robert Bruce to lead us, but I applied my mind to that task with others and thought up some of the ideas.

It was all for nothing.

The excommunication was lifted and independence was achieved, of course, by Bruce, shortly before he died; and he paid handsomely for it: £20,000. But there, you see, was the deficiency in him: he could not foresee what I did: that it could not last beyond his own life. His heir, young David, was a child of five and Randolph, who was regent, was too old and lacked Bruce's charisma and common touch.

After he died, another blow fell upon me. Bruce left pensions to his six bastards; and one of them was to my son. I knew then that he had had Eleanor at St Andrews. I should have guessed at the time but had been too much steeped in books to pay attention. Yet she had not concealed it from me much. In my heart, I knew she preferred Bruce to me; and who can blame her? He was far handsomer, stronger, far more noble and better and with the power of a king. I do not blame her; but am grateful for the time when it was me she loved, in the year just before the battle.

Because of my father, I never did return to Ardmaleish until he died there, which happened when the island was invaded again by the English; and I went only as a duty, to tidy up his affairs. I found that my mother had become a very old woman and my daughter— Eleanor's daughter—had died. A simple thing, evidently. She had been playing at the beach, fallen on some rocks and grazed her legs. These had become septic and none of my mother's poultices would draw the poison. The leg turned black and then she died in a high fever of sweating.

The boy was full grown when I saw him first. A tall, handsome youth, and for a while I tutored him, until it became clear that he had no aptitude and little desire for what I had to give. I had left it too late; should have come home sooner and then maybe I could have done something for him. I do regret this; and yet it might have been to no purpose and there were so many other affairs of state and in the world I had to attend to elsewhere. My son could have travelled with me, of course; but he was not one to leave the island; many Brandanes are like that. So congenial is the island of Bute that they never desire to face the world outside. Maybe they are right. And yet for me, it was right and necessary, and I would not have missed it for anything. I have known so many other worlds as a result of my travels.

When did it all go wrong? Just four years after Bruce's death, the English were at us again. Unhappy with the treaty of independence, they crossed our border and defeated us in battles at Dupplin and Hallidon Hill. Everything we had learned at Bannockburn was either lost or turned against us. Archers we had none; superior numbers of the English fought us on foot with pikes and we, who had so recently triumphed, were put to flight and bloody disaster. I was present and saw the whole thing; by then, an aged relic of nearly fifty, too old for anything except to comfort dying men and try, often in vain, to repair their wounded comrades. And so, what Bruce would have hated to see, Edward Balliol, son of the exiled John Balliol, was crowned king and, just like his father before him, paid homage to Edward III of England and gave over a huge area of Scottish land in the east, which Bruce and the rest of us had fought so valiantly to claw back.

I was also at Neville's Cross in 1346, when young David, flexing his muscles for the first time, was captured, shot in the face with an arrow, having been deserted by half the army, caused, some said, by his step brother, Robert, who is now the king. The irony of it is that men say a miracle was performed upon him. For after capture by the English did not his arrow magically disappear overnight? Who would pay attention to an old man who entered the prisoner king's tent early in the morning, when all around slept, and removed the arrow with a tube?

By this time, my skill in the art was extreme. I managed it while he was asleep too! A measure of the ease with which it slid out. Of course I slipped off into the crowd afterwards. Why would I want to advertise my skill? The English king would have made me follow him around to attend him until I died of it. In old age, I preferred Scottish soil to Flanders, where Edward III spent so much of his time fighting. And David never knew how it happened! Thought it a miracle and prayed to St Monan ever after, as the architect of his deliverance.

David was held prisoner in England for eleven years and only released on agreement of a ransom of a hundred thousand pounds. He was clever, of course, sweet-talked Edward into postponing several payments so that only half of it was paid before he died. And now we have Robert II, he who fled at Neville's Cross and left his brother, the king, to be captured. A gentle soul, Robert, but indecisive, and no use in the fight or even in the council chamber. A shadow of his grandfather. Maybe it is the limp he has. It has likely held him back too much, so that he never quite became the man we needed. Only in the bedchamber was he productive, but all the Bruces were.

And the English can have us any time they want, for all they have to do is come and get us as they have done so often before. It has all been for nothing, all this warring and burning and murder and pillage. Some men call it fighting for freedom, but I rather think it is fighting for folly. We might pretend to ourselves that we are independent but to the extent that it is true we suffer from the lack of what is routine in England: justice, peace and plenty. And yet it is false really, for we do depend upon them for many things—education for one; we still have no university here, a scandal it is! Anyone who wishes to be educated—

and does not a country need educated people more than anything?—must travel to the continent or England for it. And so our young men journey to Paris or Padua or Rome, those that do not creep into Oxford and Cambridge, hiding their northern vowels, as I once did myself, so that they are thought dumb. How can we make progress on our own in isolation? A child among giants, we are.

There is the French arrangement, of course, a growing reality, but it is not to our advantage; only the French profit by making England draw off troops to her northern borders to fight us when it suits the French.

Anyway, as the ransom was never paid to the English in full, they will use that against us when it suits them, as a pretext for further annexations or tribute. And so we struggle on in our lonely, uncomfortable lives, much as mine is now, in this draughty castle of Rothesay, where I must attend the ailments of the king when all else fails, condemned to exist on the scraps of life. I am too old even for medicine now. God knows I can hardly see well enough to achieve anything except to scribe. But Robert will insist on keeping me to hand in case I have something worthwhile to suggest. Alas, my reputation is not quite dead, though my body nearly is.

And yet there are no English strutting their stuff hereabouts, no Scots women are being raped and I am free to think what I like and no one pays attention. Maybe there is something in freedom after all. For a time, in 1310, I thought so. Then, anger at the English and their high-handed ways held sway over my soul.

God, my old bones are so weak now. I can hardly stand up and this ulcer in my leg gets worse and worse, as if the blood no longer flows as it used to. I must get myself down to the beach again and bathe it in the salt water. That always helps. Immersion in cold sea water has been a constant practice of mine all my life, when opportunity presents. But I grow old and stiff and it gets harder and harder to descend to the beach and harder still to climb up again. One day, I will get down there and roll in the water for the last time.'

CHAPTER 18

Edinburgh, 1996

I HAD COME TO THE END of the journal. These were the last words Bannatyne wrote, or at least all that had been preserved. A pity really, I thought with a sigh. There was so much he could still have said. I would like to have known about his meeting with Dante. That would have been at Avignon, probably, when the papal court moved there, or maybe Italy, if he had journeyed further, to one of the universities.

Sailing across the Firth of Clyde, empty now of ships, and passing the empty dockyards in the train, I wondered about the manuscript; and all the way to Waverley Station I savoured its many riches. Then, as I set foot again on Princes Street, I faced up to the question: was it true? Did Bannatyne command the archers? Was the battle fought this way? Was he right about independence being the wrong route to take? Was the manuscript of value to the Nation State of Scotland? And what did it mean to me? Should I stand for the independence party at the election?

I began by focusing on the issue: was this the journal of a medieval mind? At first I did not think so; but then I realised that Bannatyne was a genius and must be expected to be in advance of his medieval contemporaries; and, anyway, what I had just read was a translation by Tom Stewart—a modern, educated person—which he had amplified and extended for the sake of accessibility. Maybe any modern viewpoint had been introduced by him, writing in 1941. And there was so much that was new in it that Archdeacon Barbour never understood or mentioned. Of course, Bannatyne was right about Barbour. The man was innumerate, his poem full of confusions, contradictions and ignorance of many aspects of the battle—in spite of having access to people who took part—a travesty of scholarship. And Bannatyne had asked the questions Barbour had not, lacking the insight, and even provided the answers. Unquestionably, the manuscript is illuminating.

The journal explains at last what has always seemed impossible: how the success at Bannockburn was achieved. It does provide new insights, the ones that have always been missing: the role of archers; the significance of the two streams, and the meaning of the advance of the Scots pikemen on foot towards the ten great divisions of English cavalry—so that the distance between them was reduced; and that, consequently, the cavalry could not get up speed and so were unable to break through the Scottish lines—that was utterly new, a revelation! And the fact that there were just enough Scots pikemen to resist the charges of English knights in that particular confined space. The entire battle was now clear for the very first time. The decision to leave the prepared defences and march unarmoured men on foot against armoured men on armoured horses was brilliant, a masterstroke! The tactic was an idea of genius! The English cavalry were unable to deploy all at the same time. Hemmed in, only 300 could attack the 700 yard front and when they fell, obstructed the progress of those behind.

And the likelihood that Bruce, the consummate leader, had not seen all the best tactical moves himself, but had made use of other intelligences in his own force. For has it not ever been thus? Maybe Bannatyne was right: only certain kinds of very gifted minds could make these insights; and if they did, they were disqualified by their very integrity from the highest form of leadership, which must be, when necessary, manipulative, prevaricating, covert, cruel and ruthless—unacademic traits. The successful leader has a sensitivity to the needs and aspirations of his fellows and a desire, over everything else, to control and satisfy them, which the intellectual, with his ever present quest for the truth, is incapable of, and would not want to, even if he saw the necessity. Finally, power is no good if you don't win, for then you lose it; and the best leaders have been the kind of men who would do almost anything to win—devote themselves to the task, heart and soul, for years if necessary—which is why they did.

Perhaps the use the king made of Bannatyne's mind was like that of prime ministers or presidents whose most memorable speeches are written by lesser men, who never get the credit; or like intellectuals in the cabinet office who provide not only solutions to sudden difficulties but the actual policy itself. Bannatyne was a kind of chief of staff, master tactician. Of course, it took a person of extraordinary courage, charisma, persuasiveness and force to lead the troops on such a dangerous manoeuvre; only Bruce could have managed that. And only Bruce could fashion his men into such a potent, integrated fighting unit. Even the manner of his leadership was clear at last: what it was like, what it was founded upon, what it felt like to his troops.

What was my concern? Would a medieval mind have seen the world differently, even if he was a genius? Certainly, Tom Stewart had shown himself to be a novelist of sorts by his notes in his own journal on description and so forth. So perhaps, just perhaps, the Bannatyne journal was authentic. There were all these new insights into the tactics; and the mental model that had sprung fully formed from his mind for the training of archers, so that the greatest excellence in the use of the weapon was possible for the first time. All I could be sure of was that I would be unable to decide the issue, for so many pages of scholar's Latin were beyond my power to translate. I would have to give the manuscripts over to experts and allow them time to decide.

And that is what I did.

I sent a copy of a small part of the manuscript to the classics department of one of our universities, and I waited; and while I did, giving up all thought of my work for the present time—handing out my cases to others—I myself went into the history, reading the sources to see whether there was some disparity between the known facts and Bannatyne's account.

There was! I learned that Rothesay Castle had been captured by Robert Boyd in 1306, soon after the murder of John Comyn and the start of Bruce's rebellion. And yet, in the manuscript, Bannatyne reported his own attack near the end of 1312, just before the seige of Perth. What did this mean? That Bannatyne was old and his memory defective? No! For Bannatyne was at Cambridge in 1306 and could not possibly have taken part in Boyd's attack. And yet, I realised, Bannatyne might not have known about the attack for was he not, as he often admits, too deep buried in books to know what was happening elsewhere?

How then to explain the discrepancy?

I worried over it half the night and then, reading some more of the history next morning, I saw what it meant. After the battle of Methven, when Bruce fled to the west and was repulsed at Dalrigh, just north-west of Glendochart, he split his force, sending the ladies north, to safety, where they were betrayed and captured.

With a small group, he journeyed south on foot to the lands of the Earl of Lennox, with whose aid he took ship and headed past the island of Bute for the western seas, where he hid for a time, some say at Rathlin Island and others at Garmoran and elsewhere. But, and it was a vital but, an English fleet was sent in pursuit. This would have called at every castle in the region seeking information. Surely Rothesay Castle would have been recaptured and reinvested at this time by the English?

When Bruce returned, he did so by way of Arran to Carrick in the south-west mainland where, as the earl, who had grown up there, he would have had his best chance of recruiting fresh troops. Then, for a good while, the mainland was under English control, a control he was bent on ending. Would he have wasted men recapturing Rothesay? No, for it was no threat to him. Perhaps Bruce left Rothesay, and other small castles which were out of the way, until he had imposed his will on the Comyns, in Buchan and elsewhere, and as many mainland castles as he could cause to surrender.

Maybe then, the manuscript was authentic and Bannatyne had just produced a new fact, unrelated in any other source, admittedly few, often written much later, contradictory here and there, and missing out much that was so important—like this, perhaps! An inspired guess, as time would show.

I then found that educated opinion thinks Scottish bows were four feet long: much smaller than the English longbow. Was that a discrepancy? The sources have little to say about archers, even the secondary ones by later scholars. The distinguished historian, W. M. Mackenzie,[1] has the Scottish cavalry ride down the English and Welsh archers, leaving the Scots with the field to themselves—an unlikely event, as Bannatyne says, for the unarmoured cavalry should have been shot down. Then I saw that Bannatyne and the Bruces would have known about the English bow and its superior power because they had fought with the English. Was it credible then, that they did not import this knowledge into their own forces, when so much depended upon the result? Of course not! And Bannatyne was just the man to do this and force others to his viewpoint, as we have seen. How could the battle have been won with the four-foot Scottish bow against a far superior six-foot weapon in the hands of ten times as many English archers? It was impossible, unless Bannatyne's account were believed. At the very least, it seems clear, the Scottish force must have employed some six-foot bows; and having a whole year to prepare for a pitched batttle, and conscious of the need, it was such an obvious matter to arrange for as many as could be made available by such desperate, outnumbered men.

Was there a school in Bute in 1290? At first, I did not think so. Then I came across a book[2] about Ayr Academy which spoke of 'Allan, master of the schools of Ayr', in 1233. If Ayr had a school then, it was at least likely that Rothesay, with its impressive castle, strengthened after 1230, when the vikings took it by hewing the soft sand-stones, also had a school of the kind described.

What about Cambridge? The dates fitted, for the University of Cambridge began at the dispersal of Oxford in 1209, as Bannatyne explains, when there was imminent danger of the town hanging some more of the gowns, three having been perhaps but the first reprisal for the shooting of a townswoman with an arrow by a student. Some scholars went to Reading, others to Cambridge, many staying to form a new university. 'I understand it is still there,' wrote Lord Dacre, but 'what attracted them to that distant marsh town we do not know.' Leader gives the answer: 'Men from Cambridge families were probably able

---

1. *The Battle of Bannockburn*, Strongoak, 1989; first pub 1913.
2. *Ayr Academy*, 1233-1983, by John Strawhorn pub Alloway, 1983, p. 7.

to strike good bargains with their fellow townsmen for lodgings and classrooms.'[3]

Was Bannatyne's education correctly described? It was usual then to spend more time before graduating, but, if he was considered a genius, exceptions might have been made. For one thing, it might have been inconvenient and downright humiliating, to retain in class, someone who already knew much more—because he absorbed everything like a sponge—and would fire it back with interest at the luckless professor.

Was the description of Bruce correct? I discovered that a skeleton had been found under the floor of Dunfermline Abbey in the nineteenth century. Before reinterment in pitch, it was observed to have lost two front teeth and had a hole in the rib cage around the heart. It was of a man about six feet tall.

Tradition has it that Bruce consigned 'the small folk' to the rear of the army at Bannockburn and that may be true. If so, Bannatyne would not have seen them stream over the hill at the crucial stage of the battle, frightening the English into the belief that a second reserve army was approaching. Also, because of the disparity in numbers, any men or women who were available and able to fight effectively *should* have been standing with the ranks of pikemen, so a small company of female archers is not impossible, even if there is no record of it. It is not the kind of thing Archdeacon Barbour is likely to have made much of, if true—and if he knew of it. Writing sixty years after the battle, of course, he knew little.

Were the numbers at Bannockburn correct? There is some disagreement among scholars about them. The English payment rolls are taken by some as evidence that their army was under 20,000. Then the figures given by John Barbour as 100,000 English and 30,000 Scots are taken to be an accurate estimate of the ratio of one to another, leading to the conclusion that the ratio of English to Scots was about three or four to one [which seems unwise, for if Barbour's numbers are wildly inaccurate, why not his ratio?] And so the Scots army is worked out to be around 5,000. If so, the triangular plain at Bannockburn must have been enclosed by around 4,000 Scots pikemen, allowing for cavalry and archers. Yet, because the distance between the burns was around 700 yards, this means only five or six lines of pikes—not enough to halt a charge of armoured knights on armoured horses, each one weighing about a ton and with the impact and driving power of a Chieftain tank, easily able to plough through so few lightly armed men.

There was the likelihood that many knights would have fought on the English side for honour, or rewards for valour shown—not com-

---

3. *A History of the University of Cambridge*, Vol 1, Leader, D.R. pub CUP 1994, [1st ed 1988], p. 18.

pelled by service due to a feudal superior; and also, some at least of the foreign mercenaries went unpaid. Like Jean de la Moilles, a Burgundian, who, for 20,000 livres, ransomed the Earl of Pembroke who strayed onto his land, because Edward II owed him his pay. Professor Prestwich says of the battle at Falkirk, that 'there were probably two or three times as many unpaid cavalry in the English army.'[4] Maybe Bannockburn was similar.

No, I decided, Bannatyne's numbers make far more sense and they are even supported by some of the best scholars.[5] And yet, this thesis depends upon the battle taking place in the triangular plain, an area of dispute. However, the battle makes perfect sense there, and not much sense anywhere else, for the small Scots army would have been out-flanked in most other places and must have begun on the Roman Road to prevent the English advance, which restricts the second battle to a place nearby—like the triangular plain.

Even the plain itself on a map I consulted seemed to be described fairly accurately by cartographers operating centuries later. In this, there was another stream in the centre and the Bannockburn and Pel-stream curled like serpents. Yet time had passed and the terrain had changed. Anyway, what Bannatyne saw were the essentials of the field before him; he would leave out minor irregularities like a shallow rivulet in the middle, presenting no obstacle.

Everything seemed to fit and I could think of no discrepancies elsewhere. And yet, I was uneasy.

Mention of Lord Dacre[6] reminded me of the dangers of being taken in. What terrible damage had been done to his name by declaring the, so called, Hitler Diaries to be authentic, even though he had qualified his judgment with the clause 'if what people said about their discovery is true.'

Could this also be a hoax? The suggestion jolted me for a time, until I began to investigate other examples. There were the Van Meegeren forgeries of Vermeer paintings which, at first, experts would not believe were forgeries even when Van Meegeren owned up—and were only persuaded when Van Meegeren produced other examples never seen before; and the 21 Gothic saints on the walls of St Marien Church in Lubeck, accepted by every authority as genuine in 1948, but confirmed later and only because he produced numerous other examples of Picassos, Rembrandts, etc.—indistinguishable from the masters—to have been done by Lothar Malskat, a humble restorer of frescoes, who also owned up to the forgery. Was this manuscript of the same kind?

---

4. *Edward I*, by Michael Prestwich, pub Methuen, 1990, [Ist ed 1988] p. 481.
5. Such as Prof G. Barrow and Dr R. Nicholson, in their volumes of this history.
6. Hugh Trevor-Roper, Emeritus Prof. of Modern History, Oxford.

Finally, I learned of a Scottish forgery of the poems of Ossian, done in the eighteenth century by James MacPherson, who claimed to have discovered some ancient Gaelic manuscripts later shown to have been indisputably his own work. And yet the work was excellent! His art was so outstanding as to merit the description of having done 'more than any single work to bring about the romantic movement in European, and especially in German, literature . . . Herder and Goethe . . . were among its admirers.'[7] Why had MacPherson presented his own brilliant work as some one else's? Because, no one would have paid attention to it otherwise. But if it was stated to be ancient and by Ossian, every half-baked Scotsman would buy it, as if it were a newly discovered national treasure, lost before, in the mists of time.

All of this made me very careful. Then the results from the classical scholars arrived. With trepidation, I opened the large envelope with the university crest. Inside, as requested, were the copies of the pages I had sent—and a letter.

The Latin was authentic! The calligraphy was a perfect paradigm of the period 1300-1350 [which, since Bannatyne had learned his style then, fitted beautifully]; the style was 'exact, rich and elevated, as if by a distinguished medieval mind'. I laid down the letter, poured a stiff Drambuie and contemplated fresh vistas of fame and academic honours while sipping it at my old desk in the office, high above Princes Street. Saw myself elected, before an august audience, to The British Academy, The Royal Society and bedecked with honorary degrees from the finest universities the world over.

Then realism reasserted itself; and I woke up again. Who would believe the Van Meegerens were forgeries—at first? No one! Who would believe Lothar Malskat had done the frescoes at St Marien—at first? No one! And only Samuel Johnson—a genius—had seen through the Ossian poems at a first scrutiny.

I would have to be careful. Instead of the chamber at the House of Commons, I might soon appear as a laughing stock on the front page of a tabloid farce—like Lord Dacre.

I unlocked the safe and took the manuscript in my hands and surveyed it carefully, from a different point of view. Was the paper genuine? Was it made in the 14th century? What about the ink? Was it composed of ingredients of the kind available then? I did not know; and I was loathe to give the least fragment of it to anyone who might be able to tell, for fear of losing it. Shameful as it may seem, I was deeply proprietorial about it. I did not want to share my success with anybody.

Unsure what to do, I decided to investigate the nursing home for exservicemen where Tom Stewart had spent the last years of his life.

7. *Encyclopaedia Britannica* Vol 14, 1963 Edition, p. 508a.

First, though, I would visit the grave nearby, which I knew of from the legal papers.

It was the latest in the row, hundreds of others being behind it, many of the folk having died prematurely of battle-wounds, in the same place, years before. The stone was like all the others: grey granite inscribed in gold. The dates given were 1915-1996. That would have made him twenty-four in 1939 and that struck me as odd: it seemed late for someone finishing a degree in English. Twenty-two would have been usual. What, I wondered, had he done in the missing two years?

The nursing home was quiet now, so many of the inmates having passed away, and the staff constantly being reduced under the pressure of financial necessity. The blonde administrator, Mrs Merrilees, was young and efficient, however, in a neat blue suit, and when my request was stated and credentials shown, she took me downstairs into the bowels of the building, where the records of those who had stayed in the place were stored. By then, it was plain that she was an exceptional person, not only warm and charming but with a keen desire to help. This was soon to be a vital factor in the outcome.

Soon, given leave to examine it at leisure in the library, I was staring at the file on Tom Stewart. There were service records, medical reports and letters of one kind or another.

After two hours I had found nothing I could classify as worthwhile, from my point of view, and was about to give up and go home when Mrs Merrilees returned to offer a cup of coffee and enquire how I was getting on.

I explained that I was trying to understand the details of Tom Stewart's life, with a view to validating an important document. 'It's probably fruitless,' I admitted. 'I'm looking for a flaw, something that doesn't make sense. If his life is as straightforward as it seems, then there is nothing to be said.'

'So the document will be authentic, then?' she said.

'Well, not necessarily. There might still be something wrong, even if I can't see it.'

As the lady was intrigued, I told her more about it. How it was not absolutely impossible that the manuscript had been written by Tom Stewart himself and not by John Bannatyne—or even by someone else.

'And you can't prove it authentic, you can only prove it a forgery?'

I laughed. 'Yes, that's about it. Even if every aspect of the manuscript checks out, the matter is not definitely decided. But if something does not check out, then it is unreliable. I need only one flaw, one thing that doesn't add up.'

'And you would like it to be authentic?'

'Oh yes! Wouldn't you? It would be a great discovery. A national treasure.'

I sipped my coffee dreamily, wondering what to do next, whether I should give up the precious manuscript to experts, when she began to speak about the man. 'He was in a bad way for many years—all the years I knew him. Never said a word. It was the stroke, you know.'
'Did he *ever* say anything?' I said. 'I mean, before your time, perhaps.'
'I don't know. If the records do not say so, then that answers your question. A stroke can have devastating effects on speech.'

As the records were clear that he could not or would not communicate verbally, that question was decided and I said as much. But Mrs Merrilees was not satisfied by this. As she stood beside me, she adopted a far-away look, as if remembering some event in the past.
'He must have been able to get through to people,' she said at last.
'How can that be?'
'Because I have one of his books and before I had it, Dr Brown owned it. Dr Brown was the superintendent before my time.'

I asked to see the book and she invited me to her home to view it that same afternoon, after work. 'I've never read the book,' she explained. 'I bought it among a job lot from Dr Brown's effects, when his house was cleared after he died.'

Later, in Mrs Merrilees's house, I was shown into her sitting room where there was a fine bookcase along one wall. 'Books do furnish a room, don't you think?' she said, proudly. 'Even if they are largely unread. Mind you I've read some. But these particular volumes are beyond me.'

I soon understood why. It was A. E. Housman's edition of the works of Manilius, a Roman of the 1st century AD, by one of the greatest textual critics of the age—over and above his stature as a poet. Housman had been a professor of Latin at London and then Cambridge.

As I opened the first of the five volumes with trembling fingers, I had a tingling feeling of anticipation, and I was not disappointed. On the inner leaf was a printed certificate stating that Thomas Erskine Stewart had been presented with the book as his prize for winning the gold medal in Latin in his third year at university. The date was 1935!

So, he was a classical scholar! First in the honours class. And might have been capable of producing Latin of a quality which would convince experts of its medieval provenance! He must have taken a first degree in Classics before ever reading English. Then I remembered the birth-date: 1915, which meant he had graduated at 20 or 21; implying he had started university at 17 at the latest; which made him a very able scholar from the beginning. No wonder he could translate medieval Latin!

'I don't know how much these are worth,' I said, 'but I would like to have them. As a memento.' I offered her £200 and promised to return them if the real value was greater. She smiled and told me it was unnecessary, for this sum was far more than she ever expected. I pointed out that it was a first edition. 'Never mind,' said she, 'If they are worth that to you, take them with my blessing.' Her generous nature was touching; decency is so rare.

I wondered why this had not been clear before. Why was there no record of the degree in Latin? Maybe he had never taken one, become ill or had to leave because of lack of money in fourth year, perhaps. A deficiency later overcome when he changed to English; or maybe he had just fallen out with the classics department and failed to finish. Perhaps, he had even failed the final exams—an event not unknown. Housman himself had failed his final exams at Oxford!

Had he planned it from the beginning? Or was it that he had been able to translate the manuscript only because he had been such a brilliant student of Latin? I was no further forward! It was so frustrating! I was getting like Tom Stewart myself with all my exclamation marks.

And yet there were his own exclamation marks! If he had planned the whole thing—and why had he done so?—his journal, with its exclamation marks, must have been an invention, set up to trap the unwary solicitor empowered to discover the manuscript—myself. Was that possible? Of course not!

I felt convinced that the manuscript was genuine now. I had just succeeded in showing how the translation was possible, that was all. Before I left, at the front door, I said, 'I wonder how Dr Brown came by the book?'

'Maybe Tom could communicate by signs,' she said. 'Maybe he had some good days. Some of them are like that. Maybe Tom Stewart gave him the book as a present, while he was still *compos mentis*.'

That night, I drank more Drambuie than usual after dinner, and wondered again about a political career. First though, I took up the book again and noticed that, on the second inside page, Dr Brown had written his name in small handwriting, in faded pencil. And a bell rang in my brain. Had I not seen this style of writing before? And I had! In the will. The codicil had seemed to be in a hand different from Tom Stewart's. This, I felt sure, was it. I fetched the will and when I compared the two, I was sure of it. So *Dr Brown* had seen the will and had added this addendum about the object of value to the Nation State of Scotland. Well then, maybe he knew about the manuscript. Maybe the book was a gift for his aid.

Next morning, in the clear light of day, I considered the manuscript again and I knew I needed more information before announcing my discovery. I would have to give it up to be tested by others. The age of the parchment and the ink were the remaining points of concern. Finally, I realised that I might as well adopt this plan since, if I announced that the manuscript was definitely genuine, it would instantly be wanted for just such tests of verification.

Reluctantly, I selected a few pages of the manuscript which had slightly less writing than any others, though, god knows, they had been pretty crammed—to save space and cost, I expect—and sent it to the expert on parchments at the British Museum with a covering letter, explaining something of what had occurred and my problem of authentication.

And then I had to wait again!

Christmas came and went and was unsatisfactory for once. So much of my life seemed to be in the melting pot. Then the experts wrote to tell of further delays, due to shortage of staff and a backlog of work.

It was so frustrating! So, to kill time, I decided to journey back to Bute and look over the castle, the medieval chapel and the farm at Ardmaleish, in case I had missed something.

The year had just ended and the weather was cold and rainy. The castle was as dull as most Scottish castles: gaunt, empty, draughty, freezing and unwelcoming, every thing of interest having been removed centuries ago. Why, I thought, as I stood surveying its bleakness, must our heritage be preserved as a thousand empty stone coffins like this, when they could so easily be refurbished wonders, vibrant with life and interest?

Which tower had been captured first in 1312? The south west, I decided, for it would have been furthest from human habitation. But, as the place had been stripped bare, there was nothing more to learn.

Across the road, in the local museum, I found a copy of the earliest relevant document: a transfer of land from one Bannatyne to his brother, dated 1500, and in Latin. Were these descendants of my own John Bannatyne?

Later, I drove along the north shore through the village of Port Bannatyne to the headland beyond, and, parking the car, strolled down to the beach at Ardmaleish across lush fields of prime cattle and saw the place where Bannatyne and Eleanor had swum so many years before. How wonderful he had thought the experience of being in love and being loved. I envied him then, picturing the pair frolicking in the cool water.

On the way back to the road where I had parked the car, I came across the farmer, who spoke to me, and I told him part of my tale, resignedly, as if the matter of the authenticity of the manuscript could never be established for certain. He listened in silence to my explanation, took off his cap and scratched his grizzled head. 'Have ye seen the shield?' he said.

How could I? I had not looked hard enough. He led me to the gable wall of the oldest farm building and there, high up, was a stone shield. On it, two figures had been embossed on the stone on either side of a smaller shield. They were like two curved horns which crossed low down, near the points, with the wider parts uppermost on either side of the smaller shield. Out of each horn, there seemed to emanate jagged vertical lines.

'What are these?' I said, pointing at them with surprise, for I had never seen anything like them before.

'Torches,' he replied. 'They are two horns with stuff burning in the tops and those lines are flames.'

He was right. Was this the armorial bearing of the Bannatynes? A shield with two crossed torches on either side of another shield?

It seemed to fit. Maybe the shield was the family crest and maybe its importance began with Bannatyne himself. Two crossed torches around a shield would have seemed no bad emblem for a genius of war and medicine. What are torches for, but to shed light? And what had his role been all along, but to shed light into the strategy and tactics of the Scottish army and the repair of its wounded? Or was there a couple, to commemorate the two Bannatynes who had fought in the batttle and were rewarded for it?

My excitement was intense. I felt that the local facts had effectively validated the manuscript. The building might not be medieval but maybe the strange emblem had been taken from some earlier building and retained. However, I would have to wait for the expert reports. They could still ruin everything.

My last visit was to the medieval chapel on a hill overlooking the town. Inside, was a stone effigy of a medieval knight and across from it on the opposite wall, another effigy of his lady. There was no sign now of the wall having been rebuilt after the shell hit fifty years before, but then, in that time, there had been some restoration, I was told. The man was stooped over a grave in the cemetery which surrounded the chapel. He was old, white haired and frail, in a dark suit and waistcoat. He looked up at my approach and told me something of the chapel. How it had been restored by the Marquis of Bute.

'Who is the knight supposed to be?' I said, pointing to the stone effigy.

'One of the Stewart ancestors of the Marquis,' he said.

'Not Walter Stewart?' I said, with excitement, thinking of the young man who had fought at Bannockburn, married Marjorie Bruce, fathered Robert II, and helped to win back Berwick from the English.

'I don't think so,' he replied. 'Marjorie is buried at Paisley Abbey because that is where the Stewards were traditionally laid to rest.'

'But you're not sure?'

He laughed. 'No. You see, there is no tomb of Walter Stewart there any more. They say the bones have been lost.'

'So this could be of Walter Stewart, then?'

'It is just possible. If it is, the bones are lying in the crypt.'

'But you don't think so?'

'I think it's probably a son or a grandson.'

'Why would he have been interred here and not at Paisley?'

'Maybe he liked it here. A lot of folk do.'

I was excited. It could even be Walter himself, then, for Marjorie would have been interred at Paisley in 1316 and Walter, with his second wife, might have been laid down in Bute. The explanation that Walter's bones had been lost at Paisley, no matter what John Barbour said, did not bear scrutiny, given his importance. I began to tell the man something of my quest, hoping for a lead into the life of Tom Stewart. It was not to be. Fifty years was too far back for memory. But before I left him, the man said,

'Have you seen their graves?'

'Whose graves?' I said, stupidly.

'The Bannatynes. They're all buried here.' Sure enough, a few yards away were the tombstones of the Bannatynes who had died in the eighteenth and nineteenth centuries. They were the nearest gravestones, but one, to the chapel door! Other stones were so old that the lettering was indecipherable. 'The name died out in the nineteenth century,' said the man, finally. 'All the children were girls.'

As I turned away, it occurred to me ask: 'Are you quite sure you don't remember a man called Tom Stewart? He lived in that house across the road during the war.' And I pointed to the grey cottage with the grimy windows and ferns growing out of the eaves.

The man lifted his head suddenly, as if he had been shot. 'Oh yes, I do, now! You must mean wee Tommy Stewart. He was in my class at school. I remember him fine. He was the dux medalist.'

'So you knew him well, then?' I managed to say, near breathless with wonder.

'No, I can't say I did. He never played games like the rest of us. He was too clever, you see. Had his head stuck in a book all the time. A loner, even a recluse, finally. He was shot up in the war, I think. By the time I got back from the Jap prison camp, he had gone off to hospital.'

I asked many questions, but there was nothing more he could add and there was no one else still alive to ask. Then, as I walked away, the man called after me: 'I think he failed his exams at the uni. Had some kind of brainstorm, or something. Reading too many books, like enough.'

So the trip had been productive after all. I had been very lucky to find someone who had known my client and I was well pleased. Evidently, Tom Stewart had suffered a nervous breakdown of some kind during the last year of his classics course. Maybe it was even connected to his stroke, ten years later.

On the return journey, as I sat in the saloon of the car-ferry, watching the island disappear from sight into the evening murk of rain, my thoughts turned naturally to my own problem. What had the manuscript taught me? Did it have anything to convey to the present-day problems of devolution or independence or the status quo?

Bannatyne thought Scotland was better off within the union because so much could be gained by it and so much lost if it were resisted, because the more powerful neighbour would continually reassert its dominion, with consequent destruction of everything Scottish, until that resistance had been overcome. He had fought for the Scots only when there was no alternative, knowing the cause ultimately fruit-less—and was proved right. And he had done so, mainly because of English arrogance and unfair treatment of his family and friends. Resistance was necessary—inevitable—because the Scots were enslaved by Edward I.

Was that the position now? No. We are free men within the union but not slaves. Freedom is only an issue when a nation is enslaved. And yet, because of the system, the Scots could be ruled by a few Tories in the Scottish office, when the majority of Scots prefer a government of a different colour. That is the problem that devolution is designed to solve.

Clearly, Tom Stewart thought that independence was the route to take or why the talk about the Nation State of Scotland? He must have viewed Bannatyne's defection to the Scots as a sign of good sense.

I saw that the status quo would not do now. The union had failed, mainly because the English had managed it badly. Many Scots wanted a divorce because the English had shown too much arrogance, too often speaking of Britain, when there was some advantage to themselves— and of England on every possible occasion, even when Scots were responsible for the achievement. It was offensive. In government, had they taken any account of the huge Scottish majority in favour of alternative arrangements? No. They had gloated over the fact that so few of the privileged should control the lives of so many of the underprivileged: serving the interest of themselves and their class, as usual. It was an offence against democracy for years. But is it not the democracy of the union that matters? No, for the Scots did not join a union to find themselves ruled by an alien value-system they did not approve. Scotland is not in the same position as, say, the North East of England, for Scotland has been a nation for many centuries, accus-tomed to fairness within its boundaries—by the standards of its own customs. It is that very nationhood that demands a system which allows Scottish views of the time to govern its arrangements.

And as Bannatyne had observed, it was precisely Edward I's refusal to take account of the customs of Scotland that had led to the depo-sition of John Balliol and the very War of Independence itself. The same neglect was at work now!

But was devolution the answer, or separation? This I could not see then.

Returned to Edinburgh, I received a shock. A package awaited me from Mrs Merrilees. In a letter, she explained that she was enclosing another book from the box of things she had bought from Dr Brown's estate, in case it was of interest. It seemed to be a journal of some kind. Was it Dr Brown's perhaps? It might say something about his interesting patient.

Inside, I found another of the stubby black notebooks and on the first page, the date: 1944. Flicking the others, I knew the handwriting instantly as Tom Stewart's and saw that this volume, for the first time, was unfinished. The writing stopped long before the end. Was this the last journal before his illness? I read:

> *4.12.44 The work is finished now. I should be pleased and yet I'm not. Feel bloody fed up, to tell the truth. What am I going to do now for Christ's sake?*

There is no entry for the next few days. Maybe he has changed in some way. Translating the book perhaps has taken its toll.

> *9.12.44 Made it down to Home Guard HQ. No bloody good. Buggers still won't take me on. 'Have some of this navy rum, Tam,' they said. 'Take your mind off things, like,' they said. English gits, even in the HG. Bloody near didn't get back for the pain. And the rum is awful. Never could stand the taste. Rotgut.*

> *12.12.44 No whisky anywhere on the island! Not a drop. All pinched by civies and soldiers. Have they given up making the stuff?*

> *14.12.44 Christ, I dreamt I was flying up the church steeple in my kite. Woke up in a hellish sweat and had other dreams after. Feel as if am heading for a prang. What I wouldn't give for a decent dram.*

There is much more in this vein. Then,

> *19.12.44 Visited a U Boat today. Captured intact. So small it is like a toy, sitting at the bottom of the pier, so far down below, because of the tide. Miracle I got on board at all. Three ladders lashed together with ropes and a single strand of wire on either side, as a handrail, made the gangway. Of course when I put my weight on it the sag was terrific. Thought I was heading for the drink. Inside, it was bloody awful. So cramped you could hardly stand, with round doors in the bulkheads a midget couldn't climb through easily. And the walls streaming with green slime. And the smell! Oh god! Batteries they said it was. Ammonia or H2S or something, the gas. How could the Gerries live in*

this? Captain's cap still lying on chart table. Must have scarpered bloody quick. Getting up again was hell, pushed and shoved by two AB's. Every joint was agony. Lungs were so full of gas, I almost spewed up. And at the top, an English PO grinned at me, and said, 'See what we did, cock?' And it near knocked me down again. For I took 'us' as him and me, his shipmates, the AB's, and all the other jocks too. What if we had been independent? The English would have been alone. The Gerries would have rolled them over. After that, they would have gobbled us up too. Thank Christ we are together. Maybe there is something in Westminster after all.

The next pages are about the progress of the war.

23.12.44 I see now that I was wrong. We have to be in a union after all. If Scotland had been independent, we would never have been together and we would never have been able to stand against the Huns separately. It was essential for the sucessful conduct of the war that all the separate nations of Britain be completely together. Even so, we will just manage it and with a lot of help—which would never have been forthcoming to England alone. It took every Irishman, Welshman and Scot, as well as every damned Englishman, to bring it off.—And all the colonial Irish, Welsh and Scots too! Anything less would have been bloody disaster. What a fool I've been!

There is more of this, all of it very clearly written, interspersed with complaints about the lack of whisky. The absence of even one clever person to talk to is a persistent ache.

24.12.44 Went to the midnight watch service. Church was packed with women and servicemen of various kinds. Minister not much good. Spoke too fast and indistinctly, to no effect, until, finally, the bells went and the hooters sounded in all the ships at the harbour. What a racket. Worse than Gerry bombers. Then he did a simple thing. He told us to shake hands with our nearest neighbours. And by god everybody did. And they enjoyed it, even me. Reminded me I was part of the human race. 'Love thy neighbour as thyself,' he said, finally. That was all. That was enough. That was all he had to say. Came away thinking how I hate the English. Hate their strangulated accents and superior ways. But I know the man is right. They are my neighbours and I ought to love them instead. Well, then, maybe I should stick with them. Maybe we all should.

Christmas day comes and goes. A lonely, depressed time, in freezing conditions, no decent food and with snow lying for weeks. Firewood has become a vital activity: finding, chopping, carrying and storing it. But, without whisky to dull his wits, he is both reading more, and yet more depressed at the lack of a decent purpose in his life, and regret for a misspent existence.

> *3.1.45 So bloody miserable! Winston's been talking on the wireless. We are going to win for sure and he did it! He led us. And Monty and all those English public school types. And us too. But mostly them. We would have been messerschmidt mincemeat without them. And me hating them all my life. What a fool I've been; what a damn fool.*

That is the last entry.

I wondered what made him stop, and then realised that he must have had the stroke soon after. So Tom Stewart had been converted by the events of his own war, the one going on around him, to the very position Bannatyne had seen six centuries before.

I went to bed, but lay awake pondering the significance of it all. Unity of nations was strength; and without it, defeat was far more likely: subjugation by other more powerful nations elsewhere.

Did this reasoning still apply today? Of course. Was there ever a time in history when men believed they had fought the war to end all wars? Often. It was the reason so many nations were unprepared for the next one—including our own. The debacle at Dunkirk would never have occurred without that illusion. The Falklands War was won only by a short head, because we were unprepared again. A few more exocet hits and we might have been scuppered. This too, I saw: if 'love thy neighbour' is the root of our moral life, then we should be drawing together as nations, not separating into disparate units, for the sake of material or imagined psychological advantage.

Separation—and the isolation thereby—was a course set in the opposite direction to that in which, if the moral life is in control, we must inevitably proceed.

I went to sleep wondering how Europe fitted into this. A lot of folk wanted to separate from England and be a sovereign state within Europe. Was that right?

The very next morning, I heard from the British Museum. The paper and ink were fine, as far as they could see, and they had even looked at the calligraphy and pronounced it well within the limits expected in the middle of the 14th century. The style of the Latin, they assessed as first-rate—with, what is more, observable characteristics peculiar to Cambridge!

The pages were returned in the same pristine condition, and I was well-satisfied. There were questions and suggestions in their letter, of course—was there any more, how had I come by it, and so forth?—but I paid them no heed.

I was cock-a-hoop and sauntered down to the Botanical Garden for a stroll among the arboreal marvels of the place, to consider what to do next.

It was hard to decide. I could give the entire thing to the British Museum—when they might take the credit for it, or more of it than I deemed necessary; or I could announce it myself—when, by being premature, I might become a laughing stock. And yet, by now, the authenticity seemed pretty secure.

Standing between the great sequoias, caressing the rich red bark, I found myself uneasy, wary, and could not at first say why.

It was the time span, partly. Why had it taken over three years for Tom Stewart to manage this? He began in 1941 and ended in 1944. Was it the increasing dependence on whisky? No, for that was a late development. Was there a gap somewhere in his labours? No, for the journals were a continuous record of his progress. Was he at work for very few hours a day? Not that either. He was a man of great ability, with little to do; and signs, throughout, of employment at hard work, almost every day.

Was there anything I had overlooked? Any other means of checking?

There was! I had been reading secondary historical source material —because it was so concentrated and to avoid the primary sources, which were in Latin, Scots or Middle English. Should I look again at these? Why, when historians based their work on them? And these had such little detail? But there was one other source I could look at: local history, where the idiosyncrasies of Bute itself might surface at last, having been ignored in the historians' broader sweep.

I decided to return to the island again and forage in the local library.

For the last time, then, I drove to Wemyss Bay and took the car-ferry across the Clyde to Bute. For several hours I scoured the three local histories I found there for some particular thing that might stand out as an error. By nightfall, I had not finished. So I booked-in at the same hotel on the sea-front and continued my search through the night, having borrowed copies on special loan.

By lunchtime, I had found nothing to complain of, not one convincing arrow to fire into the great structure of ideas and facts in John Bannatyne's manuscript. The local histories had a fair bit about the Bannatyne family of Bute [there were others, one from Angus, author of a 16th century manuscript of poetry] but nothing before 1500. Two useful things alone emerged: 'In 1313, Bruce invaded the Isle of Man, and at the same time took the castle of Rothesay.'[8] So Bannatyne's

8. *History of Bute*, John Eaton Reid, 1864, p. 51 [Also in *Balfour's Annals* i p. 93, and *Fordun* xii 18] Rothesay Castle was also taken by the English in July, 1303, under the earl of Ulster cf *Robert Bruce and the Community and the Realm of Scotland*, by G. Barrow, p. 126. Bannatyne might not have known this, being absent then. nb

recapture of Rothesay Castle checks out after all! And the Bannatyne family first obtained possession of the estate around Ardmaleish, known as Kames, in the 14th century.[9] The one argument against, was that the name of a woman who had been married out of that farm in the 16th century was Leitch; but that was easily explained if the family had installed a married daughter there. By then, the Bannatyne men were ensconced in several farms and the nearby castle of Kames itself; one eventually reaching the peerage.

I asked myself why there was so little and found the answer: these local histories were written in the 19th century and based on even earlier secondary sources, sometimes imperfectly culled, as well as Archdeacon Barbour's poem and a few other later sources. Returning them, I came upon two newer books.

It was there that my search began to throw up inconsistencies. Such as the fact that, speaking of the Stewards, in 1298, 'as punishment for the rebellion, Edward forfeited their lands and gave them to Alexander de Lindsay.'[10] How could that be consistent with the name 'Cressingham' which Bannatyne used in reference to the Keeper of Rothesay Castle during the English period? In another, I found the statement that King Edward 'gave Hastings a Scottish earldom including Arran and Bute.'[11] This was Sir John Hastings, an English knight, mentioned in Tytler's History.[12] Did this mean that Lindsay held Rothesay Castle under the earldom possessed by Hastings? 'Cressingham' was the family name of the Treasurer of Scotland, slain at the battle of Stirling Bridge, who may have had surviving relatives.

Then in 1301, I learned that King Edward and the Prince of Wales had been at Bothwell. But Bannatyne was still in the cathedral school then, only a short distance away, in Glasgow! Was it possible he had not known of it? So deep buried in books that it made no impression upon him? The English would have been there only a day or two before travelling east and then north, but their presence should have inspired fear and trembling, for their army was bent on subduing the population of the entire country. The only other disparity I could find was that, in 1306, Bishop Robert Wishart was captured, to be sent south and put in irons in a Wessex dungeon[13] and remained a prisoner until ransomed in 1314. How then could he be in Glasgow in 1309?

9. *Port Bannatyne Past and Present*, by Archibald Brown: unpub lecture, undated, bound.
10. *The Island of Bute*, by I. S. Munro, pub David & Charles, 1973, p. 61.
11. *Scottish Islands*, by Ian Grimble, pub BBC 1985, p. 156.
12. *History of Scotland*, by P. F. Tytler, Vol 1. 3rd edition pub by Wm Tait 1845, p. 232 [1st edn 1828].
13. *Robert Bruce and the Community of the Realm of Scotland*, by G. Barrow, pub EUP 1988, p. 153.

Maybe Bannatyne meant some other bishop, Wishart's representative perhaps? And had worked out who it must be rather than remembering accurately.

The manuscript had been produced by an old man with an admittedly imperfect memory, who could not even remember the name of the castle he had been instrumental in capturing, almost single-handed.[14] So even if I could find something very wrong, it might mean nothing; it might even show that the current view of the history was at fault— which was likely, given the disagreements within it. And definitely not impossible. Bishop Lamberton, who was also imprisoned in England, had been used to carry messages to the Scottish court under parole. Maybe Wishart had been employed on the same business.

It was so frustrating! I began to feel that a decision on the grounds of the history was not to be had. That left only the physical artifact itself. Carbon dating could be performed. Carbon would be obtained from the manuscript and examined for radioactive decay and the date computed—but only at the price of setting fire to enough parchment to provide the weight—which I could not contemplate!

Still unsatisfied, I returned to Edinburgh, and for a few days I did nothing except clear up some outstanding legal matters. Then I decided to read everything again, especially the letters from the experts about the provenance of the artifact, in case I had missed something. The few pages I had given were a mixture of paper and parchment. Nothing further could be done with the paper, I was told, but the parchments, if there were enough, could be subjected to a DNA test to determine whether they came from the same or different animal skins.

It was then, looking for suitable parchments to send, that I noticed the very last page in the manuscript. It had been deliberately cut short! The writing had ended half way down and Tom Stewart had cut off the end. Why had he done this? And I saw!

So that there would be no parchment anywhere in the manuscript which was not absolutely covered in script.

Had he realised that the end paper could be used to determine the age of the manuscript? It seemed likely. Tom Stewart would know that any unused paper or parchment would be used for tests. In 1945, carbon dating was unknown, but a mind as good as his would entertain the possibility that new tests would be the outcome of new discoveries in science.

I wrote to the experts enclosing samples, with my views. And waited again.

---

14. The castle looks like Lochmaben, which was captured in just the way described. Though Bruce knew this castle well, it may have taken one of Bannatyne's ingenuity to think of the method given.

Meantime, I dithered over replying to the nationalist party. Was separation the route to take? Would it not just mean taking orders from Brussels instead of Westminster? And weren't the Europeans even less likely to take account of our Scottish concerns than the English, who at least understood us better? If there was any sense in separation, it seemed to me, it was the idea of being a vibrant, self-sustaining nation again, but one that was truly independent of every other nation—including Europe. The argument that Scots would be better off, financially and in terms of facilties like education, science, the arts etc, I thought derisory, like Bannatyne; for England had so much more to offer in everything. The first outcome of independence, I judged, would be the automatic devaluation of the Scottish pound against the English—which implied an immediate loss to us, in all transactions with them; for the stronger currency would be the one with the more secure financial base. And there was no doubt which that was: the Bank of England was a legend the Bank of Scotland could never hope to emulate.

When the letter from the experts arrived, I was helpless with excitement. I read:

> *We managed to investigate the animal skins by cutting very small pieces from the tiny margins without affecting the script. The DNA's of the skins are the same or very closely related, which supports the theory that the manuscript is genuine. However, careful comparison of the DNA's with other skins in our possession, reveals them to be from the skins of Friesian cows. We believe this breed was not imported to Britain until 1912, and was not developed until the nineteenth century.*

How could the manuscript be genuine, when it was written, some of it, on parchments made from the skins of a breed of animals which never existed until many centuries later? The skins were modern, and therefore the manuscript too! If the animals from which the skins were made could not have existed in 1375 or before, the question was finally demonstrated.

So the manuscript was not a medieval document! It was a creation by Tom Stewart himself. And I suddenly understood why. For the same reason that James MacPherson announced his own work as a mere translation of Ossian: to arouse interest in it, so that it would be read by people interested in this ancient Scottish person. And yet, MacPherson had continued to assert that his was just a translation, even after the forgery was exposed! Why? Perhaps because, having stated the lie, he felt obliged to defend it. Or maybe he so admired the memory of Ossian that he preferred to give him the credit and maybe even thought it noble to do so. Who can say for sure? Oddest of all, was the fact that if Macpherson had not presented his own work as a forgery—Ossian's work—it would not have been given a fair reading, probably would not have been published, and could not, therefore, have had the important effect it did upon the future of European literature!

Tom Stewart's motive was simpler. If he had left an unpublished novel among his things, who would have read it? Not I! And so, it would have been consigned to the waste bin like so much else lying around his house. There was no family to look out for it. All he could expect was a lawyer, like me, to have a cursory glance at his work.

It was the possibility of an object of interest to the Nation State of Scotland that had caused me to make the journey to Bute. I might not have bothered otherwise, leaving it to some minor functionary, to sell off anything of value and bin the rest. Tom Stewart's ruse had worked. I had gone looking myself and I had found it and, in case it was of national interest, I had taken the trouble to read it. And it was worth the trouble, for I had enjoyed it and it really had illuminated that distant medieval world. It might not be a window *of* that world but it was a window *into it*, made possible by Tom's knowledge and imagination. And during a war, he knew there was no hope of publishing then—or even for some time after—that was the clincher! There was no money in the country for anything but the conduct of the war— and the bare survival of those not actively involved, like himself. Leaving it for me to find was his only hope of making it known.

Had he intended the ruse to stand for ever, I wondered? Or had he left clues deliberately into the nature of the deception? The strongest disparity was the name Cressingham instead of Lindsay, for the English Keeper of Rothesay Castle near the end of 1298. The meeting with Wishart in 1309 might have been a lapse of memory.

I felt sure there would be other clues, that experts would notice, given time. Having clarified the matter at last, I took out the Drambuie and poured myself a treble. God knows, I deserved it! Tom had taken three years over the task because he had had to provide himself with authentic-seeming materials—parchment, ink and paper—to make the manuscript. Somewhere in Bute, he had used a workshop for this purpose. He would have acquired the skins from the abattoir on the island and cured them himself, or with the aid of some old tanner or leather merchant who understood the process. After so many years of changes, when so much of the town had been demolished and rebuilt, there would be no sign of it now. And he had constructed his journals with the greatest care, knowing that these at least I would read! Every exclamation mark was carefully calculated to lead me on to the manuscript and then to read it carefully. That was what he wanted above all, for he knew I would publish it.

Why did he not simply wait for a more favourable publishing climate? Because he knew he could not. That his days were numbered.

Maybe, as early as 1943, he sensed the onset of the stroke that would render waiting pointless, and this had fuelled his activity as a forger.

As I sipped the delicious liqueur, I wondered whether the investigation had been a waste of time and realised that it had not. I had found a good novel, one that illuminated history and life, then and now.

The phone rang. It was the secretary of the independence party. Would I please confirm in writing, by the first post, that I was a candidate? Of course I agreed to reply, though I still did not know whether to stand or not.

For hours, I cudgelled my brains to decide—fruitlessly. Until, lying in bed, much later in Colinton, having given it up as impossible of solution, the essential truth that Tom Stewart had seen, crashed into my mind: the injunction to everyone to love his neighbour. If that was the root of all, it meant not separating from our neighbours, but, as far as possible, combining with them. Separation was the road to isolation—real independence, anyway—not the semblance of it that absorbtion in Europe, instead of the union, entailed.

That means, I muttered to myself aloud in the darkness, that we should remain in the union and remain in Europe and play our part in uniting the many countries of the world, when opportunity arises. And yet, there was the anomaly of a Tory government in Scotland, when there were so few Scottish Tories. That was why we needed devolution: to solve that in future. Scotland had to be self-governing, within the union, for as many aspects as made good sense: like Scots law, education, etc. These should be decided by the Scottish value system, not the British one, to the extent that it was different. Bigger things, like defence, embassies etc, that could be better dealt with by the union as a whole, should be left to Westminster. The same with Europe. Folk on the periphery, like the people of Bute, should be left to control their own affairs, so far as sensible—and was far better because they alone understood the local problems and how they could be best solved cheaply, quickly and effectively—instead of waiting for folk to come from the mainland to view the problem and return to ruminate, write a report and order action. Most problems in Bute could be solved in five minutes by the local councillor, if he had the power.

In the end, separation was divorce brought about by dissatisfaction with the neighbours. It was a failure. Instead, everything—every big thing, certainly—that we do, should be in the direction of increasing and extending the brotherhood of man. That meant repairing broken relationships, taking down fences—not re-erecting them. Then, perhaps, one day, the nations of the world will live in harmony with each other.

In the morning, I phoned my refusal.

The final item in the puzzle arrived one day in a letter from Mrs

Merrilees who had come across it while cleaning out her attic where the box of oddments from Dr Brown's estate had been stored. It was to Dr Brown from a Dr Bryson, a friend in some English Hospital. In the middle of it, after several unrelated bits of news, I read: 'Glad to hear that Tom S. has been able to communicate at last. Wonder what he meant by his national treasure? Maybe he will be able to tell you next time.' The rest of the letter was about unrelated matters.

I had been right. The codicil to the will had been written by Dr Brown, after the statement had been dictated or maybe scribbled, almost indecipherably, by Tom Stewart. So the stroke had incapacitated him just before he had completed the sequence that would lead me to the mamuscript! He must have been desperate to communicate and somehow, perhaps by scribbling just well enough to be read, he had got through to the doctor, who had added the significant sentence in a legible hand which set the whole process in motion. And there had not been a next time, when Tom 'got through', which was why no record had been made of a single instance. Maybe even, the idea that he only had this last thing to do in the will had caused enough excitement and worry, in case of failure, to provoke the fatal stroke. Well, he succeeded. The book would be published now.

I tried to imagine the probable sequence of events. First Tom has nothing to do during the war and feels useless. After so many bones broken, he is in constant pain. To take his mind off it, he writes a novel about medieval times, with a political slant to independence, directed at the problem, by having a character who, initially, does not believe in it. But the more he goes into the history, the more uncertain his own position, as author, becomes.

Having finished it in a year or so, he realises there is no chance of publication and maybe even of finding anyone prepared to read it in war-time. He sees that even after the war, he might still remain unpublished. His medical condition worsens and he suspects the approaching stroke which will disable him, making publishing his work impossible. He decides to take steps to force someone to read it, in the event of his disablement, by presenting it as an actual medieval document which he has translated—like MacPherson. He translates it into Latin. Then he learns how to make paper, parchment and ink, by medieval methods, and masters the calligraphy. Now he transcribes his novel into Latin on a mixture of paper and parchment, for the sake of added authenticity: like his character Bannatyne, anything to hand would be used. So it would be a mixture.

Next, he writes up journals, using his own genuine copies to work from, and then destroys the genuine notebooks and leaves the others. Finally, there is only one thing left to do: send the lawyer, who will read the will, to look for it, and compel him to read it. How? By calling it a national treasure. Then, if the novel was as good as he believed, the lawyer would read it all and publish it. Even Tom Stewart's own immortality was assured, for he had left deliberate clues to the real identity of the author which scholars would eventually discover, assuming the secrets of manufacture were not revealed too quickly.

But one thing had not been done in time. The codicil in the will which set off the entire process. He was so shocked by the discovery that independence was not the route to take—a revelation from his own war—that he had suffered a stroke without ever changing the will.

Yet the desire to be an author who had left something of permanent value, lent him the will to overcome his disability just long enough to scrawl a message to his doctor; and that had been enough.

It would have been easy to ignore the codicil, for, unsigned, it was not legally binding and looked to be in a different hand. But none of that stopped me investigating. The possibility of a national treasure had seen to that.

After sending a full copy to my publisher, I locked the manuscript in my safe, where it could remain for now, and toasted Tom Stewart in Drambuie. I pictured him, alone and in pain, deteriorating, day by day, trying by means of literature, to convert his fellow Scots to the nationalist cause; making elaborate researches in history, paper-and-parchment making, and so forth. What a noble aim it must have seemed. And yet by the end of it, he had doubts, because of the history. And then, to cap all, mind sharpened by alcohol deprivation, he sees that the enterprise is in vain. What a shock that must have been! The stroke followed. But the ambition to present his work to the world was still strong. So strong that he had completed the paper trail, which would take me to it.

He had helped me to see many things for the first time. One day there would be a government of the world,[15] never mind Europe; the deeper reason for which is the security it brings. For where so many countries are closely intermingled and interdependent it is increasingly less likely that any one will hive off and dominate the others. Separation carries the risk of conflict; interdependence promotes understanding and even a family relationship of mutual trust, helpful to all within. A government of the world would be an upper tier designed to protect whole continents; a genuine United Nations in practice, not only in theory, with world-law, supervenient to European and British law, and the full, effective powers to discipline any particular intransigent nation and resolve disputes and problems, by force if necessary.

Then, the desperate poverty and disease of third world countries which cannot be properly addressed now because of the wall of cor-

---

15. As many philosophers, Kant and Russell among them, have argued.

ruption surrounding them, and the outcry which would greet any effort by a single country like the USA to resolve, because it was seen as cultural interference, would be overcome. For a world government would a have a duty, as well as full power, to intervene anywhere for the good of the citizens in that place, just as the government of a country does within itself.

As everything evolves, so must governments evolve in the direction of increasing unity. We should all work towards it, for then nation would not war with nation, or commit acts within their borders with bad effects for the planet as a whole, else the world's army would descend upon it. Even so, a government of the world must only take such powers unto itself as will satisfy the customs of small states on the periphery, and leave them free to solve their own particular problems, so long as their solutions are not inhumane or inefficient, for they are best placed to do this.

Then, a local Parliament would look after the district—which should be small, not large, as at present. The Parliament of Scotland would look after the districts of Scotland; the Parliament of Britain would look after the countries of the Union; the Parliament of Europe would look after the nations of Europe; and the Parliament of the World would have overall responsibility for everything on the planet and be the final arbiter, controller and power, of everything on it.

The reason why the Union is worth retaining within Europe is that the countries of the Union already have a far closer affinity with each other—and strong relationships of mutual benefit, which are likely to continue to be of value for all time—than with any other nations of Europe.

Some other books published by **LUATH** PRESS

FICTION

The Road Dance
John MacKay
ISBN 1 84282 024 9 PB £9.99

Milk Treading
Nick Smith
ISBN 0 946487 75 8 PB £9.99

The Strange Case of RL Stevenson
Richard Woodhead
ISBN 0 946487 86 3 HB £16.99

But n Ben A-Go-Go
Matthew Fitt
ISBN 1 84282 014 1 PB £6.99
ISBN 0 946487 82 0 HB £10.99

The Great Melnikov
Hugh MacLachlan
ISBN 0 946487 42 1 PB £7.95

HISTORY

Civil Warrior:
The Extraordinary Life and
Complete Poetical Works of
James Graham, First Marquis of
Montrose, 1612–1650
Robin Bell
ISBN 1 84282 013 3 HB £10.99

A Passion for Scotland
David R Ross
ISBN 1 84282 019 2 PB £5.99

Reportage Scotland
Louise Yeoman
ISBN 0 946487 61 8 PB £9.99

Blind Harry's Wallace
Hamilton of Gilbertfield
introduced by Elspeth King
illustrations by Owain Kirby
ISBN 0 946487 33 2 PB £8.99

GENEALOGY

Scottish Roots: step-by-step guide
for ancestor hunters
Alwyn James
ISBN 1 84282 007 9 PB £9.99

WEDDINGS, MUSIC AND DANCE

The Scottish Wedding Book
G Wallace Lockhart
ISBN 1 94282 010 9 PB £12.99

Highland Balls and Village Halls
G Wallace Lockhart
ISBN 0 946487 12 X PB £6.95

LUATH GUIDES TO SCOTLAND

The North West Highlands: Roads to
the Isles
Tom Atkinson
ISBN 0 946487 54 5 PB £4.95

Mull and Iona: Highways and
Byways
Peter Macnab
ISBN 0 946487 58 8 PB £4.95

The Northern Highlands: The Empty
Lands
Tom Atkinson
ISBN 0 946487 55 3 PB £4.95

The West Highlands: The Lonely
Lands
Tom Atkinson
ISBN 0 946487 56 1 PB £4.95

ISLANDS

The Islands that Roofed the World:
Easdale, Belnahua, Luing & Seil:
Mary Withall
ISBN 0 946487 76 6 PB £4.99

Rum: Nature's Island
Magnus Magnusson
ISBN 0 946487 32 4 PB £7.95

Luath Press Limited

committed to publishing well written books worth reading

LUATH PRESS takes its name from Robert Burns, whose little collie Luath (*Gael.*, swift or nimble) tripped up Jean Armour at a wedding and gave him the chance to speak to the woman who was to be his wife and the abiding love of his life. Burns called one of *The Twa Dogs* Luath after Cuchullin's hunting dog in Ossian's *Fingal*. Luath Press grew up in the heart of Burns country, and now resides a few steps up the road from Burns' first lodgings in Edinburgh's Royal Mile.

Luath offers you distinctive writing with a hint of unexpected pleasures.

Most UK bookshops either carry our books in stock or can order them for you. To order direct from us, please send a £sterling cheque, postal order, international money order or your credit card details (number, address of cardholder and expiry date) to us at the address below. Please add post and packing as follows: UK – £1.00 per delivery address; overseas surface mail – £2.50 per delivery address; overseas airmail – £3.50 for the first book to each delivery address, plus £1.00 for each additional book by airmail to the same address. If your order is a gift, we will happily enclose your card or message at no extra charge.

Luath Press Limited
543/2 Castlehill
The Royal Mile
Edinburgh EH1 2ND
Telephone: 0131 225 4326
Fax: 0131 225 4324
email: gavin.macdougall@luath.co.uk
Website: www.luath.co.uk